WAYNE D. OVERHOLSER

Twice Winner Of The Golden Spur Award!

BUNCH GRASS

"Howdy," Chuck said.

The kid with the rifle called, "Stay where you are, mister. That's close enough."

But it wasn't a boy. It was a girl, and now she stepped into view, the cocked Winchester held on the ready. She stood there, spread-legged, dressed in a man's pant and shirt and sheepskin coat, and judging from the taut, wild look about her, it would take very little to make her pull the trigger.

SUN ON THE WALL

"We're taking these men in for trial—if one of the others shoots me, I'll get you before I hit the ground, Munro. That's a promise."

Munro chewed his lip. "Glenn, you're a hero or a fool. I've been in the vigilante business a long time, and I've done my share of hanging, but I never met a man before who was a stickler for law the way you are, and was willing to back up his beliefs with his life. You've got a big future in Cheyenne—if you live."

And Jim Glenn knew, as he held his gun on the vigilante leader, that Munro did not mean him to live long—maybe two minutes more....

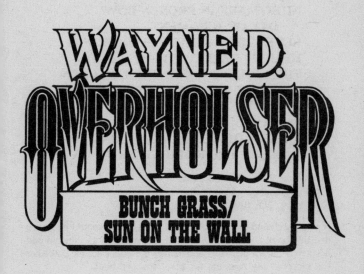

WAYNE D. OVERHOLSER

BUNCH GRASS/ SUN ON THE WALL

LEISURE BOOKS   **NEW YORK CITY**

A LEISURE BOOK®

April 1996

Published by special arrangement with Golden West
Literary Agency.

Dorchester Publishing Co., Inc.
276 Fifth Avenue
New York, NY 10001

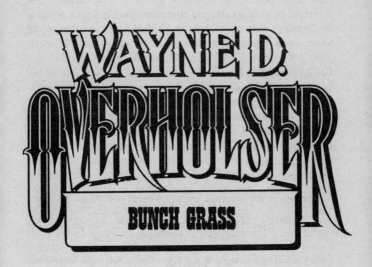

WAYNE D. OVERHOLSER

BUNCH GRASS

Wayne D. Overholser has won three Golden Spur awards from the Western Writers of America and has a long list of fine Western titles to his credit. He was born in Pomeroy, Washington, and attended the University of Montana, University of Oregon, and the University of Southern California before becoming a public-school teacher and principal in various Oregon communities. He began writing for Western pulp magazines in 1936 and within a couple of years was a regular contributor to Street and Smith's *Western Story* and Fiction House's *Lariat Story Magazine. Buckaroo's Code* (1948) was his first Western novel and still one of his best. In the 1950s and 1960s, having retired from academic work to concentrate on writing, he would publish as many as four books a year under his own name or a pseudonym, most prominently as Joseph Wayne. *The Bitter Night, The Lone Deputy,* and *The Violent Land* are among the finest of his early Overholser titles. He was asked by William MacLeod Raine, that dean among Western writers, to complete his last novel after Raine's death. Some of Overholser's most rewarding novels were actually collaborations with other Western writers, *Colorado Gold* with Chad Merriman and *Showdown At Stony Creek* with Lewis B. Patten. Overholser's Western novels, no matter under what name they have been published, are based on a solid knowledge of the history and customs of the American frontier West, particularly when set in his two favorite Western states, Oregon and Colorado. When it comes to his characters, he writes with skill, an uncommon sensitivity, and a consistently vivid and accurate vision of a way of life unique in human history.

CHAPTER I

Train Time

CHUCK HARRRIGAN reached the bottom of Monk's Hill by mid-afternoon of a raw October day, Fran Norman sitting motionless in the buckboard seat beside him, her cap pulled low over her ears, her hands in her muff. She hadn't said a word since they had left the Box N and he hadn't pressed her. Ordinarily she was a talkative girl, but today she was lost in her moody thoughts, her chin tipped down inside the collar of her coat.

The town of Norman was directly ahead of them, a cluster of houses and poplar trees at the bottom of the draw, the long slant of the bunch-grass hills rising on both sides. There was something about being down here in the bottom of a gulch that gave Chuck a smothered feeling every time he came to town, as if he were buried in a feather mattress twenty feet thick.

At times he wondered why Dad Norman had picked the top of Monk's Hill for his Box N buildings where every wind that rolled across Custer County beat at the house, sometimes threatening to flatten all the buildings on the spread. But in this country you had two choices. You could build in the bottom of a draw where you had some protection from the wind, or on top of a hill where you could see to hellangone.

Judge Castle who had started the town preferred the draw, Dad Norman liked the view, and they had argued about it as long as Chuck could remember. Actually it was the devil's own choice. Chuck didn't like wind, but whenever he came to town, he always decided that Dad was right and the Judge was wrong.

Chuck tugged his watch from his pants' pocket, glanced at it and slipped it back. "About an hour till train time," he said.

He wasn't sure Fran heard. He wondered if she was thinking about her father who had only a few days to live, perhaps hours. When they were younger he had usually been able to tell what was in Fran's mind, for they had grown up on the Box N and he knew her as well as a man could know a woman who had been raised as a sister to him, but a barrier had grown up between them, and now it seemed to Chuck that Fran purposely kept her thoughts and feelings as secrets known only to herself.

Perhaps she wasn't thinking of her father at all. For weeks she had known that her father was dying, so she'd had plenty of time to get used to the idea. Doc Logan had told her there wasn't a thing on God's earth he could do except make her father's going a little easier. But you never really got used to the idea that Dad Norman would soon be gone. He was that kind of man, a sort of balance wheel on a range that was loaded with dynamite.

Chuck was scared every time he thought about what would happen when it was over, scared so that a cold terror gripped his middle. He wasn't the scary kind, either, but when you've spent most of your life walking with a man who cast a ten-foot shadow, it was hard to know what to do when the shadow was no longer there.

Still, it seemed odd to Chuck that Fran was in this dark mood today. She was coming to town to meet Bob Neville, the man she was going to marry. Bob had been gone for more than a month, and he wouldn't be coming now if Fran hadn't written that her father had only a few days to live.

Fran had been engaged to Bob for two years. As far as Chuck could see, there was no good reason why they hadn't married, but Bob didn't seem in any hurry. He was more of a politician than a rancher, and he spent as much time in Salem as he did on his ranch. He would go a long ways, Judge Castle said. Might even be governor someday.

At times Chuck wondered if Bob regretted his bargain, if, as his ambition had grown, he had begun to doubt that Fran was the right woman for a governor's wife. Chuck was always ashamed of the thought, for he had no real grounds for it. He knew he was jealous, and he was ashamed of that, too. He could have told Fran a long time ago how he felt about her, but he'd waited too long.

They wheeled down Norman's main street, white dust rising from hoofs and wheels to be whipped on down the street by the wind. No one was on the boardwalk, but a dozen horses were racked in front of O'Toole's Bar. He recognized them, some belonging to Box N neighbors and a few to ranchers who lived south of town in the pine-covered foothills of the Blue Mountains. He wondered about it, for it was the middle of the week and these men seldom came to town except on Saturday.

Fran straightened up, glancing at the horses and then bringing her blue eyes to meet Chuck's gray ones. As he pulled up in front of the Mercantile, she asked, "What's going on?"

"Dunno," he answered as he stepped down. "I was wondering the same."

He tied the team, and coming back to the buggy, held a hand up to her. She got down, glancing again at the horses across the street. She said, "Jack Spiegle's here. Be careful, Chuck."

He nodded somberly. "I don't feel like scrapping today."

She stepped up on the boardwalk that was a foot above the street and slipped her hand back into her muff. She said, "You know how he is, Chuck. Let's not have anything happen."

He knew what she meant. Spiegle was the one man in the county who didn't like Dad Norman, and it was natural that he wouldn't like Chuck. Whenever there was trouble, at round-up or a Fourth of July celebration or a dance, Spiegle was into it up to his neck. He thrived on trouble; he wasn't happy without it. Not bad maybe, but driven by an inherent contrariness to go in the opposite direction to everyone else, so it was natural that he would dislike Dad Norman for no better reason than the fact that other folks respected him.

"I'll be careful," Chuck said. "I'll come over for you in about half an hour."

Fran nodded and swung around. He watched her go into the store, a slim, leggy girl who moved with natural grace. Not pretty, Chuck thought, if you judged a woman's beauty by perfection of features. Her nose was saucily tipped and her mouth was full-lipped and too long, and she had her faults. But she suited Chuck Harrigan and he loved her.

For a moment he stood motionless, thinking about Dad Norman who had taken him when he was five, an orphan, for his father had just died of typhoid on a little spread north of the Box N. Fran had been two then. Chuck could not remember much of his life before he had come to the Box N.

There had not been many days during the last twenty years when he hadn't seen Fran. He'd fought with her and gone riding with her; he'd fished and hunted with her. She'd always held up her end of things, more boy than girl. Dad Norman used to say proudly, but after her mother had died, she had taken over the house and proved she wasn't much boy after all.

Chuck crossed the street to O'Toole's Bar, wondering when he had fallen in love with Fran. He couldn't put his finger on the exact moment, for it had been a gradual thing, coming after they had grown up. Suddenly both of them had realized they weren't kids any more, that something had come between them.

The focal point had been the time he had kissed her after they'd come home from a dance in town. It had been an impulsive act and he hadn't felt at all brotherly. He knew at once he had frightened her and he'd been stupid about the whole business. He should have told her then he wanted to marry her. If she'd said no, he could have pulled out. Instead, he'd let it drag along and she had avoided him for a time.

Then Bob Neville had started coming around and the next thing he knew they were engaged. He would have ridden out then if Dad hadn't started going downhill. He was needed, so he'd stayed, rodding the outfit with Dad staying in the house and finally going to bed.

It would be different after Dad was gone. Fran would marry Bob. They'd throw the Box N and Bob's Mule Shoe together. They wouldn't need him. There were other jobs and other

women. Like Trudie Evans. To hell with all of it, he thought,
as he pushed through the batwings.

Neither Doc Logan nor Judge Castle was in the saloon.
Maybe he could find them in their offices, and he would have
backed through the batwings if Rusty Wade hadn't called,
"Hey, look what the wind blew in." And Barney O'Toole,
"Belly up, Chuck. The first drink's on me."

Chuck gave O'Toole a tight grin and stepped up to the bar.
He asked, "What makes you so generous today, Barney?"

Jack Spiegle, halfway along the mahogany, said, "He ain't
generous, Harrigan. You're teacher's pet, that's all."

That was like Spiegle. He was a big man, half a head taller
than Chuck and thick in the middle with more bulge than a
man of forty should have. He was grinning in the sly way he
had, green eyes pinned on Chuck's face. O'Toole shoved a
bottle and glass at Chuck, his face red, and Rusty Wade
laughed.

"That's a hell of a thing to say, Jack," Wade said. "What
kind of a teacher would Barney make?"

"Shut up," O'Toole said. "How's Dad, Chuck?"

"No better," Chuck said, and had his drink. "Thanks,
Barney."

"Have another." O'Toole motioned to the bottle. "It's on
you this time."

"I'll wait till you're generous again," Chuck said.

Spiegle snickered. "The Box N can't afford to buy drinks,
Barney. Didn't you know that?"

There was a moment of uneasy silence and Chuck knew
he couldn't leave just then. He had never actually fought with
Spiegle, but he knew he would if he stayed in the country.
He glanced at Rusty Wade, who was his best friend, and
grinned a little. Rusty grinned back, standing a few feet away
with his thumbs hooked under his belt. He was waiting, Chuck
thought. They were all waiting, and then it struck him that they
had been talking about him and Dad Norman and the Box N.

A thought occurred to Chuck, a new thought that was
startling. Box N meant something on Custer County range,
partly because it was a big outfit which overshadowed the
others, but mostly because Dad Norman was a natural leader.
When he made a decision, they all bowed to it, even Spiegle,
although he'd squall like hell about it. With Dad gone, the
mantle of leadership would fall on Chuck.

He thought bleakly that he couldn't leave no matter how
he felt about Fran and Bob Neville. These men who stood
looking at him were decent enough, probably because they'd
had to be, but with Dad gone, they'd be like a bunch of hawks
hitting a chicken pen. They'd grab their part of Box N range
if they could get it, with Jack Spiegle the first to grab, all of
them except Rusty Wade whose Three Pines lay far to the

south in the foothills of the Blue Mountains. And Bob Neville wasn't enough man to hold them off.

Suddenly impatient, Chuck said, "I get the idea I interrupted something."

Wade nodded. "You did. Jack here was orating something fierce."

Spiegle pulled a cigar out of his pocket and lit it. "Now I'll orate some more, Harrigan. What happens when old man Norman dies?"

Anyone else would have said Dad, but not Spiegle. It was clear, all right, mighty damned clear. Chuck had stepped into something. Probably Spiegle had rigged this scene, knowing Bob Neville was coming in on the train today, and that Chuck would be in town. Chances were he'd asked the others to show up.

"Mr. Norman to you, Spiegle," Chuck said.

Spiegle laughed arrogantly. "I've been waiting for this, Harrigan, waiting to cut you down to size. We've bowed and scraped in front of old man Norman for years, but damned if we'll keep doing it on his grave. You've been as big as all hell, but with him gone, you ain't gonna be big enough to cast a thin shadow."

Remembering his promise to Fran, Chuck said, "I'll let that go because I don't want trouble. Not today."

"That's right," O'Toole said. "Shut up your mug, Spiegle. You can keep all your cussedness inside you till Dad's gone."

But Spiegle had made up his mind to kick this into the open. He said, "Maybe Harrigan can shut my mug." He started toward Chuck, his hands fisted, thin face dark with the fury that had been smoldering in him for a long time and now had broken into flame. Chuck stood motionless, one hand on the bar, not liking this but seeing no way out of it.

It was Rusty Wade who stopped Spiegle. He waited until the man had gone past him, then he pulled his gun and rammed it into the small of Spiegle's back. He murmured, "Chuck and Barney are right. This ain't your day to crow."

Spiegle stood motionless, glowering at Chuck, then made a slow turn to face Wade. "I'll remember this, Rusty."

"Go to hell," Wade said. "You've got long legs, but you don't take steps as big as you figure."

Spiegle glanced along the line of men who were bellied up against the bar, fighting his temper, then he swung around. "All right, Harrigan. I'll do my orating and let it go at that. There's a family of settlers moved onto Chicken Creek. What are you gonna do about 'em?"

At first Chuck thought Spiegle was lying in an effort to keep the ball rolling, but when he turned to O'Toole, the saloonman nodded.

"That's right," O'Toole said. "A man and his daughter

named Fargo. Came in two, three days ago. Fargo was in town this morning buying lumber for a house."

O'Toole wouldn't lie. Chuck's hand on the bar top clenched. Of all the times for this to happen! It was one thing he had never understood about Dad Norman. As long as Chuck could remember, Dad had said that the day would come when the Custer County hills would be plowed and sowed to wheat, that it was cow country only because the sodbusters hadn't come yet. But they would, and he wouldn't fight them when they did.

Dad Norman had a funny twist for a rich man. He had never been rough on his neighbors; he had often gone out of his way to help them, even when it meant cutting down his own range. Still, he had prospered, and he claimed that was the reason.

When it came time to plant wheat, he'd sell his cattle and raise wheat. It had been a source of argument with everyone in the county, including Judge Castle who was considered Dad's best friend, but it had never gone far enough to cause serious trouble for the simple reason that the settler tide had not reached Custer County. Now that the railroad had been built to Norman, the settlers would come.

"Chicken Creek is on Box N range," Chuck said slowly. "What we do about it is our business, Spiegle, not yours."

Spiegle's face got redder. "That's a hell of a way to look at it. If we let one family roost in this county, they'll come by the hundreds. It is our business and you know it."

The rest of them nodded, even Rusty Wade whose ranch was so far south that he had no real stake in this. But Box N was Dad Norman. You couldn't separate them. The ranch was a symbol of the things he believed in. Every man in this room had been helped in one way or another by Dad when the rains hadn't come and grass was thin, or prices down. It seemed to Chuck that they had no right to take this attitude whether Dad was alive or not.

"If it hadn't been for Dad," Chuck said slowly, "I reckon most of you boys wouldn't be where you are now. I don't figure the Box N is gonna change its policies."

"The hell . . ." Spiegle began.

"Shut up." O'Toole pounded the bar until the glasses rattled, glaring at Spiegle, then he brought his gaze to Chuck's face. "Me, I don't own a cow, so it ain't no skin off my nose either way. I'm looking at this impartial like. Spiegle's right. You let one stay and they'll swarm in like grasshoppers."

Chuck looked at them, his eyes finally coming to Rusty Wade's face. He saw no sympathy there and for a moment he was shaken by doubt. No one, as far as Chuck knew, had asked for the railroad, but it had come just the same. The company said it had been built to tap the timber in the Blue Mountains, but steel had not been laid past Norman. Most of the men in this room had prophesied dourly that it would bring the settlers. Now they had been proved right.

A train whistle sounded north of town somewhere on the long grade of Monk's Hill. Chuck said abruptly, "I've got to meet Bob."

He went out, feeling the edge of their sullen temper. He crossed the street to the Mercantile and went in. Old man Partridge was in the back, stacking cans on a shelf. Fran was examining some cloth on the dry goods side of the room. She looked up when Chuck came to her.

"I think I'll buy some dress goods," she said. "How do you like this organdie?"

It was white with pink dots and it would look good on her, he thought. "I like it fine." He jerked a hand in the direction of the depot. "My watch must be slow."

She turned her eyes back to the bolt of cloth, feeling of it with the fingers of her left hand. A vagrant gleam of sunlight coming through a west window caught the diamond on her finger and set fire to it. She was very pale, and when she finally glanced up at him, her eyes were expressionless. The same light should be there that was in the diamond, he thought, but it wasn't. She lowered her gaze again to the cloth, her lips pressed tightly together.

"You go meet Bob," she said. "I can't make a spectacle of myself. Bring him here. I'll be in Part's sitting room."

She swung around and walked along the counter, her heels clicking sharply on the floor. He heard the whistle again, closer now, and he knew he had to go. Something was wrong, he thought, terribly wrong. Bob hadn't written very often while he had been in Salem, not as often as Fran had.

As Chuck walked toward the door, he wondered if Bob had cooled toward Fran. If he hurt her, Chuck told himself in a sudden burst of anger, he'd break his damned neck. Fran had more than her share of trouble now.

CHAPTER II

Crazy Quilt Pattern

CHUCK UNTIED the team and stepped into the buckboard. The men who had been in the saloon were drifting toward the depot. As Chuck drove past them, he wondered what Bob Neville would say about the family on Chicken Creek.

Bob's ranch was small, with only a quarter section of deeded land, and a narrow strip of range between the Box N and Spiegle's Big 10. If that range was plowed up, he would have nothing. But he might have another angle. Settlers meant votes, and next year Bob would be running for the State Senate.

Again Chuck was ashamed of his thinking. He had nothing tangible against Bob. The man was affable and friendly, a little weak maybe, but a hard worker when he worked, and completely trusted by Judge Castle. In spite of himself, Chuck was jealous of Bob, and the suspicions he had of him stemmed from that fact. It was wrong. He'd missed the boat with Fran and he had no one to blame but himself.

Chuck pulled up behind the depot and tied the team. The engine coasted down the grade and clattered past the depot, the bell clanging continuously. Not much of a train, just one baggage car and a coach.

Chuck waited at the end of the depot while the train came to a jerky stop, thinking that it wasn't his business if the railroad wanted to lose money on this spur it had built into Norman. But he hated it. If the railroad hadn't come to Custer County, the settler family wouldn't be on Chicken Creek. Life would go on as it had. Fran and Bob would get married. Chuck would keep on rodding the Box N if they wanted him. Or, and this was probably what he would do, he could ride out of the country, knowing Fran would get along.

Now, staring at Jack Spiegle's big body looming above the rest of the men who were waiting beside the track, Chuck knew he was thinking crazy thoughts. Dad Norman had said many times that only empty-headed men thought about the "might-have-beens." The smart ones took what came and made the most of it. That was all Chuck could do. Still, a sense of uneasiness lay along his spine like an ice-coated ramrod. Dad had always managed to get along without serious trouble, a talent Chuck was not sure he possessed.

The conductor called, "Norman, end of the line, Norman," and stepped down from the coach.

Suddenly Chuck was aware that Judge Castle was waiting with the others, a dour, inward-thinking man, tall and long-faced, with muttonchop whiskers and a great dignity that set him apart from everyone else in Custer County.

No one really liked Castle unless it was Dad Norman who liked everybody, and maybe Bob Neville, but he was rich and powerful, and therefore treated with respect. With Dad he had run Custer County as long as Chuck could remember, and when Bob had decided to run for the legislature, the Judge had gone out and campaigned for him.

A drummer was the first to step down from the coach, then Bob Neville with two suitcases in his hands. Barney O'Toole yelled, "Senator Neville," and the Judge demanded, "How do you like the sound of it, Bob?"

Bob put his suitcases down on the cinders and shook hands all around, grinning in the easy way he had. He was likable, Chuck thought, and he could see why Fran loved him. He had everything: good looks, an innate sense of courtesy, and a human touch that Judge Castle who owned the bank and most of the town could never quite attain.

"Sure, I'll run for the Senate," Bob said, "providing you boys want me to."

"You're damned right we do," Rusty Wade said. "Who else have we got who could call the governor by his first name?"

Bob laughed in his hearty way and slapped Rusty on the back. "It helps. I had lunch with him yesterday. The last thing he said to me was, 'Bob, you go home and tell your people we won't forget them.'"

"Maybe he don't aim to forget the plow pushers, neither," Jack Spiegle said. "We've got a family of 'em on Chicken Creek."

Chuck wasn't sure whether Bob heard or not, for in that exact instant he saw Chuck standing at the end of the depot. He pushed past Spiegle and walked quickly to Chuck, his hand extended.

"It's good to see you, boy," Bob said warmly. "How's Dad?"

"Poorly." Chuck gave Bob's hand a quick grip and dropped it. "Mighty poorly."

"Where's Fran?" Bob asked, lowering his voice.

He was concerned and anxious, Chuck saw. If anything was wrong between him and Fran, it wasn't his doing. "In the store. She'll be in Partridge's sitting room. She said she couldn't make a spectacle of herself."

Bob grinned wryly. "I should have known she'd feel that way. I'll get right over to the store."

"The buckboard's on the other side of the depot," Chuck said. "I'll get your valises."

"You don't have to . . ." Bob began.

The crowd had moved toward them, Spiegle in front. He said in a belligerent tone, "Neville, I told you we had a settler family on Chicken Creek. Harrigan allows he won't do nothing. What about you?"

The good humor had gone out of the men's faces. Even Judge Castle was watching Bob with close attention, wondering, perhaps, how good a politician he was, whether he could straddle the fence on an issue like this and still keep the friendship of the cattlemen. But if Bob was thinking of his political future, he gave no indication of it.

"It's not for me to do anything, Jack," Bob said. "We've all known it was coming. We've heard Dad Norman say for years that most of us would live to see the day when these hills were plowed and sowed to wheat."

"Well, I'll be God-damned," Spiegle said as if he didn't believe he'd heard right. "You're on the sodbusters' side."

"No I'm not," Bob snapped, "but we've got our cows graz-

ing on public land that's open to filing. The law's on the home-
steaders' side."

Spiegle slapped the butt of his holstered gun. "My law is on
my hip, Senator. I ain't giving up a square foot of grass to
nobody. If you think I'll vote for a man . . ."

"Then don't vote for me," Bob said. "Twenty years ago a
man could talk about carrying his law on his hip, but that
day's gone."

Judge Castle smiled his dour, thin-lipped smile. "I trust
you're listening, Spiegle."

"There's something mighty damned funny about this whole
business," Spiegle said deliberately. "Nobody wants to fight
for his grass. Can't be old man Norman, the shape he's in, so
it must be the girl. The thing I don't savvy is how you can
hang around Salem while Harrigan lives in the same house
with your girl and sleeps in the same . . ."

This was the one thing that would make Chuck fight, regardless of his promise to Fran. Spiegle knew that. He had
been talking slowly, apparently looking at Bob, but still watching Chuck out of the corner of his eyes, so that as Chuck
lunged toward him, he wheeled to meet the attack.

They met with a breath-stopping impact, Chuck's right
cracking the big man solidly on the jaw. It was a good punch,
snapping Spiegle's head back, but not enough to keep Spiegle
from getting his arms around Chuck.

For a time they wrestled that way, Spiegle holding his
pressure on Chuck's ribs, Chuck trying to break free. He beat
at Spiegle's sides with both fists, but they were futile blows,
lacking real power. He was too close to the big man, held too
tightly in those thick arms, and he knew that whatever he did
he had to do at once. This was Spiegle's way of fighting; break
a man's ribs, squeeze breath out of him, and when he was helpless, step back and hit him with rights and lefts until he was
down, then use his boots.

Chuck had made a mistake in rushing Spiegle, in letting him
get those big arms around him. Now, with time running out,
he had to fight Spiegle's way. He stomped down with his left
boot, the heel catching the other's instep and bringing a grunt
of pain, but the bear-like hug did not relax. Chuck kicked him
on the shin above his boot and tried to wrench free. No good.
They shuffled across the cinders, Spiegle's grip seeming to get
tighter with each passing second.

Their faces were close, Chuck's mouth sprung open, his
lungs straining for air. He saw the globules of sweat on the
big man's forehead, saw the malice and the triumph in those
green eyes. Then, without thought, his action springing only
from the sheer instinct of survival, he brought his right hand
up in a savage blow, the protruding thumb catching Spiegle's
eye.

Chuck heard the cry of sheer agony as the great arms momentarily relaxed, and he wrenched free and backed away, sucking air into his tortured lungs. Spiegle rushed at him, cursing, fists swinging in wild blows. Chuck circled, wanting only to keep out of his way until he could breathe again, and for a few terrible seconds he wondered if he ever would.

"Stand and fight, you yellow son of a . . ." Spiegle bellowed.

Chuck did, his right fist catching Spiegle on the chin and bringing his teeth together in a sharp crack. He had his breath now, and it came to him that none of the men in the ring around him and Spiegle were yelling. Not one had picked his man. They were spectators, apparently nothing more.

Spiegle made no effort to get his hands on Chuck again. They faced each other, slugging it out, hard, savage blows that jarred and hurt, and all the time Chuck was thinking of what Spiegle had said about him and Fran, and he wondered if others were saying the same thing, if the ugly suspicion was in Bob's mind. It seemed to Chuck that he had to smash Spiegle, and by smashing him, he could stop the gossip that must be on other men's tongues.

Suddenly Spiegle lowered his head and rammed at Chuck, goatlike, driving him against the depot wall. Chuck sledged him with both fists, and Spiegle backed up and charged again, driven by a kind of insane fury because he was unable to end a fight that he had thought would be an easy one for him. Chuck side-stepped, and Spiegle piled headlong into the depot, his head making a sharp crack as it hammered against the wall. A thinner neck would have been broken. As it was, Spiegle bounced back and fell on his face in the cinders and lay still.

Chuck straightened and wiped his bloody, sweaty face with his hands, and oddly enough, thought first of Fran and the promise he had made to be careful. He looked around the circle of men; he heard Rusty Wade say, "Well, that's one way to lick a man."

And Bob, "A hell of a good way, seems to me. I hope the bastard broke his neck."

It had really been Bob's fight, Chuck thought. No, maybe it hadn't been, but either way, Bob had been willing enough for Chuck to take it. Was there anything that would make Bob fight? Chuck swung around, calling, "Get him out of here. If he ever mentions Fran like that again, I'll kill him."

He stumbled toward the horse trough; he sloshed his face with the water, and then for a time stood there, breathing hard, pain knifing at him from his sides and his chest. When he walked to the crowd, he saw that Spiegle was gone. So were most of the others.

As Chuck came up, he heard Rusty Wade say, "Most of us figure like you and Chuck do, Bob. As long as Dad Norman's alive, anyhow. A few days either way won't make any difference, but waiting ain't gonna settle nothing, neither."

"You won't get hurt," Bob said. "It's us who live yonder on the hills who'll get squeezed. I don't like it any better than you do, but you can't change the law with a gun."

Bob turned toward the track where he had left his suitcases. Rusty Wade's gaze touched Chuck's face. He said, "Spiegle had a licking coming, saying what he did, but I ain't sure he's wrong, Chuck. I mean, about fighting for our grass."

Chuck didn't feel like arguing. He wheeled and walked to the buckboard, knowing then why the men who had watched the fight had not taken sides. They were decent men who, like Rusty, thought Spiegle had a whipping coming to him, but they would still follow him when the time came.

The one thing that surprised Chuck was the stand Bob had taken, but he wasn't sure what the man would do when the pinch came. He wasn't sure about the Judge, either. Then he thought, *Hell, I'm not sure of myself. Or Fran. What will we do when Dad's gone?*

Bob came with the heavy suitcases, Judge Castle walking beside him and talking in a low tone. He stopped when he was close enough for Chuck to hear.

"Get in, Judge," Chuck said. "I'll give you a lift."

The Judge looked at him in the cool, speculative way he had when he was studying a man. He said, "Licking Spiegle won't keep him from kicking up a ruckus, but what about the others? Take Rusty Wade. Can you handle him?"

"I won't even try," Chuck said. "A man has got to live by his own lights."

A thin smile touched Castle's lips. He said, "You've been raised on Dad's axioms, but even if Dad was in good health, he couldn't stop this. The settler tide has swept past us for a generation. Now it's backing up. What are we going to do about it?"

"I don't know," Chuck said, "but I don't aim to jump when Spiegle cracks his whip." He jerked his head at Bob. "Get in."

Bob climbed into the seat. "I guess we've been lucky it hasn't hit us sooner."

"I'll walk to my office," Castle said. "I need the exercise."

"Dad wants you to come out after supper," Chuck said. "I've got to tell Doc, too."

Castle shook his head. "I don't have time. I've got to catch the morning train. . . ."

"You'll come," Chuck said, "or by God I'll put a rope on your neck and drag you out there."

It was the wrong thing to say, but Chuck didn't care. Too many things had happened in too short a time, too much had piled up, and he wasn't in a mood to be polite. Castle knew how it was with Dad, and he owed this much to a man who had been considered a close friend.

Castle flushed, glancing briefly at Bob and bringing his gaze back to Chuck's face. "You've got Dad's tendency to order folks around, but I'm not ordinary folks and you're not Dad. Some work has piled up I've got to do tonight, and if I go sashaying out to the Box N, I won't get it done. When I get back. . . ."

"He won't be alive then," Chuck said. "You're coming tonight."

"Doc isn't in town," Castle went on. "He's out to the Vance place. She's having another baby. You won't get him."

"I'll get him," Chuck said. "She can have her baby some other day."

Amused, Bob said, "Babies don't wait even for a dying man, Chuck." He frowned at Castle. "You'd better come, Judge. Dad wouldn't ask it if he didn't have something on his mind."

Castle scratched his thin nose, anger a hot flame in him. Dad Norman, Judge Castle, and Doc Logan had been the first to settle in Custer County, and from the beginning, Dad had been accepted as a leader. He had always said that honey was a better weapon than a gun if you used it right, and no one, unless it was Castle himself or maybe Jack Spiegle, had resented that leadership. Now Chuck wondered if Castle was jealous and wanted to assert himself this one time before Dad Norman died.

"All right," Castle grunted. "I'll be out after supper, but remember one thing, Harrigan. When Dad's gone, the Box N will not be what it has been and you'll never be man enough to wear his boots."

"I don't aim to try 'em on," Chuck said, and backing his team away from the hitch rail, turned them sharply and drove down the street.

"Trouble," Bob breathed. "I didn't know what I was coming back to." He shook his head as if dismissing the subject. "How's Fran?"

"Waiting for you," Chuck said. "Say, you won't mind driving back to the ranch? I've got to get a livery horse and hunt Doc up."

Bob laughed, his round face losing its somber cast. "I won't mind at all. Fact is, I can't think of anything I'd like better." He glanced sideways, blue eyes thoughtful. "But there's something I want to ask, now that I have a chance. Will you stay on and run the Box N after Dad's gone?"

Chuck was silent a moment, surprised by this. He wondered if Bob knew how he felt about Fran. Probably not. Likely no one did. Even to Chuck it seemed unnatural to love a girl who had been raised as a sister to him.

"I know what you're thinking," Bob hurried on. "The Box N is your home and it's going to be hard to see it change ownership, but I wanted you to know that Fran and I will take it as a personal affront if you leave. I'm not saying this well."

He licked his lips. "I'll put it another way. I may not be here very much if I stay in politics. I'm thinking of moving to Salem when the time's right. We wouldn't worry about a thing if you were running the Box N."

They had reached the Mercantile. Chuck stepped down and tied the team, wondering if Bob was saying this because Fran had insisted on it. Perhaps it was the issue that had risen between them. He had supposed Bob would be glad to get rid of him.

Bob stood beside him, waiting for an answer. "I'd best think on it a spell," Chuck said, and wheeling, angled across the street to the livery stable.

He rented a horse and left town at once, noting that Spiegle and Rusty Wade and the others were still in O'Toole's Bar. Talking about him, probably. He stayed on the Monk's Hill road for a mile, climbing steadily, then turned east to follow the wheel ruts through the bunch grass to the Vance ranch. The bite of the wind was stronger here on the side of the hill and he turned up the collar of his mackinaw. The sun was well down toward the western horizon now, his shadow long before him.

It was a strange thing, he thought, how a man could be caught in a trap of obligation. Dad Norman had spent the last twenty years of his life making the Box N stand for something. He had been generous to a fault, and still he had prospered. Many times he had gone on his neighbors' notes at Judge Castle's bank. Or he had guaranteed payment to Partridge when someone had had bad luck and needed credit.

In a way the prosperity of Custer County was owed directly to the Box N and Dad Norman. Trust people and they'll trust you, he had said. Cast your bread on the waters and it will come back tenfold. A crazy philosophy, according to Judge Castle, but it had worked for Dad.

If he were well, it was possible he could avoid bloodshed now that the first settlers were here. But he wasn't well, and no one else could take his place. When he was gone, it would be like taking out the biggest tree in a forest. Chuck and Fran and Bob Neville were just saplings. No, everything would be different when Dad died. Jack Spiegle and some of the others would crowd in, and the fight that loomed ahead was bound to be a struggle for survival.

He wondered about the bonds of friendship, bonds that were, for most men, easily broken. Today he had seen it was that way with Judge Castle. The man was small-souled and jealous, tired of playing second fiddle. But how about Rusty Wade?

Chuck had been close to Rusty, very close, even though they lived fifteen miles apart. Chuck had often spent nights on Rusty's little Three Pines spread when he wasn't busy on the Box N, helping do the jobs that took two men to do.

Rusty couldn't afford a rider. He had started on a shoestring, and without Dad Norman's help, he'd have broken the shoestring a long time ago.

Rusty and Chuck had played together, drunk together, gone hunting and fishing together, and after Fran and Bob Neville were engaged, they had gone courting together, taking a couple of sisters to dances from a greasy sack spread far up in the pines of the Blue Mountains.

Chuck's girl, a redhead named Trudie Evans, hadn't filled the bill, probably because Fran was in his mind, but Rusty had got himself engaged, and he was going to get married the day he paid off his note to Judge Castle. He was a fool, Chuck thought, because it would be ten years the way he was going, and no girl was going to wait that long.

Rusty had more than his share of stubborn pride. He'd lose his girl before he'd change. And it was the same about this settler business. You fought for what you had, Rusty said. Nobody ever gave you a damned thing. And you were loyal to your own people or you weren't worth enough pepper to make you sneeze.

Chuck could see how it was going to be. When the time came, Rusty would probably stand with Spiegle and the others, even though he didn't have a nickel to gain either way. Bonds of friendship! Dad Norman talked about it as if it were something sacred, but judging from what Chuck had seen today, it didn't amount to a damn to most men.

He was within sight of the Vance ranch when he saw Doc Logan ride out of the yard. Chuck pulled up and waited, and when Doc reached him, he said, "Dad wants you to stop at the ranch tonight."

Doc Logan was a short, potbellied man who always wore an old black suit that was aged to the place where it was more green than black. He must have several suits, Chuck thought, because it never wore out, but if he had a dozen, they all looked alike.

He was never separated from his black bag that he carried behind his saddle, and Chuck could not remember seeing him when he wasn't tired and sleepy and slumping in the saddle when he rode, one hand gripping the horn. Not a rich man the way Judge Castle was, but a wealthy one if human affection made a man wealthy. In that way he was much like Dad Norman.

"Dad worse?" Doc asked, frowning against the slanting sunlight.

"No worse. Just wants to talk."

"Got to sing his swan song," Doc murmured. "Sure, I'll tag along, seeing as Mrs. Vance got done having her baby. Funny thing about Dad. He knows how long he's got to live, and he's bound to sing that swan song before he goes."

They rode westward, Chuck pulling the brim of his hat

low to shade his eyes. The wind was directly against them, but before they had gone a mile, it died down as it often did at sundown.

"You look puny," Doc said. "I'd better fix up something for your liver."

"Ain't my liver."

"Worried about Dad?"

"No, he'll be all right. I don't know much about God, but I know one thing. Dad's the last man I'd worry about."

"Then what is it?"

"The people," Chuck said savagely. "The God-damned selfish people. It'd be a pretty good world if it wasn't for the people."

"That's funny, coming from a boy Dad raised," Doc said in his mild way. "Dad's people. So am I. So's Fran. We're all pretty good people, if I do say so myself."

"But there's Jack Spiegle," Chuck said. "And the Judge."

Doc sighed. "Well, we can't all be angels. You need to talk, boy. Go ahead."

They had reached the road to the Box N and now turned up along it, climbing slowly. Chuck began to talk because Doc was the only man he could talk to, the man who was more like Dad Norman than anyone he knew. He told him about what had happened in town, about the settler family on Chicken Creek, and the unexpected backing Bob Neville had given him.

"You're in love with Fran, aren't you?" Doc asked.

Chuck gave the medico a sharp look. "How'd you know?"

"I know you," Doc said. "I knew your pappy before you, too. A fighting man, he was, and your ma was the best there is. Dad never was a fighter, but you've got a lot of your pa in you. It gravels you to give in, no matter what the law says."

"That's it," Chuck said. "I keep thinking about Dad and the way he's lived and what he'll want done after he's gone, and I just ain't big enough to do it."

"When the chips are down, you'll find out you are," Doc said. "That don't worry me at all. But Fran now." He shook his head. "You know, a medico gets to see what's under a man's skin, and I've seen some things in Bob I don't like."

"What's wrong with him?"

"Can't say. Just a hunch."

Something else to worry about, Chuck thought wearily. He glanced at the doctor's deep-lined, weathered face. "If you tell anybody how I feel about Fran . . ."

"I'm ashamed of you, boy." Doc grinned at him. "A good doctor never gives away a confidence, and I'm a hell of a good doctor."

CHAPTER III

Reunion

FRAN NORMAN did not understand her own feelings. All she knew was that her insides were tied up in a knot. She did not look at Chuck when he left the store; she did not know what she would do when Bob came to her. She heard the steady clanging of the bell as the train rolled into town. Just a few minutes to be alone. No more.

She went into old man Partridge's sitting room and seated herself in his rocking chair. She began to rock, her hands on her lap. He had a roaring fire in the pot-bellied heater, and suddenly she realized she was too warm. She rose, and taking off her cap and coat, laid them on the table beside her muff.

She heard Partridge come into the room from the store. She didn't want to see him or talk to him. She just wanted to be alone, and now she realized it had been a mistake to come to town. She should have stayed with her father, although he didn't actually need her.

Mrs. Benson was a good nurse and she hovered over Dad Norman the way an old hen hovers over a single chick. But Fran could have used it for an excuse. She had used it often enough to postpone her wedding day, but she wouldn't be able to use it much longer.

Partridge cleared his throat. "Can I get something for you, Fran? Won't take a minute to heat the coffee up."

"No." She took a slip of paper from the pocket of her shirtwaist and gave it to him. "Put up my groceries, Part. And cut off seven yards of that pink dot organdie."

She returned to her chair, hoping she had given him enough to keep him busy until Bob got here. But he didn't go away. He was an old woman with a woman's intuition, she thought angrily. He knew something was wrong and he wanted to help.

"Plumb cold riding in, wasn't it?" Partridge asked in his sympathetic tone that drove her wild when he used it on her. "Coffee's made and on the back of the stove. Baked a cake this morning before I opened the store. Let me get you some."

He kept standing in the doorway, his face as withered as a year-old apple. She opened her mouth to tell him to go away and leave her alone, but she didn't say anything because she suddenly realized he wasn't thinking about Bob coming back. He was just sorry about her father and he naturally supposed it was grief that was bothering her.

"I don't want a thing, Part," she said. "Go put my things up. We'll go as soon as Bob gets here."

"I'll get right at it." He started to turn and stopped. "Is there anything I can send out to your pa, any little tidbit I've got in the store?"

"No, he can't eat."

"I sure am sorry about it. I don't know how we'll get along when he's gone, I just don't know."

He left and she began to rock again. She had come very close to saying something she would have regretted. Partridge was a kindly man who knew better than anyone else in Custer County how much they all owed her father. But she didn't feel the grief people expected her to. She had been with him too long through his illness; she had seen him fail until now he was just bones and pale, gray skin covering them, hardly a shadow of the robust man he had been. She knew he was in constant pain and wanted to be released from it. No, she couldn't grieve. She would welcome death for him.

She began thinking of Bob Neville who would hold her in his arms and kiss her and she would kiss him because a woman had to kiss the man she was going to marry when he got back after being gone for a month. But he would not stir her, and that was the thing she did not understand about herself.

Bob was a good man, a kind man who would make a good husband. She was lucky, she kept telling herself. Most of the single women in Custer County would jump at the chance she had, but the truth of the matter was she just didn't love Bob the way she felt she should.

Now, thinking about how her feelings had cooled toward Bob, she admitted that Chuck was at least partly responsible. Bob had said he would put his Mule Shoe with the Box N after they were married and they'd run the two outfits together. A ranch couldn't be run by two men, so it would be better if Chuck left the country.

She had argued that Chuck wasn't just a hired foreman, the Box N had been his home since he was five and if he wanted to stay, he could. But Bob had an answer for that. Dad Norman had been more than generous to Chuck, giving him a small bunch of horses and about fifty cows, enough to make a start somewhere else the way Rusty Wade had up in the timber.

A man like Chuck would never be satisfied until he had his own outfit, Bob said. It would be better for everybody if they let him go, told him straight out he didn't owe the Box N a thing after Dad Norman died.

They had argued about it until both were angry before Bob had left for Salem, and after he had gone, she kept on arguing by mail until Bob had almost quit writing to her.

She wasn't sure how he would greet her. Maybe he'd want to call it off. But she didn't want that, either. She looked down at the diamond on her left hand. There was almost as much satisfaction in being engaged to a popular young politician as there was in being the daughter of Dad Norman.

Bob's attitude toward Chuck bothered her. In every other way he was pliant enough, bending to her will on any issue that rose between them, but when it came to Chuck, Bob was as stubborn as an old mossy horn.

She wondered if he was jealous of Chuck. He had reason to be, if he knew. That was the real reason she could not let Chuck leave the Box N. She had to have him around. She felt guilty about it, even wicked, but it was the truth.

Back across the years she had thought of him as a brother. When they'd been little, they'd romped and wrestled as kids do with no thought they were not actually related. They had gone swimming in the deep pools of Trout Creek when they had been too old to do it, but they hadn't owned swimming suits and they hadn't hesitated over a trifling question of modesty.

They had finally stopped swimming, mostly because she was afraid one of the Box N hands would stumble upon them, and she didn't want anyone else to see her naked. But they had kept on hunting and fishing and riding together. Now, thinking back upon it, she realized that the happiest days of her life had been when she'd been on one of those expeditions with Chuck, even though they'd had their share of quarrels.

Actually Chuck had been the one who had changed everything between them, although she knew it had not been his intention. Chuck always took her to dances because she had wanted him to and it had seemed the natural thing to do, but this particular dance had been a little nicer than usual. She'd worn a new pink dress she had made without his knowing about it. It had done something to her. And to Chuck.

She remembered how it had been, riding home that night under a full moon and how she had lingered at the corral when he'd put the team away. They'd started across the yard and then Chuck had stopped her. He'd put his arms around her and kissed her. It hadn't been a mild and gentle kiss like Bob's were; it had been long and breath-taking and smothering. She'd felt his teeth and his tongue and it had scared her because it had aroused a desire in her she didn't know she possessed.

Thoroughly frightened, she had beaten at him with her fists, and when he'd let her go, she'd screamed something about not ever touching her again, and she'd run into the house. As soon as she had reached her room, she realized how great a mistake she had made. It was what she had wanted Chuck to do for a long time, but at the moment she had been too upset and surprised to know what she'd wanted.

The next morning Chuck was gone. He'd spent a week with Rusty Wade, and on Saturday night they'd gone to town and got drunk and Sheriff Malone had thrown them into jail. After that he'd started going with that redheaded Trudie Evans who lived on a greasy sack spread in the mountains and wasn't fit to black Chuck's boots. She wanted to tell him that, but she'd never had the nerve.

She and Bob had sort of drifted together. She was determined to show Chuck she wasn't going to sit around and wait for him to come back to her. She wanted to go to him and tell him he hadn't done anything wrong, but she had been too stubborn to do it. Her father had often scolded her for her stubbornness, but it was a part of her, and she told herself Chuck would come to her. He never had, and when Bob began courting her, she did all she could to encourage him.

Bob's attention pleased her because he was older and handsome with a talent for turning pretty phrases and wearing the best clothes in Custer County. Besides, she had heard Judge Castle say repeatedly that Bob was the most promising young man in the county. So when he asked her to marry him, she'd said "yes" and he'd held her hands and gently kissed her. But it had never been really right, for not once in the two years they had been engaged had he stirred her the way Chuck had.

Suddenly she was aware that Bob stood in the doorway watching her. She had been so lost in thought she had not been aware of the passage of time; she had not heard him come in. She rose and stood looking at him, aware that his brown broadcloth suit and patent leather shoes and the black derby he held in his hand were perfect for him.

Bob Neville was a product of this country, yet somehow he did not seem to belong to it. That was one of the differences between him and Chuck who was as natural here as the bunch grass on the rolling hills.

He asked, "How are you, Fran?"

"I'm fine. How are you?"

He laughed as if realizing it was inane conversation for an engaged couple. "I'm fine, too." He stopped, letting her see the admiration in his eyes. "Do you know you're pretty, Fran? Funny how a bunch-grass country that has no beauty can produce a beautiful woman."

She had no illusions about her beauty and she knew he didn't mean it. He had been around other women, she thought irritably, women who had social graces and fitted the life Bob wanted to live. He had learned to say the things they liked to hear.

"Thank you," she said stiffly.

He came toward her and laid his derby on the table. He

took her in his arms and kissed her and she tried to answer his kiss. He was a good man, she reminded herself, and he deserved more than she could give him.

He let her go, murmuring, "I love you, Fran. Every time I come back I love you more than I did before."

She didn't say anything because she couldn't. She had a shocking sense of guilt over her lack of feeling for him. On their wedding night she knew she could not share his pleasure, but he would be kind and understanding and she'd feel guiltier than ever.

He lifted a small box from his pocket and gave it to her. "A little present to show how much I missed you," he said. "I picked it up in Portland between trains."

She opened it and stood staring at a small, gold watch. It was beautiful and expensive; she would wear it over her left breast the next time he took her to a dance and every other girl there would be green with envy.

"It's wonderful, Bob," she whispered. "I don't deserve anything like this."

"You deserve more than I can give you," he said earnestly. "I'm the one who doesn't deserve you, but I'll try to make you a good husband, Fran. I'll try my level best."

She put her arms around his neck and kissed him, the first time she had ever done it of her own volition, and she knew it pleased him. He patted her shoulder, smiling gently as he looked down at her.

"I've had a month to think about things," he said. "I didn't write as often as I should because I wanted to see Chuck and talk to him and get everything straightened out." He grinned in the boyish, disarming way he had that always assured her of his straight-forward honesty. "I've found out something, Fran. I can't be happy when there's anything between us."

She sat down in the rocking chair, the watch clutched in her right hand. She knew she had been wilful, but the knowledge did not make her ashamed, nor did it keep her from feeling a great satisfaction in having her way about Chuck. Then she thought wildly it wouldn't work, being married to Bob and having Chuck alone with her.

"I just had a talk with Chuck," Bob hurried on. "He's going out to get Doc at Vance's ranch, so I'm driving you home. I told him we wanted him to rod both ranches. I've got good prospects, Fran. I mean, friends in Salem who count. Before long we can move over there and I told him that when we did, we wouldn't worry about a thing if he was in charge."

She stared at the watch, shining brightly in a ray of sunlight falling through a west window. She would never leave this country for Bob, but she didn't have to tell him that now. Later she would have her way with him just as she had on this matter of having Chuck stay on as foreman.

"What did he say?" she asked.

"He wanted time to think about it."

Suddenly she began to cry. She was ashamed and she wanted to stop, but she couldn't. Bob reached down and took her hand. "I'm sorry about Dad. I shouldn't have said all this, with him like he is."

She got her handkerchief out and wiped her eyes. She hadn't cried for a long time and never in front of Bob. She said, "I'm sorry. I hate a weepy woman."

"You have every cause to cry," he said kindly.

"It's not about Dad. I . . . I guess it's about you, Bob. I don't love you the way you deserve to be loved."

So she had finally said it. She rose, and when she looked at him, she saw that his face had turned grave and disappointed. He said, "I don't ask for much, Fran. I'll wait."

She knew he wouldn't press her. It would be different after her father was gone. She said, "I guess all I need is time."

"I know," he said. "It will be all right. I know it will be because I love you."

She put on her coat and cap and picked up her muff. "We'd better start home."

She led the way into the store, Bob a pace behind her. Partridge said, "Your things are all in the buckboard, Fran."

"Thank you," she said, and went along the counter toward the front door.

"If there's anything I can do . . ."

"Nothing now, Part," she said, and went on out into the late afternoon sunlight and got into the buckboard.

Bob untied the team and stepped up beside her, taking the lines from the whipstock. He backed the team into the street and gave the horses a flick with the whip. She shivered as the wind knifed at her; she looked at the false fronts of the buildings, then they were wheeling between the houses, set behind white picket fences and rows of tall poplars.

Bob's real interest would never be in ranching, she thought. It wasn't even in this country. He would be glad to move to the Willamette Valley with its great firs and cloudy days and steady drizzles and the eternal mud.

He wanted to hold office; he wanted to go "the long ways" that Judge Castle had prophesied for him. That was one of the things which troubled her. She belonged here in the bunch grass as much as Chuck did.

She clutched the watch inside her muff, thinking of the years ahead when Bob would be building his political fences and she would be alone on the Box N with Chuck. She wanted to have her cake and eat it, too, and she could see no reason why it wouldn't work out just the way she wanted it.

She pressed a shoulder against his and whispered, "It's nice to have you back."

He grinned down at her, pleased. "It's nice to have you say that." He laughed softly. "I didn't tell you, but Chuck told the

Judge Dad wanted him to come to the Bar N tonight and the Judge said he couldn't. Then Chuck said he'd come or he'd put a rope on his neck and drag him out there. Nobody could talk to the Judge like that but Chuck."

That was right. She glanced at Bob's round, pink-cheeked face, so lacking any real strength. Therein lay the big difference between him and Chuck, she thought. He wasn't the man Chuck was and he never would be. The metal that was in him could not be tempered to hold a sharp edge.

CHAPTER IV

Death Must Wait

FROM THE TIP of Monk's Hill on an unusually clear day a man could see the triangular, snow-covered peak of Mt. Hood. It was proof that the Cascade Range was over there, and when Chuck and Fran had been children, they had often talked about taking a pack horse and riding over that way just to get a close-up look at the white-haired old mountain.

They got around to mentioning it to Dad one day and he promptly unwound like a spooky bronc. "You ain't doing no such thing," he said. "If you try it, I'll warm your bottoms up till you could fry a couple of eggs on 'em. First place there ain't no roads. Second place you'd have to swim the Deschutes. Third place you'd hit a batch of rough country and maybe run into some outlaws. No sir, you kids can do your exploring right around here."

So they had never gone. Chuck had talked to Rusty Wade about going, but Rusty wasn't much of a hand for exploring. Now, reaching the crest of Monk's Hill with Doc Logan, Chuck looked out across the tawny rolls of the land toward the sun that had dropped into a scarlet nest of clouds. He felt the urge again to have a close look at the mountains, to stick his head into a snowbank or slide down a glacier, or maybe climb to the top just for the hell of it.

He had heard Bob Neville say, "Mt. Hood is the most majestic mountain God ever made. You can see it fine from Portland if you catch a clear day." But Bob had never said anything about wanting to climb it. He was the kind who would be satisfied to just sit and look.

Chuck told himself that his trouble was the simple fact he hadn't been anywhere. He'd never been to the Willamette Valley; he had never seen the Columbia except at Umatilla where they drove their herds to the railroad. Maybe he was a drifter at heart. His father had been, according to Dad.

"Mike Harrigan sure proved that a rolling stone don't gather no moss," Dad Norman had said more than once in Chuck's hearing and probably for his benefit. "His wife and him both died when they were young, just worn out by worry and traveling."

Well, the West was full of people like that. Maybe they had died young, but if they'd lived the kind of life they wanted, what the hell? Doc had said his father was a fighting man and his mother was the best there was. If they'd lived, Chuck would probably have been as fiddle-footed as they were, but Dad hadn't raised him that way.

"Make your life amount to something," Dad often said. "Get your roots down. You ain't no good to nobody else when you're jumping around like a grasshopper in a hot skillet."

Dad had amounted to something, all right. He'd called the turn on just about everything in Custer County except the railroad. But after he was gone. . . . Chuck shook his head and glanced at Doc who was riding beside him.

Maybe Doc was right in saying there was a lot of his pa in him; maybe that was the source of the discontent which had piled up in him lately. But riding out wouldn't help. Dad had instilled a sense of responsibility in him. If he left now, he'd have a sense of guilt all his life for ducking out when he was needed.

Well, this was quite a country at that. Southward you could see the blue-black line of timbered ridges against a sky that was aflame now from the setting sun, but on the other three sides the hills rolled away into infinity, bunch-grass hills and the sky that tipped down around the horizon like a gigantic, overturned saucer.

Chuck remembered Fran's mother, who had come from the Willamette Valley, saying she couldn't stand it here with nothing to look at but the hills, and the wind beating at her until it addled her brains. It was one of the things she had quarreled with Dad about.

Mrs. Norman liked timber around her with its shadowed coolness, but it was a long trip to the Blue Mountains. They had gone once a year to cut the winter's supply of wood. To her that annual trip was something to look forward to, the same as Christmas had always been to Fran and Chuck.

Monk's Hill had struck Dad Norman right from the first moment he had seen it. Fran loved it, too. Chuck was sure of that. She had been born here; she didn't know anything else. But if she married Bob, she'd go with him. Maybe she wouldn't complain as her mother had, but she wouldn't be happy.

They rode into the Box N yard, Chuck realizing that all his thinking had accomplished nothing except to add to his confusion. But he'd play it out because he was trapped by his sense of obligation to Dad and Fran. The buckboard was yonder by the big barn, so Fran and Bob were here. He'd have to tell Bob something. He'd stay for a while if they really wanted him.

"I'll put your horse up, Doc," Chuck said as he dismounted. "Go on in."

"Reckon the Judge will show up?"

"He'd better," Chuck said.

Doc swung down and rubbed his backside. "I'm getting old, Chuck. Too old to keep trying to save folks' lives and fetching babies into the world and giving advice." He laughed. "Giving advice is the best part of my business. I hear all the gossip. If a girl gets pregnant when she's got no business being that way, I'm the first to hear it and then I can hand out my pearls of wisdom." He shook his head, frowning. "Not that it helps a damn."

He walked toward the big, square house, set here on top of the hill behind a row of slender poplars which Dad Norman had planted to please his wife. The house was a landmark that could be seen from a dozen hilltops, shiny white because Dad painted it every year as regular as he drove a herd of Box N steers to Umatilla.

Even the house had its place in Custer County, Chuck thought as he watered the horses at the log trough beside the windmill tower. The neighbors could see it during good times and bad, when the grass was green in summer, or the land drab and gray with the death that was winter. It was the nerve center of the Box N, a sort of symbol to anyone who was in trouble and needed help. Dad Norman had known that and he'd found satisfaction in the thought.

Chuck stripped the horses and turned them into a corral. Hod Davis who had worked for Dad as long as Chuck could remember came out of the barn and looked at the livery horse Chuck had ridden. He said, "You're getting down to cases, riding that hunk of wolf meat."

"You can take him back to town, come morning," Chuck said. "We don't want nobody to see him. They might think he belonged to the Box N."

Hod gave it a moment's thought as he chewed on his quid of tobacco, then shook his head. "Naw, I don't reckon even Jack Spiegle would allow that critter was a Box N horse. Things just ain't that bad."

"Any change with Dad?"

Hod shook his head again. "No change."

Chuck glanced at the old cowboy, wondering if he had heard about the settler family on Chicken Creek. Even Hod wouldn't understand. How could anyone understand, patting the plow pushers on the back and saying, "Sure, go ahead and take our range. Turn the grass under. Maybe we'll buy some plows ourselves."

Nobody except Dad Norman would figure that way, but Dad had always been able to look ahead farther than anyone else. He was right, too, and that was the part that hurt. Call it progress or changing times, or whatever, but it would happen just as sure as the Lord made little, green apples. It was too bad He wasn't letting Dad live long enough to get Custer County through the changing years.

"Reckon I'd better see if I can rustle supper," Chuck said, and walked toward the cookshack.

Old Broadhorn Baylor, who had cooked for the Box N as long as Hod Davis had ridden for it, did his usual amount of grumbling about a late meal, but he finally set something out. While Chuck ate, he thought about Broadhorn and Hod who had worked for Dad so long. It was all part of the same pattern, the same problem. They'd be lost if the Box N folded. Chuck wondered if Dad had thought of that.

He was on his third cup of coffee when Judge Castle rode up, tied and went in. A moment later Bob Neville appeared in the doorway. He said, "We're all ready for the palaver, Chuck."

"I ain't stopping it," Chuck said.

"Hell, you're part of it," Bob said. "Come on."

Chuck finished his coffee, not wanting to go but knowing there was no way out of it. He put the cup down, glancing at Bob. The dusk light was so thin Chuck couldn't see his face clearly, but his chubby body made a round shape in the doorway.

He had never seen Bob in a fight, had never seen him drunk, had never seen him lose his temper. Even his voice was smooth and soothing, like a tune played on the newfangled graphophone Dad had bought a year ago.

Chuck pushed himself upright from the bench alongside the table. Doc was right. Bob wouldn't do for Fran, or for any woman with the vitality she had. It wasn't jealousy that made him think that, he told himself. He knew Fran. That was all. If she married Bob, it would be like a man who needed a shot of whiskey trying to make out with a drink of tepid, skim milk.

He walked across the yard, wondering if Bob would bring up the matter of his staying on after Dad died, but nothing was said. They went into the living room, Chuck nodding at Judge Castle who nodded back, his long face barren of expression.

A crackling fire was going in the fireplace. Doc stood with his back to it, hands folded across his fat little belly. Fran was sitting on the orange love seat across the room from him. Chuck moved to the fireplace and warmed himself, thinking that the chill which gripped him was not due so much to the cold October night as it was the prospect of facing the next half hour.

There was an awkward moment of silence, Chuck glancing around the big room with its expensive furniture that Dad had bought years ago in The Dalles: the heavy mahogany table, the plush-bottom chairs, the black leather couch, the love seat.

Chuck remembered how pleased Mrs. Norman had been when the freight wagons rolled in and the furniture was carried into the house. That was the only time he had ever seen her kiss Dad.

Even the furniture had its part in the whole pattern, as representative of the Box N as the big house. It wasn't particularly beautiful, but it was comfortable, and it gave the living room an air of honest hospitality. No pretense, and none of the studied elegance with which Judge Castle had furnished his house in town.

Every piece of furniture showed signs of wear which was natural since Fran and Chuck had been raised in this house. Chuck could not remember a single time when either Dad or Mrs. Norman had said to be careful, you'll scratch the furniture.

Mrs. Benson came out of Dad's bedroom, starched dress rustling with each movement. She said, masking her face against the grief she felt, "He's ready."

"Just one thing," Doc said in a low tone. "No argument no matter what he says. He's got himself geared for this. I don't reckon he's got another twelve hours of life." He looked squarely at Judge Castle. "No argument."

The Judge stroked his muttonchop whiskers, glaring at the doctor, then lowered his eyes. "I didn't come here to argue, Doc."

Fran led the way into the bedroom. She had arranged chairs around the bed so all of them could be seated. She took the one beside her father, and reaching out, gripped his skinny hand. A pink, hobnailed lamp on the table near the head of the bed gave out a shaded light.

Chuck took a chair at the foot of the bed, purposely because it was shadowed there. He preferred to think of Dad when he was big and robust and ruddy-faced, overflowing with the good, strong juices of life. Now he was a long, slight bulge under the blanket, every bone in his face trying to break through the gray, tightly drawn skin of his face. Only his blue eyes and big hands reminded Chuck of the Dad Norman he had known all his life.

Dad was propped up by a mass of pillows. He looked around, smiling gently, and it surprised Chuck to see so much happiness in his face. It had not been there the last time Chuck had seen him. Doc was right. Dad had geared himself for these few minutes and then his strength would be gone.

"This is good," Dad said, "awfully good to have in this room the people I love."

"You know we love you, too," Fran murmured.

Chuck bowed his head. He was choked up as he knew he would be. He hoped he wouldn't have to say anything, for he could not keep his voice from betraying the emotion that gripped him.

His own father was only a vague blur in his mind. Dad Norman had been his father in everything but birth, and that wasn't important except for the character traits that had come down to him. Even those had been shaped by Dad Norman.

"I know you do," Dad said. "And Chuck. Doc. And Mrs. Benson. But I dunno about the Judge and Bob. I've had a lot of time to think on things, lying here inside these damned walls, and I want to say some of the things I've been thinking."

"I don't love you like Fran does, but . . ." Bob began.

"Of course not," Dad said. "Let me do the talking. I'm ready to die, and I'm looking forward to what's ahead. I don't know what it'll be like. Never gave much thought to God till here lately and I haven't got Him figured out. I reckon you have to hunt for Him, and I didn't do it."

"I think you have," Doc said softly. "What's more, I think you found Him."

"I dunno. Anyhow, I ain't troubled about it. What I've been wondering about is what makes folks tick. Me, I never even figured out why I done the things I did. Take Doc here, doing his damnedest for folks and not getting paid most of the time and wasting his life here in the bunch grass. Lucky if he gets some sleep in his saddle and if his mare gets him home òr where he's going. Why, Doc, why?"

Surprised, the doctor scratched his bald spot. "I'm like you, Dad," he said. "Never gave much thought to it, but I guess that when a man decides he wants to be a doctor, he allows that's the way he's got to live."

"We came here better'n twenty years ago," Dad said. "You could have gone to a bigger town and had it a lot easier. The Dalles. Or Baker City. But you don't have the answer no more'n I do. Well now, it's different with Bob. I figure love is something you can shape a little. Not much, but a little, so Bob shaped it some, knowing Fran was going to inherit a damned fine ranch."

Chuck was shocked, for it was a brutal thing to say and it wasn't like Dad. But there was nothing wrong with his mind. He must have been driven by some inexorable inner urge, or he wouldn't have said it, knowing he was leaving a bad memory in Bob's mind.

"Dad . . ." Fran whispered.

"I know, honey, I know," he said. "I've never told you how to live and I ain't gonna try now. You've got a lot of horse sense and that's something I've been proud of. If Bob's the man you want, then he's the one I want you to have. Well, like I was saying, me and Doc and the Judge were the first ones here. I drove in a herd of cows, Doc nailed up his shingle, and the Judge plotted out the town and named it after me. Why, Judge?"

Castle sat hunched forward, long-fingered hands on his knees, his face dark with anger. Or guilt. Chuck couldn't tell which, but when he glanced at Bob, he was sure of what he saw there. Bob was caught, the expression on his face that of a kid trapped with one hand in the cookie jar.

"I thought it would please you," the Judge said. "If it didn't . . ."

"Sure it did, with me having my share of vanity like most folks, but that ain't telling me why."

"We've always been friends," the Judge said. "I didn't have any other reason. I just thought you'd like it."

"I've been wondering about something else," Dad said. "How'd you sweet-talk the railroad company into building into Custer County?"

He said it in a low voice, but the effect was the same as if he had shouted. Castle jumped, his face a dull red. He yelled, "By God, I didn't . . ."

Doc slid low in his chair, and swinging a foot up from the floor, kicked the Judge in the seat of the pants. He said, "Sit down."

Castle dropped back into his chair, mumbling, "I'm sorry, Dad, but I didn't have anything to do with the railroad coming in here."

Chuck, watching this closely, sensed there was something he didn't understand, but he thought Doc caught it. Friendship, he thought bitterly, tied together by selfish interest. Then he felt Dad's eyes on him, questioning, warning him against this man who had supposedly been his best friend.

"I ain't got much time left," Dad said, his voice so low that Chuck had to lean forward to hear what he said. "You all know how I feel about the future of this country. We've used the grass ever since we came, used it without paying a cent to nobody, but it's gonna be wheat land, every acre that's fit to plow. We'll wind up with nothing but our deeded land. I reckon I'm glad I won't be around to see it."

He was looking directly at Chuck, and Chuck knew this was for him. He was being given an obligation that would burden him long after Dad Norman was gone, but he felt no resentment. He owed him too much. Then he wondered if Dad was thinking of Fran, knowing there were some things he could do for her that Bob Neville was not capable of doing.

"When they come, Chuck," Dad went on, "don't fight them. Don't have their blood on your hands. I know how you feel and how you think, and you'll hate like hell to see Box N busted up, but the law's on their side."

Dad licked his dry, thin lips and rolled his head on the pillow to look at Fran. "I've got better'n twenty thousand dollars in the Judge's bank. It'll take some time to get everything squared around, so I've put the money in your name. You can draw on it to pay the crew and Partridge and anything else that comes up."

His head dropped sideways on the pillow and Doc came

to the side of the bed. Chuck was on his feet, outstretched hands gripping the two brass balls that were atop the bedposts, clutching them so tightly that his knuckles were white, but he was not even aware he had hold of them.

He thought Dad was dying, and then he saw he was wrong. Dad's eyes were on him again, and there was something in them that reminded Chuck of the time when he'd been a kid and a horse they were breaking had thrown him.

"Climb on him again," Dad had said. "The only time a man gets licked is when he walks out on a tough deal."

It had been wicked. Chuck's nose was bleeding and he had lost a hunk of hide on one leg as big as the palm of his hand; he was thoroughly shaken up and sick in the stomach and scared. Fran, watching wide-eyed between the corral poles, had cried out, "He's hurt, Dad." But Chuck had got back into the saddle and that time he'd ridden the horse and he'd learned something.

"I always meant to adopt you, Chuck," Dad was saying, "but I just had too many irons in the fire and I never got to it. Now I'm making up for it the only way I can. I made out a new will the other day. Box N goes to you and Fran, share and share alike." He tried to smile, a faint quivering of his lips. "I'm tired." He looked at Fran.

"You've been a fine daughter. God bless you."

She bent down and kissed his cheek. She whispered, "And you're the best father a girl ever had."

Dad held out his hand to Chuck who came around the corner of the bed to grip it. He whispered, "Good riding, Son."

"You, too," Chuck said, his voice trembling, and he wondered how Fran could be as calm as she was.

Mrs. Benson, standing back in the shadows, was crying, and even Doc who had stood beside a hundred deathbeds, was blinking hard. Dad said, "Don't grieve for me, any of you. I'm gonna ride up to the good Lord's throne on the biggest black stallion He's got in Heaven and I'll be waiting there in the saddle for the rest of you."

"Let him sleep now," Doc said.

Chuck walked out ahead of Bob and the Judge, then Fran left the room with Doc, leaving Mrs. Benson there. Chuck started toward the foot of the stairs to go to his room. He wanted to be alone. Dad was right. No one should grieve for him. This was the night for him to die. He wouldn't have to watch Box N break up. Then Chuck wondered if he'd heard about the family on Chicken Creek.

"Chuck."

He turned at the foot of the stairs. Doc was walking toward him, unashamed of the tears that had left their splash on his cheeks. He said, "There goes a man," and Chuck nodded. Doc hesitated, wanting to say more and not finding the words, then he said in a low tone that was only for Chuck's ears, "Get the mail tomorrow."

He walked away, leaving Chuck staring at his back and puzzling over his cryptic order. The Judge was standing beside the fireplace, gaunt body more stooped than usual, but Bob was in the middle of the room, gripping Fran by both shoulders and shaking her.

"He's out of his head," Bob was shouting in a voice that was almost hysterical. "It wasn't fair, what he said about me. He's always been prejudiced against me. I love you and I never thought about you owning the ranch. It wasn't fair . . ."

Doc grabbed his arm and yanked him away from Fran. "Shut up, you damned fool. You're yelling loud enough for him to hear."

"I know, Bob," Fran said, and taking his hand, led him to the leather couch. "You've got to forgive him. He's dying. Don't you understand?"

Bob dropped down on the couch and leaned forward, holding his head in his hands. He wasn't a politician now; he wasn't much of anything, Chuck thought, just a kid caught with his hand in the cookie jar and trying to lie out of it.

Chuck climbed the stairs to his room, hearing the familiar squeal of the steps under his weight, and he wondered if Bob was capable of loving anyone but himself. Then, for the first time, he realized how much he hated Bob Neville.

CHAPTER V

Dawn Ride

CHUCK LIGHTED the lamp on his bureau and closed the door. He walked around the room that he had occupied since the house had been built. The furniture had come from his home: a gilt, metal bedstead with much of the paint peeled away, a tall bureau with a marble top that his mother must have taken pride in at one time, the cheap mirror which always gave him the impression that the skin had been laid on his face in a series of ridges and valleys, and the rawhide-bottom chair.

That was all except for his father's Henry rifle that leaned against the wall, a few odds and ends Chuck had picked up when he was a kid like the chunk of petrified wood he'd found one summer when they had gone to the mountains, and the tintype of his mother on the bureau. He had no picture of his father, and the only thing he could remember about him was the bushy beard the color of a dry corn stalk.

He picked up the tintype and studied it. His mother had been very young when it was taken, probably when she was married, and she had been pretty. Suddenly he felt a strange emptiness which was unusual because he had never been one to feel sorry for himself. He had always realized he'd been lucky, raised by the Normans as he had, but now he felt a little cheated. He wished he had known his mother.

Replacing the tintype, he walked to the window and opened it. He looked out. The stars and the thin rind of a moon were covered by clouds and the smell of the first snow was in the air. He hoped it would warm up. He didn't like the idea of snow being on the ground when they buried Dad.

He lowered the window, shivering, and took off his boots and pants. Maybe he should have stayed downstairs. No, he might do something he would be ashamed of later, like taking a poke at Bob. Fran had enough trouble. And there was the Judge, sullen because of what Dad had said, stripped down to his selfish nakedness by inference rather than direct statement.

Chuck wondered how Dad had known the Judge was responsible for the railroad coming to Custer County. But that wasn't important. Dad had hinted at something else which still eluded Chuck.

He blew out the lamp and went to bed, but he didn't sleep. He heard someone ride away, probably the Judge; he heard stairs creak and the murmur of voices in the hall. Fran was giving Bob the third bedroom at the end of the hall. After they were married, they would share Fran's bedroom which was next to Chuck's. He swore softly, knowing he could not remain in this room after that. But maybe they wouldn't be married. Dad had done all he could to break it up tonight. It might be enough.

Chuck began thinking about Fran and some of the crazy things they had done when they were younger and not really aware that they were unrelated by blood, that she was almost a woman and he was close to being a man.

Dad and Mrs. Norman never knew, he was sure. Not that they would have cared except that they wanted Fran and Chuck to get a night's sleep. There were many nights when they hadn't. Fran would come into Chuck's room and play cards on the bed. Or she would read. She read aloud better than he did, so she had done most of it.

He had liked *The Last of the Mohicans* better than any other book, and he remembered how they had stayed up night after night until it was finished and he had thrilled at the exploits of Natty Bumppo and Uncas. He grinned when he thought of Mrs. Norman worrying over the way he and Fran had yawned at breakfast, so tired they were late starting to school.

Sometimes they had just talked. About what they'd do when they were grown. Fran was set on being a bear hunter and Chuck would be a United States Marshal. He'd clean out all the bad men in the West and return to Norman a famous man with a brace of gold-plated .45's, and everybody in Custer County would be on hand.

Chuck reluctantly agreed to let Fran ride beside him. They'd have a brass band. Norman would be a big town by that time, probably bigger than Portland, and the sidewalks would be crowded with cheering people, thousands of them.

Or they'd talk about the last fishing trip they'd made and how the biggest trout wouldn't get away next time. Or about school and old man Whittsley who was the meanest teacher they ever had. He kept a leather strap in his desk that he loved to use, and he had used it on Chuck the day Chuck left a snake in the top drawer of his desk.

The snake incident gave them something to talk about for months afterwards. Sometimes they'd get to giggling until they were out of breath. They'd tell it to each other over and over, about how old Whittsley had jumped ten feet right into the air when he'd yanked the drawer open and seen the snake. He'd hit the wall behind him and sat down and leaned against it, his face as white as a Halloween ghost.

Chuck had got a real tanning out of it. Reno Vance, the oldest of the Vance brood, had tattled on him. Afterwards he'd licked the stuffing out of Reno. He'd never liked Reno after that, and the fact that he was riding for Jack Spiegle added to his dislike.

There were other things, like tying a rope to Chuck's bed and going out of the window. They had that idea every spring when the grass greened up and the nights were warm. Usually it was just after a rain when the land was rich with the smell of growing things and it was fun to run through the wet grass in their bare feet.

Chuck was still awake when he heard the door open. He sat up, calling, "Who is it?"

"Fran. I couldn't sleep." She closed the door and came to the bed and sat down on the edge. "You don't mind?"

"No." He put his shoulder blades against the wall, looking at her slim shape in the darkness. "It's been a long time."

"A long time," she agreed. "Sometimes I wonder what happened to us. I've been lying in bed so wide awake I thought I'd never go to sleep, and I got to thinking about how it used to be. You know, talking all night and playing cards and everything."

"That's funny. So was I. Remember old man Whittsley?"

She giggled. "I'll never forget him." Then she was silent for a long time. Finally she said, "But it's gone, Chuck. It doesn't seem so funny now. I feel kind of sorry for him, trying to teach you anything."

"You weren't any better," he said. "If there was any devilment going on, you were into it."

"Half boy, half girl," she whispered. "Oh Chuck, it's all

behind us, and the half boy part died a long time ago. I guess it was the night you kissed me."

"I'm sorry. I didn't know how it was going to be." He stopped, knowing he couldn't tell her how it had been with him and how he had felt about her. Still felt, for that matter. Not with Bob's ring on her finger and Bob sleeping down the hall.

"You don't have anything to be sorry for," she said miserably. "I've always been ashamed of the way I acted. Sorry, too, after it was too late."

He reached out and touched her. She didn't have anything on but her silk nightgown, the only silk nightgown she owned. He wondered why she was wearing it tonight. She gripped his hand and put it against her face, whispering, "He'll die tonight. Or tomorrow. Doc says he knew, and it was a miracle he had the strength to say what he did."

He pulled her to him and she laid her head against his chest and began to cry. This was the first time she had talked to him like this since she and Bob had announced their engagement, the first time he had seen her cry since her mother had died. He held her that way a long time, knowing it was good for her to cry.

He wanted to tell her he loved her, that she couldn't marry Bob because he wouldn't make her happy. He would take her away. She would have to live his kind of life and she wouldn't like it. She wouldn't even have as good a life as her mother had had.

She murmured, "I needed that. I'm sorry for myself, I guess, but I'm glad Dad's giving you half the ranch. I'm selfish, Chuck. I've been afraid you'd leave after Dad was gone, but now you'll have to stay."

If there was anything left of the Box N to stay for, he thought. He said, "I didn't know how Dad felt about Bob. You can't . . ."

"Don't say it," she whispered. "Dad was wrong. I know Bob loves me. He never once thought of marrying me for the ranch. I know, Chuck. I tell you I know."

So there was no use to tell her how he felt. If he said anything against Bob, she would defend him and Chuck would simply drive a wedge between him and Fran. But there was one thing he had to say, and he would never find a better time.

"Look, Fran," he said carefully. "I ain't saying Bob don't love you or that Dad's right about him. I'm just thinking about what he wants to do and what you want. It won't work."

"I've thought of that," she admitted, "but I'll make it work. Maybe I can change him."

"You know you can't. Why don't you give his ring back?"

"I gave my word," she said.

He could make no answer to that. Sort of funny, the way it was working out. If there was anything Dad had taught the two of them, it was that very thing. A promise was sacred.

Once given, it was not to be broken.

Tonight Dad had left no doubt about how he felt, but Chuck wasn't sure he would have told Fran to break her promise if the question had been put directly to him. Now, holding her slim body against his, he realized that Bob should be the one to break it up. It would never be Fran. But Bob wouldn't. He had too much to gain.

"Seems to me the question is whether you love Bob," he said. "Do you?"

She was silent for a long time before she said, "Yes. I feel sorry for him. I mean, he needs me, and he's good and gentle and I'd hurt him if I gave his ring back. But I'm wicked, Chuck. Down inside me I'm wicked because I love you, too."

She turned in his arms so that she faced him; she brought a hand to the back of his neck and pulled his head forward and kissed him. His arms were tight around her, holding her, and she was kissing him the way he had kissed her a long time ago, hungrily as if none of Bob's kisses had ever satisfied her. He felt her tongue, the hot pressure of her demanding lips, and there was nothing else for either of them but this moment.

Outside a man yelled, "Harrigan."

Fran drew back, breathing hard, and the moment was gone. She whispered, "Who is it?"

"Sounded like the sheriff," he said. "What do you suppose he's doing here?"

Fran ran to the window and looked down. Chuck followed her, and he saw that the front door was open, letting a long finger of lamplight splash across the yard. Doc stood there talking to Mike Malone, the Custer County sheriff. Doc was arguing and motioning for Malone to go away, but Malone, a square-shouldered bulldog of a man, was shaking his head.

Raising the window, Chuck called, "I'll be down as soon as I get my clothes on."

He lowered the window and fumbled along the bureau top until he found the matches. He lighted a lamp and looked at Fran, the silk nightgown clinging to her slender body. Her blonde hair, touched by the lamplight so that it seemed almost red, hung down her back in a long, smooth mass. Her arms were folded across her breasts, hugging them, and she was smiling gently as if that kiss would always be a bright, warm memory.

"I needed your strong arms tonight, Chuck," she said.

He put on his shirt and buttoned it and pulled on his pants. She stood there watching him, and he thought with a fierce rush of bitterness that this was wrong. He had given her strength to face tomorrow, but not all the other tomorrows that would include Bob Neville, for he was a man who would take of her strength without giving anything in return.

He tugged on his boots and rose. "You can't marry Bob. I won't let you."

The smile lingered at the corners of her mouth. "We'll see things differently in a few days, Chuck." She hesitated, and then said softly, "But I'm sorry Malone came when he did."

"I tell you I won't let you marry Bob," he said. "I'll kill him first."

Her face was grave then, and troubled. "That wouldn't help. Maybe we'll find the answer in time, but we don't have it yet."

He left her then and went down the stairs. He could hope that something would happen. That was all, just hope. Fran was right. He hadn't found the answer yet.

Malone was standing in front of the fireplace, holding his hands out to it. He swung around when he heard Chuck, his great shoulders sagging with weariness. He said, "We've got a ride to make. Pull on a coat and get a gun."

Chuck had no great respect for Mike Malone. The man was serving his third term as sheriff, and he'd been all right because nothing serious had happened during his nine years in office. He had been hand-picked by Dad Norman and Judge Castle, so, with Dad gone, he would look to the Judge for his orders.

Chuck glanced at Doc who was slouched on the couch, his chin dropped to his chest as if he were bone-weary. "Any change?"

"He's sleeping," Doc answered. "I doubt that he ever wakes up."

Malone said irritably, "Let's ride, Chuck."

Chuck swung to the lawman and was silent a moment, studying his square, muscle-ridged face. "Funny time to ask me to take a ride, Mike."

"Doc's here and there's nothing you can do," Malone said in a cranky voice. "You're Box N now. It's up to you."

"What is?"

"Getting that bunch of settlers off Chicken Creek. I just got back to town from the mountains when Reno Vance rode in and told me. If we don't move 'em now, we never will."

"Then you never will," Doc said. "You know what Dad's always said."

Malone threw out a big hand, irritated by what Doc had said. "Talking is one thing. Actually having 'em on your range is something else."

"Not to the Box N," Chuck said.

Malone scowled at him. "Take another look at this business. I can't do nothing till they break the law. You can. If you don't, Spiegle and some of the others will start throwing lead, and I don't know where we'll wind up after that."

Chuck walked past Malone into Dad's office, thinking that the sheriff was right. After Dad was gone, Spiegle and the Vance tribe and some of the others would make far more trouble than a band of land-hungry settlers. He took his gun belt off the wall and buckled it around him, wishing he had ridden over to Chicken Creek after he'd got Doc. But he hadn't. It was a chore he had to do sooner or later, so he might as well go with Malone.

He lifted the bone-handled .45 from leather and checked it, his mind going back to what Dad had said about the Judge bringing the railroad to Custer County. The notion kept nagging him that there had been something more to it than Dad had actually said. It was even possible that the Judge had brought the settlers to Chicken Creek, that it tied in somehow with his interest in the railroad.

As Chuck eased his gun back into the holster, the thought struck him that what he said to the settlers would depend upon the kind of people they were. But regardless of that, he had to make some sort of gesture tonight so that Spiegle would not have any excuse to start the ball. Later on Box N would be forced to make a stand, one way or the other, and he reluctantly admitted to himself that he was the man who would decide what that stand would be. Malone had been right about that, too.

Chuck put on his mackinaw and returned to the living room. He said, "Let's ride, Sheriff," and they went out into the cold night. Chuck found a lantern in the barn and lighted it. While he was saddling his buckskin gelding, he felt the sting of the first snow carried in on the wind.

"Something funny about this, Mike," Chuck said as they rode out of the yard. "These settlers coming in this time of year and Dad in the shape he's in. I don't like the smell of it."

"Me, neither," Malone said sourly. "Looks like they'd come in the spring when they could plant a crop and have some good weather to get settled in. Hell, they'll freeze to death afore they know it."

They angled northeast across the bunch grass, the wind blowing straight from the north. It was within an hour of dawn, but now the night was inky black, so dark that Malone and his horse made an indistinct shape beside Chuck. They dropped down the north side of Monk's Hill, crossed Dutchman's Gulch, and started up the next slope.

Chuck thought of saying something about the Judge and decided against it. As long as the Judge was high man in the county, Malone would be cagey, but he liked his job. If Castle got himself out on a limb, Chuck doubted that Malone's loyalty would stand the strain.

"I tangled with Spiegle today," Chuck said.

"I heard about it," Malone said. "That jasper is sure ornery. I reckon I've had him in the jug more times than any other five men in Custer County."

There was no more talk until they reached the top of the next hill. Dawn was at hand and the snow had stopped, leaving a thin covering on the ground. Chicken Creek was directly below them now, and by continuing in the same direction they had been following, they should hit the creek not far from the settlers' camp.

Suddenly Malone said, "Doc told me you're getting a half interest in the Box N. You had it coming, working for the old man the way you done."

Chuck was surprised. It wasn't like Malone to be happy about another man's good luck unless he had his own ax on the grindstone, and Chuck couldn't see how his ax fitted. Finally he said, "I don't savvy why you give a damn."

Malone laughed shortly. "Well sir, I've got my reasons. If Box N goes under, all the other ranches this side of town will, too. You can be a pretty tough hombre when you want to, and I figure you will, seeing as you've got an interest in the Box N. You take Bob Neville now, hell, he's all right for the legislature, but he ain't man enough to keep the settlers off Box N grass, and marrying Fran ain't gonna put any hair on his chest."

They were silent again as they rode down the long slope to the creek, the sun slowly breaking through the clouds so that it was full daylight by the time they reached the stream. Chuck saw the wagons to his right, and he swung up the creek toward them, Malone beside him.

All the way down the long hill Chuck had been thinking about what the sheriff had said. His opinion of Bob Neville was just about the same as everybody else's. Bob was liked. He'd get most of the votes from Custer County when he ran for the State Senate, but they would have no confidence in him when it came to something like this. Malone had his ax on the grindstone, all right. If the settlers flocked in and made a majority by the time Malone was up for re-election, he'd lose his star simply because he represented the cowmen's interest.

Chuck was still thinking about it when Malone said, "Easy, Son. There's a kid back of one of them wagons with a Winchester lined on us. It don't look good."

Chuck saw the kid and the rifle; he saw five men who had drawn back from their fire and made a long line along one of the wagons. They were carrying guns and they made no effort to hide their hostility. A cheap-John outfit, Chuck thought, judging from their work horses that were held in a rope corral on the other side of the creek.

The men had a tough look about them. They were proddy enough to start throwing lead if they had an excuse. Chuck pulled up twenty feet from the fire, a vague suspicion that had been in his mind now taking definite form. He had seen hundreds of settlers during the drives north to Umatilla, and he had never known one to carry a gun.

"Howdy," Chuck said.

The kid with the rifle called, "Stay where you are, mister. That's close enough."

But it wasn't a boy. It was a girl, and now she stepped into view, the cocked Winchester held on the ready. She stood there, spread-legged, dressed in a man's pants and shirt and sheepskin coat, and judging from the taut, wild look about her, it would take very little to make her pull the trigger.

CHAPTER VI

Gypsy Fargo

MALONE SUCKED in a long breath, then he shouted, "Throw that damned rifle down. I'm the law."

"Speak your piece," the girl called, "then get to hell out of here. We ain't done nothing to get the law after us."

The middle man of the five laughed. He was small and knot-headed, his face scarred and as ugly as sin. He leaned forward and spit a stream of tobacco juice into the fire that sizzled ominously. He said, "Better do like she says, boys. Gypsy's the best man of the bunch of us, and that's saying a lot on account of us Fargos are fighting sons from a way back."

Chuck dismounted, leaving his reins dangling. He said, "Cold morning. Mind if I warm up at your fire?"

"You're damned right I mind . . ." the girl began.

"Easy now, Gypsy, easy," the little man said. "Put that rifle up and give 'em a cup of coffee. It is a cold morning for a fact."

Malone remained in the saddle. Chuck glanced at the girl. He had never seen anyone like her. Wild as all hell, and proud, like a small, forest animal that has no lack of courage but is suspicious of everything.

She had the blackest eyes Chuck had ever seen, and she laid them on him, direct and penetrating. Then, as if not sure she was doing the right thing, she leaned the rifle against the wagon wheel, and coming to the fire, picked up the coffepot and filled two tin cups.

She stepped back, still eyeing Chuck. "Warm up, mister," she said flatly. "Get that coffee inside your gut, then vamose."

"Gypsy," the little man said reprovingly. "That ain't no way to be neighborly."

Malone stepped down and came to the fire. "Was that girl mine," he said, "I'd take a quirt to her and teach her some old-fashioned, cow-country manners."

"She ain't your girl," the little man said, "and I don't cotton to being told how to raise my kids. If you don't like her manners, ride on."

Chuck picked up a cup and drank the scalding coffee. "We'll ride after we get warmed up." He held out his hand to the small man. "I'm Chuck Harrigan, ramrod of the Box N. Heard you folks was camped here."

"I'm Pete Fargo." The little man shook hands. "We're all Fargos here. That's my boy Lon." He nodded at the young man who had stood beside him, then motioned to the others. "My brother Hank and his boys, Phil and Doby."

Chuck shook hands all around. "Mike Malone, the Custer County sheriff," he said, nodding at Malone.

The sheriff gave them a short nod and picked up his cup. He was tired and cranky, and the reception the Fargos had given him had not sweetened his temper. Chuck had not shaken hands with the girl who had moved back to the wagon wheel. She kept on staring at him as if trying to probe his mind, then for no reason that was apparent to Chuck, she laughed.

"So you're Chuck Harrigan," she said. "We've heard of you. Heard of the Box N, too."

"You're on our grass," Chuck said.

"We know it," she snapped. "We're not camping, neither. We're settling. Now what are you fixing to do about that?"

"Run us off," Lon Fargo murmured. "That right, Harrigan?"

"Maybe," Chuck said.

"I'll tell you something," the girl said flatly. "You ain't running us nowhere."

Pete Fargo shoved his hands into his pockets and teetered back and forth in his spike-heeled boots. "That oughtta be plain enough, Harrigan. I'm surprised you showed up with just the sheriff. We figured you'd come helling over the ridge with your whole damned crew, but no, you ride in meek as Moses." He leaned forward and spit into the fire again, throwing an exploratory glance at Chuck. "You're right, Gypsy. He won't run us nowhere."

Thoroughly angry, Malone burst out, "Then I'll do the running, mister. This is cow country. Get to hell out of it."

Lon stepped forward, a hand on gun butt. He was taller than his father, but he had the same narrow, wolfish look to his face. No good, Chuck thought, none of them unless it was the girl. She seemed to be a different breed of cat. He liked the way she stared at him, unabashed and unafraid.

"No use beating around the bush," young Fargo said. "Pull your irons if you're aiming to push. If you ain't, clear out."

"We ain't pushing this morning, but there's some things I'm curious about." Chuck glanced again at the girl. Eighteen or nineteen, he thought. Raised with men and allowed she was as tough as any of them. He asked, "How'd you folks happen to come here?"

He was looking at Gypsy, but it was her father who answered. "The railroad. That's why. Custer County would have been settled a long time ago if it hadn't been a hell of a haul to the railroad. Good wheat land. You can tell it by looking at it." He wiped a hand across his mouth, still teetering on his heels. "All cowmen are alike. They use government land like the Lord had given it to 'em. Well sir, He didn't."

"I know that," Chuck said. "For years my boss has said we'd see the day when these hills were plowed and sowed to wheat. In the long run the country will be better off. More folks living here. More business for the town. But that day ain't here yet, and we don't aim to help it along."

The Fargo men showed their surprise, brittle eyes on Chuck as if they didn't know quite how to take this. The girl said, "Maybe you figure to ride out and then come back and shoot us when we ain't looking."

"No, that ain't my size," Chuck said. "Staked out your claims yet?"

"That we have," Pete said. "Right down along the creek, five quarter sections. Come spring we'll plow." He took a long breath, a little easier now that he saw there would be no trouble. "You best get one thing through your noggin, friend. If we have to fight, we'll fight like hell."

"Any reason for you settling on Chicken Creek?" Chuck asked.

"Judge Castle, he said . . ." Lon began

His father slapped him across the mouth. "Shut your tater trap." He glared at Chuck. "We looked the country over and we liked it here. Water. We're out of the wind some. And the land on both sides of the creek looks good."

Chuck nodded, masking his face against the satisfaction that warmed him. He had cast out his bait and caught a bigger fish than he had expected to. "All these hills have good land. You ought to know what you're up against, though, coming this late in the year. Our winters are mean."

Pete jabbed a finger at a pile of lumber. "We'll make out. We'll get our shacks up before bad weather hits . . ."

Chuck heard the girl cry out. That was the only warning he had. Lon lunged at him, his fists swinging, a right catching Chuck on the side of the head. The blow jarred him, but it was too high to be damaging. He ducked a left, blocked another right, and then, thoroughly angry at this unprovoked attack, stood his ground and sledged young Fargo with a looping punch that knocked him back on his heels.

The other Fargo men yelled encouragement to Lon, but the girl screamed, "Stay out of it, Phil. You, too, Doby, or I'll plug both of you."

For an interval Chuck and Lon traded blow for blow, but Lon, considerably smaller, took more punishment than he gave. Suddenly frantic, he swung a wild uppercut that missed by half a foot. He left himself wide open, and Chuck caught him with a hammering right that knocked him flat on his back. Glancing toward the wagon, Chuck saw that Gypsy was holding her rifle on Hank Fargo and his boys.

Chuck should never have taken his eyes off Lon, carelessness that came close to costing him his life, or at least a vicious beating. Lon had fallen near the creek. He jumped up, his right hand gripping a rock twice as big as his fist, and threw it as Chuck turned toward him.

Chuck jerked his head sideways, the rock missing him by inches. He was off-balance for a moment, and Lon, sensing this momentary advantage, drove at him in a desperate effort to end the fight with a single blow. He got in one solid punch that rocked Chuck's head. It was his best, but it wasn't enough. He fell against Chuck, hugging him and trying to smother his blows, but Chuck grabbed a handful of hair and, yanking his head back, hit him on the sharp point of his chin. Lon's grip relaxed, and Chuck stepped away and let him fall. He was out cold.

Chuck saw that the girl was still holding her rifle on her uncle and his sons. He looked at Pete Fargo. "You're a pack of wolves," he said. "You'd all have jumped me if your girl hadn't held them off. Now I'm supposed to owe her something, I reckon."

Pete tipped his head forward and spat at Chuck's feet. "Jumping you was Lon's idea, not mine. He got a licking, and that was fair enough. And as far as your advice is concerned, keep it to yourself. We'll make it through the winter all right. I already seen Partridge in town. He'll give us credit for all the grub we need."

"You're lying," Malone shouted. "Part wouldn't do that. He'd lose every customer he's got."

"Dust along," Pete said wearily. "Go on. Git."

Chuck walked to his buckskin and mounted. He saw that Gypsy had leaned her rifle against the wagon wheel again, and he wondered what they would do to her for holding the rest of them off his back. Lon was sitting up, glaring at him, his eyes filled with a deep and passionate hatred.

"If you freeze to death or starve, Fargo," Chuck said, nodding at Pete, "don't expect help from nobody. Maybe we won't keep you from settling here, but the country will whip you before spring."

"Go on, I said," Pete shouted. "You, too, Sheriff."

"Don't give me orders," Malone said. "I know your kind, living off somebody's beef until you get your start. Now I'll tell you something. The first steer you butcher will get you a rope necktie, and I won't stop nobody from yanking the rope."

The Fargos said nothing until Malone was in the saddle, then Pete called, "We don't have to steal nobody's beef, Sheriff. All we want is to be let alone."

Malone leaned forward, one hand gripping the saddle horn. "You won't be. Harrigan was talking for himself. The other boys don't see it his way. They'll come over the hill all right, and they'll be throwing more lead'n you ever saw before."

Malone and Chuck swung their horses, but they had not gone ten feet until Gypsy called, "Harrigan."

They pulled up and looked back. She ran toward them, the hostility gone from her brown, little face. She asked Chuck, "You know where Bob Neville's Mule Shoe is?"

"Sure. He's a neighbor of ours."

"Will you take me to his ranch?"

"Don't do it, Harrigan," Malone said ominously. "You've done enough damage, pussyfooting around . . ."

"Me, pussyfooting around?" Chuck said. "What were you doing, Mike, when her brother jumped me? I didn't notice you keeping that bunch off my back."

For a moment Malone's sullen eyes locked with Chuck's, then he wheeled his horse and rode away. Chuck looked down at the girl's upturned face, anxious and with no trace of the tough defiance that had been there a few minutes before. He wondered if Bob was into this, too, along with the Judge. These people weren't ordinary settlers. They looked more like outlaws. Maybe the Judge, for some reason of his own, had hired them to settle on Chicken Creek because the Box N wouldn't run them off.

If the Fargos stayed through the winter, they would break the ice and the word would spread. When spring came, settlers would cover the hills like a plague of locusts. But if the Fargos failed, the grass might be saved for a while at least.

Looking into the girl's anxious face, frantic with the waiting, the idea that the Judge and Bob had had a hand in bringing the Fargos here grew in Chuck's mind until it became a certainty. He owed the girl this much, and more. Besides, her friendship was worth having.

"All right, I'll take you," Chuck said.

The girl whirled, calling, "Wait till I saddle up."

She roped and saddled a bay gelding. Chuck noticed that the saddle horses, held in another rope corral above the wagons, were good stock, a fact which bore out the conclusion he had already reached. Genuine settlers would not invest their money in expensive riding horses, even if they had any extra money which was not likely.

The Fargo men stood around the fire, watching the girl as if faintly amused. Lon was on his feet, a hand touching his bruised face, his eyes telling Chuck he would not forget the beating he had just taken.

When Gypsy mounted, Chuck motioned up the hill and put his buckskin across the creek. Gypsy caught up with him a moment later. He looked back and saw that Lon had drawn his gun, but Pete was twisting it out of his boy's hand. At that moment Chuck had been as close to death as he had ever been in his life. For some reason Pete had not wanted him to die, perhaps because it was not part of the Judge's plan.

Chuck breathed easier when he and Gypsy were far enough up the slope to make accurate shooting impossible. Gypsy made no effort to talk. She rode well, Chuck saw. This was additional evidence that the Fargos were not bona fide settlers, just a tough family Judge Castle had stumbled onto.

"You know Bob pretty well?" Chuck asked.

"Real well," she answered.

"How much did Judge Castle pay you folks to settle on Chicken Creek?"

She looked at him, dark eyes mocking. "Who the hell is Judge Castle?"

"You know, all right. Your brother let the cat out of the bag."

"Lon knew he'd talked too damned much as soon as Pa cracked him one. He got mad then. That's why he jumped you. Got a hell of a temper, Lon has. Had to take it out on somebody and you were handy."

"Why did you horn into it?" Chuck demanded.

"I don't love you, Harrigan," she said quickly, "if that's what you're thinking. I had two good reasons. They'd have killed you. The sheriff wouldn't have stopped them. He don't have a spoonful of sand in his craw. You could sure tell that."

"What were those reasons?"

"This is one. I figured you'd take me to Bob's spread." She laughed shortly. "It ain't much of a reason, is it? I could have asked somebody else. Well, it was mostly on account of killing you would have caused hell to bust loose. We aim to stay on Chicken Creek, but Lon, he never looked that far ahead in his life."

They topped the hill, the wind slashing at them with needle-sharp claws, then they dropped down the south slope, the Mule Shoe buildings directly below them. Gypsy had buried her face in the collar of her sheepskin, but here the wind tapered off and now she reached up and turned her collar down.

"That's Bob's layout." Chuck pointed to the buildings. "I don't reckon you'll find him home today."

"I'll wait." She glanced at him, biting her lower lip. "You ain't like I thought you'd be, rodding the Box N and finding us on your grass and all. I'm sorry I acted the way I did when you rode up, but we'd been expecting trouble and we thought that was it."

Now that she had lost some of her wariness, Chuck saw that she wasn't bad looking. She just needed to put on a dress and fuss with her black hair that hung down her back in a long braid.

A few minutes later they reached Mule Shoe, a small ranch that made no effort to pretend it was either large or prosperous. Bob Neville probably made less money than any other rancher north of the mountains. He hired one hand named Dake Collins who did most of the work because Bob was gone more days than he was home.

When Bob was here, he kept the place up, for he was a fastidious man who hated disorder. Now, glancing at Gypsy, Chuck saw she was aware that the place was run down. She was staring at the corral. The manure that should have been forked out weeks ago was piled high.

"Bob's been gone," Chuck said.

"I know," she said, and swung down.

She went into the log cabin that had been built years ago before there was a sawmill in the country. She didn't knock; she just shoved the door open and went in. Funny, Chuck thought. She acted as if she owned the place.

He decided she did know Bob as well as she pretended, and he wondered what she thought of the place. Just the cabin, a slab shed, and a pole corral that held a couple of saddle horses. There was a small pile of wood beside the chopping block. Maybe Collins had gone to the mountains for a load of wood. If he hadn't, he'd better go soon, or he'd be fighting snow up to his neck.

The girl appeared in the doorway. "It's a hog pen," she said angrily, "but I'll make something out of it. What kind of a lazy, good-for-nothing does Bob hire?"

"You can see," Chuck answered. "Can you get back to camp?"

"I'm staying here." She looked at the corral and then the slab shed, her face bitter with disappointment. "This ain't what I expected after listening to Bob, but it's better'n what I've been used to." She brought her dark eyes to Chuck's face. "In case you haven't guessed, me'n Bob are getting married."

No, he hadn't guessed. There was nothing she could have said which would have surprised him more than this, and she must have seen the expression of shocked incredulity on his face.

"That's right," she said. "If you see him, tell him I'm here and I'm cleaning up his damned old shack. Tell him he'd better get over here and not keep me waiting."

He rode away, having more than enough for his mind to chew over. It was possible the girl was lying right down the line, but he didn't think so. Even with all her gall, it was hard to believe she'd move in and say flatly she and Bob were getting married.

There must be something between them. He wondered what Bob would say when he told him. And Fran? He couldn't tell her, he decided bleakly. She wouldn't believe him if he did.

The sun was noon high when Chuck reached the Box N. The sky had cleared, and the snow was gone even from the shaded sides of the buildings. As he offsaddled, Bob came out of the house and walked rapidly toward the corral. When he reached Chuck, he said, "Dad's gone. Died about an hour ago."

Chuck nodded and put his buckskin into the corral. He felt no shock, no sudden rush of grief, only worry and a heavy burden of responsibility. He turned to Bob who was eyeing him expectantly. He asked, "How did Fran take it?"

"About like you are," Bob said. "I guess you're both glad it's over since it had to come."

"Yeah, it had to come." Chuck rolled a smoke. "I've been thinking about what Dad said last night. About you."

"He was wrong," Bob said. "Dead wrong. I've loved Fran for a long time, and I'd keep on loving her if she didn't have a nickel."

Chuck fished a match out of his pocket. "Funny thing happened this morning. I met a girl named Gypsy Fargo. She's at your place. Says she's gonna marry you."

Bob's mouth sprung open. He gripped a corral pole, his eyes glassy, his face turning green as if he were about to lose his dinner. He breathed, "You're bulling me."

"Go see."

"I will. Damn her, I never promised . . ." He choked and lowered his gaze. "You won't tell Fran, will you?"

"That's your chore."

"I'll never tell her." He glared defiantly at Chuck. "It isn't true. I just met the Fargo girl last spring. She . . . she's trying to get money out of me, that's all." Then, for some reason, his anger settled on Chuck. "If you fetched her here to break me and Fran up, I'll kill you. You hear me? I'll kill you."

Wheeling, Chuck strode toward the house. It was true, he thought. Bob had lied with his mouth, but his eyes and face had told the truth. If Chuck didn't do something, Fran would be hurt. He wondered why Bob had threatened him, for certainly Bob knew he had never heard of Gypsy before, and then he wondered if Bob was capable of killing him, or any man.

He thought, *Maybe I'll have to kill Bob to keep him from killing me.* But if he did, Fran would never speak to him again.

CHAPTER VII

Cat's-Paw

BOB NEVILLE saddled a black gelding and left Box N at a run, heading east and hoping Chuck would think he was going home. He knew he should have gone in to see Fran and tell her he had to get over to Mule Shoe, but he'd be back tomorrow. Right now there were two things he must do and neither would wait. He had to see Judge Castle and he had to see Gypsy.

He swore bitterly, filled with the poison of his hate for Chuck Harrigan. He knew that Chuck was a better man than he was, at least in the ways that counted in the bunch-grass country. Chuck was a cowman, a good rider, a fighting man: solid qualities that were rated high in Custer County.

But there was something else about Chuck that was less tangible. When Bob turned downslope toward town, he pulled his black to a walk. Then, with his heart slowing down and his feeling for Chuck less virulent, he thought carefully about this other element in Chuck's makeup. It was, as nearly as he could mentally phrase it, a steadfast devotion to Dad Norman and the things he had believed in.

In this regard Dad's death would not change Chuck. If Chuck stayed, the Box N would go on just as it had, and in time Chuck would hold the same position in the county Dad Norman had. Even if Bob married Fran, he knew he would never run the ranch. Even if he wanted to, he would never be the boss.

That brought him to what Dad Norman had said last night. For the two years he had been engaged to Fran, the old man had always treated him courteously. Not by a word or gesture or inflection of his voice had he shown his distrust. But last night he'd skinned him alive, and even now Bob could not be completely sure how Fran had taken it.

Bob's pride was hurt more than anything else. He knew his talents as well as he had measured Chuck's. Pretending was one of them. Charm, a talent for wearing clothes, a sense of proper word selection: all of these tied in with his ability to pose as something he wasn't.

He had supposed that only Judge Castle really knew him, but he had been wrong. All this time Dad Norman had been sizing him up and he'd pegged him right. It hurt and worried him. Maybe even Fran sensed something phony about him.

He had never been able to pin her down to a wedding date, but he would now. She couldn't go on using her father's illness as an excuse. If he didn't marry her soon, she'd slip away from him, and every dream and plan he had would blow away like smoke.

On top of everything else, Dad Norman had left half the Box N to Chuck. That was the final straw. He had been sure he could talk to Chuck about staying but work it so he wouldn't. Now it couldn't be done. No man was fool enough to walk out and leave half a spread. The bonanza days of the Box N were gone, but even if all these hills were plowed and sowed to wheat, the deeded land on Monk's Hill would be worth a fortune.

He was in Norman now and he looked up at the long, tawny slope to the south, then turned to stare at the hill he had come down, exactly like the other. The sameness of this country bothered him as much as the loneliness. You could ride ten miles north or east or west, and except for the town, you'd be looking at exactly the same thing you saw right here.

He had to get out or go crazy. If it hadn't been for Judge Castle's glittering promises, he'd have left years ago. Now, any way he looked at it, he was stuck for several more years. Next fall he'd try for the State Senate. After that, well, if his luck held, he'd run for a state office.

He had his political connections, but they wouldn't pay off yet. That was why he needed Fran and the Box N. Both would help him politically here in the bunch-grass country. Even after the county was settled by wheat farmers, it would still help because the Box N wouldn't fight them, and he could pose as their champion.

As he reined up in front of the bank and tied, his mind swung to Gypsy Fargo. Judge Castle was to blame for her being here. Everything had been working out fine except for what Dad Norman had said last night, and that wouldn't be fatal. Now the fat was in the fire, and it was up to the Judge to get him out of the jam he was in.

He climbed the stairs to Castle's office over the bank, his heart hammering. For the first time in his life he was going to be tough. He'd tell the Judge exactly what he had to do. He'd been a yes man too long. If he were Chuck Harrigan, he thought wildly, he'd beat hell out of the Judge.

Castle's stenographer sat at the desk in the outer office. When she saw Bob, she said, "I'll tell the Judge you're here . . ."

"Don't bother," he shouted at her, and crossing the room, yanked the door open to the Judge's private office. He went in and slammed the door, banging a picture on the panel walls. He stood there, glaring at Castle who looked up from his desk.

"Nobody comes in here like that," the Judge said evenly. "Not even you, Senator."

"To hell with you and your grand way." Bob knew his face was red and he wasn't at his best, as angry as he was, but he couldn't help himself. "You're a fool, Judge, a God-damned fool, and I'm the one holding the sack because you had to go ahead without asking me or telling me or anything."

The Judge leaned back in his swivel chair, his dignity ruffled. For a moment he was silent, his mouth pursed out, his long face ugly with smoldering resentment.

·"You can apologize, Senator," he said. "I don't know what's eating you, but I'll remind you that you need me a hell of a lot more than I need you."

"I don't think so." Bob dropped into a leather-covered chair and put his trembling hands on his knees. "You need me all right because I know enough to blow you sky high. You never gave my welfare a thought. Why should I give yours any?"

"What are you talking about?"

"Several things. This business of Harrigan getting half the Box N for one. Where does that leave me when I marry Fran?"

"I'm beginning to wonder if you'll ever get your loop on her," the Judge said tartly. "If I was engaged to a girl for two years, I'd see she got off the . . ."

"How you play your cards is one thing," Bob snapped, "and how I play mine is another. I'm asking you about that will."

Castle's bony fingers tapped the mahogany desk top. "I'll take care of it."

"You heard what he said last night. How can . . ."

"Never mind how. I'll do it. Is that what you came helling in here about?"

"No." Bob leaned back, a little sick and weak, now that his rage was passing. "I'm sorry for what I said. It's just that everything was lined out, but now hell's to pay. Gypsy Fargo is in my cabin waiting for me. She told Harrigan she was going to marry me."

Castle scratched his long nose, grinning a little. "So that's it. Well, I knew you were seeing her, but I didn't know it had gone that far. So you've got two women."

"Thanks to you for bringing the Fargos here," Bob snapped. "Sure, I saw Gypsy, but I never intended marrying her."

"Just talked yourself into her bed. That it?"

"I wasn't the first man," Bob said thickly. "What the hell! I suppose you're a paragon of virtue?"

"Not exactly," the Judge said. "But I'm not married and I don't intend to be. That makes you and me different."

"The hell it does. If Gypsy hadn't showed up on this range, it wouldn't have made any difference."

Castle's laugh was a soft, taunting sound. "One woman on this side of the mountains and one on the other, but as long as they stayed that way, you were safe." He shook his head. "No, Senator, I never claimed to be a paragon of virtue, but I never let my women get together, either."

"This was your doing, not mine."

"You'd better keep me informed on your love affairs. You knew what I planned to use the Fargos for. Why didn't you stay away from the little bitch?"

Bob stared at the floor. He knew, all right. He would never have met Gypsy if the Judge hadn't taken him to see the Fargos. He had gone back, and he'd had the inside track because he was the Judge's friend. Or at first it had been that way, but later it had been strictly between him and Gypsy, a matter of making her love him. He had succeeded too well.

But it had worked both ways, for he had never known a woman with the fire and passion that Gypsy possessed. Even when he had come back and seen Fran, his thoughts had been on Gypsy and he wasn't sure he would ever get her out of his mind. He had two women, all right, one he needed and one he wanted, but he had his tail in a crack because it had never occurred to him that Gypsy would come with her menfolks to Custer County.

Castle rose and took a cigar from the box on his desk. He walked to the window and stood with his back to it, eyes on Bob as he lighted the cigar. He said, "Now that you've cooled down, let's take a look at this, Senator. We need each other. I grant that, but I don't want to hear any more talk about you blowing me sky high. Understand?"

"I didn't mean . . ."

"All right," the Judge said curtly. "Our partnership is one of convenience, not of friendship, but you should know as well as I do that it can go on indefinitely to our mutual advantage. This mess with Gypsy is your fault, not mine, but I'll help you get out of it." He took a wallet from his pocket and counted two hundred dollars in greenbacks. "Send her back home. Promise her the moon if you need to. Just get her out of the country before she sees Fran."

Bob rose, and walking to the desk, picked up the money. He put it in his pocket, not sure he could work it, but at least he was getting some help which was more than he expected. Maybe he could get her to take half the money. He could use the rest himself.

"I'll see what I can do." He turned to the door and then swung back. "What are you going to do about Harrigan?"

"I don't know," Castle admitted. "He's got to be handled. Some way!"

"Spiegle?"

"Possibly. Spiegle may take care of it without me having to nudge him. Or we may have to use Pete Fargo."

"He's got to be killed," Bob said, trying not to let his voice tell Castle how strongly he felt about it. "The sooner the better. Fran leans on him.'"

"You've got one asset with a hell of a lot of liabilities," Castle said in a cranky tone. "You've got a smooth tongue. You ought to be able to get them quarreling and then she'll lean on you."

Bob stood motionless, one hand on the doorknob. There was no trace of good humor in Castle's face. It was dark and forbidding, and he knew that Castle was thinking of himself again, and of Dad Norman whom he hated. Bob hesitated, wanting to say one more thing, to convince Castle how important Chuck's death was, but the time for it had passed. Still, there might not be a better time.

"He's got to be killed," Bob said again. "It's for your interest as well as mine. If he lives, he'll be Dad Norman all over again."

Castle threw out a hand in a sudden, violent gesture. "You

think I can't read the writing on the wall?" He laughed sourly. "Maybe you'd like to pull the trigger." He shook his head.
"No, you're too yellow for that. You're yellow right down to
the heels of your fancy shoes. I said you had just one asset.
Now get out of here and use it."

Anger was in Bob again. He could not defend himself
against the charge of being yellow, but he knew that Judge
Castle was no different, or he would not have remained in
Dad Norman's shadow all this time. He walked out, ignoring
the girl who was staring at him with the frightened eyes of
one who has just heard a man defy God.

He went down the stairs to the street, finding some satisfaction in the fact that he'd had enough self-control to keep
from telling Castle what he thought of his courage. He could
afford to be a cat's-paw as long as it suited his interest. Once
he had made his own future secure, he could cut the strings
that bound him to the Judge.

Mounting, he rode out of town, following the Monk's Hill
road for a mile, then swung east. In spite of himself, he could
not ignore the tingle that the prospect of seeing Gypsy again
aroused in him. For a time he considered what would happen
if he broke with Fran and married Gypsy. It would make his
position solid with the Fargos. When spring came, the settlers would move in. Before a year was out, they'd be in a
majority and he'd have their votes.

No, it wouldn't do. For one thing, the Judge would blow
up. He wasn't ready to come into the open. Besides, Bob
needed the Box N and the money Dad Norman had left for
her in the bank. If he handled Fran right, she'd let him have
all he needed.

All! He rolled the word around in his mind. A good prospect. A very good prospect if he was rid of Chuck Harrigan.
So he had to get rid of Gypsy and he began thinking about
how it could be done.

When he reached the ranch, he saw with irritation the
signs of Dake Collins' shiftlessness. His anger flared and he
told himself he'd fire the man. He knew at once he wouldn't
for the simple reason he couldn't find another man who
would remain alone as much as Collins did and work for the
pittance he paid the fellow.

He dismounted, noting that the wagon and team were
gone. Probably Collins was in the mountains getting wood.
It was past time, he thought. He swung toward the cabin
and stopped. Gypsy stood in the doorway, her shoulders
against the jamb, her round breasts rising and falling with
her breathing, her dark eyes showing her pleasure at seeing
him again.

For a moment they stood looking at each other, the girl
smiling as if aware of the power she had over him. She said,
"You're slow getting here, Lover."

He moved toward her, trying to hate her because of what her presence would do to his plans, but he couldn't. Fran would never mean to him what this girl did. When he was a step away, she backed into the cabin. He followed her and saw at once that she had cleaned the room up. There was a pie on the table, coffee smell filled the air, and there was a pan of biscuits on the back of the stove.

Gypsy kept moving so that the table was between them. She said, "This is the first time I ever saw you when you couldn't talk."

It was the first time, too, when he couldn't think of the right thing to say, so he said, "I'm hungry."

"That's fine." She pouted. "Real fine. You haven't seen me for weeks. I clean your damned old boar's nest up and cook you a meal and all you can say is you're hungry."

He knew he was lost if he took her in his arms and kissed her, and that was the only thing which would satisfy her. Angry at himself, he blurted, "You shouldn't be here. I didn't know you were coming."

"I shouldn't be here?" Her eyes sparked with quick anger. "Now that's a hell of a way to talk to your woman. Why shouldn't I be here, I'd like to know."

"Because this is mighty touchy business, your folks settling on Chicken Creek. If people knew . . . I mean, about you and me . . ."

"Ashamed of me?" she asked, her voice deceptively soft. "You want a woman with a lot of geegaws and a ribbon in her hair and some money in the bank. That it?"

"My political future . . ."

"Who gives a damn about that?" she flared. "You sang a different tune when you wanted to bed down with me. Let's have it plain without none of your fancy trimmings. Are we getting married or ain't we?"

"Not now." He pulled the money out of his pocket that Castle had given him, not holding any of it back. "Look, Honey. Take this and stay in the Willamette Valley until we get things straightened out."

She stared at the money and then lifted her black eyes to his face. She raised a hand and brushed a rebellious lock of hair back from her forehead. "Well," she breathed, "I guess that makes me the damnedest sucker in the state. I believed you, all that hogwash about loving me and having a fine ranch. Here it is, a greasy sack spread if I ever saw one. And now you think you can buy me into leaving the country."

She stalked to the wall and grabbed her hat off a peg and jammed it on her head. He said, "Now don't . . ."

She stood in the doorway, her dark little face twisted with bitterness. "Mister, if there's anything I hate, it's a God-damned liar, and you're it." She jabbed a forefinger at him. "Something about this is fishy, so fishy it stinks. You're bak-

ing your own little pudding, ain't you? Well, I'll find out
what it is, and so help me, I'll spoil it if it's the last thing
I do."

She flounced out of the cabin and mounting, galloped
away. He looked at the money in his hand, then threw it on
the table and sat down, his knees too weak to hold him. He
had lost her and she'd see to it that he lost Fran.

He was sick, sick with frustration and hopelessness and a
sense of impending disaster. Then he thought of Chuck who
had brought Gypsy to the cabin, Chuck who was the kind of
man who was never helpless no matter how tight a squeeze
he got into, and as he thought, the poison of his hatred
started working in him again.

He began wondering if he had the courage to pull the
trigger. He would fix a lot of things if he did, including
Judge Castle's opinion of him. He got up and left the cabin,
considering how it could be done without danger to himself.
Now, filled with hard purpose, he told himself he had to do
it, and he was not afraid.

CHAPTER VIII

Girl Alone

FROM a living room window Fran watched Chuck and Bob
talk at the corral; she saw Chuck turn and stalk toward the
house. She could always tell when he was angry, but there
seemed to be no reason for it now. She had sent Bob out to
tell him about Dad. She didn't move when Chuck came in.
She remained by the window until Bob had caught and saddled a horse and ridden out of the yard.

"Where's he going, Chuck?" she asked.

"Home, I reckon."

She watched Bob until he was out of sight, piqued by the
fact he had not come in to say good-bye or tell her where
he was going. Chuck was standing in the middle of the room.
She knew he was looking at her, and suddenly she whirled
to face him, irritated by his silence.

"Well?"

He took off his mackinaw and she saw he was carrying
his gun. He threw the mackinaw down on a chair and laid
his Stetson on top of it. He moved to the fireplace, asking,
"What do you mean by 'well'?"

She was trembling, closer to hysteria than she had ever
been in her life before. She cried, "You went off with Malone
last night, and when you get back, I send Bob out to tell you
about Dad and he rides off. What happened? I've got a right
to know, haven't I?"

He remained by the fireplace, his gray eyes fixed on something across the room. He seemed to be considering her question and finding the answer difficult to arrive at, and her irritation grew. She screamed, "Answer me."

"Me and Malone went to see the settlers on Chicken Creek," he said slowly.

"Did you tell them to get off?"

"No."

"Why didn't you?"

"They haven't broke no laws yet."

"But they're on Box N range," she said hotly. "It's your ranch, too. You can't just stand here and let them have it."

Slowly his eyes came to meet hers and she saw the misery that was in them. "You heard what Dad said last night."

She sat down on the leather couch. For a long moment she was silent, waiting until she could regain control of herself. She knew what was wrong. It was simply the relief from the tension of waiting all these months for her father to die. She had thought she would be glad to see him go because it would release him from pain, but she wasn't glad at all. She was alone, terribly alone.

Chuck had left with Malone. Today she had needed him when she'd sat beside her father's bed and watched him die. Bob hadn't been any help. He'd tried. He'd said the words, but something had been wrong. Chuck could have helped.

"He's dead," she said dully, "but we're alive and we can't let everything he worked for just . . . just go up in smoke."

He didn't say anything. She knew he didn't want to argue with her just now, but his silence angered her because she sensed his resistance to her will. She had never been able to change his mind once it was made up. Perhaps that was the reason she clung to Bob.

She got up and began walking restlessly around the room. If she didn't do something she was going to blow up and scream at him again. Mrs. Benson came in from the dining room to call, "I've got your breakfast ready, Chuck."

"Thanks," he said, and followed her into the kitchen.

Fran sat down on the couch, and pulling her legs up under her, smoothed out her skirt. There were times like this when she felt she didn't really know Chuck, not the way she knew Bob.

Calmer now, she remembered how often her mother had said the same thing about her father. They had seemed to be in love with each other, but she remembered how many times their wills had clashed and her mother had bruised herself against Dad's resistance. They'd make up after her mother had had a crying jag, but the residue of those quarrels had been like a corroding acid, leaving a wound that even time never fully healed.

She had been young, too young to really understand, but

she remembered her mother telling her, "I just can't understand why your father does the foolish things he does."

The strange part of it was that many of their quarrels had been over some generous act of her father's. Like guaranteeing payment of a store bill so Partridge would continue to give credit to some poor family, perhaps the Vances. Time had always proved her father right. Fran could not remember a dozen times when he had lost anything.

Dad had not been above taunting his wife by saying, "Just goes to prove that a man sows what he reaps. Bread cast upon the water, you know." But he never proved anything to Fran's mother. They would go through it all over again the next time the situation came up.

Fran wondered if she was being like her mother. No, this was different, a question of survival. They couldn't just give up. But that was the part which didn't make sense. Chuck had his faults, but lack of courage was not one of them. He had never ducked a fight in his life.

She remembered watching one time when he had tangled with a new puncher. She never did find out what the trouble was over, but it must have been something terrible. Chuck fought like a crazy man. He was knocked down five times, but he kept getting up and he finally won because he didn't have sense enough to know when he was licked.

Dad had paid the puncher off. He rode away, so groggy he had to hang to the saddle horn with both hands. Chuck had a black eye and a cut lip and a bloody nose. He was too tired to stand up, but he got on his horse and rode off with the crew.

Fran remembered she had been horrified and repelled by the fight, but she had not been able to turn around and walk off. She had seen the blood and sweat rolling down their faces; she had heard the grunts and oaths and the solid thud of fist on flesh and bone, but she'd stayed out there by the poplar trees until it was finished, then she'd gone into the house and she'd been sick.

She had a horrible feeling she was not being true to her father's memory, but she couldn't change. If Chuck wouldn't fight, she would. She'd hire gunhands if she had to. She'd arm the Box N riders. She'd see there wasn't a single settler left on Chicken Creek. But she'd have to wait until after the funeral.

Suddenly she remembered she had not sent for a preacher. She put on her coat and went out to the corrals where young Johnny Bain was working with a filly. She called, "Johnny."

He came to her at once, wiping a hand across a sweaty face. He was the youngest of the crew of four that Dad always kept through the winter, and although he had worked for the Box N a shorter time than the others, she did not doubt his loyalty any more than she did Hod Davis who had come to the bunch-grass country with her father.

"I reckon it ain't right," Johnny said apologetically, "working this way with Dad just gone, but I've got to do something."

His freckled face was smeared with dirt, and she saw he was expecting a scolding. She said quickly, "It's all right, Johnny. I want you to do something. Ride over to Condon and get Rufus Mattingly to preach the funeral. It'll be day after tomorrow. In the afternoon."

He bobbed his head, relief breaking across his face. "I'll sure do that, ma'am, but supposin' he can't come?"

"He will if he isn't sick. He thought a lot of Dad."

"I know, ma'am," Johnny said, and swung around.

She walked back to the house, bending her slim body against the wind. When she shut the front door behind her, she saw that Chuck was sitting at the kitchen table, his head bowed as if he were too tired to get up. She took off her coat and hat and went into the kitchen.

Mrs. Benson called from the pantry. "Make Chuck go to bed, Fran. He's worn down to a nubbin."

Fran sat down across the table from Chuck. "He's a big boy, Mrs. Benson, too big to listen to me."

Chuck straightened up and grinned at her. "Dunno about that. Why don't you tell me to go to bed and see what happens?"

"I will when you tell me what you said to Bob that made him leave the way he did."

Chuck drew the makings from his pocket and rolled a cigarette, his head tipped down so she couldn't see his mouth, but she felt his resistance build up in him. She saw this whole thing more clearly now, and she realized there must be some good reason for Chuck acting this way.

He struck a match and lighted his cigarette. He said, "Ask Bob."

She rose and came around the table and sat down beside him. She said, "Chuck, I just don't understand you. If we don't do something about the settlers, we'll lose all our friends."

"We've already lost Jack Spiegle."

"I didn't mean him. I mean Vance and Rusty Wade and the ones that count."

He looked at her through the spiraling smoke of his cigarette. "Were you with Dad when he died?"

She nodded. "He just quit breathing." She was silent, thinking about it, and then she added, "It was kind of nice, the way he went, peaceful and happy looking."

"Maybe he'd had a look at the big, black stallion he was gonna ride," Chuck said. "Well, I'm just hoping I can face the Lord someday with the kind of writing in the book Dad had."

There was more in his mind, she thought, and it all tied up with what he was going to do about the settlers on Chicken Creek. She had the answer, then, to the question that had been puzzling her about Chuck. He was trying to think what Dad would do, and when he decided, he'd do it, come hell or high water, losing friends or keeping them. In that way he was as much like Dad as a son could have been.

"Hod took the body into town," she said in a low voice. "Doc said he'd take care of everything. We're having the funeral day after tomorrow. Hod took the livery horse back to town, too." She paused, and then added, "I just sent Johnny to Condon for Mattingly."

Chuck nodded. "Dad would have wanted him."

She thought about the preacher in Norman who would probably think he should preach the funeral, but Dad had despised him for the shallowness of his thinking. Once he had come out to the Box N to talk to Dad about his soul and how it could be saved, but when Dad had asked him if a man shouldn't look to the saving of his own soul, the preacher had cursed him in a flare of anger and walked out.

But Mattingly had always been welcome on the Box N. He had usually sat up with Dad until after midnight talking about man's relationship to God and to other men, and out of those talks there had grown a bond of understanding that had been a fine and beautiful thing to see. Mattingly had visited Dad several times after he had become bedfast, and when he left, he had always said to Fran, "I have never met a man who knows God the way your father does."

Fran blinked back the tears that suddenly threatened to run over. She rose, and walked out, calling back, "Go to bed, Chuck."

"Reckon I better," he said.

She put on her coat and hat and went outside. She should help Mrs. Benson, but a restlessness was in her. She saddled her bay mare Lucy and rode east along the top of the hill. Strange how old memories kept crowding her mind today. Like her mother saying, "So terribly many hills. They're like a bunch of butchered hogs, lying beside each other. As far as you can see. I wish we had some trees besides those poplars. A fir. Or even a pine."

Dad had brought some pine seedlings from the Blue Mountains, but they had died. Looking eastward, Fran thought her mother had been right. Nothing but hills as far as she could see. At this time of year they did look like the round, scraped carcasses of butchered hogs.

She looked southward at the mountains, a long, uneven line against the sky, and she remembered how her mother had loved the trips they had taken there for wood. As soon as she returned, she'd start planning next summer's trip.

Fran reined up and looked back. The sky was depthless, swept clean of clouds by the wind, but far away she could see the tiny triangle that was the tip of Mt. Hood. "Just a cloud," her mother always said skeptically. "You can't see that far."

But it wasn't a cloud because it was always in the same place. She wished she had sneaked away with Chuck and gone to see what it looked like, up close.

She swung back to the Box N, wanting to go on to Bob's Mule Shoe and ask him why he had left the way he had. But she was afraid to. She didn't know what she might find. If Chuck had brought bad news, Bob would tell her.

He needed her. For some reason she found the thought distasteful. Then she realized she had never found it distasteful before. In a way it had given her pleasure. But today Chuck was in her mind, clawing at it like a cockleburr.

Everything was wrong, she thought desperately. She could never leave the Box N. No matter how successful Bob became, she would hate every minute she was in the Willamette Valley. Well, she just wouldn't go. She'd stay here, with Chuck.

Chuck! Always Chuck. Even when she quarreled with him, she still respected him. His stubborn strength, his vigor, his courage that was never showy but could not be doubted, even his puzzling and incredible devotion to the principles her father had believed in.

She was excited when she thought of their kiss last night. If Malone hadn't come. . . . She wished he hadn't. It was just as she had told Chuck. She loved both him and Bob, and what kind of woman did that make her.

She brought the mare up into a gallop, the wind quartering at her from the north, sweeping the tall bunch grass in long waves so that it looked like wheat ready for the binder. Wheat! Brown stubble. Gray, plowed land. It would never be the same again, this view across the endless hills. It couldn't happen. She couldn't let it happen.

When she galloped into the ranch yard, Hod Davis came out of the barn in his awkward, bowlegged walk. His face was very grave when he said, "It's all taken care of, Fran. Doc, he said he'd get the word out to everybody."

"Thanks, Hod."

She stepped down and handed him the reins. His face reminded her of this country, his skin the color of old rope. He was even built like a rope, long and tough-muscled, taller than Chuck by three inches. He was part of the Box N just as she was, and the corrals and the barn and the house and the poplar trees. If the Box N broke up, Hod would die because there would be no place left for him.

"I fetched the mail from town," he said. "It's on the front room table."

She only half heard. She gripped his arms. "Hod, do you know about the settlers on Chicken Creek?"

He looked past her, his faded blue eyes on something far away, or maybe nothing at all. Chuck had been that way in the house awhile ago, and she remembered her father had often been the same before he had become bedfast. The country did something to men, she thought, or the wind, or maybe it was just being alone so much with a horse between their legs and the sky overhead.

"I reckon everybody knows," Hod said in a mild voice, his eyes still fixed on that faraway thing, if it was anything.

"What are we going to do?"

He brought his gaze to her. He gave her question a moment's careful study, then he said, "Why, I guess that's up to Chuck." He pulled free from her grip and led the mare to the horse trough.

Fran whirled toward the house, her body caught in a spasm of crying. What kind of men were they? She would get no help from the crew, not if she had to go over Chuck's head. It would have been the same if Dad was alive.

She pushed the front door open and went in, feeling the rush of warm air. She closed the door and leaned against it until she was done crying. The house was so silent it seemed empty. It would be a long time before she was used to her father being gone.

She hung her coat and hat on the antlers, then saw the mail and glanced through it. Circulars and catalogs and the weekly *Custer County News*. There was one letter addressed to Chuck. It was postmarked Norman. She puzzled over the handwriting that was almost an illegible scrawl, and it was some time before she recognized the doctor's writing.

Chuck would be upstairs asleep. She tiptoed across the dining room and glanced into Mrs. Benson's bedroom. She was asleep on the bed, worn out by the night's vigil. Fran studied the letter again, trying to think of some reason for the doctor writing to Chuck. Then it came to her. She remembered early in the week when he had been here to see Dad and he had come out of the bedroom and asked for some paper, an envelope, and pen and ink. He had gone back in and closed the door.

For a long time Fran stood there fighting her conscience, and lost. She went into the kitchen where the tea-kettle was puffing steadily on the front of the range. Carefully she steamed the envelope open and slipped it inside her blouse. She went into the pantry, dropped a spoonful of flour into a cup so she could make paste to reseal the envelope, and stealthily climbed the stairs, hoping she wouldn't meet Chuck.

For an instant she paused in front of his door, listening to his snoring, then she went into her room. She set the cup on the bureau, and going to the window, drew the letter from her blouse. Even then she hesitated, realizing she had never done anything as despicable as this before, but she reasoned her doubts away with the thought that it might involve the future of the Box N.

She drew the folded sheet of paper from the envelope and began to read. It took her a long time to make out the scrawled handwriting, and when she was finished, she replaced it in the envelope and laid it on the bureau beside the cup. Stiff-legged, she walked to the bed, her heart hammering as if it were going to explode, then everything inside her broke and she fell face down on the covers and cried as she had not cried since she was a little girl.

CHAPTER IX

The Shot in the Night

CHUCK WOKE, feeling as if he had been dragged up forcibly out a deep, black pit. Someone was tapping on his door. He wanted to yell to whoever it was to go away, then he heard Mrs. Benson call, "Chuck, are you in there?"

"Yeah." He sat up. "What's wrong?"

"Supper's cold," she said. "You'd best get up. Fran's asleep, too, I guess."

He saw that it was dark and he was ashamed of having slept so long. He said, "I'll get Fran up and we'll be down in a minute."

For a time he sat on the edge of the bed, rubbing his face and not wanting to get up, not wanting to face what had to be faced. He thought of the Fargo girl, of Bob who had asked him not to tell Fran, and his saying it was Bob's chore. Chances were he wouldn't tell Fran.

He thought of Fran being here on this bed with him last night. He swore softly and got up. She had said she was wicked, that she loved both him and Bob. To Chuck's way of thinking, that was impossible. She just hadn't sorted out her real feelings, or maybe she was too upset by Dad's long illness to know how she felt.

Then he remembered their quarrel when he had got back from seeing the Fargos. She expected him to run them off. That hurt more than anything else that had happened because she was Dad Norman's daughter and she should have understood how it was with Chuck. She should have wanted Dad's ideas carried out even more than Chuck did who was no blood kin. But she didn't. She just couldn't see the long-run shape of things that were to come.

He went into the hall and tapped on Fran's door. When there was no answer, he turned the knob and opened the door. In the thin starlight coming through the window, he saw her sit up in bed; he heard her scream.

"It's me, Fran," he said quickly. "Supper's ready."

"Go away." She jumped and ran to the bureau. She yanked a drawer open, threw something in, and jammed the drawer shut. "Wait outside."

When he hesitated, she shoved him into the hall. "I'll be down in a minute," she cried hysterically. "You go on."

She slammed the door in his face. He went downstairs, not understanding what was the matter with her, then he wondered if Bob had seen her and distorted what he had said about Gypsy Fargo. Funny thing, he thought, how a man could grow up with a girl and think he knew her, and then all of a sudden find her as changeable as a March wind.

He walked into the kitchen and pumping a pan of water, washed his face. He ran a comb through his hair, and looking at himself in the mirror, saw that he needed a shave. But it would take more than a shave to make his rough-featured face as handsome as Bob Neville's.

He turned to Mrs. Benson who was dishing up the food at the stove. "Bob been around this afternoon?"

"No." She gave him a questioning glance and turned back to the stove. "I took a nap, though. He might have dropped in for a minute."

Bob wouldn't drop in for a minute, Chuck thought as he sat down at the table. He waited until Mrs. Benson poured his coffee. She was a middle-aged, white-haired woman, gentle and understanding, and she had done far more for Dad during his illness than Fran had. She had never complained about anything since she had come, and now as she sat down across the table from Chuck, he sensed how much this year of security had meant to her.

She looked at him briefly, biting her lower lip as if wanting to say something, then she blurted, "Maybe it isn't seemly for me to ask this right now, but I mean, do I have to rustle another job?"

"As far as I'm concerned," he said, "you can stay here as long as you want to, but I sure don't know what Fran will say."

"She's terribly upset," Mrs. Benson said. "That's why I didn't want to ask her."

They heard Fran cross the dining room. She came in, saying, "I didn't intend to go to sleep. I'm sorry. I haven't been much help today."

"It's all right," Mrs. Benson said. "You just sit down and eat."

Fran dropped into her chair at the end of the table, completely ignoring Chuck. He saw that she had been crying and she had not taken time to put her hair up. It was tangled and frizzled, a contrary lock bobbing against her forehead. She was always one to take pride in her appearance, but she had not even bothered this evening to remove her riding skirt and blouse and put on a house dress.

She filled her plate and toyed with her food, her eyes on her plate. Presently she said, "I guess I can't eat."

"I'm not hungry, either," Mrs. Benson said. "I loved your father, too."

Fran put her fork down. "I haven't told you how much we appreciate what you did for Dad."

"She was just asking about whether we'd like for her to stay," Chuck said. "I don't know about you, but I told her I'd like . . ."

"You should know about me," Fran said, her voice sharp-edged, her eyes avoiding Chuck's. "You'll have a home on the Box N as long as you want it, Mrs. Benson."

For a moment Mrs. Benson sat motionless, her head bowed, then she jumped up and ran to the stove, dabbing at her eyes with a corner of her apron. She brought the coffeepot to the table and filled Chuck's cup, and when she returned to her chair, she gave Fran a quick, warm smile.

"I'm kind of choked up tonight," she said. "I do want to stay." She swallowed. "Thank you, both of you."

"It's our place to thank you," Fran said.

Chuck finished his pie and leaned back in his chair. He rolled a smoke, thinking that Fran had a lot of her father's innate decency and common sense. Their troubles would ravel out, someway, if there was time.

He heard glass tinkle to the floor from the east window; he heard the snap of a bullet as it passed close to his head and the slap of it as it ripped into the opposite wall. Still, it took a second for him to realize what had happened, then the distant crack of the rifle came to him.

Chuck spilled out of his chair, yelling, "Get down, both of you." When Fran didn't move, he reached up and pulled her out of her chair. "Don't you know what happened?"

She struggled upright to a sitting position, staring blankly at him. Mrs. Benson was on the floor, looking at them under the table. She asked, "Was that a shot?"

"Sure was," Chuck said. "Didn't miss me by more'n a gnat's eyebrow, neither. Stay down."

It was the closest to death he had ever come in his life, and he was trembling, now that he had time to think about it. The shot had been fired at considerable distance by someone out there in the grass who had been afraid to come close enough to the house to be sure of hitting what he had aimed at.

Chuck crawled to the dining room. He got to his feet and ran across it. The room was dark, but the lamp on the front room table was lighted. He had no time to be careful, but he didn't think there was any danger now. The bushwhacker wouldn't hang around. A man who'd try a job like this would be short on guts. Chuck plunged across the living room into the office, grabbed a rifle off the wall, and ran out of the house.

The crew was stringing out of the bunkhouse. Hod Davis yelled, "Who fired that shot?"

"Stay out of the light," Chuck called, and sprinted across the yard to the dark shadows of the poplars. "I don't know who it was, but he came damned close to getting me."

They crowded around him, Davis saying bitterly, "Don't we have enough trouble without this?"

"Listen," Chuck said.

They could hear the beat of horse's hoofs far to the east along the crest of Monk's Hill, then it was smothered by distance. Davis said, "He ain't hanging around. A brave man, that gent."

"Who do you reckon it was?" Curly Grow asked.

"Spiegle, maybe," Chuck answered.

"Them settlers . . ." Ike Long began.

"No," Chuck said. "I was over there this morning. They're a tough outfit, and maybe they wouldn't be above taking a shot like that, but I didn't make 'em no trouble. I'm the last man they'd want plugged."

There was a moment's silence, the three cowhands thinking this over. Then Davis said, "What are we gonna do about them plow pushers?"

Sooner or later the question had to be asked and there was no use evading it. Whatever happened, these men would stick, but they had a right to know what was coming. The trouble was Chuck didn't have the answer, either.

"Hod, you came to these hills with Dad," Chuck said. "You knew him better'n me or Fran. What would he do?"

"Let 'em alone," Davis said bitterly. "He'd have fought any cowman to hell and back who tried to grab a blade of grass, but he always claimed he'd never buck the sodbusters."

"So we sit around," Ike Long said, "and let 'em take pot shots at us."

Long was not much older than Chuck, a proddy man who always claimed that if you had to fight, you'd best knock the other fellow on his behind before he got in a good lick. He had said what was in all their minds, and he might as well have added that it wasn't like Chuck to let them bang away and not do anything.

"No sense cracking any caps till we know who this was," Chuck said. "I had some trouble with Spiegle yesterday. If it was him, we'll make this country too hot to hold him. We'd better have somebody stand guard tonight. Tomorrow night, too. I'll take it till midnight."

"I'll take the next guard," Davis said. "Wake me up."

They drifted back to the bunkhouse, Chuck knowing they weren't satisfied. He returned to the porch and sat down with his back against a post, his rifle across his lap.

The more he thought about Spiegle, the less likely it seemed to him that he was capable of dry gulching a man. But it could have been young Reno Vance who rode for Spiegle. He hadn't been in town the day before, but he'd know what had happened. Maybe he'd taken on this chore without orders from Spiegle, thinking he'd fix himself so he'd be solid with his boss.

Then Chuck thought about Bob Neville. Bob had plenty of reason for wanting him dead. If he'd managed to get rid of the girl, Chuck would be the only one who knew about her.

He was still thinking about Bob when Fran came out of the house. She called, "Chuck," and he said, "Here."

She sat down beside him. She said, her voice trembling, "I was too dazed to realize what had happened, but after you left, I checked where the bullet hit the wall and the window it broke. You were right in line."

"That ain't news to me," he said.

"Who would do a thing like that?"

If he said Bob, she'd blow sky high. In time this might be what he needed to prove to Fran that Bob was a poor sample of a man, but it would take proof, good solid proof, and he didn't have it.

"Might have been Spiegle," he said.

She laid a hand on his arm. "Chuck, you haven't told me what you said to the settlers. If you warned them to get out, they'd. . . ."

"I didn't," he said.

She sat there another moment, her hand still on his arm, and he had a brief hope that everything was going to be all right between them, that this attempt on his life might be the means of bridging the gap that had opened between them. Then, without another word, she rose and went back into the house.

He sat there a long time, then he got up, and carrying the Winchester, walked toward the barn. There was no sense in going out in the grass where the man had been. In the darkness he would find nothing. Tomorrow he'd have a look.

He made a wide circle around the buildings and the corrals and returned to the porch. The light had gone out in the bunkhouse. Presently the lamp in Fran's room died, then in Mrs. Benson's, and there was a tight, nerve-pricking silence broken only by the thin cry of the wind around the eaves and the bark of a coyote from some distant hill.

He had not expected trouble until after the funeral. Spiegle was sure to do something then, but what he would do was a question. In any case, Chuck was certain he was not one to act alone. He would do all he could to bring the others in, and if he succeeded, there would be hell to pay.

The faint hooting of an owl came to Chuck. He stood up and listened, his head cocked. It came again, and this time he was sure. Rusty Wade was out there in the grass somewhere. They had used an owl hoot for a signal when they were younger, and both of them had been good enough to fool most folks.

Chuck circled the corrals, and when he was some distance from them, he called, "Rusty."

"Right here, boy." Rusty laughed. "Been quite awhile since

we played this game. I was afraid you were asleep and I'd have to throw a boot against your window."

"Why didn't you ride in instead of . . ."

"Because I've got something to tell you," Rusty said bluntly, "and if it got back to Spiegle and the others that I was blabbing to you, they'd work me over good."

Rusty made a vague shape ahead of Chuck in the starlight. He could not see his face, but from the tone of his voice, Chuck knew he was worried. He was caught in a squeeze, not quite sure where his loyalty should lie.

"You might have got a few buttons shot off your shirt," Chuck said. "Somebody took a crack at me while I was sitting at the table tonight."

"The hell." Rusty was plainly jolted by that. After a moment's thought, he asked, "Got any notion who did it?"

"Spiegle maybe. Or Reno Vance."

"How long ago was it?"

"I dunno. Couple of hours, maybe."

"That'd make it about nine. Well, it wasn't neither one of them. We was palavering in O'Toole's Bar right then. Just about every cowman in the county was there but you and Bob Neville."

It helped nail down what Chuck already suspected about Bob. He asked, "What was the palaver about?"

"Spiegle called the meeting," Rusty said. "He'd talked to Malone about you being easy on the settlers. Malone wasn't there. He won't be around when the blow up comes, neither. He'll be shooting his winter's supply of venison."

"What'd you do?"

"It's what I came to see you about." Rusty lighted his cigarette, the match flame throwing a brief light across his freckled, worried face. "None of us cotton to the way you handled that Fargo bunch. A tough outfit, Malone said. Even had a tough girl who held a Winchester on you."

"Did he mention the slip one of 'em made about Judge Castle?"

"No. What kind of a slip?"

"I got the idea Castle fetched 'em in."

"You're loco. He don't have no stake in this."

"I ain't so sure about that, although I don't savvy what kind of a deal he's working on."

Rusty was silent, apparently thinking about this, the tip of his cigarette a red glow in the darkness. "Something funny going on," he said finally. "Well, I ain't said what I came here to say. Spiegle claims that if the Fargo bunch stays till spring, we'll be licked. Sort of a test, Spiegle says, because they'll show every damned plow pusher in eastern Oregon that we won't fight."

"Well?"

"Hell, they've got to go," Rusty said in exasperation. "I don't savvy the way you're taking this."

"I'm taking it the only way it can be taken. It's like Bob Neville said at the depot yesterday. The law is on their side. If we fight 'em, we break the law."

"Malone . . ."

"It ain't just Malone," Chuck cut in irritably. "Use your noggin. We'd have a U. S. Marshal in here and Malone can't top him. Stay out of it, Rusty."

Rusty dropped his cigarette stub and rubbed it out with his toe. "Maybe I will," he said sourly. "Ain't no skin off my nose either way, but it gravels me to sit on my behind while it happens."

"It's happened wherever crops can be raised," Chuck said, "and some places where they can't."

"I still ain't said what I rode up here to say. Now I'm gonna say it. You're a damn fool, Chuck. Anybody but you can see you're betting on a busted straight. Pull out of the Box N. Let Neville do the worrying. He's the one who's marrying Fran."

Chuck laughed shortly. "That ain't my size and you know it."

"You've got a few cows of your own," Rusty argued. "There's a good spot for a little ranch east of my place. Round up your cows and move onto it. We'd be neighbors."

In that moment Chuck was sorry for the doubts he'd held about his friendship with Rusty Wade. It was real, one of the few good, solid things that had been left during these hours when the old life he had known for so long had been cut away from under him.

"Thanks," Chuck said in a low voice. "It's a good thing for a man to know he's got one friend."

"You've got damned few," Rusty said. "The boys figure to run the Fargo outfit over the hill and then they're shoving their cows onto Box N range. Spiegle says you're just bluff. If a man won't fight sodbusters, he won't fight nobody."

For a moment Chuck had been tempted. His half interest in the Box N would not have held him, not if Fran was bound to marry Bob Neville. But now his natural stubbornness took hold of him. He said, "I'll hang and rattle, and before I'm done, I'm gonna jam every word Spiegle's said down his God-damned throat. I never did like that bastard."

"You are a fool," Rusty said hotly. "You could have a good life for the taking. Trudie's just sitting around hoping you'll show up again, although why she's in love with a bullhead like you I don't know. You could do a lot worse."

That was true. He could do a lot worse for a wife than Trudie Evans, but he couldn't go back to her. He said, "I'll still hang and rattle."

"All right, rattle yourself right into a pine box," Rusty said angrily. "I'm done talking to you."

He wheeled away, and presently Chuck heard the beat of hoofs as he rode down the hill. It would never be quite the same with Rusty, he thought bitterly. He walked back to the house, an all-gone feeling in him. He had just lost one of the few good things that had been left to him. Then he wondered how great a price a man should pay for his loyalty to someone who was dead.

CHAPTER X

The Funeral

THE FOLLOWING DAY was a slow one for everybody on the Box N. Hod Davis fixed the bullet-shattered window in the kitchen. Fran spent the day working over the kitchen range with Mrs. Benson, for tomorrow there would be people to feed. Many who attended the funeral would come for miles.

It was a strange day to Chuck, one that had to be worn down to a nub and somehow lived through. He had the weird feeling he was living in a period of suspended time until Dad Norman could be buried and then life would begin flowing again.

About noon Johnny Bain got back from Condon with news that Rufus Mattingly would be there to preach the funeral. Then, at supper time, Bob Neville rode in. Chuck met him in the yard, strongly tempted to accuse him of the shooting, but Bob gave him a cool nod, and hurried into the house. Well, there was no use to say anything about it now. Bob would try again, and Chuck might have the proof he needed, if he was still alive.

Chuck had spent most of the morning going over the ground where he thought the bushwhacker had stood when he'd fired the shot. He finally turned up a .30-.30 shell, which proved nothing at all because it was the most common rifle on the range. He found horse tracks between clumps of bunch grass, but there was nothing distinctive about them.

Chuck ate supper with the crew, a silent meal, each man staring morosely at his plate. When he was done, Chuck walked across the yard and on past the barn and corrals and stood alone on the crest of the hill, the cool wind running past him, the tall bunch grass bowing before it. All around him the hills seemed to reach to infinity except in the south where the mountains loomed against the horizon in a great blue-black mass.

Staring upward at the darkening sky, he thought of Dad Norman riding the big, black stallion that belonged to the Lord. He shook his head, bringing his eyes back to the earth, the hills still touched by the dying sunlight, the gulches black with heavy shadow. Dad Norman would never help him again, never advise him, never point the way to the path leading out of a trap of trouble as he had often done in the past.

From now on it was Chuck Harrigan against everybody else, or so it seemed to him it must be. Inside the big house Bob Neville would be talking to Fran in his smooth way, charming her, for that was his gift, a talent Chuck did not possess.

The temptation to ride out with his half dozen horses and shirttailful of cows and join Rusty Wade was a strong urge in him. He could have a good life for the taking as Rusty had said. His half interest in the Box N was not enough to keep him here, for he had never been one to set a great store on wealth. Neither had Dad, although he had become one of the richest men in the county.

He returned to the bunkhouse, thinking grimly that he had to hang and rattle just as he had told Rusty he would. He could not escape from the accusing look he imagined Dad would give him if he left, the words he knew Dad would say, "I thought I had raised a man, but you're riding out because it's the easiest thing to do."

He stepped into the bunkhouse and told the crew they'd keep a guard out tonight and he'd take it until midnight again, although the thought was in the back of his mind that there was no need for it, not with Bob Neville here on the Box N.

Neither Bob nor Fran were in the living room when he went in to get the Winchester, so they must be upstairs. Before he could get out of the house, Mrs. Benson stopped him. She was tired, he saw, so tired she was ready to drop, but her conscience was burdened by something she had to say.

"Chuck, I know you and Fran better than I do my own children. I haven't seen any of them for years, but I've seen you and Fran almost every day since I came here." She paused, her work-hardened hands fluttering a little as she searched for the right words, then she hurried on, "Dad was not one to say anything to Fran about Bob because he said she was too stubborn to be changed by words."

She paused again, and he said harshly, "Well?"

She shrank back, hurt by his tone, and he heard her long, indrawn breath, then she made herself go on, "He was sure Bob was a weak man. You know how hard Dad was to fool."

Once more she seemed at loss for words, and he said again, "Well?"

"You've got to keep her from marrying him," Mrs. Benson said. "I know what's wrong with both of you. You're in love with each other, but you can't get rid of the feeling that it isn't quite right to be in love because you were raised together, and you've thought of each other as brother and sister."

She was dead wrong, he thought. She didn't know about Fran coming into his room and lying down on his bed, about her kiss that for the moment at least told him so clearly she wanted him. There was no way out of this, he told himself as he looked at Mrs. Benson's pale face, a vague oval in the twilight, no way out unless Fran found it herself.

"Dad was right about Fran being stubborn," he said. "If I threw Bob out of the house, or even if I went upstairs and told them I knew what he was, I'd just fix things up good."

He walked past her into the dusk, leaving her standing there. He knew that if Fran did marry Bob, he would always blame himself for letting it happen, even though he could not think of anything he could do to stop it.

At midnight he woke Hod Davis and gave him his Winchester. He went into the house, blew out the lamp in the front room, and wearily climbed the stairs. He lay down, wondering briefly if Fran would come to him again. A foolish and wishful thought. He knew she wouldn't.

In the morning he helped Hod Davis dig the grave in the little cemetery on top of the hill east of the house. His parents were buried there, and Mrs. Norman, and a cowhand who had died a year ago from injuries he'd received trying to break a bad horse.

The day was warm for October, the sky clear, the wind not as strong as it usually was. He leaned his shovel against the metal fence when the grave was finished, glancing at Davis' weather-beaten face, and he sensed that the old cowboy was feeling Dad's loss as strongly as he was. They walked back to the house in silence, Chuck remembering he had hoped the night it had snowed that it would warm up. It had. Maybe it was a good omen.

People were already coming on horses and in wagons and buckboards and buggies. Rufus Mattingly was there. He shook hands with Chuck, but he didn't say anything. Mattingly was like that. He understood a man's feelings.

Ike Long and Curly Grow had fixed a table by laying planks across a pair of saw horses. Fran and Mrs. Benson brought food from the house, several of the other women helping her including Trudie Evans and her sister Nona.

Bob stood talking with Judge Castle. Old man Vance and his flock were here. So was Jack Spiegle. Rusty Wade and most of the little ranchers from the mountains. Once Trudie, passing Chuck with a heavy pot of beans in her hands, smiled and spoke briefly to him, and hurried on as if not wanting to press herself on him.

After they finished eating, Doc came in a wagon with Dad's body. There were not many flowers this late in the year, but some of the women had fixed bouquets of artificial flowers made from brightly colored paper. That seemed an omen to Chuck, too.

This was an artificial ceremony, for nothing that was said or done today would change a single thing about Dad Norman.

But they had to go through it, and the fact that so many had come was a great tribute to him, greater than all the prayers and songs and Mattingly's sermon that was still to come.

Chuck asked the members of the crew to act as pallbearers with him and Doc Logan. They carried the coffin to the side of the grave, the people packed tightly all around it, so many that twenty or more had to remain outside the metal fence.

Mattingly asked the preacher from Norman to give a prayer. Professional courtesy, Chuck supposed, and the man took advantage of his one opportunity, praying long and loudly about the glories of Heaven and the fury of Hell for those who were not saved.

Chuck listened with growing impatience. When the man was done, Chuck had more fire and brimstone in his nostrils than he had of the fine fragrance of Heaven. He had the impression the preacher was saying Dad wasn't saved, and he was trying to scare his audience into coming to church. But if that was the choice, Chuck told himself, he'd take the fire and brimstone. He'd prefer riding beside Dad who'd be on that black stallion, even if it was as hot as Hell.

A mixed quartet sang several songs, ending with *Shall We Gather at the River*. Mattingly talked then, a big man endowed with gentle dignity, his kind eyes almost lost behind the bushy brows, his great beard fluttering in the wind. Before he had finished his first sentence, the sourness that the prayer had aroused in Chuck was gone.

Mattingly talked about Dad and God. He said Dad knew God; he walked with Him and talked with Him, and his life, as long as Mattingly had known him, had been shaped by that knowledge of God.

Mattingly paused, his eyes on Jack Spiegle and Reno Vance who stood beside him, then moved on to Judge Castle and Bob Neville.

"I am proud to say that Dad Norman was my personal friend," Mattingly continued. "As long as I live, I shall treasure the talks I had with him. Many of them lasted far into the night, and although I was always faced with a long trip the next day, I never begrudged the lost sleep because Dad had given me so much to think about.

"I believe I am qualified as well as any man to say what Dad believed in and what he would do under any given circumstance if he had lived. He was a cowman and a good one, but he was like no other cowman I ever met.

"The difference lay in his vision, for I have met other men in various walks of life who lived as good a life as he did. Because he had that vision, he knew these hills would be lost to him and to you who run cattle on them. He often said that he hated to see it come, but when it did, he would not use a gun to hold his grass. He said a dozen families had their living from these hills now, but the day would come when a hundred families could live as well as the dozen do now."

Then he bowed his head, and raising a great hand, prayed briefly. He stepped back, and the crew moved past him and began filling the grave. The crowd drifted away, but Chuck stood there, and he saw that Fran and Mrs. Benson and Bob had remained.

When the grave had been filled and earth was a gray, round mound above it, Hod Davis set a tailgate of a wagon into place. That morning young Johnny Bain had carved on it, "Thomas Jedediah Norman, 1841-1899. May he rest in peace."

Mrs. Benson knelt beside the grave and arranged the flowers over it. Fran stood at one side, her head bowed, and she did not see Mrs. Benson move back and motion for the crew and Mattingly and Bob Neville to return to the house. She went with them, and Chuck walked around the grave to stand beside Fran.

It seemed to Chuck that the noise of the people leaving came from a great distance. Apparently Fran didn't hear them. Suddenly she dropped on her knees and prayed in a voice so low that Chuck was unable to hear her words. He could not swallow. When Fran rose, he tried to say something, but no words came from his tight throat.

"I know," Fran breathed. "I've shed a lot of tears the last few days, and now I guess there just aren't any more tears to shed."

He nodded, looking away at the endless roll of hills that went on and on until there was only the sky, and he could see the dark shapes of horses and men and plows on the sides of the hills. Then there would be wheat, green at first, and later more golden than the ripe bunch grass, and finally the stubble.

Houses, with smoke rolling up from chimneys through the long winter months. The wind would still blow, and there would be dust when the land was dry, and the air would be dark with it. He would hate all of it as Fran would hate it. Dad, too, if he had lived, but it would come.

"You've got Dad's look on your face," Fran said. "I remember how he used to stand and just stare as if he could see down through the years."

They walked away, Chuck pausing to shut the iron gate, and he wondered if Fran's attitude had been changed by what Mattingly had said. By the time they reached the house, most of the people were gone, but Mattingly had waited.

When they came up, he said, "At a time like this my grief is for the ones who live. When it's a man like Dad, my grief is all the greater because he will be missed far more than the average person." He cleared his throat. "Is there anything I can do?"

"No," Fran said. "We want to thank you. We can't in words, but I think you know."

"Yes," Mattingly said, "I know."

He walked away. Fran went into the house, and Chuck would have followed if Rusty Wade had not called to him from the poplars. He saw that Nona and Trudie were with Rusty, and he walked toward them, not wanting to, but knowing he could do nothing else.

"I'm sorry." Trudie gave him her hand, brown and hard with calluses. "I'm awfully sorry because I know how you felt about him."

"Thanks," Chuck said.

Trudie withdrew her hand. She said, "You can't reach out and touch a person at a time like this, so I won't try. It's something you have to live through until time has healed the wound, but there is something I'd like to say. I envy you for having known him the way you did."

He saw her, then, for the first time, not just a red-headed girl who worked outside with her father as much as she helped her sister Nona in their cabin, not just a girl from a greasy sack spread who was wearing a cheap calico dress because she had nothing better and never had known anything but poverty and hard work. She was much more than that, an honest girl who loved him.

He saw genuine sympathy in her hazel eyes, in the sweet shape of her mouth, and he felt a bitter self-condemnation for having kissed her and held her in his arms, letting her hope for something he could not give her.

She swung away from him, asking for nothing. As she walked toward her horse, Rusty said, "If you change your mind, remember what I said." Then he followed Trudie, Nona walking beside him, and Chuck watched them ride away, traveling south toward the mountains, and presently they were lost from sight beyond the crest of the hill.

He thought of what Dad had said that night about Bob, that love is something you can shape, and Bob had shaped his love for Fran because she was going to inherit a damned fine ranch. Maybe a man could shape his love; maybe he should never reach for something which was beyond him.

He turned toward the house, shaken by what Trudie had said and the way she had said it. He wished he could take Fran out of his heart and put Trudie there; he wished he could just ride away and forget everything that bound him to the Box N, but he couldn't.

CHAPTER XI

The Ghost Letter

WHEN CHUCK went into the front room, he saw that Fran, Mrs. Benson, Doc, and Bob were seated, but the Judge was standing by the fireplace, cranky and impatient because he had been held here longer than he wanted to be.

"I've been waiting for you," Castle said. "I'll read the will in the morning in my office at ten o'clock. You and Fran and Mrs. Benson will have to be there." He nodded at Bob. "You'd better come, too, since you and Fran will be married in a few days. Is the time and place agreeable to all of you?"

All of them nodded except Mrs. Benson who said, "I'd rather not come. This is family business and I'm just hired help."

"You're much more than that," Fran said quickly.

"You have to come," the Judge said indifferently. "You've been remembered in the will."

He walked out, holding his dignity around him like a dark, impenetrable coat. He had not been touched by what had happened this afternoon, Chuck thought. Probably he was glad Dad was gone. He was the big one in Custer County now; he would play his own game in his own way with no man holding a tight rein on his ambition.

Chuck looked at Fran. "He seemed to know about your wedding. Have you set a date?"

"No." She frowned at Bob. "Why would he say a thing like that?"

"I don't know," Bob said as if troubled. "But I won't go in the morning if you'd rather not have me."

"I want you there." Fran chewed on her lower lip, nervous tension showing in the tight lines of her face. "It's just that he was taking too much for granted."

Bob took her hand. He said gently, "We've been putting it off, but there isn't anything holding us apart now, is there? I mean, you could set a date, couldn't you?"

"Yes." She glanced at Chuck as if wondering whether he was going to say anything, then she added defiantly, "I will set it, Bob, right after the will's read."

"That's the best news I've heard, honey." Bob rose, visibly relieved. "I've got to be getting along, but I'll be in town in the morning."

As she got up to follow him outside, Doc asked, "You get the mail yesterday, Chuck?"

"No."

"Hod brought the mail," Fran said, not meeting Chuck's

77

eyes. "There was a letter for you, but I forgot all about it. I'll get it."

Doc seldom spoke with malice, but he did now. "I'm thinking you wanted to forget that letter, Fran."

"I did not," she flared, and flouncing past him, went up the stairs.

"You were leaving, Bob," Doc said. "I didn't aim to keep you."

It seemed to Chuck that Bob had lost ten pounds in the last two days. His face wasn't as round and rosy-cheeked as it had been. He was worried, and now he gave Doc a look of pure hatred. He asked, "Which string of the fiddle are you playing, Doc?"

"The hunch string," Doc said. "You don't fool me a little bit, Bob, and if Dad hadn't figured Fran was in love with you, he'd have told you he wasn't fooled, either."

Fran came down the stairs and handed the envelope to Chuck. She said nervously, "I'm sorry I forgot this."

As Chuck took the letter, Bob said, "I've got to go, Fran."

"I'll walk to the corral with you," she said, and hurried out of the house with him.

Chuck studied the envelope, recognizing Doc's handwriting, and when he turned it over, he saw that it had been steamed open and hastily resealed. Not a good job, for there were several small lumps of flour paste along the edge of the flap.

"It's been opened," Chuck said.

Doc swore. "Fran did it. Dad dictated that letter to me a few days before he died. He was too weak to write it himself. Go upstairs and read it, Chuck."

"Thanks, Doc," Chuck said, and turned to the stairs.

"I'm never sure when it's the right time to say what you have to say," Doc said, "but maybe there's no use waiting for the right time to tell Fran that Bob's just no damned good. I'd better take the bull by the horns . . ."

"No," Mrs. Benson said sharply. "You'd only make it worse. I know how she feels, and I know how Dad worried about her. We've just got to pray that something will happen so she can see for herself."

Chuck stopped halfway up the stairs. "I thought you wanted me to do something."

"I was wrong," she said miserably. "None of us can say anything, but they aren't married yet. I'll go on hoping until they are."

Chuck went on to his room, thinking that the most useless thing in the world was to just sit around hoping for something to happen. He closed the door and crossed to the window. Ripping the envelope open, he drew the letter from it and unfolding the sheets, held them up so the fading afternoon light fell upon them. It took a long time to read it because he had to struggle with Doc's poor handwriting, but he eventually made it out.

Dear Chuck,

I cannot take my pen in hand because I have put this off so long that my strength is gone. I'm asking Doc to put it down for me because he is a man we all trust. In many ways I have been foolish to the point of stupidity because I have believed I should look for the good in others and that the good will overcome the evil in the long run.

Doc says I'm an impractical idealist and there will be hell to pay when I'm gone because I've kept people from doing what they wanted to do. The Judge is a case in point. He never stood against me because I'm his biggest depositor, so it was to his advantage to pretend to agree with me.

I've grown pretty sentimental, lying here in bed this way, and because it's hard for me to say the things I feel most deeply, I'm taking this method of letting you know you have been all I ever wanted in a son. It seems wrong, but I have loved you more than I have Fran. I wanted a boy more than anything else in the world, but my wife would not have any more children after Fran came. I also want you to know that since you are not actually my son, you do not owe me or my memory any obligation. Your work on the Box N has squared anything you feel you owe me for your raising.

I had hoped to live long enough to see the change that is bound to come to Custer County, not because I want to see it but because I believe I could keep that change from taking the violent course it has usually taken in other places. Perhaps you can prevent bloodshed, although I can't tell you how to do it.

If any man is responsible for the trouble I am afraid is inevitable, the man is Judge Castle. I can't prove it, but I am convinced from things he has said that the railroad would not have been built at this time without his conniving.

He stands to profit by it because he owns the bank and most of the town. If the population of Custer County is tripled as it will be when the settlers come, he will have more business for his bank and the town property will increase in value.

I said you have no obligation to me or my memory, but if, of your own free will, you decide to make a fight, watch the Judge and Bob who is the Judge's man. This brings me to the real reason I am having this written.

I wish I could die with the assurance Fran would not marry Bob, but we know how stubborn she is. If I told her she couldn't marry him, I would make her more determined. I have always found it hard to talk to her just as I found it hard to talk to her mother. I love Fran, but her mother often told me I didn't understand women. Perhaps she was right. All I know is that my life with her was not a happy one. Even you, growing up in our home, did not have any idea how it was.

I do not want you to feel that I am leaving Fran as a burden to you. There was a time when I hoped you would marry. I don't know what came between you. I do know that sometimes even love is not enough.

I hope that you will find a way to make Fran see that Bob is not the man for her. If you can't, don't worry about it. Each of us must live his own life and suffer for our mistakes. I have always believed we get just about what we deserve.

This letter is not written with the words I would have used if I could have held the pen, but it says what I wanted to say, so I am signing it.

Dad.

The labored signature did not look like Dad's. Staring at it, Chuck thought it must have taken a tremendous effort, weak as he was, to write those three letters. He put the folded sheets back into the envelope, his throat as tight as it had been at the funeral this afternoon.

The words weren't Dad's, but the ideas were, and Chuck thought of him lying there, ashamed of his weakness because he had always been a proud and self-reliant man. Still, he had forced himself to tell Doc what he wanted to say because he had to tell Chuck these things which he could not put into words.

Dad had said Chuck was not to be burdened with a debt of obligation. Still, the obligation was there. It took more than a letter to wipe out a debt, but the part about Fran was out of his hands. He was even more helpless than Dad had been.

For a long time Chuck stood at the window. Bob had left. Presently Doc drove away. For a few brief moments the light of the setting sun was a blinding glare on the hill tops, the gulches slowly darkening, then the last bright light was gone, and scarlet banners glowed and faded above the western horizon.

The letter in his hand seemed a ghostly thing, and he had the weird feeling Dad had spoken to him from the grave. His natural inclination had been to fight to preserve the Box N, but it would be a mistake. Regardless of what Fran did or said, there must be some other way out of this.

Mrs. Benson called supper and he went downstairs. Fran, pale-faced and jittery with nervousness, said nothing while they ate. Chuck pulled the blinds before he sat down. Bob would try again, but probably not in the same way he had before.

When they finished eating, Chuck said, "We can look for

trouble, now that the funeral's over. What does Bob say about the settlers?"

Fran ran the tips of her fingers across the oilcloth, her eyes lowered. She said, her voice so low it was barely audible, "The same as you, but for a different reason. He says we'd set ourselves against the law."

"What do you say?"

She kept on running her fingers across the oilcloth, her face pallid in the lamplight. She said finally, "I won't do anything just now."

"On account of what Bob says?"

"Yes."

So it was Bob who was holding her back. He asked, "You're bound to marry him?"

"I've been engaged to him for two years. I can't keep putting him off." She looked up, her blue eyes defiant. "It isn't right, you hating him like you do. Why, Chuck, why?"

He hesitated, tempted to tell her about Gypsy Fargo and his certainty that Bob had tried to kill him, and knew at once it was not the time. Now, looking at her mouth, downslanting at the corners, he found it hard to believe that this was the girl he had grown up with.

"It's because I know him," Chuck said.

"I never thought you could be so small and cheap," she flared. "I know him, too. He's good and kind, and he doesn't deserve to be hated." She swallowed. "Don't you ever try to hurt him. Do you understand that?"

Mrs. Benson rose and left the room. Chuck sat there, staring at Fran and wondering what her feeling had been when she'd read Dad's letter. Then he remembered she had been crying. Perhaps she had not known before that her father had found it hard to talk to her, and it must have been a shock to know he had loved Chuck more than he had her.

Suddenly he was angry, so angry he wanted to reach across the table and shake the stubbornness and defiance out of her, shake her until she was ready to listen to reason. But he couldn't do that if he shook her to death.

He rose and strode out of the house, afraid to trust himself if he stayed. He got his Winchester out of the bunkhouse, pausing to tell the crew they would keep a guard out again tonight, and walked away into the darkness.

The wind held the breath of winter, but Chuck did not feel it. He thought about Trudie who had somehow made him realize she wanted him without telling him in words, Trudie who would put no price upon her love.

Out here, with the buildings lost in the velvet blackness, there was just the sky and the stars and the wind, and a world of bunch-grass hills. It was still the way God had made it, lonely and vast and beautiful to those who could see and feel its beauty, but man would not leave it that way.

A coyote barked and another answered, and a faint tingle ran down Chuck's spine. It seemed to him that he was closer at this moment to Dad than he had ever been in life, Dad who maybe now had the answers to the questions he could not answer when he was alive, the questions he had talked to Rufus Mattingly about so many times until dawn.

There was something for a man here on top of the hills, something far removed from the scheming of Judge Castle and the brutality of Jack Spiegle and the clever lies and deception of Bob Neville.

Dad must have sensed that vague something. Probably he had never named it or defined it, but it had shaped his life and his beliefs. He had not been afraid to die. But still the answers did not come to Chuck Harrigan.

He dropped to his knees and tugged at a clump of bunch grass. It was as tall as his knees, dry and heavy with seed, and deeply rooted, rich with nutrition and symbolic of the strength and vitality of the land itself. He rose, not really wanting to yank it from the ground to blow away and be wasted. It had use and value, it had meant something to Dad Norman that wheat would never have meant.

That was the part Chuck could not understand. But Dad had. Men would come with their plows, a hundred families living on the same amount of land where a dozen lived now. Maybe that was the way God wanted it and Dad had understood. It was the understanding which had given him compassion, and compassion had made him the man he had been.

Chuck walked back to the house, Trudie touching his mind again. He pictured her, red hair, hazel eyes, a strong, round body. It was only this day he had understood her, asking for so little, waiting for something he could not give her. He was sorry he couldn't. There was no justice in it, and he blamed himself.

When it was midnight, he woke Hod Davis and gave him his Winchester. He went to bed and slept, and when he woke, it was daylight. His lips and tongue and mouth were dry; he felt wrung out as if drained of all emotion.

He got up and dressed. The will would be read today, but that would be only the beginning. It was the rest of the day and the following days he didn't want to face, if Rusty had been right. When he went downstairs, he found that breakfast was ready. He looked at Fran; she spoke to him coolly and impersonally. She seemed like a stranger to him.

CHAPTER .XII

The Will

THEY LEFT the Box N for Norman shortly after nine, using the two-seated hack. Fran sat beside Chuck, bundled up in her heavy coat and cap, her hands in her muff, a buffalo robe across their laps.

Mrs. Benson sat behind. Fran listened indifferently when Chuck told Mrs. Benson to get into the front seat with them. She laughed as she climbed into the back seat, saying she was too big in the Chuck-knew-what, and he was just being polite to suggest such a thing.

Fran was glad Mrs. Benson hadn't sat up here with them, for Fran would have been squeezed in the middle and she didn't want to be that close to Chuck. He did not look at her, and when she glanced sideways at his face, it seemed to her his profile was becoming more hawk-like every day.

She was startled, remembering her father had looked that way at times when he was facing some trouble he didn't know how to settle. Right now she could easily believe Chuck was a blood relative, but perhaps his expression was the result of close association with her father, or maybe it was caused by the fact that Chuck thought about things the way her father had.

The sky was clear, the sunlight very sharp on the tawny, bunch-grass carpet that rolled out across the hills as far as she could see. The wind was with them again, chill and blustery even when they dropped off the top of Monk's Hill and wheeled down the slope toward Norman. Once she glanced back at Mrs. Benson who smiled and said, "You've got cherries in your cheeks this morning, Fran."

"Frozen ones," Fran said, and turned her head to stare at the twin lines wheels had cut through the grass.

The hurt inside her was a steady ache, and she had never been free from it since she had read her father's letter to Chuck, a letter which had not been intended for her eyes. It was the most completely wrong thing she had ever done in her life, so wrong she could not even rationalize it in her thoughts.

But it was not a sense of guilt over having done something wrong that hurt her; it was the new, terrible knowledge that she had never really understood her father and he had not understood her. She found it inconceivable that she had been oblivious all her life to this fact which now seemed so plain. That was why she had cried after she had read it, why she had been almost hysterical and had screamed at Chuck when he'd come into her room that evening to tell her supper was ready.

Some of the sentences clung to her mind and ran through it like a bitter refrain. "We know how stubborn she is. If I told her she couldn't marry him, I would only make her more determined." What was wrong with being stubborn, she asked herself? And why shouldn't she be determined? Dad had been terribly unfair to Bob. If he'd been so sure something was wrong, he should have told her.

"I am not leaving Fran a burden to you." He had no reason to write that to Chuck. She'd taken care of herself from the day she'd been big enough to walk. She had never been a burden to anyone, to Chuck least of all.

"Each of us must live his own life and suffer from our mistakes." That was exactly what she was going to do, and if she made a mistake, she wouldn't grumble or go howling to Chuck for sympathy. She'd marry Bob. She'd set the date today for sometime next week.

And that other sentence which was the worst of all. "It seems wrong, but I have loved you more than I have Fran." It was wrong, she told herself, terribly wrong because she had loved her father in a way she had never loved her mother. Now, after he was gone, she found out she had not been first with him.

She glanced at Chuck again when they reached the bottom of the grade and hit the gravel road that followed the gulch. She hated him because he had taken the place that should have been hers.

Chuck had not shaved that morning, the stubble giving his face a sort of fierce, bristly look. He was so much like a dormant volcano that might erupt at any time. Bob never gave her that feeling because she could handle him, but she had never been able to handle Chuck even when they were children, not when his mind had once been made up.

It was all his fault, she thought with growing anger. That time he'd kissed her. The trouble had started then. Before that nothing had been wrong except the ups and downs that two kids were bound to have who see each other every day. And the other night when she'd gone into his room. That was his fault, too. He could have sent her away. And then this business about the settlers!

Suddenly she wished her father had not given Chuck a half interest in the Box N. They would never be able to make decisions together. He'd browbeat her, but she wouldn't give up to him. All right, she was stubborn, but she didn't care. She wasn't going to sit around and watch Box N break up.

When they reached the edge of town, Fran knew what she had to do. She'd borrow money from the Judge and buy Chuck out if she had to. She'd get rid of him. She'd marry Bob and she'd shame him into fighting, law or no law. They'd take the crew and they'd run the settlers off Chicken Creek.

Chuck left the team at the livery stable. When they came back into the street, he said to Mrs. Benson, "You go on up to Castle's office. Me 'n Fran have some business with Partridge."

"It's almost ten," Fran said coldly. "I don't have any business with Partridge."

She stared at him, hating him and hoping he could see it in her eyes. Mrs. Benson walked away, leaving them glaring at each other. He didn't explain anything. He just stood there, spread-legged, his hands at his sides, his eyes locked with hers. Suddenly a feeling of futility gripped her. It was like trying to stare down a pillar of rock.

"Partridge is gonna say something you need to hear," Chuck said finally. "You'll go if I have to carry you."

"Don't try it," she flared. "I won't be bullied."

But she whirled and walked toward the store. He'd do just what he said he would. He'd pick her up and carry her, and no amount of kicking and screaming would change her. This wasn't the time to make a stand against him, she thought, not out here in the middle of the street where everybody could see her defeat.

They'd talk about it for weeks, Dad Norman's daughter who was engaged to Bob Neville, juicy gossip that the townspeople would pass from one drooling mouth to another. Well, she had some dignity if Chuck didn't.

They went into the store, Fran pulling her hands out of her muff and turning down the collar of her coat as the warm air rushed at her. Partridge walked toward them, an old, stoop-shouldered man with the good years behind him. He must have sensed from their stormy faces that something was wrong, for his voice was troubled when he said, "Good morning."

"Howdy," Chuck said. "Part, we don't have time to beat around the bush. The settlers on Chicken Creek told me you had promised them credit so they could get through the winter. That right?"

The old man was taken aback. He began to tremble, eyes shuttling to Fran's face, then he walked to the counter and put a hand on it for support. "I never ask you why you run the Box N the way you do. You have no right . . ."

"Answer me."

Partridge's wrinkled face was gray. He lowered his gaze, the corners of his mouth beginning to twitch. "It's true."

"You were always careful about who you gave credit to," Chuck said, his words beating the old man like blows of a club. "Many a time Dad came in and said he'd guarantee payment for some cowman who was down on his luck."

"I know he did," Partridge said, still staring at the floor.

"A generous man, Dad was. I guess we'll miss him more'n . . ."

"Listen, Part," Chuck cut in. "I don't want to be hard on you, but you're gonna give this to us straight. Why are you taking a chance on a bunch of settlers you don't know nothing about?"

"I knew you wouldn't run 'em out of the country. They'll get a crop next summer . . ."

"Almost a year from now." Chuck grabbed a handful of the storekeeper's shirt and shook him. "Why, Part? You're telling us, or by God I'll beat it out of you."

"Chuck, stop it," Fran cried. "Are you out of your mind?"

"No, but Part was when he gave that settler bunch credit." Chuck shook him again. "There's something wrong with this deal, and he's telling us what it is."

Fran struck Chuck on the side of the face, the blow making a sharp, vicious crack. "If you don't let go of him I'll get the sheriff and . . ."

"No, Fran, I'll tell him." Partridge licked his lips. When Chuck released him and stepped back, the storekeeper pulled a bandanna out of his pocket and wiped his sweaty face. "The Judge told me to. He promised to make it up if the Fargos couldn't pay next summer."

Chuck looked at Fran, his face bone-hard. "You're a little too handy with your hand. You crack me again and I'll turn you across my knee, and don't you forget it."

Fran was too shocked to pay any attention to what Chuck said. She was staring at Partridge, her lips parted. This was something she could not believe. She had no love for Judge Castle. She had disliked him even when she'd been a child and he'd come out to the Box N and brought her candy and jiggled her on his knee, trying too hard to be friendly.

She'd had nothing against Castle. It was just that her child's intuition had cut through his pretense of friendship. She had always been polite because he was her father's friend. But this thing Partridge had said was ridiculous. It had no bearing on her feeling about Castle. His business was with the cowmen of Custer County, and she could think of no reason for him to make a friendly gesture toward people who were the cowmen's natural enemy.

"Why, Part?" she whispered. "Why would the Judge help those people?"

"He didn't tell me," Partridge said bleakly. "He just told me what to do, and well, I'm too old to fight him."

"Come on," Chuck said, and turned to the door.

She went back into the wind again, wondering where she had made her mistake in her judgment of Chuck. He hadn't actually said he wasn't going to run the settlers off, but he'd talked about what Dad would have done. There wasn't the slightest doubt in her mind what her father's attitude would have been.

"Why didn't you tell me you were going to fight the settlers?" she asked angrily.

"I didn't say a word about fighting. There's something fishy about this mess and I'm gonna pull the fish out where you can see it. I've got a hunch you won't like what you see, neither."

As they climbed the stairs, she suddenly remembered what Dad had said in his letter about the Judge and how he would profit from a settler invasion. It could be true, although it was hard to believe Judge Castle would turn traitor to his own people. Then she thought about Dad saying Bob was the Judge's man. But that was impossible.

"Don't drag Bob into this," she said when they reached the hall at the head of the stairs.

"I ain't dragging anybody in," he said curtly, "but maybe he'll pop in all by himself."

Chuck led the way into Castle's outer office. The girl at the desk smiled and nodded at the door marked, "Private." She said, "He's expecting you."

Fran followed Chuck, afraid of what was going to happen, afraid that these next few minutes would prove her wrong all down the line and that her father and Chuck were right. But no, she couldn't be that wrong about Bob. He was sitting across the room from Castle's desk, and he smiled the instant he saw her. Ignoring Chuck, he said, "Good morning, Fran."

"Good morning, Bob." She went to him, so filled with the certainty she was right that she bent and kissed him. "You asked me to set our wedding date. Will next week do?"

He glanced at Chuck who was standing in the middle of the room, scowling. Fran wasn't sure, but she thought she saw a trace of malice in Bob's eyes. Then he brought his gaze to her, his smile very tender. He said, "Honey, that would be fine."

"Maybe we can arrange it for the last of this week," Fran said. She knew at once she had spoken too loudly. "But we haven't made my wedding dress. That's the only thing." She turned to Mrs. Benson who was sitting by the window. "Do you think we could be ready by the last of the week?"

"No," Mrs. Benson said quickly. "We have a lot of things to do. We don't even have the material. You want everything to be right, Fran."

"Our business this morning is the reading of the will," Castle broke in, his voice sharp-edged. "Will you sit down, Fran. And you, Harrigan."

"Next week, Bob," Fran gave him a bright smile and drawing up a chair, sat down beside him, her hand in his.

Chuck dropped into a chair and leaned back, his long legs stretched in front of him. Fran, glancing at him, thought she had never seen his face quite as grim and filled with hard purpose as it was now.

Castle had a legal-looking sheet of paper on the desk in

front of him. He nudged it with the tip of a long finger, eyes
pinned on Chuck's face as he made a show of his displeasure.
He said, "You're late, Harrigan. You owe us an apology."

"Harrigan never apologizes," Chuck said. "We're here now
and you're in a hurry."

"Quite right." Castle cleared his throat. "I will not take
long. Dad had me attend to this matter some months ago when
he realized he would not live through the year. It is a fair will,
although I realize some of you will be disappointed because
of the things Dad said the night before he died."

· Castle cleared his throat again, plainly nervous, his gaze
touching Chuck's face briefly. "I have only one explanation to
give. He wasn't himself that night, and apparently he had convinced himself he had done something he hadn't done at all."

Fran leaned forward, squeezing Bob's hand. Something
was wrong. Perhaps Chuck had guessed. He must have by
this time, for there could be little doubt about what Castle
was trying to say in a roundabout way. Suddenly she was
ashamed of the thoughts she'd had on their way to town about
getting rid of Chuck. Box N needed him, needed him desperately.

"I don't understand, Judge," Fran said.

"You will in a moment." Castle lifted the sheet of paper
from his desk, drawing his cloak of dignity about him which
most people found impressive and often intimidating.

The Last Will and Testament of Thomas J. Norman. In
the name of God Amen: I, Thomas J. Norman of the
County of Custer and State of Oregon, being of a sound
and disposing mind and not under any restraint of the
influence or representation of any person whatsoever do
make, publish and declare this my last will and testament in
manner following that is to say—I give and bequeath to
persons herein mentioned: One Ada Benson who has
worked so hard to make my last days comfortable, one
thousand dollars in cash. To Charles Harrigan I bequeath
one thousand dollars with the thought that he may desire
to start a ranch of his own. To my dearly beloved daughter, Frances Helen Norman. I bequeath and give the re-
mainder of my property, real as well as personal.

I hereby appoint Judge Lucius Castle of Custer County
State of Oregon my Executor of this my last will and
testament.

In witness whereof I have herein to set my hand and seal
the fifth day of June, the year of our Lord one thousand
eight hundred and ninety-nine.

Thomas J. Norman

Castle laid the paper back on the desk. He stroked his
muttonchop whiskers, glancing covertly at Chuck to see how

he was taking it. In this moment of vast silence, it seemed to Fran that everyone in the room must hear the pounding of her heart. She had never in all her life experienced an interval of time which seemed as unreal as this.

"It isn't possible," she whispered. "Dad must have made out another will since June."

"I would know if he did," Castle said severely. "Dad did deposit all of his cash in your name as he told you, so you can draw on it if there are any immediate obligations."

Now, staring at the Judge's bland, horsy face, it seemed to Fran she saw complacency there, an expression of satisfaction as if he had outsmarted someone. She said, "Half the Box N goes to Chuck. It was the way Dad wanted it."

"Of course," Bob said with great heartiness, "unless he feels he would rather not be burdened with Box N's troubles." He shook his head, frowning. "But I don't understand. Dad was so sure he had left half the Box N to Chuck. He must have mentioned it to you, Judge."

"No, I heard nothing about it until he mentioned it that night." Again his eyes swung to Chuck's grim face, apparently not understanding Chuck's silence. "I'm sorry, Harrigan. I simply put it down to the vagaries of a dying man's mind."

Fran rose. She started to tell Castle to draw up a deed that would name Chuck and her as owner of the Box N, then the thought struck her that Castle might be right. Perhaps Dad had not been as sound mentally that night as she had thought. It would account for what he had said to Bob. It might account, too, for the letter he had dictated to Doc, for his telling Chuck he loved him more than he did Fran.

Mrs. Benson said in a small, frightened voice, "Chuck, there's something wrong."

"Yeah," Chuck said, "there's something wrong, but I don't reckon we can prove it."

Suddenly Fran was aware that they were looking at her, even Bob, expecting her to say something, to do something. But now, staring at Chuck's hard-set face, the thought struck her that he was glad to be out of this. The will had relieved him of all responsibility as far as the Box N was concerned. He could take his thousand dollars and his horses and cows and start his own place just as Bob had often told her he would do.

"You can't walk out on us, Chuck." She said it because they were waiting for her to say something, but her voice lacked conviction even to her own ears, and she added hastily, "We need you, Bob and me."

He grinned at that, the first grin she had seen on his lips for hours, but it was a little sour as if he knew no one else would see any humor in what she had said.

"I didn't say anything about walking out." He rose and faced Castle. "You're a purty sharp hombre, Judge. You knew the Box N wouldn't fight the settlers, so you had the first bunch move onto our range. If they made it stick, we'd have 'em coming in by the hundreds next spring, and then you figured it'd be safe to let us know how you stand."

"I don't know what you're talking about," Castle said in a hurt voice. "I had nothing to do . . ."

"Stop lying," Chuck said testily. "You got your toe caught in a bear trap. One of the Fargo boys let it out about you when I was talking to 'em, and this morning I got some real proof. Partridge told Fran and me that you ordered him to give the Fargo bunch credit. I guess any damn fool can figure it out from there."

"You're lying," Castle breathed, his face turning red.

"No," Fran said. "I was there."

"Then Partridge lied."

"He didn't have no reason to." Chuck leaned across the desk. "We wouldn't lift a hand against bona fide settlers, but the Fargos are toughs you fetched to Custer County and we're gonna run 'em off Chicken Creek. When this gets out, you're finished around here."

"Why, God-damn you," Castle shouted, and yanked a drawer open.

"Lift that gun and you're a dead man," Chuck said. "Go ahead. I'd just as soon do the job now as later."

But Castle didn't lift the gun. He didn't want to die, Fran thought. He said, "I suggest you leave the country, Harrigan. I shall advise Fran to pay you the thousand dollars Dad left you so there will be nothing to hold you."

"If I left now, I'd never be able to face Dad in the hereafter. When I do leave, if I ever do, it will be after you're dead, or broke and crawling across the hills on your belly."

Chuck wheeled and stalked out. Fran raised a hand to her throat; she wanted to call out to him, but no sound came from her. She wasn't thinking clearly, she wasn't feeling anything. Suddenly she had been thrown into a pit of puzzling uncertainty.

"Get rid of that troublemaker, Fran," the Judge said.

Bob put his arm around her. "The Judge is right. Chuck hates me because you love me. He'll try to kill me. You'll see."

She slipped out of his embrace and left the office, Mrs. Benson following her. She heard the Judge say, "Just a minute, Bob. I have a chore for you that must be attended to today." As she went down the stairs, she remembered Chuck threatening to kill Bob before he let her marry him, and now Bob said Chuck would try.

When they reached the boardwalk, Mrs. Benson said, "Do you want to see if Partridge has the material for your wedding dress?"

She realized with a start that she had promised Bob they would be married next week. She shut her eyes, leaning against the wall of the bank building. She said, "No, not today."

CHAPTER XIII

Trouble in O'Toole's

CHUCK HARNESSED and hooked the team to the hack, thinking he might as well have tied the horses in front of the bank, but he had supposed the reading of the will would take much longer and he had wanted the horses to be sheltered from the biting wind.

He got into the seat and drove out of the stable, sick about this whole business because it was all mixed up and his own course wasn't clear to him, not after the Fargos were driven off Chicken Creek. In a way he was glad the will did not leave him half the Box N as Dad had said.

He was surprised at his own reaction, now that he had time to think about it. His feeling was one of relief as much as anything. He was puzzled, too, for he could not understand why Dad had said he had left one will when he had actually left another.

Chuck was sure of only one thing. Castle had been wrong in what he'd said about "the vagaries of a dying man's mind." Dad had been in full possession of his mental faculties that night. Chuck had known him too long to be fooled.

"Chuck."

He pulled up, recognizing O'Toole's voice. He waited while the saloonman hurried toward him, impatient at the delay because he saw that Fran and Mrs. Benson were waiting in front of the bank. When O'Toole reached him, he asked, "What's up, Barney?"

The saloonman hadn't taken time to put on his coat. He was in his shirt sleeves, his apron still around him. He shivered, his red face redder than usual. He said, his teeth chattering, "You'd better stay in town today."

"Why?"

"I ain't gonna stand out here and freeze to death," O'Toole said. "Come inside if you want to talk."

"I don't want to talk," Chuck said harshly. "I just want to get out of this damned burg."

"All right," O'Toole said, and wheeling, started back toward the saloon.

Chuck hesitated a moment, knowing that O'Toole was not a man to get excited over nothing. Chuck called, "I'll be in pretty soon," and O'Toole turned to nod and hurried on to get out of the cold.

Chuck drove along the street to the bank and stepped out of the hack. He said, "I've got to stay in town. I reckon you can drive back, Fran."

She gave him a sharp glance. "Are you going to make trouble for Bob?"

"Maybe."

She frowned, biting her lower lip the way she did when she was bothered by something. She was silent until she climbed into the hack and took the lines. Then, with Mrs. Benson in the seat beside her, she said, "If you know anything against Bob, really know anything, you ought to tell me."

He studied her worried face, sensing an uncertainty of purpose that was not like her, and he made a sudden decision. He asked, "Would you believe me if I told you he was the one who tried to kill me the other night?"

Her eyes widened. She asked incredulously, "You mean that?"

"Do you believe it?"

"Of course not," she cried. "Bob's got his faults, but he's not a killer, and you're pretty small . . ."

"Would you believe he's got another girl who says she's going to marry him?"

"A lot of girls would like to marry him," she said indignantly, "but that doesn't mean he's done anything wrong."

"You'd best get along," he said. "You've got a cold ride home."

Swinging sharply around, he walked to the saloon. He went inside and watched her leave town. She hadn't believed either accusation, but he felt he had done the right thing. At least he had given her something to think about.

He walked to the big heater in the middle of the saloon, took off his mackinaw and Stetson and laid them on a poker table, and held his hands over the stove. No one else was in the saloon except O'Toole.

"Want a drink?" the saloonman asked.

"No."

O'Toole poured one for himself. "It sure poisons a man. Dunno why I sell it."

"It's a living, ain't it?"

"Not one I'm proud of." O'Toole set his empty glass down. "I'm thinking about getting rid of the place and buying an outfit."

"That'll be worth waiting around to see."

O'Toole walked to the stove. "Staying in town?"

Chuck rolled and lighted a smoke. He said, "For a while."

"Well then, I'll tell you the boys are meeting again this afternoon. Spiegle is still working on 'em about that bunch on Chicken Creek. He didn't get anywhere while Dad was alive, but he will today."

Chuck drew on his cigarette. "Spiegle and Judge Castle in cahoots?"

O'Toole scratched a fat cheek, surprised at the question. "Now why would you ask that?"

"Just wondering."

"Hell, I don't see any reason why they should be."

No use to tell the saloonman what the reason was, Chuck thought. He glanced at his watch. After eleven. He sat down at a poker table and began playing solitaire. O'Toole watched from where he stood at the stove.

It had been an impulsive question, but now that he had time to think about it, Chuck decided there could be something to it. By nature Spiegle was a troublemaker. If he worked up a ruckus, it would be to Castle's advantage. Some of the smaller ranchers would sell and get out rather than be involved in a range war, and no one but Castle had money to buy. Range land was one thing, wheat land another. This was the time to buy before values went up.

When it was noon, Chuck and O'Toole went across the street to the Top Notch Café. As they were eating, O'Toole said, "Jack Spiegle is the only man I know of who likes to fight just for the hell of it."

If Chuck had made a good guess about Castle and Spiegle, there was more to it than that, but no one was likely to figure it out. Spiegle's nature was too well known. Folks would put it down to his natural cussedness just as O'Toole was doing.

"You're taking the long way to say something, Barney," Chuck said.

O'Toole sawed off a bite of steak with a dull knife and putting it into his mouth, chewed on it, his jaw muscles working. Finally he said, "When the king dies, you've always got some folks who start thinking about a revolution." He sawed on his steak again. "What I'm saying is that the Box N can't just sit on Dad's reputation."

"So I've got to lick Spiegle again."

"That's it, only you might get the licking. Spiegle might have Reno Vance jump you, and Reno's a hell of a tough hombre."

"I don't give a damn about who sits on the throne," Chuck said, "but I owe Dad too much to let a lot of folks get hurt for nothing. Maybe this is a good day to whittle Spiegle down so he'll stay down."

"Maybe," O'Toole said, and was silent.

Riders began drifting into town as soon as O'Toole and Chuck returned to the saloon, many of them from the fringes of Custer County range. Old man Vance came in with some of his boys. Rusty Wade showed up, and finally Spiegle and Reno Vance made their appearance.

Chuck moved to the far end of the bar and waited. The others, even old man Vance who had been helped many times by the Box N, spoke coolly to Chuck, or ignored him. Rusty was the only one who came to him.

"Didn't figure you'd be here," Rusty said.

"Why?"

"Spiegle aims to take all the boys who'll ride with him and hit that bunch on Chicken Creek. I didn't think you'd stand for it."

Chuck knew it wasn't just a proposition of getting rid of the settlers. The prestige of the Box N was at stake, and what happened today here in the saloon would shape the future. Chuck said, "I won't. We'll tend to the chore ourselves."

Rusty's freckled face showed his surprise. "That's the damnedest thing I ever heard you say. I was half a mind to agree with what you said the other night about taking the law into our own hands."

Spiegle shouted, "Drinks are on me, boys. Belly up."

They crowded against the bar, the run of talk coming to Chuck. Spiegle tossed a gold piece to O'Toole, ignoring Chuck just as he had from the time he'd come in, but now Reno Vance walked toward Chuck, swaggering a little as if he felt important because he rode for Spiegle.

"You ain't drinking, Harrigan," young Vance said belligerently.

He was pushing for a fight. It was in his voice, in his manner, in the tough, brittle expression in his eyes. Spiegle had planned it well, Chuck thought, foreseeing the possibility that Chuck would hear about the meeting.

"You never were any good, Reno," Chuck said. "Remember the time you tattled to old Whittsley about me?"

Reno Vance was younger than Chuck, but he was bigger, and working for Spiegle had given him some of the older man's bravado. He shoved his big face close to Chuck's, shouting, "You're a damned liar," and drove a fist at Chuck's jaw.

Chuck ducked the blow, for he had expected it, and he jumped at Vance, his right fist cracking him in the stomach. Vance jack-knifed, his breath jolted out of him, and Chuck hammered him on the chin. Vance went down.

No one but Rusty had seen or heard what had taken place, but now they crowded along the bar, Spiegle yelling, "Get up, Reno. Get up and bust him." And Rusty, "Give him your boot, Chuck. He sure as hell asked for it."

But Chuck stood motionless, not wanting to do anything to turn these men against him. Too much depended on this, and what would happen later between him and Spiegle.

Slowly Vance got to his hands and knees. He shook his head, swearing, then he made a headlong dive at Chuck's legs, his arms extended. He wanted to make a wrestle out of it on the floor where his weight advantage would help him, but Chuck sidestepped and Vance missed and hit flat on his belly.

"You want to rest?" Chuck asked.

Now, furious because of his failure, Vance jumped up and drove at Chuck again, his right swinging up in a terrific uppercut that missed by inches. Chuck sledged him in the face with a left, moving around, and still Vance came on. Chuck went back, his fists flicking out in sharp punishing jabs that closed an eye and bloodied his nose.

The crowd had formed a circle around them, and now someone shoved a poker table behind Chuck. He heard Rusty's warning yell too late; he spilled across the table and went down in the clutter of chips and cards. Vance fell on him and they rolled over, neither getting a good hold on the other. Vance was on top of him, his right getting Chuck by the throat, and for one horrible moment Chuck thought he was finished.

"Get his eyes, Reno," Spiegle yelled. "Gouge 'em out."

Chuck grabbed a fistful of Vance's hair and yanked. He saw the thumb on Vance's left hand jab at his right eye. He twisted his head; the thumb drove against his temple. He yanked harder on Vance's hair; he tried to arch his back and roll the man off, but Vance clung there, still choking him, his left drawn back for another try at Chuck's eye.

Vance's legs were spread, and Chuck lifted a thigh in a hard, up-driving blow that caught the bigger man in the crotch and brought a howl of pain out of him. For an instant his grip on Chuck's throat relaxed and Chuck got a good breath. He was still pulling Vance's hair, and now he brought his other fist down on the back of Vance's neck.

Chuck rolled the man off and struggled to his feet, sucking air back into his tortured lungs. The shouts of the crowd seemed a long way off, and for a moment the room whirled and tipped, then, as Vance slowly got off the floor, Chuck's vision cleared. Now he did the pushing, driving at Vance and leaving himself wide open to get in a finishing blow.

Vance was hurt and he was slow. He clubbed Chuck with a right that had lost its power, and as his fist fell away, Chuck got him squarely on the jaw with a pile-driving blow that knocked him cold. Chuck watched him go down, and it took a moment for his dazed mind to grip the fact that it was finished.

Rusty slapped him on the back. "A good fight, boy. You ought to pass the hat. It was worth a dollar apiece to see it."

"Not from me," old man Vance yelled. "What the hell is the matter with you, Harrigan?"

Chuck swung to the bar. He poured a drink and gulped it, then he turned to Vance who was staring at him with cold hatred. Chuck rubbed his hands against his pants, closed them and opened them. He had jammed up the knuckles of his left, but his right would grip a gun.

"He called me a liar and swung on me," Chuck said. "What did you think I was gonna do, stand there and let him knock my head off?"

He moved away from the bar, the men falling back. Reno Vance was sitting up, too dazed to know exactly what had happened. Chuck was watching Spiegle, and he saw worry in his face. Reno Vance had a reputation as a barroom fighter, and Spiegle had not doubted that his man would win.

"I don't believe Reno swung on you first," Spiegle said. "It's my guess you started it."

"No," Rusty said. "I saw what happened. Chuck told it straight."

Spiegle's gaze shuttled to Rusty's face. "So you've gone over to Harrigan. I figured you would. I told you the other day . . ."

"This was your idea all the way," Chuck broke in. "Don't try to lie out of it. What are you up to?"

"You know damned well," Spiegle bawled. "We're riding to Chicken Creek and we're running them sodbusters plumb to the Columbia."

"And when you get back, you'll try grabbing a piece of Box N range," Chuck said. "All right, you can make your try right now. The Box N is still the Box N."

Chuck stood five feet from the bar, right hand close to gun butt, eyes pinned on Spiegle's big face, and then, quite suddenly, the push seemed to go out of Spiegle.

"This don't call for gunplay, Harrigan," Spiegle said, his voice strangely mild.

"The hell it don't. You wanted trouble the other day. Now you've got it, mister. Real trouble this time. What are you gonna do with it?"

Spiegle wheeled to face the other men who had dropped behind him. "He's holding up for the sodbusters, boys. Are we gonna stand for it?"

A redhead named Vickers yelled, "By God, no. We'll . . ."

"Stay out of it, Vick." O'Toole produced a double-barreled shotgun from behind the bar and lined it on the redhead. "This ruckus between Harrigan and Spiegle started the day Bob Neville got back. Now let 'em have it out."

"I've got my iron on Reno," Rusty said. "You don't need to worry about him putting a slug in your back, Chuck."

Silence then, so tight and oppressive that it seemed to have weight and substance. Chuck's eyes did not leave Spiegle's face. He had boxed himself into a corner; he either had to fight or crawl. Suddenly a man behind Spiegle lunged forward to get out of the line of fire. The rest followed like sheep when one makes a break, even the redhead Vickers.

O'Toole asked, "You throwing in your hand, Spiegle?"

The big man hit the bar with an open palm. "I know what Harrigan done the morning he went to Chicken Creek with Malone. Sure, he licked one of the kids, but he left 'em there. Maybe it was on account of that bitch of a girl they've got with 'em."

"Make your play," Chuck said, "or get down on your belly like a worm and crawl."

Spiegle must have seen then that he couldn't get out of this. Still, he stood motionless, his bronzed face showing his indecision. Sweat broke through his pores and ran down his cheeks. Someone, it sounded like Vickers, said in disgust, "Let's go home."

Spiegle's hand swept downward for his gun. Chuck made his draw; his Colt swung up, the hammer back. He felt the hard buck of it run up his arm, and through the cloud of smoke he saw Spiegle go back on his heels and fall, his gun that had not been fired dropping from his hand.

Chuck moved toward him, the hammer of his gun back again. Spiegle had been hit in the left shoulder. His gun was on the floor within reach of his right hand, but he didn't make a try for it. He lay there, cursing and groaning, blood spreading across his shirt front.

"Get the doc," Spiegle begged. "I'm bleeding to death."

"You can walk," Chuck said. "For a man who can talk as big as you can, you're sure short on guts."

"Vickers, you and Sampson tote him over to Doc's office," O'Toole said.

The two men came forward and lifted Spiegle to his feet. They got him out of the saloon, half carrying him, half dragging. Rusty, moving up beside Chuck, said, "You can shoot straighter than that. You should have killed him."

"You've changed sides." Chuck eased the hammer of his gun down and holstered it. "Maybe you done some thinking."

"Maybe you have, too. You quitting the Box N?"

"Not today." Chuck looked at the men crowded against the saloon wall. "How many of you boys allowed you'd move in on the Box N?" They were silent, abashed and puzzled, with no certainty of purpose in them. "Maybe it don't look so good now. Well, get one thing straight. Box N will stomp its own snakes as long as I'm rodding the outfit."

Old man Vance glanced at Reno who had crawled to the back wall and was leaning against it, thoroughly cowed and beaten, then he licked his lips and brought his gaze to Chuck. "But you wasn't doing nothing. You can't blame us . . ."

"I sure do," Chuck said. "The Fargos were on Box N range, not yours."

He picked up his hat and mackinaw and put them on. He walked out of the saloon and turned along the boardwalk to the livery stable. He'd have to rent another horse to ride home. Home! Hell, he didn't have any home, not the home he'd had for twenty years. Then, for some reason, he thought of Rusty saying he should have killed Spiegle, and he wondered why he hadn't.

CHAPTER XIV

The Dry Gulcher

CHUCK RENTED the same horse he had ridden the day he'd gone after Doc at Vance's ranch, ignoring the hostler's gibes about Box N being fresh out of saddle horses, and left town at a gallop. Hod Davis and the rest of the crew hadn't said anything, but he knew they were wondering what he was going to do about the Fargos. Well, they'd find out tonight, if Fran didn't fire him before then.

He pulled his horse down to a walk as soon as he was out of town, taking the Monk's Hill road without conscious decision. Dad was dead now and buried. Chuck could not go to him for advice as he had so often during the past months when Dad had been unable to leave the house. Doc. O'Toole. Rusty Wade. Good, solid friends, and the cynicism with which he had regarded friendship a few days ago was gone. But good friends or not, he had reached the place where he could not lean on anyone.

Now, thinking ahead to what must be done, it seemed to him the Box N had one major asset which must be used for all it was worth: the prestige that Dad Norman had given the ranch. Chuck was satisfied with what he had done today. The way he'd handled Reno Vance and Jack Spiegle had added to that prestige. No one would try stealing Box N graze.

He scowled, staring at the slope of the hill ahead of him. There wasn't any sense in worrying about the future of the Box N, or Fran either, if he was going to lose his job. If Fran married Bob, and there seemed to be no way to stop her, Chuck wouldn't be around any longer than it would take him to pack his war bag. It amounted to the same thing, whether he was fired as Castle had advised Fran, or whether he just quit.

Now, almost at the crest of Monk's Hill with the ranch not far ahead, he realized that he was wrong. It did make a difference how he left Box N. If he was fired, it would have to be Fran who made the decision, and that meant cutting off all the roots that had bound him here. He'd probably start drifting just as his father apparently had done.

He was so completely lost in his thinking that it took a moment to realize a rifle had actually cracked and a bullet had slapped through the crown of his Stetson. He wheeled his horse, dropping low in his saddle and pulling his gun. He could do nothing else. There was no cover here on the side of the hill. If he tried to run, he'd get the second bullet in his back.

Chuck cracked steel to his horse, eyes sweeping the grass

in front of him, but he didn't spot the dry gulcher until the man fired again and he saw the puff of smoke before the wind caught and destroyed it.

The man was lying in a shallow depression just below the top of the hill. He must have been seized by panic, for the second bullet was wide. He had only a fool's cover. Probably the last thing he had expected was for Chuck to wheel his horse and come charging at him this way.

Chuck fired, his bullet kicking up dirt to the right of the dry gulcher. Chuck fired again. The man jumped to his feet and started running up the hill, right arm dangling at his side. He moved with the desperate urgency of a jack rabbit that can feel the hound's hot breath on his rear. The instant he gained his feet Chuck saw that it was Bob Neville.

Chuck yelled, "Stand still, Bob, stand still."

But the man went on as if he thought he could outrun a bullet. Chuck fired a third time, laying the slug in front of Bob. He didn't stop, but when he reached the top of the hill, Chuck caught up with him. He swung his horse against him, crowding him, and Bob stumbled and fell down. Chuck reined up and looked down at the fallen man.

"Don't shoot me." Bob, belly-flat on the ground, turned his head to stare over his shoulder at Chuck, and he screamed again, "Don't shoot me."

This was Bob Neville, stripped of all gallantry and charm, his once handsome face distorted with fear of instant death. This was Bob Neville, bushwhacker who had made the mistake of missing what had been an easy shot, an absolute coward now with sweat rolling down his face and mingling with saliva that drooled from the corners of his mouth.

"I wish Fran could see you," Chuck said.

Again Bob screamed, "Don't shoot me."

"Why not?"

Chuck had two loads left in his gun, but he had no desire to pull the trigger. At the moment he felt only disgust. Bob Neville, as Dad Norman had known, was no man at all. With his luck run out, he was nothing more than a piece of flesh, all spirit and pride gone out of him.

"I can't defend myself," Bob cried. "I left my rifle back there."

Then a burst of fury burned through Chuck when he thought how close he had been to death for the second time at this man's hand. He shouted, "You God-damned bastard, you try to shoot me in the back, but you figure I can't plug you because you can't defend yourself."

The fury grew until Chuck had to fight an insane desire to get out of the saddle and kill Bob with his hands. The moment passed. He couldn't do it. Maybe it was the same as it had been when he'd shot Jack Spiegle in the shoulder instead of through the heart.

"Get on your feet," Chuck said in a low voice. "Start walking to the Box N."

"My arm's broken," Bob whimpered. "I'm bleeding."

"You're walking," Chuck said, "or I'll wind this up quick."

Bob got up on his knees and struggled to his feet. He started toward the house, Chuck following on his horse. He was weak and a little sick, the fury beginning to die in him. One good thing would come of this, he was thinking. Fran would know now, and he'd make Bob tell her about Gypsy Fargo.

"Hustle," Chuck shouted at him, and prodded Bob into a run.

They reached the Box N that way, Bob staggering and cursing in a plaintive voice, his clothes that were usually so immaculate covered with dirt and grass. Blood was a steady dribble running down his arm.

"Into the house," Chuck swung down. "Into the house. This is your day to talk."

Bob's knees gave under him and he fell on his face. Chuck nudged him with the toe of a boot. "Get up. Or crawl. Keep moving."

Bob struggled to his feet, making whimpering sounds like a hurt animal. They reached the porch and Chuck threw the door open, calling, "Fran."

Bob went down again, spilling forward on his face as Fran ran into the living room. She saw the gun in Chuck's hand and the blood dripping from Bob's fingers, and her face went white. A scream came out of her, a terrible, shrill sound, and she ran to Bob and knelt beside him.

"He tried to kill me," Bob whispered.

She looked up at Chuck, and he was shocked by what he saw in her face. The possibility that she might not believe him had not entered his mind, but in this moment he knew she wouldn't. The proof he had brought was not proof at all to her. Bob Neville, wounded and bleeding and groaning with pain, aroused all her sympathy.

"You said you'd kill him to keep me from marrying him," she breathed, "but I never really thought you'd try. Have you gone completely insane?"

"He tried to dry gulch me," Chuck shouted at her. "You think I'd bring him here if I'd tried to kill him?"

"Get the doctor," Fran whispered. "Ride to town and get Doc. That's the least you can do."

"He's got some talking to do first." Chuck's words hammered loudly against his own ears. "He's gonna tell you how he tried to kill me that night when we were sitting at the table . . ."

But Fran wasn't listening. She ran into the kitchen, crying, "Mrs. Benson, find one of the men. Send him to town for the doctor, then come and help me with Bob."

Bob, still lying where he had fallen, turned his head to look up at Chuck. He had stopped whimpering, his lips squeezed together, white, rigid. He forced himself to say, "It backfired, Harrigan. You've lost her for good."

A sense of futility beat against Chuck's mind. He holstered his gun, remembering he had told her he'd kill Bob to keep her from marrying him, words which now convicted him in Fran's mind. She ran back into the room. "I'll get the bleeding stopped, Bob. You'll be all right. Chuck, help me get him to the couch."

But Chuck didn't move. He stood there, dazed, watching Fran as she tugged at Bob who either wouldn't or couldn't move. Bob said, "Chuck's a crazy killer. When the will was read and he found out he didn't get half the ranch, he decided to kill me so we couldn't get married. I told you he'd try."

"Malone will arrest him," Fran said. "Can't you crawl, Bob? If you could get to the couch . . ."

"Just get him off the ranch, Fran. Get rid of him. Pay him the money he's got coming like the Judge said and tell him to stay away from here."

No use, Chuck thought as he stared at Fran, no use to talk to her, to reason with her. No use to do anything now. She had stopped trying to lift Bob. She sat on the floor glaring at Chuck, hating him, afraid of him. She was in a state of shock, her mind closed.

But he tried. He asked, "You want to hear what really happened?"

"I don't want to hear any of your lies," she said in a voice that had the bite of a down-striking quirt. "Go away. Don't ever come back."

"But you don't know . . ."

"I know he wouldn't try to kill anyone and I know you shot him. You ought to be in jail."

Chuck leaned against the door jamb. For a crazy moment he had the feeling the floor was tipping up in front of him, that this was a nightmare and he'd wake up in a minute. But there would be no waking up from this. The sky had fallen on him. He had nothing left. Nothing.

"Give him his money," Bob said. "If he ever comes back, I'll swear out a warrant and he'll go to jail."

She got up and ran into the office. There was something about Bob that touched her, his need for her, his helplessness. Chuck walked into the kitchen, stiffly as if his joints had lost their flexibility. He found a flour sack and filled it with food, not really knowing why he was doing this or where he would go, for he was thinking of Fran, and wondering.

She had said once she loved both him and Bob, but she wasn't even willing to listen to what Chuck had to say. She instinctively went to Bob's defense just as she always had if Chuck tried to say anything against him.

When he returned to the front room, she was standing by

the table, a check in her hand. Tight-lipped, she said, "If it was just me, I'd send for Malone, but Bob says to let you go. That ought to show you the kind of man he is."

"Ask him who Gypsy Fargo is," Chuck broke in. "Ask him where he was the night somebody shot at me."

"Get out." She jammed the check into his coat pocket. "Just get out."

He said wearily, "The things in the bedroom are mine, and there's some cows and horses on Box N range that belong to me. I'll be back for them."

He left the house, passing Mrs. Benson who was hurrying across the yard from the barn. She cried out, "Chuck, what happened?"

He passed her without saying a word, his face stone-hard. He led the livery horse to the corral and stripped gear from him. He caught and saddled his buckskin gelding, tying the sack of food behind the saddle. He mounted and sat there for a moment, his eyes sweeping this familiar scene.

There was still a weird sense of unreality about all of this, a crazy nightmarish feeling as if he were trying to wake up and couldn't. He'd been caught in a wild flood and tumbled end over end. He was helpless, no footing, nothing to hang onto.

He had felt this way once when he'd been a boy. Thanksgiving night after a big dinner. He remembered he'd screamed for help and Fran had run into his room and she'd shaken him back to consciousness. But Fran would never do anything for him again, and there was nothing he could do for her, or the Box N.

Hod Davis and Curly Grow were riding in off the range. He turned his buckskin south, not wanting to talk to them, to try to explain something which couldn't have happened and yet had. His shadow rode long beside him and the wind snapped at him with its sharp teeth, but he did not feel it. He was feeling nothing, nothing at all.

It was not until he reached the bottom of Monk's Hill that he realized he was going to Rusty Wade's place. He was going there because he had no other place to go.

CHAPTER XV

Three Pines

TWILIGHT CAUGHT Chuck before he reached the edge of the timber. He had been climbing steadily for an hour, and then he was among the pines, the wind making a high sound in the tops of the trees above him.

Darkness seemed to come at once, the road a narrow alleyway running upslope between two banks of timber. Black walls flanked the road, a narrow strip of sky above that showed a few stars. A sudden, wild feeling of panic crowded into him and set his heart to hammering. He wanted to yell, to get out of the timber, to run. He fought down the crazy impulse, but out of the red, frightening flashes that struck his mind, one thing came clear. He could not live in the timber.

He had no thought of time. He kept climbing until he reached the meadow that held Rusty's buildings, and when he saw the light in the cabin, he called out. The door swung open, Rusty standing there, lamplight throwing his shadow into the yard.

"That you, Chuck?" Rusty shouted.

"Yeah, it's me. Got a drink?"

"You bet I have." Rusty ran to him. "What the hell happened?"

"Plenty." Chuck was cold, his teeth chattering. "I need a drink."

"Go on in. I'll put your horse up."

Chuck stumbled into the cabin and stopped just inside the door. Trudie Evans was there with her sister Nona. They stared at him blankly, for they had never seen him like this. Trudie ran to him and gripped his arms. "Chuck, what happened?"

He jerked free from her and walked to the stove. They had just finished supper, the dirty dishes still on the table. Trudie stood where he had left her, silent and hurt, and Nona, who had far less patience than Trudie, said sharply, "You look like a stepped-on pup, but you've got no call to come in here and start snapping at . . ."

"Shut up."

He hugged the hot stove, giving the girls his back. They began clearing the table, ignoring him, and presently Chuck was aware that he was sweating. He took off his mackinaw and Stetson, but he remained by the fire, his hands over the stove.

When Rusty came in, Nona said tartly, "Sleep walking. Or drunk. I can't tell which, but whatever it is, he's no sweet . . ."

"Nona," Trudie said sharply.

Rusty walked across the cabin to the shelves in the corner. He found a half-filled whiskey bottle and gave it to Chuck who grabbed it and took a long drink. He handed the bottle back and wiped his mouth with the back of his hand. He asked, "Got room for me?"

"You know I have." Rusty turned to the girls. "I'll take you home. Chuck and me will do the dishes after I get back."

Chuck was still huddled over the stove when they left. The Evans place was on up the mountain not more than a quarter of a mile from Rusty's Three Pines. He'd take them home while Nona spoke her mind about a man who had walked big and proud when he had Dad Norman to lean on. Now he was crawling on his belly. Chuck picked up the bottle and took another drink.

Women, hell. Let Nona talk. And Trudie. But she wasn't like Nona. Or Fran who wanted a man she could run. Well, she had one. She could see what it got her. Then the whiskey began working in him and he felt better.

Thinking clearly now, he realized he had brought this on by impulsively taking Bob to the Box N. He should have taken him to town and thrown him into jail. But Mike Malone had gone hunting. Up here somewhere. Probably at the Evans place, for that was where he stayed when he went after his winter's supply of meat.

After Fran had time to get over this, she'd start thinking about it. She might even doubt Bob's story. If Chuck had someone to back up what he'd said. . . . Then his thinking took another turn. If Bob decided to press charges, Chuck could wind up with his tail in a crack.

He grabbed his mackinaw and ran out of the cabin. He yelled, "Rusty," and heard Rusty call, "Here." Chuck put on his mackinaw and ran across the meadow. The lighted windows of the Evans cabin were not far ahead in the timber.

When he reached them, Nona asked tartly, "Get scared, being left by yourself?"

"Nona," Trudie said, her tone sharper than usual. "If you don't halter your tongue . . ."

"Where's Malone?" Chuck asked.

"He's here," Trudie answered. "He got his buck today.'"

"I want to see him," Chuck said, and hurried on toward the Evans' cabin, Trudie running to keep up.

"She ought to lay a single tree across his noggin," Nona shouted. "He's not worth her worry."

Chuck slowed up. He said, "She's right. Quit worrying about me."

"I wish I could," Trudie said. "If I knew what had happened . . ."

"I'll tell Malone," Chuck said, and they walked on up the slope, the timber closing around them.

When they reached the cabin, Trudie opened the door and went in. She said, "Sheriff, Chuck's here."

Old man Evans, a skinny, goat-bearded man who was a better hunter than he was a cowman, sat at the table with Malone, a bottle between them. Malone rose when he saw Chuck, scowling. He had run out on the trouble he had expected and now he sensed that Chuck was bent on taking him back to it.

"If you figure I'm going to stop Spiegle and that bunch from hitting your settler friends . . ." Malone began.

"Shut up and listen," Chuck said. "You ain't here because you don't want to stop the cowmen. You know Judge Castle is into the deal up to his neck and you don't want to buck him."

Malone sat down, his big face red and hard set. "I don't know nothing of the kind."

"You heard the slip young Fargo made," Chuck said. "But that ain't why I'm here. Neville tried to dry gulch me and I shot him in the arm. I took him to the Box N and Fran believed his yarn that I'd tried to kill him."

Malone was tired and a little drunk, and it took a moment for the full significance of what Chuck had said to penetrate his consciousness. Rusty and Nona had come in and had heard what Chuck had told the sheriff.

"So you're on the dodge," Nona said with satisfaction. "The great Harrigan is a ridge runner now."

Rusty shook her arm. "Shut up." He moved up to stand beside Chuck, eyes on Malone. "Better get back on the job, Sheriff."

"You've got no need to worry, Harrigan," Malone said, the tension going out of him. "If you just winged him . . ."

"It ain't altogether that," Chuck broke in. "I want you to take a look at where it happened. Tell Fran what you see. It was just before the road hits the top of the hill. He was lying in a little gully to the east."

"I know where it is," Malone said.

"He took two shots at me. You'll probably find his Winchester there. His horse ought to be on the other side of the hill."

"I ain't starting tonight," Malone said harshly.

"Tonight," Rusty said. "If you're afraid of the dark, I'll go with you."

Old man Evans laughed, his beard wiggling comically. "Afraid of the dark, Mike?"

Stubbornly, Malone said, "I ain't gonna be pushed . . ."

"I'm pushing you," Chuck said. "You've got to be there at sunup. Bob will get there ahead of you if you don't. Maybe he has already."

Evans nodded agreement. "Usually I don't give a damn what happens to the bunch-grassers, but I'm your friend, Mike. If you want to be sheriff, you'd best act like one. Quite a few folks are wondering why they voted for you."

"I don't blame them," Nona said.

Malone rose, sour-tempered, but lacking the will to stand against all of them. "All right, all right. I'll get moving."

Evans lighted a lantern and they left the cabin. Rusty and Nona drifted out after them. Trudie said, "I know how it's been. Rusty told me." She paused, her round face troubled, then she asked in a low voice, "You love Fran a great deal, don't you?"

"I thought I did," he said wearily.

He dropped down on the homemade couch, looking around

the cabin that was almost barren of furniture. Trudie's father had built a lean-to that was the girls' bedroom, the only concession he had made to them. Chuck wondered how long Nona would wait for Rusty, and why Trudie had waited for him at all. But maybe the answer was here. The girls had known nothing but stark poverty.

"Love's a two-way proposition, Chuck." Trudie walked to the couch and sat down beside him. "It would be foolish to love her if she doesn't love you."

"A lot of folks are foolish," he said, "but it's more'n that. It's Dad and the Box N and the notion I've got that I ought to . . . well, he knew the settlers were coming and he didn't want 'em to make trouble. What I mean is, I figure I ought to try to do what he'd have done if he'd lived."

"But Fran isn't part of that."

"No," Chuck admitted, "she isn't part of that."

He glanced at Trudie, and he could not help thinking how different she was from Fran who was happy when she was receiving something or having her own way. Maybe that had been Dad's trouble with Fran's mother.

"What are you going to do?" Trudie asked.

"I don't know. Haven't thought much about it."

"You've got to think about it. What will you do if she sends for you?"

"I don't know that, either." He rose and looked down at her. "You're good, Trudie. I knew all the time, but . . ." He stopped. He had said too much already. He would not hurt her again. "I reckon I'd better slope along."

"You were right about a lot of folks being foolish," she said. "I'm the last person who should talk about love being a two-way proposition."

He wheeled and walked out of the cabin, fighting the impulse to take her into his arms and kiss her. Right now he wanted her because she was kind and gentle and she understood how he felt. Then the truth hit him with a jolting impact. That was exactly the way Bob seemed to Fran.

Malone and Evans were tying Malone's buck to a pack horse. Chuck circled them, not wanting to talk, and when he reached the meadow, Rusty caught up with him. They walked in silence until they reached the cabin, then Chuck said, "Put that bottle up. I don't need it now."

Rusty laughed. "I guess Trudie done you some good. Nona's got a tongue as sharp as a butcher knife that's honed down so you could shave with it, but Trudie now, she's a comfort to have around."

That was true, Chuck thought, but Trudie hadn't done him any good. Dad had written in his letter that sometimes love was not enough, but all the other things weren't enough without love, either.

Chuck stayed with Rusty for three days, helping him snake

poles down from the ridge to the west. He was building a new corral, and Chuck was surprised to hear him say that he'd paid off most of his note to Judge Castle.

Rusty had had a good year. He'd thrown in with Evans and some of the other mountain ranchers and they'd driven a pool herd to Umatilla. Nona had worn him down, convincing him that his notion about getting out of debt before they were married was a foolish one. They'd set a date the first of next month.

"I've got good prospects for once," Rusty said with satisfaction. "A fair to middlin' calf crop, plenty of hay to winter on, and I'll have about fifty steers to market come fall. Hell, I wouldn't swap places with Bob Neville or old man Vance or anybody on the hills."

But when Rusty wanted to take a look at the place he had in mind for Chuck's ranch, Chuck refused to go, and he refused to talk about what he was going to do. He had a wild hope Fran would send for him, and he wanted to be free if she did. He told himself that proved he was crazy, but he kept on hoping.

"I tell you this is the best life a man can have," Rusty said repeatedly. "You ain't a man to go on working for somebody else. Sure, you'll never get rich up here, but you'll be your own boss, and by hell, that's something in my book."

It was, too. Chuck couldn't get around that. Even if he had stayed on the Box N to rod it for Fran and Bob Neville, he wouldn't have been satisfied. Not over the long haul. But the mountains weren't for him.

He continued to work for Rusty, always listening for horse coming up the grade, always hoping. Then, while he v eating dinner with Rusty the third day, Hod Davis rode in on a lathered horse, his weathered face bleak.

"Doc sent for you," Hod said. "Saddle up."

Doc, not Fran. Chuck stood in the doorway, a shoulder against the jamb, the hope that had briefly surged through him when he had first seen Hod slowly dying. He said, "To hell with Doc."

Angry, Hod snapped, "Fran needs you. Doc says you've got to come."

Rusty shoved past Chuck. "There's beans on the table, Hod. Want me to saddle another animal for you?"

"I wish you would," Hod said. "I've got to get back."

Something had happened, something that must have been pretty damned bad, judging by the look on Hod's face. Chuck sat down while Hod filled a plate and began to eat.

"I ain't going till I know," Chuck said.

Hod glanced up. "Well, it ain't purty, but you've got to know, all right. Dad was a good man, the best one I ever knew, but he was weak when it came to women. I don't claim to know nothing about 'em, neither, but by God, if I'd been married to Fran's mother, I'd have lodgepoled her and made a good squaw out of her. Lately now it seems like Fran's getting more and more like her ma. What happened is gonna be good for her, if she's got any of Dad in her."

"You telling me, or ain't you?" Chuck demanded hoarsely.

"I'm getting to it. Fran, she set her head on marrying Bob right off. It was gonna be early this morning so they could take the train to Portland and have a honeymoon, although he wouldn't have been no good, having a busted arm like he's got. We were all in the living room, dressed up in our store duds. Doc was there. And the Judge. The preacher from Norman, he was fixing to tie the knot when that Fargo outfit walked in."

Hod got up and filled his coffee cup. "We were all standing around, not looking outside or nothing. Didn't see 'em ride up. They left their horses on the other side of the barn and walked to the house. Either they hit it lucky, or they waited outside and listened. Anyhow, the preacher got to that place where he says if anybody knows a reason why this here couple shouldn't be spliced, it's time to speak up or forever hold their peace. That was when they came in, the girl in front. The Fargos had their guns out. Hell, we couldn't do nothing. We didn't come to a wedding toting our irons."

Hod snickered. "You should have seen Bob's face. Funniest thing I ever seen. If there'd been a hole in the floor big enough for a mouse to crawl through, he'd have been diving for it pronto. The girl says, 'You're damned right there's plenty of reason why they shouldn't get married and I ain't holding my peace.' She walks right up to the preacher as smart as all hell, her hips a-swinging nice and purty. She wasn't ashamed, neither. She says, 'Bob Neville's got to marry me. I'm carrying his baby, and he's gonna see the baby has a name.' Hell of a way to say it before everybody, but them's her exact words."

Hod drank his coffee, the good humor gone from his face. "Fran, she faints. Fell flat on her face. Doc and Mrs. Benson toted her into Dad's room. The Fargo girl's pa shoves his iron into Bob's back. He says, 'This ain't a shotgun but it'll work. You gonna marry Gypsy, or do I blow a hole in your backbone?' Bob allowed that was the thing for him to do, so the preacher hitches 'em up, and they lit out for Bob's place."

Chuck rose. "What about Fran?"

"Dunno. Doc came out of the bedroom and said to get you. He claims you can do something for Fran, but he couldn't, so I'm fetching you." He glared at Chuck as if expecting trouble. "You goin'?"

"I'll saddle up." Chuck walked to the door and then turned back. "Did Malone show up?"

Hod nodded. "He couldn't find Bob's horse or his rifle, but he located the place where he'd been laying for you. A couple of shells and a lot of cigarette stubs. The grass showed somebody had been there, all right, but Fran was too bullheaded to believe him. I reckon she would now, though."

Chuck left the cabin. Rusty was bringing a saddle horse for Hod. He asked, "What's up?" Chuck told him, and Rusty asked, "You gonna go crawling back?"

"I've got to see her," Chuck said. "After that . . . hell, I dunno."

Rusty laid a hand on Chuck's shoulder, his face grave. "Since you've been here this time, I've found out a couple of things. Trudie ain't right for you, and these mountains ain't your kind of country, but there's one thing I do know. If you go crawling back to Fran now, you're licked. A man's got to have some pride with a woman the same as anything else."

"I've got to see her," Chuck said again, and went on to the corral.

CHAPTER XVI

The Tempering Flame

FRAN LAY on her father's bed when she regained consciousness. The door was closed. The silence was oppressive. A weight seemed to be pressing against her chest, so heavy that she had to struggle for each breath. Her hands were clenched at her sides, the nails biting into her palms.

She stared at the ceiling. Her wedding day! Wedding day! Wedding day! She screamed it over and over and she began turning on the bed, her fists beating at the pillow.

"Here, take this."

It was the doctor, propping her head up. She tried to fight him, but she couldn't get away from his arm that held her shoulders upright. He slipped a pill into her mouth. He said, "Drink this, Fran. Easy now."

She tried to spit the pill out, but he held a glass of water to her mouth. Some of it spilled down her chin. He kept the glass there, saying softly, "Relax, Fran. Ease up." The next thing she knew her mouth was full of water and she swallowed and the pill went down.

He lowered her head and stepped away from the bed. She looked at him. His face was blurred. His pudgy body was ten feet wide. The voice was the doctor's, but this man didn't look like him. She heard Mrs. Benson whisper, "What can we do, Doc?" And Doc's voice, "She'll be all right after she sleeps. This is the best thing that ever happened to her."

The best thing! Doc was crazy. The best thing! That girl! The Fargo men! Guns in their hands. The awful, guilty look on Bob's face. What would Dad have said if he had been here? But Dad was riding the Lord's biggest black stallion. She was glad he wasn't here. Glad! Glad! Glad! Then she was asleep.

It was afternoon when she woke, slanting sunlight falling on her bed. She shivered, and Mrs. Benson said, "I'll get a quilt and put it over you."

Mrs. Benson left the room. Fran seemed to be swimming up through a gray fog, slowly, as if the weight of the fog held her here on the bed. Mrs. Benson returned with a quilt and spread it over her, then Doc was there, looking down at her, his face grave.

"How do you feel, Fran?" Doc asked.

"I don't feel," she said. "I don't feel anything at all."

He put a hand on her cheek and made a clucking sound as if satisfied. "No fever." He lifted her wrist and counted her pulse. "A little fast, but it's all right. You're going to be all right, too."

Everything that had happened that morning flooded her mind and she began to shiver. "I'll never be all right."

"Could I bring you something to eat?" Mrs. Benson said. "A bowl of soup?"

"No."

Doc pulled up a chair. "I tell you you'll be all right. Funny thing about this, Fran. I'm not a praying man usually, but I prayed for something like this to happen and it did. The good Lord's up there, if we stop and think about Him and try to work with Him instead of against Him."

She lay on her side, looking at him. She remembered the weird impression she'd had of him awhile ago, his face blurred, his body ten feet wide. He looked all right now, just as he'd always been, his little potbelly, his kind face, the old green-black suit.

Mrs. Benson left the room, shutting the door behind her. Doc said, "I sent for Chuck."

Her heart missed a beat and then began to pound. She whispered, "He won't come."

"He'll come. Be along any time, I reckon." Doc pulled his chair closer to the bed. "Fran, I'm going to talk to you. I'm going to hurt you, but it's got to be done. I can't help you by operating on you or giving you medicine. Maybe what I say will."

"Chuck won't come," she whispered. "I drove him away."

"He'll come all right, but what happens after that is up to you. I want you to think back and tell me what turned you against Chuck. Don't lie to me. That'd be the worst thing you could do."

She closed her eyes. "I was never against Chuck."

"You're lying," he said sharply. "Don't forget I've known you all your lives. I watched you grow up, playing together like a couple of pups. And then something happened. What was it?"

She was silent a long time, thinking of the last dance he'd taken her to and how he'd kissed her and how frightened she'd been, and then she thought of the weeks when she kept hoping he would come to her and she could tell him she shouldn't have acted that way and the kiss was all right. But he'd started going with Trudie Evans, and then Bob had begun taking her places.

"All right," Doc said gently. "Don't tell me. Just think about it. But there is one thing you've got to tell me. Do you love Chuck?"

Still she was silent. She could see it now that it was too late, her stupidity and selfishness. She could have changed all of it, but she hadn't. She could not deny, even after what had happened, that Bob had appealed to her. Maybe it had been ambition, wanting a man who had a sort of charm and wore good clothes and had a gift for saying pretty things. Chuck had none of these qualities.

Then she remembered her feelings when Bob had come back to Norman this last time, and her crazy idea she could have them both. It hadn't seemed crazy then, but it did now. She had never given much thought to whether it had been right or wrong. And going into Chuck's room that night, but she thought about it now, and she was glad Malone had come when he had.

"You've got to answer that question," the doctor said, "or I can't do anything for you. I'll meet Chuck when he comes and I'll send him back."

Back to Trudie Evans? She cried out, "Yes, I love him, and there never was a time when I didn't. But there were things about Bob I liked, things Chuck didn't have."

"That's better," Doc murmured. "But the things you liked in Bob weren't really important, and the things you liked in Chuck were. That right?"

"Yes, I guess that's right," she said, "but when Chuck came in with a gun in his hand and Bob was wounded, I remembered he'd said once he'd kill Bob to keep me from marrying him, and I thought that was what he'd tried to do."

"You closed your mind and you wouldn't listen," Doc said. "After that you were too proud and stubborn to back up, even when Malone told you what he'd found."

No use to lie to him. He knew her too well. She said, "No, I couldn't back up."

He leaned forward, his hands on his knees. "What did you think when you read Dad's letter to Chuck?"

He knew her all right. She turned her head on the pillow to look at his earnest face. He had said he was going to hurt her and he had. He must know how she felt. She had never

done anything as cheap as reading that letter, nothing that had
made her as ashamed as it had. She might as well admit it.

"It was the nastiest thing I ever did." She paused, thinking
about it, and then because she suddenly wanted to talk, she
hurried on, "But there was something else. I didn't know Dad
couldn't talk to me. I mean, I had always felt we were honest
with each other. And he said something about me being a
burden to Chuck . . ."

She couldn't go on. She turned her head and began to cry.
Then, minutes later, she wiped her eyes and said defiantly,
"You know now. I won't be a burden to anybody. I just won't.
I knew I wouldn't be to Bob because he needed me more than
I needed him."

"But Chuck has always been stronger than you have." The
doctor smiled. "Now you're being honest and that's good. But
you see, Dad didn't mean it the way it sounded to you. That
letter was for Chuck. Dad wasn't sure how Chuck felt about
you. If he married you out of a sense of obligation, you
would have been a burden, but if he married you because
he loved you, you wouldn't be. Does that make sense?"

She had never thought about it that way before. She said,
"Yes, I guess it does."

"Now then, I'm going to tell you something else that's been
wrong with you. You couldn't know about it because your folks
always put up a front when they were with you and Chuck, but
I know all about it because Dad used to come to town and
talk to me, sort of unload. Your mother was a very selfish and
wilful woman. She hated this country and she wanted to go
back to the Willamette Valley, but Dad, well, you know how
he loved the Box N and the hills and everything, and he took
a lot of pride in what he had done here."

She nodded, not understanding yet what he was getting at.
"Yes, but Ma . . ."

"Wait," Doc broke in. "That's the part I want to tell you.
It got so she wasn't a wife to him. She slept with him, all right,
but there might as well have been a mountain between them.
You see, she thought she could force him to make a move, but
he wouldn't, even for her. That's what he meant when he said
love wasn't enough. He loved her a great deal at first, but by
the time she died, I think he must have hated her.

"You see, Fran, there's one thing you've never understood
about men. If a man is worth a damn, he's got to be stronger
than his wife. He wants a woman who believes in him and
understands the things he's trying to do and who's big enough
to give in to him on the important things."

Doc rose and walked around the bed to the window. "Mrs.
Benson doesn't want you to know, but I think you should.
After she lost her husband, Dad used to go to town to see her.
Your mother thought he was playing cards, but he'd stay with
Mrs. Benson until midnight or later before he came home. She

was everything your mother should have been and wasn't. I'm not sure why Dad and Mrs. Benson didn't get married unless they were afraid you and Chuck would figure out how it had been, and Dad didn't want to destroy the illusion that everything had been fine between him and your mother."

She lay there, staring at Doc's broad back, shocked by what he had said, but she did not doubt it. She had seen the way Mrs. Benson had looked at her father, Mrs. Benson who had done so much for him those last months and who had said a few nights ago that she had loved him.

The doctor came back to the bed. "I told you it's up to you about Chuck. You can be like your mother, or you can decide you love him enough to let him take the lead on things. Make the big decisions." He spread his hands. "A man like Bob can be henpecked, but men like your father and Chuck can't. I don't mean for you to crawl to him. Just be willing to admit there are a few things he knows more about than you do."

He walked to the door and opened it. "I'm going to town. You'd best get up and fix your hair. The first thing you say to Chuck will decide everything between you."

She lay there a long time after he left, thinking about her mother saying that a woman had to stand up to a man or she'd lose her rights. If she let him, a husband would get to thinking she was a slave. Well, her mother had fought for her rights, and she'd made a failure out of her marriage.

Now, thinking of Bob, Fran knew how terribly right Doc had been in saying that the things she had liked in him were not important. She was well rid of him. For the first time she saw him as a weak and cowardly man who had tried twice to murder Chuck, a cheap and unfaithful man who had never dreamed his affair with Gypsy Fargo would catch up with him.

She rose and went upstairs to her room. For a long time she sat in front of her mirror working on her hair. It had begun to rain, and when she went downstairs and stood in the open doorway, she watched the rain come down and smelled the scent of sage that came in on the wind. It had warmed up, and she had a strange feeling that it was spring and she should be running through the grass barefooted, with Chuck.

But it was dusk and Chuck hadn't come. Then she was afraid. He would not come. Doc should have talked to her a long time ago, but she knew instantly it wouldn't have done any good. She wouldn't have listened. It had taken the thing that had happened this morning to humble her, and now it was too late.

CHAPTER XVII

Betrayal

BOB NEVILLE had lived with his cowardice all his life, but no one else had known until the Fargos had broken up his wedding to Fran and forced him to marry Gypsy. Now he was finished. He could never win another election in Custer County. But that wasn't the worst thing. He had lost a fortune when he had lost Fran.

Judge Castle would wash his hands of him. He was faced with nothing but hard work on a ten-cow spread that he'd lose when Castle's plans materialized. More than that, he was saddled with a wife he didn't want and a batch of tough in-laws who had measured him for size and found him mighty damned small.

He rode beside Gypsy who sat her saddle in the proud way of a woman who has succeeded in what she set out to do. He glanced at her, hating her so much he was sick with it. When she felt his eyes on her and looked at him, he quickly turned his head to stare at the road in front of them.

"You don't seem to be real happy for a man who just got married," Gypsy said. "Hell, I did you a good turn. I'll make you a better wife than that Norman woman."

He didn't say anything. What was the use? His broken arm ached with a steady, painful throbbing. He hurt all over, right down into the bottom of his belly. So close, he thought, so close to getting what he'd wanted. He'd played every card with the finesse of a skilful gambler, turning Fran against Chuck, telling her to forgive him even if he was a greedy man who had gone out of his mind.

He'd been very clever with Fran, telling her over and over how much he loved her; he'd let her have her way on every issue that had been raised, even to promising to stay on the Box N and give up his political ambitions. He'd promised to run the settlers off Chicken Creek. He never intended to keep his promises, but the immediate problem was to get married.

It had worked out right down the line. She hadn't even believed Malone when he'd showed up that morning with a yarn about someone lying on the grass for hours waiting for Chuck to come along. All right, Bob had said, maybe one of the settlers had aimed to dry gulch Chuck, but he'd left before Bob had showed up.

He'd been riding along, he'd said, headed for the Box N when Chuck started cutting loose at him. He'd grabbed his Winchester and fired a couple of times in self-defense. Chuck had knocked him out of his saddle and his horse had spooked and gone over the hill. Johnny Bain had found his horse and the Winchester the evening before and brought them in.

Fran was the only person who had believed him, but she was the important one. Malone couldn't prove anything against him. He cursed himself for missing that one clear shot he'd had at Chuck, but he'd never been a good marksman and he'd had buck fever.

He was filled with revulsion when he remembered the horrible, clawing fear he'd felt when Chuck had wheeled his horse and come straight at him. Panicky, he'd lost his head and thrown his rifle away and started to run, then the numbing impact of the slug hitting him. All of it was a nightmarish memory he wanted to forget.

In time he could forget it. He had the compensating certainty that he was smarter than anyone else in the bunch-grass hills. The fact that he had been able to turn defeat into victory and get rid of Chuck proved it.

If the damned Fargo bunch hadn't showed up. . . . He blamed Judge Castle. He'd get square with him. But maybe it wasn't worth it. Maybe the best thing to do was to sneak away when Gypsy was asleep some night and ride out of the country.

He still had the money Castle had given him to get Gypsy off his neck. Not much, but enough to start somewhere else. His greatest talent was making people like him, and he could do that on another range just as he had when he had come here.

He was still pursuing that line of thinking when they rode into his yard. He reined up and swung down, awkwardly because of his broken arm, noting absently that Dake Collins had brought a load of wood and had gone back to the mountains for another.

Gypsy was out of the saddle then. She said, "You don't need to hang around, Pa. This is our honeymoon."

Pete Fargo leaned to one side and spit and wiped his mouth. He was the ugliest man Bob had ever seen, and the most vicious. Castle hadn't been half as cute as he'd thought, or he wouldn't have brought a wolf pack like the Fargo bunch to Custer County. He'd have been smarter if he'd brought in some genuine settlers.

"I dunno about that," Pete said. "This bucko ain't happy about the way things went this morning."

"He will be," Gypsy said confidently. "I told you that. I'll make him forget the Norman woman before sundown."

"Maybe," Pete said. "Maybe not. I've got just one thing to say, Neville. You treat Gypsy right, or I'll skin you and hang your hide on your own door. Savvy?"

Bob stared at the man, his usually pink face a dark red. He showed Pete Fargo how much he hated him and he didn't care. He said, "I married Gypsy, not you or her brother or uncle or cousins. Now get to hell off my ranch and don't ever come back."

He wheeled and walked into the cabin. Gypsy called, "I'll put the horses up. I'll never do it again, but this is special."

Bob sat down at the table. Never in all his life had he been so completely humbled as he had been today, never had he felt so helpless. He had to get out. He hated to leave his ranch which was worth something. He had a few horses and some cows. Well, he'd let Gypsy have the whole layout.

If he stayed, he'd be reminded of today's failure as long as he lived, and that wasn't good for a man. He had been proud of his talents, feeling a little condescending to men like Chuck who had a core of toughness he lacked, and to men like Dad Norman and Doc Logan who had the weakness of feeling compassion for others. He had never doubted his ultimate success and he didn't now. All he needed was a new country and new people.

He was vaguely aware that the Fargo men had ridden away, then he heard Gypsy chopping wood and a moment later she came in, dropping her armload behind the stove. She said, "I'll get dinner. You're hungry, ain't you, Bob?"

He didn't answer. He sat hunched forward, his good arm on the table, fist opening and closing. She said sharply, "Answer me."

Still he said nothing. She came to the table and looked at him, brushing a rebellious lock of hair back from her forehead. A wilding if he had ever seen one. She hadn't even cared enough about her looks to put on a dress when she had come to make him marry her. He had known all the time what she was, raised with men until she thought and talked like men, and he wondered what he had ever seen in her.

"Let's get one thing straight," Gypsy said in a strained voice. "I made a bargain when I stood up in front of that preacher this morning and I'll keep my part of it, but there's one thing I won't stand. That's a God-damned sullen bastard who just sits. Now answer me. Are you hungry?"

"I'm hungry." He swallowed, and then asked, "How did you find out about me and Fran?"

She laughed. "Why, it wasn't hard. I knew you had something up your sleeve, so we asked a few questions in town and we got the whole story."

"And you wound up ruining every prospect I had," he said morosely.

"Because I don't have a big ranch for you to marry," she said scornfully. "You should have thought of that when you got into bed with me and made all them pretty promises. You see, I believed them."

"You made a bad bargain. You didn't get what you thought you did."

She shrugged. "I got what I thought I did, all right. Right

now you're sore as a bear with a boil on his tail, but you'll get over it." She turned to the stove and built a fire. "I heard Castle talk about your future and what was going to happen in Custer County, so I figured that would suit me fine."

"You fixed it so I don't have any future." He watched her slice bacon into a frying pan, a sense of outrage growing in him until he could not keep from shouting at her, "I won't stay here. I've got nothing to stay for."

She whirled and shook the butcher knife at him. "You've got a wife. You can get one thing through your smart head right now. You walk out on me and I'll kill you. I've got a little pride, too."

"Not much, judging by what you did today."

She smiled and turned back to the bacon. "A woman has to use any weapon that will work. I've lived like a man until I'm sick and tired of it. I could have married a long time ago, but any man I could have had would have been another tough drifter like my own family."

"You're used to that kind of life," he said dully. "You won't like it here."

"You bet I'll like it. I've never had a home, not even one as good as this. Just a wagon or a tent, riding all over the country while Dad and the rest of 'em traded horses or rigged up a horse race or maybe knocked a bank over when we were down on our luck, then dodging like hell and being afraid of every stranger we ran into on account of he might be a lawman. I've had enough of that."

He drummed his fingers on the table, wondering just how hard it would be to get away from her. If her family had lived the way she said, they'd know every owlhoot trail and hideout in the West. They'd have friends. They could trace him.

Then he thought about the baby she was going to have and a feeling of absolute despair gripped him. He'd have everybody against him if he went off and left her. If her folks caught him, they'd hang him and nobody would lift a finger.

He asked hoarsely, "When are you going to have your baby?"

"Your baby?" She had shoved the frying pan to the front of the stove and now set the coffeepot beside it. "Why don't you say our baby?"

"I won't claim him," Bob yelled at her. "What do you think I am?"

"One of these days I'll tell you, but this ain't the day." She began setting the table. "Maybe it'll make you feel better if I tell you I'm not having a baby, yours or anybody's. I told you a woman had to use any weapon that would work, and I couldn't think of anything else that would."

He stared at her, his blood pounding in his temples. It took a moment for him to really grasp what she had said because he was too upset and jittery to think clearly. Then it hit him.

He'd been taken in by an old dodge, taken in by a scummy bunch of ridge runners because a girl was tired of her kind of life and wanted a different one so badly she'd do anything to get it.

"And I'll tell you something else," Gypsy went on. "I've fought men to keep them out of my bed ever since I was big enough for them to want to crawl in with me, but you're the only one who ever did. I don't know if that means anything to you, but it does to me."

He wasn't seeing her clearly now. Red dots were running across his eyes. He began to tremble, a fury taking hold of him that he had never felt before. Everything gone, and for nothing. He was going to kill her. It didn't make much difference because he had to run anyhow, and he'd get a rope if they ever caught him. But he wasn't going off and let her laugh at him the rest of her life.

His Colt and gun belt hung from a peg near the door. He rose; he made a slow turn toward the door, then he jumped toward it and yanked at the gun. It jammed in leather, and he lost a precious second getting it clear because he had only one hand to work with.

He heard her scream something at him, but he didn't know what it was. He had the gun clear of the holster then, and he eared the hammer back and wheeled toward her. He heard a shot that wasn't from his own gun. Something struck him in the back like the blow of a club and he fell forward, his head hitting hard against a corner of the table. After that he felt nothing, just blackness that reached up and pulled him down and down, and finally that was gone, too.

Pete Fargo, standing in the doorway with a smoking gun in his hand, said, "Well, you had your way and see what it got you. Get him into bed, you said, and you'd make him forget what you'd done to him. Now maybe you're satisfied."

She stared at Bob's body, a hand clutching her throat. He had meant to kill her! She had never given that possibility a thought. She had been so sure she could manage him, once they were married. She couldn't go on living the way she had, but now it would be the same old life all over again.

She began to scream. Pete walked to her and slapped her sharply on the cheek. "Shut up. We're on the dodge again in case you've got enough sense to figure it out."

She stopped screaming. Pete went through Bob's clothes, found the money Judge Castle had given him, and grunted as he put it into his pocket. He said, "Come on. Nothing else worth taking, I reckon."

The bacon was burning, smoke filling the cabin. She stumbled outside, unable to think of anything, to say anything. Running again, leaving their wagons and teams over there on Chicken Creek, getting nothing out of this but the few dollars that had been in Bob's pockets. Her father would never let her forget she'd spoiled the best deal they'd ever had.

Pete shut the door. "I'll saddle your horse," he said.

She waited there, trembling and scared and unable to believe the roof had fallen in on her. Her father led her horse to her as the rest of the Fargo men rode up. Her brother Lon said, "Looks like you had it figured, Pa."

"I had it figured all right," Pete said. "Start letting a God-damned woman have her way, and you've got trouble." He motioned to Gypsy. "Climb on. We're sloping out of the country."

"I'm staying," Gypsy cried. "I was his wife. This place belongs to me."

Pete snorted as he stepped into the saddle. "All right. Stay here and keep his carcass company if you want to. But just try to figure out what you're gonna tell the sheriff. He don't like you much. And with Castle being Neville's friend, hell, if you've got a lick of sense, you know where you'll land."

He was right. She mounted, then saw that her father was looking at Bob's horse in the corral. Lon said, "Everybody in the country knows that horse."

"Yeah, better leave him," Pete said reluctantly, and turned his mount toward town.

Gypsy fell in behind the men, her head bowed, and they rode for a mile, no one talking until Lon asked, "What are you fixing to do, Pa?"

"Castle promised us five thousand for coming here," Pete said. "I'm going after it."

"We haven't earned the money," Gypsy cried. "We weren't to get it till spring."

Pete hipped around in his saddle and glared at her. "I'm getting it anyhow. Ride the other way if you don't like the smell of this."

She hated them, hated everyone of them because they'd dragged her all over the country. They'd used her in every way they could, and she hated them for that. But they were all she had.

"Means knocking the bank over," Lon said.

She stared at her brother's back. Another robbery. Killing, maybe. More riding and dodging with fear always with them. She heard her father say, "Maybe not. Castle don't have much guts if I've got him pegged right. He ain't gonna cotton to the notion of me telling around why we're here. I figure he'll cave."

"What if he don't?" Lon asked.

"You boys stay on the street in front of the bank," Pete said. "If you hear a shot, move in and grab. It'll go smooth as silk if we handle it fast."

"The sheriff . . ." Lon began.

"Oh hell," Pete snapped. "You seen him that day on Chicken Creek. He don't amount to nothing."

Gypsy knew then what she had to do. It was the best of two bad choices. If she went with them, she'd be hunted. Whatever the future held for her, it wasn't going to be that. She'd made that decision a long time ago. It was the reason she had insisted on going to the Box N that morning.

She wheeled her horse and struck north. She'd stop at their camp and load a pack horse with all the food he could carry and she'd keep riding until she was a thousand miles from here.

Lon yelled, "Gypsy's pulling out."

She heard her father curse her, heard him call, "We'll hit for the Blue Mountains and then angle over to the Snake River. You can find us." She didn't look back. She didn't want to find them, she didn't want to see them again, and she knew she never would.

CHAPTER XVIII

Spring in October

CHUCK AND HOD DAVIS rode fast after they left Rusty's place. Clouds had moved across the sky, low and heavy with moisture. It would rain before sundown, and now, with the afternoon still young, the timber thinned the half light until it seemed like dusk.

Even after they had left the pines and were dropping down the long grade toward the gulch that held the town, the light was still so thin that it gave the weird impression the day had died before the sun had set. Later, sometime during the night, it would turn cold, and there would be snow instead of rain, possibly an early blizzard that might have tragic results.

All of this was a vague disturbance on the periphery of Chuck's consciousness. The safety of Box N cattle was not his problem. Perhaps it never would be again, but he said nothing to Hod about it, for he had the feeling the old cowboy had assumed he was coming back to stay.

Chuck wondered what Hod and the rest thought about working for Fran. Maybe she'd bring a stranger in to be foreman. If she did, the Box N would never be the same again. The old loyalty would be gone.

Funny about a thing like that. You never develop the kind of spirit that had always characterized the Box N by setting out to develop it. It was a sort of miracle that only a man like Dad Norman could perform. It had found its roots in his character; it had not resulted from anything he had said or done, but from what he was. Fran, if she insisted on running roughshod over everyone, could destroy in a few weeks what Dad had spent a lifetime building.

They reached the gulch, the town not far east of them. Hod reined up, calling, "Hold on, Chuck." The wind was running in hard from the west, or they would have heard the gunfire sooner. Now the sound came clearly to both of them, and Hod threw a questioning glance at Chuck.

For a moment Chuck was caught in a bog of indecision. He wanted to see Fran, and the sooner he saw her the better. The last three days had been hell, waiting when plain, cold logic told him he had nothing to wait for. Maybe he didn't have anything now to wait for, but he had to find out.

Chuck felt a compelling desire to ride on, but the amount of firing sounded as if a small battle was taking place in the streets of Norman, and the only real fighting man in town was Barney O'Toole. The presence of the Fargos in the county was what bothered Chuck. It would be about their size to raid the town and maybe tackle the bank, and it was possible that the thing which had happened this morning on the Box N had brought about a split between them and Bob Neville and Castle.

"Well?" Hod asked.

"We'd better have a look," Chuck said. "Won't take long if we find out it ain't our put in."

Hod nodded. "That was my way of figuring it."

They turned toward town, putting their horses into a run along the gravel road. Chuck reined up before they reached the business block. Some of the firing was coming from the bank, but most of it was from the hotel.

Hod, pulling up beside Chuck, said, "Now how are we gonna tell which side we're on?"

"We'll try the hotel," Chuck said, "and maybe wish we'd gone the other way."

They swung off Main Street and turned down an alley that went behind the hotel. Chuck couldn't tell whether they had been seen or not. No one had fired at them, which didn't prove anything either way, but if they hadn't been seen, there was a fair chance they could get into the lobby and find out who was there.

They left their horses ground-hitched in the alley, and moved along the hall that led to the front of the hotel, guns in their hands. The door into the lobby was closed. "Guess we'll find out whether we got our neck into a loop or not," Chuck said in a low tone. Turning the knob, he shoved the door open.

Malone and two townsmen were standing at the front windows behind barricades of mattresses. Hod let out a whoop. "We guessed right," he crowed.

Malone wheeled, his gun palmed. Chuck yelled, "Hold it, Mike," and Malone lowered his gun.

"You damned near got your tail shot off," he said peevishly. "I didn't know you were in town."

"Heard the shooting and figured we'd better look into it," Chuck said, and crossed the lobby to Malone.

The townsmen nodded at Chuck and Hod and went on firing their Winchesters, a plain waste of ammunition, it seemed to Chuck, for they weren't aiming. They were just banging away as if they were afraid the men in the bank might charge across the street.

Malone glared at Chuck. "Who do you think we've got holed up over there?"

"I was wondering."

"That damned Fargo bunch, that's who. I knew all the time they were outlaws. Should have chased 'em off Chicken Creek . . ."

"You're saying you were right and I was wrong," Chuck broke in impatiently. "Now tell me what happened."

"They rode into town awhile ago," Malone said, "peaceful and mild-like. Pete Fargo's kid held the horses. Three of 'em stopped on the walk in front of the bank and Pete went upstairs. I came here from my office to watch 'em, figuring it didn't look right. Pretty soon I heard a shot and Pete came high tailing down the stairs. The Judge, he got to a window and yelled he'd been shot, then he disappeared. I got Pete. Then the kid who was holding the horses threw a slug at me. He missed and I got him, and the other three ran into the bank when their horses spooked and went tearing down the street."

"The girl with 'em?"

"Didn't see any sign of her."

"So you got three badgers in a hole and don't know how to get 'em out. That it?"

"That's it," Malone said. "O'Toole and a couple other boys are in back of the bank so they can't get away, but come night, they'll wiggle out and we'll lose 'em."

"Why don't you go in after 'em?" Chuck asked, grinning.

"I'll deputize you to go," Malone snapped. "It's your fault they're here."

"Not the way I figure," Chuck said. "Come on, Hod. This is the sheriff's business."

"You stay here," Malone bellowed. "I need all the men I can get. Besides, Doc's upstairs. If them varmints figure out there's a stairs inside the building, they'll go up and get Doc and use him for a hostage. Then we'll be in a hell of a fix."

"Doc." Chuck grabbed Malone's shoulder. "What'd you let him go over there for?"

"I didn't let him," Malone said. "He went as soon as he heard the Judge had been shot."

"I'll get him," Chuck said. "Give me two, three minutes to get to the end of the block and then open up with every gun you've got."

"Chuck, you lunk-headed . . ." Hod shouted.

But Chuck had already run out of the lobby and down the hall. It had begun to rain, and as Chuck ran along the alley, the rain became a downpour. He raced past the backs of the drugstore and a jewelry store and turned to follow the wall of the building to Main Street.

He was fully aware of the chance he was taking, and there wasn't a man alive he'd do it for except Doc Logan. The trouble was Judge Castle wasn't worth a hair on Doc's head, but Doc wouldn't think of that.

The hard rain coming at this moment was a piece of luck for Chuck. It drew a misty curtain across the street, and now with four guns hammering from the hotel, there was a good chance Chuck could reach the other side of the street without drawing any of the Fargo fire.

He lunged away from the corner of the building where he had briefly waited until Malone and his men had started their firing. He sprinted across the street, the dust rapidly turning to mud, and reached the opposite side without drawing a bullet. He ran along the boardwalk, hugging the front of the building, and turned into the opening at the bottom of the stairs that led to Judge Castle's office.

He paused a moment, sucking air into his lungs. The firing had died down. He climbed the stairs, but before he reached the hall, he remembered that the Judge had a gun and it was possible Doc had taken it to defend himself.

"Doc," Chuck yelled. "Where are you?"

Doc came out of Castle's front office. He stopped, staring at Chuck in blank amazement. "What in blue blazes are you doing up here? They might have plugged you when you crossed the street."

"Didn't you think of that when you came?"

"That was different. The Judge had been shot . . ."

"No different, Doc. Fighting ain't your size. I figured I'd better give you a hand in case that bunch of coyotes found the back stairs. You'd make a good ticket out of town."

"I've been scared of that," Doc admitted, "but I couldn't get out. The Judge's stenographer is in there and she's so scared she's crazy. She won't budge."

That was like the Doc, Chuck thought. He'd stay and get killed rather than walk out on a frightened girl. He asked, "The Judge alive?"

Doc shook his head. "He was when I got here, though, and he wanted to talk because he knew he was done for. Told me some interesting items. The wedding this morning didn't pan out. Pete Fargo told him Bob went out of his head and tried to shoot the girl, but Fargo was on hand and he got Bob."

There wasn't much Chuck could say to that. He didn't care one way or the other about Bob, now that things had turned out the way they had. He said, "Saved me the trouble, I reckon."

"That isn't all. The Judge admitted he'd fetched the Fargos here to spend the winter so other settlers would be encouraged to move in next spring. He had a hand in the railroad coming, too, just like Dad figured. The thing was Castle promised Pete Fargo five thousand if they'd hang on till spring, but Pete knew he was finished hereabouts when he plugged Bob, so he asked for his money. The Judge said nothing doing and when Pete got nasty, the Judge went for his gun and Pete drilled him."

"Nothing wrong with this county a few good funerals won't cure," Chuck said.

"That's right," Doc agreed. "Here's something else. The Judge didn't destroy the last will Dad made. It's still in his safe. I had a look at it. Gives half of the Box N to you just like he said. Now there's one more thing that's hard to believe. I ain't sure I believe it myself, but maybe it answers a question Dad asked about why the Judge would get mixed up in the railroad business when he had all the money a man could need."

Doc stopped and scratched his nose, watching Chuck who remained silent, his eyes on the other end of the hall where the stairs came up from the rear of the bank. He didn't want to stand here talking with the job not even started, but he didn't have the heart to go off and leave Doc who was so full of what he'd learned that he had to talk.

"It's the damnedest thing," Doc went on. "The Judge said he'd always envied Dad for the good will he had. The Judge knew folks didn't like him, maybe because they owed him money, so he figured he'd change things. He was going to get the settlers in here and help them out just like Dad had done with some of the little ranchers. He was going to be their friend. What do you think of that?"

"I don't think anything of it," Chuck said. "Maybe he was lying, and if he wasn't, he was just fooling himself. Dad had something in him the Judge didn't have and never would."

"I thought of that," Doc agreed, "but he was dying, so I didn't tell him. Well, it just goes to prove that a man isn't satisfied with what he's got."

"I reckon not," Chuck said, and started down the hall.

"What are you up to?" Doc shouted.

"I'm aiming to run Malone's badgers out of their hole for him."

"And get yourself plugged?" Doc bellowed. "Listen, you chowder-headed fool. You've got something to live for, not die for. You ride out and see Fran . . ."

Chuck went down the stairs, thinking he wasn't going at this the way Dad would have. Maybe it was part of his father in him, some heritage which had come to him through his blood stream that had not been blotted out by Dad's raising. He was a Harrigan, not a Norman. He knew Doc wouldn't go with him as long as the girl was here and there was still danger, so he was doing the only thing he could if he wanted to be on his way.

Every step he took brought a squeal from the stairs that seemed deafening to him, but it was not likely anyone below would hear him. Rain was hammering on the roof and guns were roaring from the street end of the building.

He could not see anything, for the opening below him was black dark. He had to open the door at the foot of the stairs, and he knew that anything could happen then. His gun was in his right hand, and when he reached the bottom, he paused for a moment to listen.

He could not hear anything from the other side of the door. The stairs led into a small room that opened into the bank. It was here that the teller and Castle had their conferences, unseen by the waiting customer in front.

As he remembered it, the room had only a desk and a couple of chairs, but there was a window through which a man could look into the alley and the vacant lot behind the bank. If O'Toole and some of the others were back there, one of the Fargos was bound to be in this room watching the men who blocked their escape.

Picturing in his mind the relationship between the window and this door, he was sure he was within ten feet of anyone in the room. The man would be looking the other way. Apparently the Fargos didn't know that this door led upstairs. Probably they had thought it opened outside and had not given it a second thought.

Chuck felt for the knob with his left hand, found it, and turned it. The door was locked. He swore softly, not knowing what to do. He had planned to throw the door open, hoping that sheer surprise would accomplish his purpose.

Then, impelled by a sudden rush of impatience, he brought the muzzle of his gun to the lock and fired. He kicked the door and it banged open. Hank Fargo wheeled from the window, so shocked by surprise that he lost the one precious second he could have used to shoot Chuck.

Chuck fired point-blank at Fargo, the bullet knocking the man off his feet. Chuck lunged into the room; he saw that no one else was there. Fargo, hard hit in the side, had dropped his gun. He reached for it, then pulled his hand back when Chuck yelled, "Hold it."

One of the Fargo boys was running toward the back. Chuck waited, and the boy stopped flat-footed in the doorway that opened into the bank, his eyes on the bore of Chuck's gun. "Drop your iron," Chuck said.

"Do what he says," Hank Fargo muttered. "I don't know how the hell he got here, but he's here."

The boy dropped his gun, swearing bitterly. "Of all the damned fool . . ."

"Shut up," Chuck said. "Your string's run out. Call the other one in." When Hank remained silent, Chuck said, "If you don't get a doctor, you'll bleed to death. You can't get anywhere hanging tight. Malone hasn't got anything much against you three. It was Pete that got the Judge, and Pete's dead."

"Yeah, I guess our string's run out at that." He raised his voice, calling, "Phil, come in with your hands up."

Chuck waited until the other boy appeared in the doorway, his hands high. Then shouted, "Doc, come down here." He moved to the edge of the window. "I've got 'em; Barney. Go around and tell Malone."

Doc came clattering down the stairs, black bag in hand. Chuck herded the boys into the front of the bank, and a moment later Malone ran in, Hod and O'Toole and the others behind him. Chuck said, "You figured I was to blame for this, Sheriff, so I dragged your badgers out of their hole."

"Why, I didn't mean . . ." Malone began.

"How'd you pull off a stunt like this?" O'Toole cut in. "I figured we'd be here all night."

"Luck," Chuck said, and started out of the bank. "Let's ride, Hod."

"Hold on." O'Toole caught up with Chuck and walked across the street with him. "I'm gonna be your neighbor. Been wanting to get out of the danged saloon for a long time, so I bought Spiegle's ranch. He's on his way out of the country now with Reno Vance. Good riddance, I say."

"It is for a fact," Chuck agreed, "but what does that make you, getting out of a good business and taking on a ranch when you know we'll have settlers in our hair in another year or so?"

"Makes me a smart man, talking Spiegle into leaving the country." O'Toole's red-veined face creased in a grin. "I ain't above raising wheat, but I lean to cattle. I'll fence my deeded land and I'll summer in the mountains. Lot of talk about setting up a government forest and giving grazing permits."

"Might work at that," Hod said.

"Hell yes," O'Toole said. "The cattle business ain't done in this country, not for a man who works it right."

Chuck nodded and jerked his head at Hod. "Let's mosey."

It was still raining when they left town and took the Monk's Hill road. Chuck, thinking about what O'Toole had said, knew it was the only answer for a man who wanted to stay here and run cattle. It meant a lot of changes, but a ranch that had as much deeded land as the Box N had could survive. Whether Fran would agree to the changes was another matter.

Twilight came early with the low clouds and the rain. They

rode past the place where Bob had tried to kill Chuck, then they were on top. Hod said, "I'll go on in."

Chuck saw Fran running toward him and he reined up and swung down. She was soaked, her dress clinging to her slender body, and for a moment he had a feeling that winter had passed and it was spring, and he was thinking of his boyhood, of running through the grass in his bare feet with Fran beside him.

There was no holding back in her when she reached him. Her arms were around him, squeezing him, her wet face pressed against his shirt, and she said over and over, "Doc said you'd come. He said you'd come."

He hugged her, and then she lifted her face, and she told him everything he wanted to know with her kiss. She drew back, suddenly abashed, and whispered, "Trudie?"

"No."

That was all he needed to say. He was sorry about Trudie, but if she was bound to wait, she had no one to blame but herself. She'd find another man in time. It was different with him. He knew as he had always known that for him there would never have been anyone but Fran.

"Don't ever think you are second choice with me," Fran said, "even if it looks that way. I've always loved you. It was just that . . . that . . ." She swallowed. "I can't really tell you how it was except that I'm terribly glad that you're back. I'll crawl on my hands and knees if you tell me to."

"I won't."

"We're wet," she said. "I never saw a wetter rain. Let's go in."

"Wait till I get my boots off," he said. "I want to walk through the grass barefooted."

"You're crazy. It isn't spring."

"Who's crazy? Look at your feet."

She laughed, a good, rich laugh, the first he'd heard from her for a long time. She said, "Chuck, we'll have the craziest kids."

"We sure will," he said. "I figure they'll all be born barefooted."

WAYNE D. OVERHOLSER

SUN ON THE WALL

CHAPTER I

Paul Lerner was finishing his second cup of breakfast coffee in the Windsor Hotel dining room when Alex Dolan, editor of the *Rocky Mountain News*, stepped through the door, glanced around until he saw Lerner, then came directly to his table.

Dolan offered his hand, asking, "How's the roving correspondent this morning?"

"Tired." Lerner shook hands and motioned to the chair across the table from him. "Had breakfast?"

Dolan nodded. "I'll have a cup of coffee with you, though. Have any luck in Meeker?"

"No." Lerner signalled the waitress, asked for coffee for Dolan, and went on. "It's the same old story. A little band of Utes come over into Colorado from Utah to hunt. A white man runs into them, gets scared, and takes a shot at them. Then he runs like hell and tells everybody there's an Indian war."

Dolan's coffee came. He reached for the sugar, questioning eyes on Lerner. He asked, "You're free now and looking for another job?"

"I'm free and I'm going to stay free and I am not looking for a job. I had enough riding in the stagecoach to make me feel like I've been through a meat grinder." He started to lift his coffee cup to his mouth, then set it back in the saucer, his eyes narrowing. "Oh no you don't. I don't know what you've got in mind, but I'm not taking the assignment no matter what it is."

"Yes you will," Dolan said. "You're the only man for it. You won't have to even look at a stagecoach. Just get on the train and ride it to Cheyenne."

Lerner shook his head. "No! I'm not hungry yet. When I get hungry, I'll look you up."

"It'll be too late then," Dolan said. "As a matter of fact, I'm not even sure there's a story in what I'm talking about, but I want you to check it out. We like to run historical accounts of the Rocky Mountain region if the source is reliable, and I think this one is."

Dolan paused, watching Lerner, who was lifting his cup to his mouth again, and added, "I'll pay you for your time. If you get a story, I'll pay you for that."

"Why me?" Lerner demanded. "You've got a dozen reporters. Send one of them."

"No, I want you," Dolan said. "This is the kind of thing you specialize in, and you do it well. The average reporter would go to Cheyenne, twist a few arms, bull headfirst into whatever he finds, and wind up in a Cheyenne callaboose. You've got compassion and tact, and if I'm any judge, that's what this job needs."

Dolan paused again, knowing he had to choose his words carefully, then went on. "Besides, you don't have a regular job, so since you free-lance, you've got time to work all the angles. You might even get a book out of it. The man I'm talking about had a good deal to do with the Cheyenne Vigilantes."

Anticipation replaced the expression of negative determination on Lerner's face. He had been engrossed in the vigilante organizations in the West for several years and had hoped to write a book about them. Dolan, he knew, was aware of his interest and had baited his trap with that information.

"Well now," Lerner said cautiously, "maybe I would like this job. What am I supposed to do?"

"You're to interview Jim Glenn. He's Mr. Cheyenne himself. I don't know whether they believe in God up there in Wyoming or not, but they sure as hell believe in Jim Glenn. I'm uncertain what you'll do after you see Glenn, but you'll probably interview more people. Of course it's Glenn's story I want, but chances are you'll have to talk to some others to round it out."

Lerner reached into his coat pocket for his pipe and

tobacco pouch. "I've heard of Jim Glenn, but I'm a little hazy about him. He's a cripple, isn't he?"

"That's right. He's been in a wheelchair for more than twenty years. He lives alone except for his servants, a man named Ron Ballard and a housekeeper named Ella Evans. He was one of the first settlers in Cheyenne and for a while he had an exciting life. That's the part we want. Then he was shot and got his spine busted up so he's paralyzed from the waist down, but all through these years he's done a lot for Cheyenne. He's given a big chunk of his money away to libraries and hospitals and schools and the like. I've read about the shooting and the trial of the man who did it, but there's a lot that never came out. This is the time to get it."

"Why?"

"His health's failing. Apparently he hasn't got long to live. He's only forty-six, but chronological age doesn't have much to do with it."

Dolan watched Lerner tamp tobacco into his pipe and light it, then went on. "What triggered me on his story was a letter I got from him last week. He said he thought he had something to say and he wants it published in a book or newspaper, or anything else where folks can read it. I knew you had gone to Meeker, but I kept thinking you'd be back any day, so I waited."

Lerner slouched in his chair, pulling on his pipe. This was the kind of assignment he loved, but it wouldn't do to appear too eager. He said casually, "I'll think about it, Alex. I've been looking forward to getting back to Denver and just sitting around and—"

"You're not going to sit around thinking about it very long or I will send one of my men up there," Dolan said sharply. "Now you get up off your behind and pack up and hike over to the depot. If you get a move on, you can catch the morning train that'll put you into Cheyenne by noon. I don't know whether Glenn's alive or not. All I know is that I've waited a week and I'm sure as hell not going to wait another week. Or even another ten minutes."

Lerner saw from the editor's expression that he couldn't

play hard-to-get any longer. "All right," he said. "I'm on my way, but what do I use for money?"

Dolan grunted and took his wallet out of his pocket. He counted out fifty dollars and handed the bills to Lerner. "That's expense money." He drew a piece of paper from his wallet. "His address is 2202 Ferguson Street. I copied it down for you. And don't blow that money on a good hand in the first poker game you see."

"I wouldn't think of it," Lerner said blandly as he pocketed the money and the address. Then he asked, "Why did he write to you? There are some good Cheyenne newspapers that would be glad to get his story. The *Daily Sun*. Or the *Daily Leader*. Seems to me I've heard that he's been hard to interview."

"He has," Dolan admitted. "He said in his letter that he hadn't been in any hurry about it because he hadn't thought about dying. I guess he's like most of us, thinking everybody else was going to die but him. Anyhow, he's been going downhill and he decided it was time he did something. He wrote to me because he's heard of me. He said he didn't want to talk to any of the Cheyenne reporters because they were too close to home and they'd think they knew more about what happened years ago than he did. Some of them were around in those days. Besides, they might slant a story in a way he wouldn't like."

"A prophet is not respected in his home town," Lerner observed. "He's probably right."

"Oh, one more thing," Dolan said as Lerner rose. "He ended his letter by saying the sun was on the wall. I don't know what the hell he was talking about."

"I don't know, either," Lerner said, "but I'll find out."

He left the dining room and hurried along the hall to the stairway, his feet silent on the lush Axminster carpet. He spent only a few minutes in his room packing his shaving gear and a change of clothes into an overnight bag, then took the elevator. He left the hotel by the Larimer Street entrance and ran toward the depot, knowing he had very little time.

He brought a round-trip ricket and sprinted across the

depot and on toward the tracks. The train had begun to move as he swung up on the back steps of the rear car. He went inside, panting from his run, and dropped into a seat after stowing his bag in the rack.

He was more tired than he had realized. Every muscle in his body still ached from the jolting he had received when he'd ridden the stagecoach from Rifle to Meeker and back to Rifle. There should be a law against stagecoaches, he thought bitterly.

He tipped his hat forward and put his head back against the red plush seat. Closing his eyes, he thought about the way Jim Glenn had closed his letter: "The sun is on the wall." Lerner had never heard the statement before and it didn't mean any more to him than it had to Dolan. What the hell had Glenn meant?

CHAPTER II

Lerner went directly to the Inter Ocean Hotel in Cheyenne and took a room. The Inter Ocean was older than the Windsor in Denver, having been opened in 1876, but it had been improved in 1884—only five years ago—with new wallpaper, elegant chandeliers in the lobby, and a twenty-five-foot cherrywood bar. Lerner had stayed here before and knew the rooms were comfortable enough and not at all like the primitive quarters he'd had in Meeker.

He ate dinner and then walked the six blocks from the hotel on the corner of 16th and Capitol to 22nd. He turned to his left and walked one more block to Ferguson and found that he had reached the Glenn house. He could have picked up a cab, but the June day was pleasantly cool with little of the blustery wind that was typical of Cheyenne, so he had enjoyed the walk. And he had needed it to work the kinks out of his legs.

Lerner paused on the corner to study the house. Cheyenne had in the past been called the richest city for its size in the United States. That may or may not have been true, but certainly this section of Ferguson Street had rightly been termed "millionaire's row."

Jim Glenn's house properly belonged with the other fine houses on the street, many of them built by rich cattlemen during the prosperous years before the "big die" and the decline of the price of beef.

The house was designed in Queen Anne style, with a pointed roof and three tall chimneys. There were two large porches on the Ferguson Street side with several stained-glass windows between them. One of the porches was almost covered by lush vines which had grown up over a trellis to the right of the steps.

An iron fence mounted in cut stone ran along the street sides of the house, which, with its yard and barn, took up a full quarter of the block, as did most of the houses in this part of town.

Lerner smiled as he opened the metal gate, stepped through, closing the gate behind him, then walked up the curving path toward the front door. There were few houses in Denver any finer than these on Ferguson Street in Cheyenne. Some were larger and more ornate than the Glenn house, but he doubted that many had cost more. He wondered what sort of man Jim Glenn was, or the others, for that matter, who would build houses as ostentatious as these.

He had not quite reached the porch steps when a big man appeared from the shrubbery where he had been working. He moved in front of Lerner, blocking his path, and said in a low, deliberate way, "Mr. Glenn ain't well and he ain't having no visitors."

Lerner was irritated as he wondered why he had come all the way from Denver to see a man who was too ill to receive visitors. He started to turn; then, because the irritation grew and became anger, he asked, "Why did he write to the editor of the *Rocky Mountain News* to send a reporter up here if he's too sick to have visitors?"

"I don't know—" the man began.

"I'm well enough to see him," a man called from the porch. "Let him come in, Ron."

The man moved aside and motioned toward the porch. He mumbled. "I was just following orders," and returned to his work in the shrubbery.

Lerner stepped up onto the porch and saw the man who had called. He sat in a wheelchair, having been hidden from Lerner by the vines. Now he held out a claw-like hand as he said, "I'm Jim Glenn. I didn't know who you were. Fact is, I almost gave you up because I wrote to Alex Dolan more than a week ago. Our mail service is abominable. I believe it gets worse every year."

"My name's Paul Lerner," Lerner said as he shook

hands. "I'm not actually on the *News* staff. I'm a free lance reporter, picking up assignments wherever I can. I was out of town for a week. Dolan waited until I got back because he thought I was particularly suited for this job."

Lerner understood why Jim Glenn was concerned about telling his story now. He looked seventy rather than forty-six. He was so thin that his gray, parchment-like skin seemed to have been pulled tightly over the bones of his face. At one time he must have been a very large and strong man, judging from the size of his bony frame and the big knuckles of his hands, which still had enough strength to give Lerner a firm grip.

His hair was completely white and his voice had the quavery tone of an old man, but his eyes, which were boldly fixed on Lerner's face, were as bright and sharp as a chipmunk's. His mind, Lerner told himself, was as quick and nimble as it had ever been.

"Tell me one thing," Glenn said. "Just why are you particularly suited for the job of interviewing me?"

"Why, I don't know," Lerner said, surprised by the question. "I guess it's mostly that I'm interested in the history of the Rocky Mountain region. I've interviewed a good many pioneers in Colorado, particularly the fifty-niners. I've written their stories largely for the *News,* although I do write for other newspapers, too."

"I see," Glenn said, his eyes narrowing thoughtfully as if he were not sure that Lerner was the man for the job. "Sit down, my friend." He motioned toward a chair. "Would you like something to drink?"

"No thank you," Lerner said.

"Good," Glenn said. "I don't drink any more. I guess I've had too much in my time. The lining of my stomach must be gone. Feels that way when I take a drink these days."

"There's one more thing," Lerner said, "along with the fact that Dolan's regular reporters were probably busy and couldn't be spared. I've been interested in the Vigilante organizations in Denver and the Montana mines, thinking that there was likely some connection. Might be tied in with a lodge, too. This connection might be true with the

Cheyenne Vigilantes, although they came a little later. Dolan said you knew a good deal about them."

"A little, my friend, a little." Glenn's gaze had not left Lerner's face, but now he turned his head to look through the network of vines at Ferguson Street and the slowly drifting dust cloud that rose behind a buggy that had just passed. "I'm not sure that I have anything to say that's worth hearing, but I have lived in Cheyenne from almost the first day of its existence . . . I was involved with some of the exciting historical events in the early days. I also believe that those months were filled with interesting personal incidents, but whether my story is worth telling is a decision you'll have to make."

He frowned, his thin lips pressed tightly together. He reached into his coat pocket for a cigar and handed it to Lerner, then took one himself and bit off the end. He raised it to his nose, smelled of it, rolled it between his finger tips, and finally reached for a match.

"Mr. Lerner, I'm not sure you're my man," Glenn said, "although I'll have to settle for you because time has run out for me. I look like an old man, and sitting in this damned chair for more than twenty years is enough to wear any man down to a nubbin. You see, I have already written my story. Now I'm going to leave it up to you as to what happens to it . . .. I don't have any idea how well I've done. If you take the job, you'll have to go over it and correct the spelling and punctuation and the like, and maybe improve some of the writing. My housekeeper copied it for me and she writes an adequate hand. Her grammar is good, too, so it may be that when she copied the manuscript, she cleaned up my mistakes. Maybe you won't have to do much with it."

He struck the match, fired his cigar, pulled on it a moment, then went on. "We'd better get one thing straight, Lerner. You've written about the fifty-niners and the excitement of those days that went with their discovery of gold and the vigilante hangings and the Civil War and all of that . . . Now I'm not saying there was no excitement in my first years in early Cheyenne, but I am saying that I had a bigger and better reason for writing about my life than excitement. I'll be damned if I'll let you take all of that out and build up the fighting and screwing and such just to make your story more sensational so you can get a newspaper to buy it."

Lerner's heart sank. He had never run into a situation like this in which his story was already written before he had even heard it. He doubted that, even with his housekeeper's help, Jim Glenn had written anything people would read.

This meant that Lerner would have to rewrite it from scratch and embellish it with whatever other information he could find out about the first months of Cheyenne's history, when Glenn had been a participant in the making of that history. It would have been easier to have taken notes from an interview and written it himself. Still, he was not one to overlook a nugget in the pile of country rock, and there just might be a nugget or two in this pile.

"I won't take it out," Lerner said mildly, "but what was your reason for writing your life story?"

"My own satisfaction in trying to be honest," Glenn said, "although I have another lofty reason which I gave myself as I wrote it. I've made some God-awful mistakes that I've never forgiven myself for. I want other people to read about them so they won't make them. Of course most men and women are too stubborn or too stupid to learn anything even from their own mistakes, but that's their problem, not mine."

He took his cigar out of his mouth and looked at it thoughtfully. "You see, Lerner, we humans are so selfish and narrow-minded it's beyond all reason. My father understood this and accepted it and lived by his own lights. I didn't understand it until I had to sit here in this miserable chair and look out there at Ferguson Street hour after hour and day after day and month after month and watch people go by, or have them come to my door and ask for money for every damn thing you can imagine. When I finally got it figured out, I knew I had to tell other people . . . I guess I'm a kind of crusader, maybe as bad as the loud-mouthed preachers who keep shouting that we're going to hell if we don't get baptized all right and proper. Most people, including me, don't listen to them, and I guess they won't listen to me, but like I said, it's their problem if they don't listen. I've done all I can."

"I'm a little thick-headed today," Lerner said, "but I still don't savvy what it was you figured out."

"Why hell," Glenn said as if it were plain for everybody to see, "it's what the Bible says about reaping what you sow, only I say it a little different. A man ought to know that if he interferes with other people's lives or their happiness or their rights, and for his own pleasure, it's going to come right back on him. Even if he makes an honest mistake it'll come back ... After all these years I'm not sure I made a mistake."

He stopped and wiped his face with a handkerchief. He sighed. "You know, I give out so damned quick any more it's pathetic."

He reached down beside his chair, picked up a bell and rang it loudly. A moment later a middle-aged woman in a starched black dress came out of the house and stood looking disapprovingly at Lerner.

"This is the reporter I sent for, Ella," Glenn said. "Fetch my manuscript. I'm going to give it to Mr. Lerner."

"You're getting tired, Mr. Glenn," she said. "I'd better wheel you inside—"

"Go on and do what I said," Glenn ordered, raising his voice. "I know I'm tired, but I've got to do this while I can."

She turned, her dress rustling in protest, and disappeared into the house. "You know, Lerner," Glenn said, "at one time I had a lot of money. I built this house trying to keep up with the Careys and the Kellys and the rest of them. I gave money to some good causes, and now it's been pared down. Just this house and a few shares of stock left and several thousand dollars in cash and some town property. Here's Ron Ballard and Ella Evans—who have been taking care of me for years—expecting to inherit a fortune, which they've earned, but I don't have it to give them. Now isn't that a hell of a note?"

Lerner sensed a tough kind of honesty about this man.

Suddenly he wanted to read what he had written. He didn't care how much rewriting he had to do. Tough, basic honesty was a rare commodity. Most of the men he had interviewed held themselves up as paragons of virtue and courage. Before this moment Lerner had not been sure he would take the manuscript when the woman brought it to him. Now he knew he would.

A moment later she came sailing out of the house, handed a cardboard box to Glenn and sniffed as she stared at Lerner. "You'd best leave now, mister," she said. "Mr. Glenn is tired."

"My God, Ella," Glenn shouted, sudden anger putting a depth to his voice that it had lacked before, "I'll tell him when to leave. You go on about your business and leave me to mine."

She made another noise, more of a snort than a sniff this time. Turning with another great rustling of her skirt, she stomped back into the house. Glenn opened the box and took out a sheet of paper. He handed it to Lerner, saying, "My life during the first months in Cheyenne was bound up with several people. It's hard to tell where my responsibility for my mistakes ended and theirs began. We all made them and somehow our lives got tied up in a kind of crazy pattern. The trouble was things got out of hand before I realized it. When I was writing this I kept trying to think what would have happened if I had done something different or made a different decision at any of the critical points in my life. Or if one of them had."

Lerner looked at the paper. There were three names: Cherry Owens Lind, who lived five miles from Cheyenne up Crow Creek; Nancy Rush, who lived in a white frame house on the corner of 16th and Russell; and Frank Rush, who was in the Territorial prison in Laramie.

"Who are these people?" Lerner asked. "I mean, why did you give these names—"

Glenn raised a hand. "I'm going to tell you," he said as if irritated by the question. "I just hadn't got to it. These three people are still alive. I haven't seen Cherry for a long time. Twenty years or more. Nancy comes by to visit me quite often. I haven't seen Frank since the trial. I'm not even sure he's still in prison, but I thought the warden or someone there could tell you where he is."

Glenn settled back, his eyes closed. He went on wearily. "I want you to talk to them after you've read what I've written. Maybe they won't talk to you, especially if they know what they say might be published, but go see them anyhow and in the order I have their names listed. You have to make a judgment concerning the events I've written about after you hear what they've got to say."

"I don't see why it's up to me to make a judgment," Lerner said.

"Well, I'll tell you why," Glenn said. "I may have been lying faster'n a horse can trot. You're going to have to decide. Otherwise you'll just be taking my word. Besides, they were familiar with most of the things that happened to me, but they saw those events through different eyes. Actually, they helped create most of the events I'm talking about. You'll need their viewpoints to round out my story. Now I'll tell you it's time for you to go. I'm so damned tired I can't think straight."

"All right," Lerner said, "I'll talk to them. I'll report back to you after I see them."

"If I'm still alive," Glenn said.

Lerner rose and walked to the steps, then turned, realizing that Jim Glenn might not be alive when he finished interviewing the three people. "You said something in your letter to Alex Dolan about the sun on the wall. He didn't know what you meant and I told him I'd find out."

"You'll know when you've read my story," Glenn said. "I mention it because it was one of my father's favorite sayings."

"Good day, sir," Lerner said. He walked rapidly along the path to the gate and let himself into the street.

As he returned to the hotel, he thought again that he had never before been in this situation, his story already written by the man he was to interview and three more people to see. He wondered if these three had written their stories, and if they would say anything basically different from what Glenn had written.

He would have to tell them he was going to write down what they said. Perhaps it would appear in the *Rocky Mountain News* and later in a book, so the chances were that they would say they had no intention of having their private lives dragged out before the eyes of thousands of readers. But he had promised Glenn he would see them, and he would. Then he wondered if Jim Glenn had a premonition of death. He'd heard of people who had. The thought occurred to him that perhaps in some way Glenn had kept himself alive until he had been able to turn his manuscript over to another man who was capable of doing something with it.

He went to his room in the Inter Ocean Hotel, opened a window, then filled and lighted his pipe, and settled down to read. The woman's handwriting was excellent. He had no trouble reading it, and once started he did not stop to go down to supper until he had finished.

CHAPTER III

I, James Glenn, could begin by saying, as Charles Dickens had one of his characters say, that I was born. I certainly was, in the bedroom of a small farmhouse in Missouri not far from St. Louis. When I was older, my father told me it was a hard birth, with my mother's labor pains lasting for hours. He thought she was going to die. After seeing her suffer so long, he resolved that he would never make her go through it again, and as far as I know, he never had sexual relations with her after that.

He didn't talk to me about sex, but I suspect that he lacked the drive most men have. It was not, of course, the kind of thing a father would discuss with his son, but I am quite sure he did not have any women after my mother died. I failed to inherit his ascetic temperament. After I grew up, I did my share of drinking and fighting and whoring, and I am afraid I was the source of a good deal of concern to my father.

I do not remember very much about my mother. She died when I was six years old, so she had some influence on my life. I have retained a mental picture of her. However, the picture may not be very accurate. Possibly most of it came from what my father told me about her. He worshipped her, he idealized her, and of course when he talked to me about her, he always made her out to be a sort of earthly angel.

I do know that my mother was not very strong. She made me take naps in the afternoons and she always lay down with me. She was very blond, with blue eyes and a pale skin that never tanned, although she had a garden and spent a good deal of time out of doors in the sunshine. I've always thought of her as being virginal and virtuous and very, very beautiful in an ethereal sort of way. She was indeed an earthly angel.

One of my most poignant memories as a child was standing beside her grave and listening to the preacher tell what a splendid woman she had been, and then spend the next ten minutes begging God to save her soul. It was a clear April day, with a brisk wind, and I remember thinking that the wind would carry her soul right up into Heaven.

Right or wrong about her, she was a very good woman, and my attitude in this regard has influenced my opinion of the "good women" I have known.

My father raised me. He died in the spring of 1867, eight years after we reached Colorado. I left his house soon after we moved to Colorado, and made my own way from that time on, but he did more to shape my life than anyone else, particularly between the ages of six and sixteen.

I know he loved me very much, partly because I was all he had of my mother. Sometimes he would talk to me for half an hour at a time on all kinds of subjects including religion and politics and people in general. Philosophy, too, and most of all, I think, the moral code or system of ethics that each of us take for ourselves.

I didn't have to say a word to prime him. All I had to do was sit quietly and listen. At the time most of what he said was wasted on me, but it wasn't wasted in the long run because in later years much of it came back to me.

It seemed to me then that he was a strange man. I guess he was. In many ways I didn't know him at all. That may sound crazy, but the truth is I never knew the inner man. I have a conviction that he did not know himself. I think he always lived for other people, first my mother, and then me. I also think he lived for causes, particularly the Free Soil movement.

My father hated slavery with a passion I never knew him to feel about anything else. He could not, of course, continue to live in Missouri, which was a slave state, so after my mother's death he sold the small farm he owned and moved west into Kansas. We lived there for ten years until we moved to Colorado.

My father was a hard worker. I remember how he told me repeatedly that when the sun rose high enough to shine on the east wall of the house, it was time to be up and doing. In winter he would not let me stay in bed that long because the sun was lazy during the cold months, he would say, and didn't rise until it was late.

During the spring and summer months, when the field work had to be done, he would say to me while I was still in bed, "Get up, Jimmy. The sun's on the wall." He was seldom harsh with me, but this was the one thing that made him lose his temper. I soon learned, after a few painful sessions in which his razor strap and my backside made contact, that I would feel better if I got up when he called me the first time.

Along with being a hard worker, he was also a gambler. The combination seems to me an odd one. Not that he ever had much to gamble with when I was a boy. He would try, though, even if the bets were for small amounts. He would bet on which bird would fly first if two were sitting on a fence. He would bet on the date the first killing frost would come or when the first snow would fall or whether our cow's calf would be a bull or a heifer.

He was also a very religious man, apparently never considering the possibility that gambling might be contrary to religion. Obviously it was not contrary to his. I will admit that he had a peculiar religion, and although it seems to me that all religions are peculiar, his was more peculiar than most. He had absolutely no use for the itinerant preachers who floated through the country in those days, particularly those who preached hellfire and brimstone sermons, and nearly all of them preached that type of scary sermon.

I have never understood why the preachers put out that kind of teaching. My father often said the same thing. I cannot accept the explanation that they believed it. If they had thought about it at all, they would have seen that it didn't add up. Maybe they never thought about it, but simply accepted it because it was what they had been taught. Or perhaps they sensed that it was what the people wanted to hear and they were not anxious to disappoint their listeners, so they preached "the word" and "good, gospel sermons."

Anyhow, my father always claimed that preachers were the laziest men alive and were the worst kind of parasites, coming around and wanting you to put them up for the night and give them a big evening meal and let them have the pick of everything on the table including the breast of the chicken. They did not, of course, intend to pay for anything.

My father always gave them short shrift as soon as he found out they were preachers. He'd just point down the road and say, "Git. You won't have any trouble finding a sucker who'll put you up." He'd shake his head as the preacher mounted and rode away. He'd say, "I just don't savvy how they can do it, move in on you and take the best of everything and lie about God while they're doing it."

My father always got furious about the way the preachers and the churches treated Negroes, even using the Bible to prove that black people were inferior and created by God to serve white people, and to go from there and say that slavery was God's way of taking care of the blacks.

"You can twist anything to make it prove what you want it to prove, and that includes the Bible," he would say. "The white people act superior even in church, not letting the Negroes worship with them. You'd think that having to sit beside a black man is going to send you right down to hell."

I've thought about it a good deal, but I have never decided how much my father influenced me and shaped me into the man I became. Of course it's not the kind of thing that can be measured. I am sure my father did nothing to diminish my appetite for lusty living. He never lectured me about it, something for which I am thankful.

He was a philosopher of sorts, and since I have a tendency to run in that direction, I suppose he gave my thinking some direction. I have read a great deal, although books have always been hard to come by. I think my father's influence was the greatest in this area, perhaps in setting up my sense of values and establishing some of my basic virtues, such as my desire to work and my belief in being honest in all things. Also in the more abstract beliefs in God and man, and in man's relationship with man.

As I said, my father's greatest weakness was gambling, and although I have done some gambling, I never particularly enjoyed it. I mean, I could take it or leave it, but my father couldn't. On the other hand, women have always been my weakness. I could never turn one down until I became an invalid, and then it was only because I had no choice.

As far as I could tell, women meant nothing to my father after my mother's death. All of this proves nothing, I guess, except that what is one man's meat is another man's poison, even if the men are father and son.

CHAPTER IV

By the time I was sixteen, when we left Kansas, I was a big, strong boy who could keep up with my father in any kind of physical work, but he refused to involve me in his other activities. For instance, he was mixed up in the border fighting between the Free Soil men and the Border Ruffians who kept making trouble by coming across the line and burning houses and barns and sometimes murdering the anti-slavery Kansans. I mean, I think he was involved in the fighting, but he never talked about it, so it was something I could only guess at.

I had never considered my father a fighting man, but in looking back on our last years in Kansas, I have a feeling he did his share of fighting and he probably belonged to one of the secret Free Soil societies that flourished in Kansas during those bloody years.

He would be gone for two or three days at a time, leaving me to take care of the chores. He always warned me when he left to keep my eyes open for strangers and my gun handy, and to head for the house if anybody showed up that I didn't know.

The house was built of logs and was a sort of fort with heavy doors and strong bars and thick shutters for the windows. Underneath was a cellar. A tunnel led from it to the cut bank of a nearby creek. If we were ever pinned down and the Border Ruffians succeeded in burning the house, we could get away through the tunnel and probably escape by hiding in the weeds and brush along the stream.

Before my father left on one of these trips and after he came home he always gave me a sort of lame reason for being gone. I never questioned him, because I thought he'd tell me if he wanted me to know. Probably it was better that I didn't know, because I couldn't tell anything if I didn't know it.

We heard a great deal of John Brown in those days. I don't know how much my father had to do with him, but it may have been a good deal. I only saw him once, when he rode past our farm and my father stood in the road talking to him.

I was close to Brown for only a few seconds. As soon as I walked up, my father sent me away to do some chore that didn't need to be done right then, and the one sharp memory I have of him was his fierce eyes. They were the eyes of a zealot, a fanatic.

Somehow I found it hard to put my father in the company of a man like that. He was too gentle, too mild, and yet there were times when he got worked up about slavery and the brutal crimes that some of the slave owners committed. During those times, which did not come very often, I saw in my father's eyes the same wild expression I saw in John Brown's eyes.

I suppose that all men of John Brown's caliber are finally crucified in one way or another. They are John the Baptist men who make way for the Lord, and without them I suspect that man would never progress in a humanitarian way.

I'm sure my father was more of a zealot than I suspected at the time. He may even have been a conductor on the Underground Railroad, but I never knew for a fact that he actually brought slaves to our farm. However, we did have a cave in the side of a hill on the upper end of our place. My father ordered me to stay away from it, saying there were outlaws in the country who sometimes sought refuge there and it was dangerous.

Once I was caught in a violent storm and couldn't get back to the house before it hit, so I sought shelter in the cave. I found plenty of evidence that someone had been there recently. I never said anything to my father about what I had found, but I thought then and I still think that slaves, not outlaws, used the cave.

At any rate, he was never caught. If he took part in the fighting he was never wounded. He was very restless the last year we lived there and kept talking about leaving. I suppose he worried about getting caught or being shot. Anyhow, when the news of the discovery of gold in the Pike's Peak area reached us, he decided to move out there and get rich. It sounded like good adventure to me, so I was all for it.

He sold the farm, bought a herd of horses, and prepared to set out for the gold fields. Before I knew it, we were headed west over the Smoky Hill Trail. I guess there isn't anything that's more of a gamble than buying and selling horses, and I never knew of any kind of man who could look you right in the eyes and lie faster than a horse trader.

My father, being honest, was at a disadvantage, but he had a way of being silent on certain matters that he didn't want the other man to know. Perhaps that was a form of dishonesty, but my father could accept it and keep his moral code intact.

He hired two men and we took the horses through to Denver without much trouble or loss, although the last hundred miles of the Smoky Hill Trail were tough ones, and many a man lost his life in that stretch. We weren't slowed down by women and children, and we had no wagons, so we moved fast. We didn't have any run-ins with either Indians or horse thieves—just lucky, I guess—and ended up in the Elephant Corral in Denver with one of the best horse herds that ever made it up the Smoky Hill.

Everything in Denver was high, but my father expected that. He sold most of the horses at a good profit, keeping one saddle horse, a sorrel, which he gave me, and one team of work animals. He bought a wagon and looked around for a place to settle.

He had no use for Denver, which was tough and wild, and he didn't want to go to one of the mining camps. Eventually he decided on Golden, which was right at the foot of the Rockies where Clear Creek comes out of its canyon. He built a small house and had a big garden, and

made a living freighting with his team and wagon between
Golden and the mining camps.

I was seventeen the following spring. My feet were too
itchy to stay home, so I told my father I was leaving. He
took it pretty well, better than I had thought he would.
Knowing me as well as he did, I suppose he expected me
to do exactly what I did. I'm sure the signs were there to
be read, and he was a sensitive man. He handed me one
hundred dollars and asked me to write once in a while so
he'd know where I was.

I had to do it, and I have never been sorry that I left
home, but I didn't find the world as much of an oyster for
me to open as I had expected. I went to Black Hawk and
worked in a mine, but I couldn't stand being in a dark
tunnel day after day. I had to be out in the sunlight and
feel the wind on my face.

I quit my mining job and went to work in a store in
Central City, but I couldn't stand counter jumping either.
Eventually I discovered that I could sell all the firewood
in Black Hawk and Central City that I could cut, so I
chopped and hauled wood most of the time I was in
Colorado.

My first big problem was a place to live. I solved it by
building a small cabin in the canyon north of Black
Hawk. Of course I didn't get rich cutting and hauling
wood, but I was outside and I made a living. I had time
for myself, too, if I wanted to go fishing.

The truth was I couldn't stand the regularity of a job
working for somebody else and having him boss me
around all the time. During the bad winter weather, when
there was too much snow on the ground to cut wood, I
managed to swallow my pride and work for a carpenter in
Black Hawk. Although I rebelled as I always had when I
was working for daily wages, I disciplined myself and
kept my job. I was glad later on that I had the training.

After the Civil War broke out we heard all kinds of
wild stories about an army of Texans that would be
invading Colorado, moving north from New Mexico.
They wanted the Colorado mines, and unless they were
stopped they'd march right on north into Montana and

grab those mines. By that time, of course, they would have cut California off from the rest of the Union and they'd have had the mines there, too. The South didn't have the wealth that the North had, and the gold they'd have from the western mines might have saved them.

Anyhow, the last thing I wanted was for a bunch of wild-eyed Texans coming into Colorado and telling me what to do. I knew enough of what the Border Ruffians from Missouri had done in Kansas. Along with a number of men from Black Hawk and Central City, I joined the First Colorado Volunteers in the fall of 1861 and started learning how to be a soldier in Camp Weld, which was two miles south of Denver.

I guess we were a pretty wild bunch. None of us took to soldiering very well. If I rebelled against the regularity of an ordinary job, I would naturally be more than rebellious when I had to suffer army discipline and believe me I suffered.

Everyone in Denver, I think, was made happy by the orders we received on February 13, 1862, to march south. We moved out of Denver on February 22, the day after a Union army in New Mexico had been beaten in the battle of Valverde.

The march south was no picnic. Until we reached the Santa Fe Trail the road was more of a path than a real road. The weather, as my father often said, was cold enough to freeze the balls off a brass monkey.

When we reached Pueblo, we heard for the first time about the defeat at Valverde and that the Rebel army was marching up the Rio Grande. After we got that news, we knew we had to move because it was going to be up to us to stop the Texans. Most of the regulars that had been in the West had been called East. Even with several inches of snow on the ground, we made forty miles a day.

As we were climbing Raton Pass, we had word from Fort Union that the Rebels had occupied Albuquerque and Santa Fe, and would soon be attacking Fort Union itself. We made some kind of record after that, I guess. Carrying nothing but our arms and blankets, we marched through the darkness to the Cimarron River in New Mexico.

We had to stop when we reached the Cimarron because we were simply worn out. Some of the horses pulling the baggage wagons actually fell dead in their harness. We had covered ninety-two miles in the past thirty-six hours, so it was understandable that we were dead tired.

The weather was still bitterly cold. After we rested, we went on to Fort Union, reaching it March 10. We had covered more than four hundred miles in thirteen days. We remained at the fort for twelve days, resting and receiving regulation uniforms. Arms and ammunition, too. The officers decided it was a good time to start drilling us again, but we'd come to fight, not to drill, and we didn't like it any better than we had at Camp Weld.

We had our wish about fighting two weeks later. We left the fort, marching south, and ran head on into the Rebel column in Glorieta Pass. I guess the Texans figured it would be easy enough to take Fort Union, and it probably would have been if the First Colorado Volunteers hadn't been there to stop them. I don't think they even knew we were in New Mexico, so I guess they were somewhat surprised when they met up with us.

We whipped them in two battles, one called "Apache Canyon," on March 26, the other "Glorieta," on March 28. I've met Texans after the war who claimed we didn't whip them at all, but I guess that's like a Texan.

The truth is these battles were very important, sometimes being referred to as the "Gettysburg of the West." The Texans turned around and went home, their commander, General Sibley, arriving at Fort Bliss near El Paso during the first week in May. How anyone, even a braggy Texan, could call that a victory for them is beyond me, but then, I'm not a Texan.

The regiment continued in service in Colorado and neighboring territories through the rest of the war, but I took a bullet in my left leg in the last fight. Although it wasn't a particularly serious wound, it was painful and it was enough to get me sent back to Denver and out of the regiment, which was fine with me. I'd have gone crazy sitting out the rest of the war with no fighting to do.

I had left my saddle horse with my father in Golden. I stayed with him until the soreness was gone from my thigh and I was able to work. He didn't have much to say about what he'd been doing, but he was never one to talk about his personal exploits.

Before the firing on Fort Sumter and in the early months of the war there had been a good deal of Confederate sentiment and intrigue in Colorado, and I suspect my father was involved in some of the activity against the secessionists just as he had been in Kansas. In any case, the trouble had been pretty well settled around Denver by the time I got back from New Mexico.

My father, of course, was glad to see me come home mostly in one piece, and he was sorry to see me leave to return to Black Hawk. He was lonely, and although he never said so, I'm sure he wanted me to stay with him, but now that I felt all right, my feet were itchy again and I had to go.

He continued with his freighting business, usually showing up in Black Hawk at least once a month. He always stayed overnight with me, so we were never out of touch very long.

CHAPTER V

When I'd left Black Hawk to volunteer, I had nailed the door to my cabin shut and had put shutters on the windows. I knew something was wrong, the evening I came back, as soon as I was in sight of the cabin. The door was open, the shutters were off the windows, and smoke was pouring out of the chimney.

I'd heard plenty of stories about men jumping mining claims, but jumping a cabin was a new wrinkle to me. At first I was puzzled and surprised, and then shocked, and finally I was mad. The closer I got, the madder I got. It was a hell of a note, I told myself, when a man goes off to war to fight for everybody who stays home all safe and snug, and then finds that somebody has grabbed his home while he was gone.

I stepped out of my saddle and went into the cabin without knocking or hollering howdy. Two miners were sitting at the table eating supper. They were filthy, and the inside of the cabin was a dirty mess; it smelled worse than any pigpen I had ever seen or smelled.

One of the men yelled, "You never learned no manners, did you, just walking in—"

"It's my cabin," I said. "Git out."

"Oh no, we ain't doing no such thing," the second one said. "We found the place empty, so we moved in."

"Possession is nine-tenths of the law." The first one grinned as smug as a cat licking up spilled cream. "You've only got one-tenth, mister."

By that time I was in a killing rage. It's a miracle I didn't pull my gun and shoot both of them where they sat. Instead, I stomped up to the table and banged their heads together. I did it three or four times until I got a good solid crack that took the fight out of them, and then I threw them out. That gave me nine-tenths of the law and left them with one-tenth.

I grabbed up some dishes and threw them at the men. There was a big bowl filled with hot beans. I guess they'd just taken it off the stove. Anyhow, I hit one man in the face with them, the beans running from his forehead clean down to his chin. He took off down the road howling like a turpentined dog. The other one almost ran over him before they got out of sight.

I yelled at them, "Git out of camp and stay out."

It was a comical sight, I guess, but I was too mad to see anything funny in it. They were running so fast and making so much noise I don't think they heard me, but I never saw them in Black Hawk again, so it seems they took my advice whether they heard me or not.

I didn't feel like starting to clean up that night, so I cooked my supper outside and slept outside. I started trying to make the cabin livable again in the morning. I never had been much on cleaning house, but I cleaned that cabin. It took me three days of throwing stuff out and scrubbing with lye, and I still didn't get rid of that sickening, insidious stink. It lingered for days.

I fetched my team and wagon from the man I'd left them with, but it took me a while to work up customers for my wood. When the snow got too deep late in the fall for me to continue cutting wood, I went to work again for the carpenter I'd worked for before I'd volunteered.

That was the way my life went until the first of October, 1866. All the time I kept thinking I'd save enough money to start some kind of business of my own. I had saved a few hundred dollars, but by that time I realized I was never going to make it if I didn't hit something big. Otherwise I'd be like thousands of other men I'd seen come and go in the mines and spend their life working for wages. I didn't intend to do any such thing, but the trouble was I couldn't see anything big coming my way in Black Hawk or Central City.

There was always the opportunity to invest in a poker

game, but my savings had come too hard for that. I had
plenty of chance to buy mines, but that, too, was more of
a gamble than I wanted to take. Prospecting wasn't for
me, either. I couldn't tell country rock from rich ore and I
didn't have any real desire to learn the difference.

I'd decided it was my last year cutting wood. I didn't
know where I was going, but I knew I was going. I
talked to my father about my future. He didn't have any
good advice to give me, although he offered to take me
into his freighting business, which had been more prof-
itable than my wood-cutting. I was too restless for that, so
I thanked him and said no.

He told me he had over one thousand dollars saved and
I could borrow it if I found something I wanted. Well, I
hadn't found anything, and the more I thought about it,
the more I was convinced that it didn't make much
difference whether I stayed in Black Hawk or went to
Denver. I needed capital and that was the truth.

I'd worked in a store long enough to know I didn't
want that. I'd had all the farming I could stomach back in
Kansas. I even thought about buying and selling horses,
but I didn't know horses well enough or the tricks of
horse traders, so I realized that the first good trader I ran
into would cheat me out of every cent I had.

I would have liked to own a stage line. Or some kind of
contracting business—house-building, for instance. But
even if I borrowed from my father, I wouldn't have
more than fifteen hundred dollars, and that wasn't enough
to set me up in any kind of business.

On the first day of October I fell into a job I hadn't
expected. I came back to my cabin after delivering a load
of wood in Central City and found two young women
waiting for me. They'd driven a buggy up from Black
Hawk and were just about ready to leave when I got
there.

They introduced themselves as Rosy and Flossie Martin. They were identical twins, good-looking, blond, blue-
eyed, and on the plump side. They were dressed fine and
fancy in black silk dresses that rustled in quiet luxury
every time they moved, bonnets with long drooping

plumes, and red shawls that gave them a dignified, respectable appearance and made them look older than they were.

I studied one and then the other, and decided I was seeing double. They looked that much alike. They wore pins on the front of their dresses, one with the letter *R*, the other with the letter *F*. Later on, when I knew them intimately, I discovered that Rosy had a big brown mole on her left buttock. When I was in bed with one of them, that mole was the only way I had of telling which one I had. When they were dressed, I couldn't tell them apart unless they wore those pins.

I guessed their profession, but I wasn't real sure until they told me. They were honest and saw no point in not informing me right away. Rosy said, "We're whores. There are plenty of other names folks call us, especially the women, but when you get right down to cases, that's what we are."

"Do you have any scruples about working for us?" Flossie asked.

"Not a bit," I said, but I'll admit I was taken back a little by their frank announcement.

"We want a house," Rosy said. "We think men like to be reminded of home even if we're not their wives."

"That's right," Flossie said. "We've got an organ. I play real pretty and Rosy sings real good, so every evening before we transact any business, we'll entertain 'em. That's why we're not gonna set up our place alongside all the other ones. We don't want to get a bad name."

"Hell no," Rosy said. "We're going to have us a dignified business and we ain't gonna stand for nobody being rowdy. If they are, we'll throw 'em out."

I kept looking from one to the other just as I had been. It was the damnedest feeling, kind of like looking at a woman's face and then turning and seeing it in a mirror. I still didn't know what they wanted, so I said, "It sounds good, but what's all this got to do with me?"

They seemed surprised. Rosy said, "We told you. We want you to build us a house. We've bought some land in the canyon below here. We want the house good-sized: two bedrooms, a front room, and a kitchen. A good, big front room that'll have room for the organ and several men. They'll have to sit in it and wait their turn."

"And a privy, of course," Flossie said. "Behind the house."

"A woodshed, too," Rosy added.

"And maybe a small barn," Flossie said, nodding as if dreaming about the whole business. "We're gonna have us a nice horse and buggy. We talked to a man in Black Hawk and he said you'd been working at being a carpenter for several winters. We've got money, and you can take some of your pay in trade."

I wasn't so anxious to do that, though later on I did. Anyhow, the money sounded fine. I said, "I've always worked for somebody else, but I can do it."

"Good," Rosy said. "Start tomorrow."

"In the morning bright and early," Flossie added. "We want the house well enough along to give us shelter before the cold weather sets in."

"Better build the privy first," Rosy said.

"That's right," Flossie agreed. "We're going to live in a tent and watch you build the house."

They were the damnedest pair I ever ran into, but I told myself they just might do all right. Actually I didn't care whether they did or not as long as they had the money to pay me. I hired a man I'd once worked with and we staked out the positions for the buildings and hauled lumber and got started.

We had good luck with the weather and got the house framed up and the doors and windows in before the first bad storm hit us late in November, but it took us a good part of the winter to do the finishing work. By the time we had the wallpaper on and the painting done, we were ready for spring.

We got paid, all right, and I landed another house-building job in Black Hawk, so I kept my man and went right on working. Almost every evening as I went back to my cabin, I stopped at the Martin house and had a cup of coffee with Rosy and Flossie. They had the organ sure enough, and Flossie could play pretty well and Rosy could sing, but they were better cooks than they were musicians, and once in a while they asked me to stay for supper.

Their business was fine right from the start. They gave the men a touch of what they had left back home before they came to Colorado to get rich in the mines, which mighty few of them did. The girls sang some of the old sentimental songs. When I'd spend an evening with them I was surprised how many of those tough old miners would break down and cry like children when Rosy sang "Just Before the Battle, Mother" and "Tenting Tonight."

Most of the men were Civil War veterans and they'd sung these songs themselves. Then Rosy would sing "Juanita," and when she got to "Weary looks, yet tender, Speak their fond farewell," there would be few dry eyes in the room.

The craziest side of the girls came out one Sunday afternoon when we were sitting in the kitchen drinking coffee and eating one of Rosy's chocolate cakes. Rosy was the one who liked to cook and Flossie liked to sew, and both of them wanted to get married.

"Why don't you marry one of us?" Rosy asked. "We'd make you a good wife."

"Sure we would," Flossie added. "We've had lots of practice with men."

I wanted to laugh, but I didn't dare risk it. They'd have run me out of the place if I had. It was plain they were deadly serious. I almost choked on my coffee trying to keep from snorting. Finally I asked, "Who do you think would marry a whore?"

That made them mad. Rosy said hotly, "We ought to chase you up the road to your place."

"If I knew where the broom was, I would," Flossie said, "and I'd hit you over the head every jump you made."

"Where do you think men on the frontier got their wives?" Rosy demanded.

"I'll tell you," Flossie said. "They got them out of whorehouses, that's where. And they made good wives and mothers."

"If you really want to get married," I said, "why don't

you get out of your profession? You could find work in Black Hawk or Central City."

"Work?" Rosy demanded. "We don't want to work."

"Hell no," Flossie added. "What we're doing is better than working."

I wasn't so sure about that when I stopped in one evening in May. Rosy looked as if she'd been through a meat grinder. One eye was swollen shut, her nose was twice the size it usually was, and on one side of her face she had the biggest, most painful-looking black-and-blue bruise I ever saw on a human being in my life.

I asked what had happened and Flossie said, "She don't feel like talking much, so I'll tell you. That damned, mean Bully Bailey done it last night. They went into her bedroom and pretty soon I heard her scream. I ran into her room. A couple of men who were waiting in the front room were right behind me. All we saw was Bailey's hind end going through the window."

Rosy's lips were all puffed up, and she had trouble talking, but she managed to say, "I always was afraid of him."

"We don't usually do business with that kind of man," Flossie said, "but we didn't know he was that bad. He just fooled us."

"Now we've got to close down for a while," Rosy said with regret. "I can't let anybody see me this way."

I started looking for Bailey. I knew the bastard and I was surprised when Flossie said that Bailey had fooled them. There wasn't any doubt about the kind of man he was. He was big, taller than me and twenty-thirty pounds heavier. He was a wicked barroom fighter who would gouge a man's eyes out if he could. I'd seen him whip smaller men than he was, but I had never seen him tangle with a real good small man or one that was bigger than he was.

His real name was Roscoe Bailey, but folks always called him Bully because that's exactly what he was. He didn't like it one little bit, but once the name got hung on him, he couldn't stop people from calling him that.

I found him just after dark in the Western Star. He was

bellied up against the bar, wedged in between a couple of
his cronies. I didn't say anything to him. I just went up
to him and grabbed him by a shoulder with my left hand
and yanked him around to face me, then I let him have it
right square on his nose.

Well sir, you should have seen the blood fly all around
him in a bright red shower. It was just as if you'd squeezed
an overripe plum in your hand. He let out a squall of
pain. Anger, too, I guess. He shook his head and came at
me like a bull, his big fists flying.

I ducked a wild punch and hit him on the chin. It
stopped him, but he stayed on his feet, weaving a little
and kind of pawing at me. I kicked him in the crotch and
I think I must have knocked his balls about six inches
higher than they were. He bent over and froze there. I
guess he hurt so much he was paralyzed.

"Get out of camp," I said. "If I see you around here
again, you'd better go for your gun because I'll kill you.
I'll cut your head off and give it to Rosy Martin to hang
on her wall."

He didn't move even then, but the men he'd been drinking with came to him and grabbed his arms. They practically carried him out through the batwings. I started
toward the door to see if they had left or were fixing to dry-
gulch me and then I saw my father standing in the front of
the crowd. I didn't even know he was in Black Hawk.

He'd never seen me like that before. He'd probably
never seen me fight anybody. His mouth had sprung open
and he was staring at me as if he didn't know who I was.
Maybe he didn't; maybe for a few seconds I had not been
the son he had raised.

"Let's go home," I said. "I haven't had any supper yet.
Have you?"

He shook his head. He followed me out of the Western
Star and walked up the canyon past the Martin house and
on to my cabin. He didn't say a word all the way there.

CHAPTER VI

I built a fire and put the coffee pot on. I warmed up some left-over beans and fried bacon, and made biscuits. I set the table and put out a jar of honey, and all the time I was doing this my father sat on a chair at the table and looked at me. I had a funny idea that he wasn't seeing me, and then it struck me that it wasn't the fight that was bothering him. I didn't have any idea what it was, though.

As soon as I had everything on the table, I said, "It's ready. I'll bet your tapeworm is hollering at you."

He didn't say a word until we started to eat. Then he sat staring at his food for a moment before he said, "You handled that big fellow good. You went after him like a mad grizzly."

"I was mad enough," I said, and told him what had happened.

"If that woman is a whore, she's got to expect some of that," he said. "Not that I condone it. It's just that now and then you find a man who's that way."

"Not if I can help it," I said. "Both women are popular in camp. I'll kill Bailey if he shows up in Black Hawk again and he knows it. He likewise knows that no jury would convict me of murder."

He shrugged and started to eat, but his heart wasn't in it. After a while he asked, "Got any ideas yet about what you want to do or where you want to go?"

I shook my head. "No."

"I've been thinking about the railroad that's being built across Nebraska and ought to be in Wyoming pretty soon. Maybe it is now. I don't know. Anyhow, there's bound to be some good-sized towns spring up along the railroad where there's nothing but prairie now. If you'd take my money and put it with yours, you could buy some property cheap. It's bound to go up."

I hadn't thought of that. It made sense. The railroad would bring people West who would farm or raise cattle, and it would give them the means of shipping their produce back East where the big markets were. More than that, a lot of other people would come with the ranchers and farmers: storekeepers, lawyers, doctors, school teachers, newspaper men, and a lot of others. Why hell, the belt of country along the railroad would be settled and booming in just a few years.

The more I thought about it, the better it looked to me. I'd never been real excited about the mining country. It was a take-out kind of industry that didn't put anything back. Sooner or later the gold or silver or whatever metal was being mined would be gone and the camp would be deserted. Farming and ranching were different—the land would always be there and they wouldn't leave ghost towns all over the country the way mining would.

"You've got a good idea," I said. "I'll think about it some more and maybe head up into that country. I'm ready to quit here as soon as I finish building the house I'm working on. It's about done. You'd better go with me."

"No," he said with more emotion than the suggestion called for. "I've got a feeling that my race is about run. I won't live through the summer, so I might as well stay right here."

I don't know when I had heard anything that shocked me as much as that. I put my fork down and swallowed. All of a sudden I had a crazy kind of hollow feeling in my belly. My father was my only close living relative. I guess there were some cousins back in Illinois, but I didn't know them and I didn't want to.

"Now look," I said. "You're not fifty years old. Most men are in the prime of life at your age. I've never known you to be sick. What are you talking this way for?"

He didn't look at me. He went on eating, taking one slow bite after another. Finally he said, "Well, Jimmy, I'm not superstitious. At least I don't think I am, and I never put any faith in folks who claimed to have second sight, but lately, say the last month or so, I've had some notions about dying. Came on me pretty fast. Dreams, mostly, but they're so real I can't get them out of my mind."

"Dreaming about dying doesn't mean you're going to die," I said. "I don't like to hear you talk that way."

I felt like laughing or crying or just getting up and walking out of the cabin. I don't think anything that had happened to me since I was a child had bothered me like this. I took a drink of coffee and discovered that my hands were shaking. It was so bad I actually spilled some of it, and my cup wasn't full, either.

Even though it all sounded crazy to me and wasn't like my father, who had always been a sane and stable man, I couldn't entirely discount what he had said. I remembered there had been men in the First Colorado Volunteers who had had premonitions that they were going to be killed. They had, too—every one of them.

My father pushed his plate back, his food only half eaten. "It really isn't important, Jimmy. Life is a transient thing as far as this earth-plane is concerned. I've had a good life. Eight happy years with your mother and the good years while you were growing up in Kansas. I haven't seen much of you after we moved here, but I've known what you were doing and where you were. I've been proud of you, too. I know you're the kind of man who'll get along and be able to take care of himself."

He had picked up his fork and was starting to poke at a piece of bacon. Then he put the fork down and raised his head and looked squarely at me. He said, "Jimmy, the sun's on the wall for you."

I knew what he meant, all right. He'd said something like that too many times when I'd been a boy for me to mistake his meaning. He was absolutely correct. I'd spent enough time here in Black Hawk cutting wood and building houses, and now it was time to get on with my life somewhere else, a place where I could make it count.

"Yes," I said. "I'll be on my way as soon as I finish my obligations around here."

"I was thinking about Julesburg," he said. "Right now they say it's hell on wheels, and I guess it is, but they'll settle down after the end of track is pushed on West. It might turn out to be quite a city."

"It might," I said, but I wasn't at all sure. It seemed to be too far away from any place of importance to become a city.

"I finally had a run of luck," he went on. "That's what I'm working up to tell you. I've been a great one to piddle around with little bets. You know that, of course. I've won some and I've lost some, and all the time I kept working and saving when I could. My gambling never amounted to much and I've always come out about even, but a few days ago I decided to try for the big one, so I went into Denver and got into a big poker game."

I had trouble believing what I was hearing. This wasn't like him, either. The little bets like wagering fifty cents on which bird was going to fly off the fence first was his size, not the big poker game. I knew he had played some, but I also knew he wasn't particularly good at it.

I'd watched some games here in Black Hawk and Central City and I'd seen some big winners, professional gamblers who knew when to press their luck and when to pull back. It seemed to me it was a matter of intuition and the big ones knew when to trust it.

I've talked to some of these gamblers. The interesting part of it is that none of them can pin it down and tell exactly what the feeling is or why and how intuition works the way it does. The trick is to know when to trust it, and even if they can't describe the feeling, they can and do recognize it.

The more I thought about it, the more certain I felt that my father did not understand this or had not done enough big-time gambling to recognize the feeling if it did come to him. I didn't know what a run of luck meant to him, or even what he called big-time gambling. It might be winning or losing fifty dollars. Anyhow, I puffed hard on my pipe and waited.

For some reason he was having trouble telling me about it, maybe because he sensed I found it hard to believe. I'm sure he realized that what he had done was not his customary behavior. Maybe he had even surprised himself, and then I remembered what he had said a little before about living through the summer.

Right then I realized why he had done it. The way he saw it, he wasn't going to live long enough to put together any sizeable amount of money. His savings, like mine, had dribbled in too slowly, so he had decided on the big play—but I still didn't know how big was big.

He'd sat back in his chair all this time without saying anything. He'd been staring into space and probably not seeing anything. Now he raised a hand to his chin and began feeling the deep cleft that was there, a sign that he had something important to say. I'd seen that gesture too often to be mistaken, so I knocked my pipe out and filled it again and waited for him to go on.

"Well," he said finally, "I took all but about fifty dollars of my savings and went to Denver. I had twelve hundred dollars, and with that kind of money I could pick my game. The funny part of it is that I still don't know exactly why I did it or why I drifted into the saloon I did, but when I walked up to a table, I knew it was the one where I wanted to play.

"At first my luck was just average, and then I began getting the big hands. By sunup I was two thousand dollars ahead. I cashed in and came home and put all of it under the hearthstone. You'll find it there when the time comes. You'll have enough to make the big gamble, and that's what you've got to do."

"I don't know what to say," I said, and I didn't.

There was a strange, unreal feeling about the whole business, my father thinking he was going to die soon and going on this gambling spree and then coming here and telling me about it. I got up and went around the table and laid a hand on his shoulder.

"We haven't been together as much as we'd both like,"

I said, "but I can't face this dying business. It's been good to know that I had a place to go when I got out of the army or any other time when I needed it."

He put a hand up on mine and patted it, but he didn't look at me. I guess both of us were about ready to start crying. It was a new feeling for me. Neither of us was what I'd call sentimental. We'd never talked like this to each other before in our lives. It was a moment before we could speak, and his voice trembled when he did.

"You know, Jimmy," he said, "we make too much of death. Actually, there is no death. We keep right on living. I want you to think of it that way because I know it's true. I never understood that until lately, but I do now."

I pulled my hand away and stepped back. He rose and said, "Let's clean up the dishes and go to bed."

We did, but for some reason I couldn't sleep. I had always felt that my father was a strange man, but this was too strange. Something had happened to him and I didn't suppose I'd ever know for sure what it was. I felt positive it had been more than a dream, but he would have told me if he'd wanted me to know.

I guess it was the way it had been in Kansas when he'd been involved with the Free Soldiers and the Underground Railroad. He didn't want me to get into trouble over his doings, so he didn't tell me about them. Maybe he just found it hard to talk about himself. I knew that what he had said tonight had not come easily.

There are so many things a man experiences but cannot describe in words. It's like the professional gambler who often knows when to push his luck and when to back away but, like I said, he can't tell how he knows. I think it was that way with my father regarding the experience he'd had. All I knew as I lay awake staring into the darkness was that it had been a very profound one.

We had breakfast in the morning and shook hands. Neither of us said anything more about what had happened or had been said the previous evening. I guess we were drained dry.

Three days later a neighbor of my father's rode all the way from Golden to Black Hawk to tell me that he had died of a heart attack. They'd found him sitting in a chair in the kitchen, slumped over the table.

CHAPTER VII

My father's neighbors had been very fond of him. They had taken care of the funeral arrangements before I got to Golden. I slept in his house the first night I was there, although one neighbor, a lanky Missourian named Carew, came over at dusk and asked me to stay with him and his family. I thanked him and said that I'd rather be by myself, and he seemed to understand.

I didn't look for the money that night. It would wait. Too, I was afraid more of the neighbors would drop in to offer their sympathy. Several of them did. They all spoke highly of my father and said what a good neighbor he had been. I did not have the feeling they were saying this just because he was dead. You get a feeling about things like that, and I was convinced they were sincere.

The funeral was the next afternoon. The preacher came by in the morning. I didn't like him at first, but then I just didn't like preachers. I had decided that if he used the funeral service as a means of converting those of us who were sinners, I'd get up in the middle of the service and walk out. I told the preacher how I felt in plain, direct language that he couldn't misunderstand.

He stared at me, shocked, I guess. He said, "Mr. Glenn, I believe you would walk out."

"You bet I would," I said. "I was only six when my mother died, but I remember what the preacher said. He ranted and raved and threw his arms around. It was all about hell. If there was ever an angel who walked this good green earth, it was my mother. Hell had no place in her funeral service."

The preacher was thoughtful for a moment, then he asked, "Have you been saved, Mr. Glenn?"

"Of course I have," I answered. "So has my father. He didn't go to church, but he read the Bible. It's yonder on the table. Take a look at it and you'll see he mighty near wore it out reading it. I was taught by him. I don't go to church, either, but we know a little bit about the nature of God. That's why we know we're saved."

"You sound as if your father was still alive."

"He is, isn't he?"

I don't suppose anybody ever argued with the preacher or contradicted him. I guess some preachers would have jumped down my throat and worked me over verbally, but he didn't. He didn't answer my question, either. He kept looking at me in that thoughtful way he had. Then he asked, "If you know something about the nature of God, you must know what His dominant characteristic is."

"I do," I said. "It's love, and if God is love as the Bible says, He sure wouldn't prepare an eternal hell and cast people into it because they didn't do just what He thought they should. Like getting baptized, for instance, and doing it by a certain procedure."

"Immersion, for instance?" he suggested.

I nodded. "That's right."

"You don't think it makes any difference to God what you do?"

"Of course it does," I said, "but we're not going to be condemned for eternity on account of what we do in one lifetime. There's too much difference in the way we're born. I was lucky with an angel mother and a loving father, but how about some savage Indian who never heard of God? Or a Negro who was born and raised in slavery? Or some sick, ignorant kid born in a family of drunks? I could go on, but you get the point. If God is anything, he's a just God."

"I do indeed get the point, Mr. Glenn." The preacher rose and, walking to the table, picked up my father's Bible. He added quite casually, "You are very much a chip off the old block. You were not home very much, so you don't know that your father and I were very good friends. As a matter of fact, I think I am the only preacher he was ever really friendly with. I often dropped in for an evening and we'd sit up until midnight talking about some of these very things. I must admit he made a good case for his point of view."

He put the Bible back on the table and smiled slightly. "I will miss him a great deal, mostly because I find so few men who force me to stretch my understanding. It's very easy to fall into a rut and ·preach a safe and sound doctrine. He taught me that I had a greater obligation than that, and I have tried to meet it. I tried to persuade him to come to church because I felt he needed the fellowship, but he never came, so perhaps he didn't."

He walked to the door, then turned back, his face grave. "There is one thing I must tell you because I believe I knew him better than anyone else in Golden. He was very proud of you and he loved you very much. He knew you would never get any more schooling. It wasn't necessary for you, he said, because you would educate yourself. He thought that book learning often made men impractical, and as a result they live in the clouds. You are a practical man, he said, very independent, and you'll make your own way. No matter what happens to you, you will always be able to take care of yourself."

His smile returned then, and he added, "There will be no mention of hell today."

The neighbor, Carew, stopped for me after dinner and took me in his carriage along with his wife and children to the church. The service was not a long one. There were the usual songs and prayers and scriptures, but the preacher's short talk was what I was to remember.

He kept his word. There was no mention of hell, though he did talk about Heaven—not the usual golden streets and harps and angels, but a place of peace and love. He never said my father was there, but I did not for a moment doubt his conviction that it was true. He also said that death was not the end of anything, but a continuation of life.

He talked briefly of his personal loss and the community's loss as well. I could find no fault with anything he

said. I knew that if my father was there to hear—and I
had a strange feeling he was—he, too, would have
approved of all the preacher said.

Afterwards I rode beside Carew to the graveyard. I
heard the last prayer, the last song, and I saw the coffin
lowered into the grave; then some men stepped up with
shovels in their hands and started filling it. The first rock
that hit the coffin made a strange, echoing sound. A sob
shook my whole body when I heard it. I turned quickly
and walked to Carew's carriage and stood there. I had
been able to detach myself from the fact of death, but that
empty sound was too much for me.

It struck me that the daily business of living was lonely
and too often as empty of meaning as that hollow sound
of the rock hitting the coffin. For the first time a keen
sense of regret stabbed me like a thrust of lightning. I
could have spent more time with my father. He always
visited me and slept in my cabin and ate his meals with
me when he came to Black Hawk. I could have ridden to
Golden and spent some time with him, but I had not been
here for more than a year.

The preacher shook hands with me and said he hoped
we would meet again. Carew returned to the carriage with
his family. He waited until the rest of the neighbors had
filed past and shaken hands with me, then we got into the
carriage and he drove back to my father's house.

On the way I asked, "Did he have any heart attacks
before this last one?"

Carew gave me a sharp look, perhaps thinking it was
something I should have known. I didn't try to defend
myself, though. If my father had wanted me to know, he
would have told me. Besides, it was none of Carew's
business.

"Yes, he'd had several over the last two years," Carew
said. "Most of them were minor. At least, they didn't lay
him up very long, but he had a bad one last fall. We all
thought he wasn't going to make it."

"Why didn't you send for me?"

"He said not to," Carew answered. "I don't know
why."

So that was why he had told me what he had about not living through the summer. I said, "Then he knew he didn't have much time."

Carew nodded somberly. "Yes, he knew. I tried to get him to stop working. He had some money. He could have lived quietly here and spent a little time working in his garden every day. He'd have made out all right, but he said no, that wouldn't do for him. He'd wear out, but he sure didn't aim to rust out. He told me that more than once. I said he could go and live with you, but he said he guessed neither one of you would like that."

I didn't say anything. He was right. We both liked the way we had been living. I honestly believe he would have preferred death to living with me and being dependent on me. It was something the preacher would have understood, but Carew did not. He looked at me accusingly, as if I were to blame for my father's death. By his lights I was, but not by mine.

He pulled up at the front door of my father's house and I got out and thanked him. He drove away, not saying anything. He had done his duty; he didn't want to see any more of me. Most folks felt the way he did, I guess. And then I had a weird sensation. I thought my father was standing beside me telling me not to worry about what Carew and the rest of the neighbors thought. I wasn't. I mentally thanked him for raising me the way he had.

I guess I had not fully realized before how much alike we had been: non-conformists, loners, independent thinkers, and, most of all, men who did not want to depend on anyone else. I went into the house, feeling good. I did not have the slightest sense of guilt, even though Carew and the other neighbors considered me guilty of gross neglect.

I built a fire and cooked my supper. As soon as it was dark, I barred both the front and back doors and hung blankets over the windows. I didn't know how many people in Golden were aware that my father had been lucky in Denver, but there were bound to be some thieves in Golden. I didn't want any of them watching me through a window.

As soon as I had the room ready, I lifted the hearthstone. Under it was a hole containing a number of canvas sacks. I moved them to the table and emptied them, and then I was looking at the biggest pile of gold and silver and greenbacks I had ever seen in my life. I counted it, and then I simply sat and stared at it, thinking of all the things I could do with that much money.

There was more than thirty-five hundred dollars. My father had been right. I could buy a good many lots in any of the railroad towns. If I picked the right one, I would be rich. If I picked the wrong one, I'd be broke. So I was going to gamble, but my bet wouldn't be a piddling fifty cents on which bird was going to fly off the fence first. It would be for all or nothing.

I put the money back under the hearthstone and lowered it into place. I didn't touch it again until I had sold my father's house, team, wagon, and personal things, retaining only his watch and a few small items that were keepsakes more than anything else. The last night I slept in the house I took the money out from under the hearthstone. I placed the gold in a money belt I had bought that day; the rest went into my saddlebags.

I wound up my affairs in Black Hawk as fast as I could, but it was well into July before I was done. By this time I had more than five thousand dollars—closer to six, I guess. I stopped at the Martin girls' house and told them good-by. They kissed me and cried a little and said they'd miss me. Not just as a customer, either, and didn't I want to marry them before I left and take them with me.

"You think I'm a Mormon?" I asked. "What would I do with two wives? I doubt that I could handle one."

"Marry just one of us and the other one will go along as a friend of the groom," Rosy said.

"Yes, that'd be the way to do it." Flossie bobbed her head in agreement. "I would make you a mighty intimate friend. Two women are twice as much fun as one."

"I'll bet they are," I said. "And twice as much trouble, too. I'd sure have problems. If you took your pins off, I wouldn't know which one I'd married until you were undressed."

"Oh, I undress easy," Rosy said.

"So do I," Flossie added.

"Yeah, for the first man who rode by with two dollars in his pocket," I said.

I got out of there then, thinking that if I ever did get married, it would be to a girl of virtue. I rode to Golden and turned north. I had been hearing recently about a new town named Cheyenne in the southeastern corner of Wyoming that was going to be a division point on the Union Pacific. It just might be the place I was looking for.

As I rode, my thoughts drifted back to Rosy and Flossie. They were indeed a strange pair. I had a notion they might turn up in Cheyenne. Business had been slow in Black Hawk all winter, but it was bound to boom in an end-of-track town.

The Martin girls were business women if they were anything. They'd retire someday as rich women, I thought. They'd move to some town where they weren't known, pass themselves off as rich widows, and end up respectably married.

All of a sudden it struck me funny and I began to laugh. Suppose only one of them got married and the single one lived with the married one. If Rosy got rid of that mole, the husband would never know which one he was sleeping with.

CHAPTER VIII

The first night I camped on the bank of the Poudre just below Fort Collins. I rode directly north the next day, but I didn't find Cheyenne. I didn't know how many miles I had ridden, and I didn't know where the territorial line was.

I began to wonder if I'd gone right past Cheyenne. It couldn't be much of a town yet, so I began to worry. It might have been on the other side of some ridge I'd passed. Maybe I was getting farther away from it all the time. I'd be in Fort Laramie the next thing I knew. That really wouldn't happen, of course; the fort was about one hundred miles north of Cheyenne. I was thinking crazy because I was irritated by my failure to find the town.

Late in the afternoon I saw a ranch to my right and I reined toward it, thinking I might be smart to stay the night there. At least I'd find out where Cheyenne was. When I reached the buildings, I decided it wasn't much of an outfit.

The house was a shack—no more. The log barn was better, not large, but well built and tight, and would give horses ample protection in bad weather. The pole corral was equally well built and tight. It struck me that whoever owned the spread had put out much more effort for his animals' comfort than his own. I was dead sure of one thing: there were no women here.

I reined up in front of the shack and sat my saddle for a moment, just looking around. I couldn't see any cattle, but there were six horses in the corral: one bay, two sorrels, and three blacks. They were fine-looking, leggy animals that could cover a lot of miles in a day. My sorrel

was the same horse my father had given me when we
arrived in Denver. I hated to sell or trade him, but he was
getting old and I was going to have to buy another mount.

A small, meandering stream flowed past the barn and
shack. A short distance downstream the owner had built a
dam. A good-sized pond was above it, holding more than
enough water to irrigate about forty acres of meadow. He
would get a good crop of hay, and I judged the grass was
about ready to cut. I guessed that the stream would dry
up later in the summer if the weather stayed dry, but the
pond was big enough to furnish drinking and stock water
all year.

I sat there a good five minutes, but nobody showed up.
I decided no one was home, but I hollered "Hello" on the
off chance that someone was around and hadn't seen me.
Sure enough, the door banged open and a man came out
of the shack rubbing his eyes.

"I was sleeping and didn't know anybody was here," he
said. "Get down and rest your saddle."

I had no way of knowing what I was getting into or
whether anyone else was on the place. If I'd had my
druthers, I'd have stayed the night in Cheyenne, but I was
tired and my horse was worse off than I was. Still, I
hadn't made up my mind when I asked, "Where's
Cheyenne? I figured I'd be there before now."

He jerked a thumb toward the north. "It's another five,
six miles. Your horse looks plumb tuckered. Better spend
the night here. I like company and I don't mind telling
you it gets damned lonesome. I've been here two years
and if you ask me why I settled in this God-forsaken hole,
I won't tell you because I don't know."

He was as tall as I was, a good six feet, his face as
brown as the leather of my saddle, with more lines in it
than I could count. It was what I'd call a weathered face.
It reminded me of some ancient cliff that had been eroded
by wind and weather for centuries. He was about my age,
maybe a little older, with faded blue eyes and corn-col-
ored hair that hadn't been combed lately and stuck out in
all directions.

I stepped down and held out my hand. "I'm Jim Glenn," I said. "I was hoping to get to Cheyenne tonight."

"Ed Burke here," he said, shaking hands. "This prosperous-looking spread is the EB. You wouldn't know it, but I'm a rich cowman." He winked as he threw out an arm in a grandiose gesture. "The range as far as you can see belongs to me. Nobody else is fool enough to claim it. That's why it's mine. All I need is some cows. I've got a herd that's grazing on the other side of yonder ridge." He grinned wryly. "All ten of 'em."

I seldom responded favorably to a man the moment I met him, but I liked this Ed Burke right off. I prided myself on being able to judge men, and although I wasn't always right, I had a pretty good average. I'd learned by hard, bitter lessons.

Black Hawk and Central City always had a lot of floaters. When I'd started to cut and haul wood, I had been taken in by some of them who promised to pay, but after they got the wood they'd manage to put me off by one excuse or another. Before I knew it, they'd left town still owing me. Of course they'd burned up a load of free wood.

As I grew older, I got meaner. The last year I lived in Black Hawk I didn't lose a nickel. One reason was that I had a reputation for being mean and nobody figured it was smart to cheat me. Another reason was that I'd learned to pick my customers.

I never really knew how I judged a man or what kind of measuring stick I used. I guess it was mostly just a feeling. Now it struck me that Ed Burke was all right. I had a crazy idea that I'd like to stay here and throw in with him. I had enough capital to buy a fair-sized herd, and if Cheyenne was destined to grow into a city, it would furnish a market close at hand. Even if it didn't, the railroad would be here and shipping cattle to Omaha or Chicago or St. Louis would be no problem.

Once the idea hit me, I could see a lot of possibilities. For one thing, there was less gamble in a cattle ranch than there was in buying town lots when it's anybody's guess what the town is going to do. I wasn't fool enough to say

anything about it, though. I'd look Cheyenne over first
and get a little better acquainted with Burke before I made
him a proposition.

"I ought to keep riding," I said, still not sure what I
wanted to do. I guess my trouble was that I'd made up
my mind I wanted to get to Cheyenne before dark and it
was hard to unmake it. "If Cheyenne is only five, six
miles, I could—"

"If you're thinking you're gonna find a city," Burke
interrupted, "you are mistook. You'll find a few people
and some tents and shacks, and a lot of street markers and
stakes showing where the streets are. But city?" He shook
his head. "Hell no. You probably won't find no bed and
no place to stable your horse. I'll go throw another
antelope steak into the pan. You take care of your horse."

I decided to stay. Cheyenne would be there in the
morning. I still wasn't sure why I had taken a liking to Ed
Burke. Saying I had a feeling about a man wasn't any
answer. Why did I get a feeling? I thought about it as I
watered my horse. I offsaddled and rubbed him down and
turned him into the corral, and all the time I kept asking
myself that question.

I finally decided I liked him because I had a natural
sympathy for him. He'd settled here with a tall stack of
hopes and he hadn't cashed in on them. He didn't even
have a good working ten-cow spread. Chances were he
hadn't had enough money to stock his range when he
started and he didn't see any better chance yet.

I stood looking at his horses and a question popped
into my mind. He didn't need six horses as good as these
to operate the kind of outfit he had. Those animals could
be driven to Denver and sold for a sizeable chunk of
jingle. Why didn't he do that and take the money and buy
some cows and a good bull?

Not that it was any of my business, but it seemed to me
he wasn't really smart—more of an idealist than a practical man. I knew the world was full of men like him who
struggled all their lives to get their heads above water and
worked their tails off while they were doing it, and never
quite made it.

When I went into the shack, it was hotter than the hinges of hell's front door. He had a good fire going, coffee boiling, and a pan of antelope steaks sizzling. The smell was enough to start my mouth watering and my stomach to rolling around. It had been a long time since I'd eaten dinner. It hadn't been much of a meal anyhow, just crackers and cheese and a can of peaches.

Burke motioned to a chair at the table. "Sit down," he said. "This ain't gonna be no banquet, but there's plenty of what there is." He stopped in front of the stove and stared unabashedly at me for a good minute, then he said, "I don't usually ask a man his business, but I'm going to ask you because I might be some help. Why are you headed for Cheyenne?"

"To buy lots," I said. "I'm not sure Cheyenne is the place, but somewhere along the railroad there's going to be a big town. I aim to get rich off the lots I'm going to buy."

I expected him to give me the horselaugh. It sounded pretty stupid to my own ears when I told it plain out that way, trying to get rich so easy. I was a practical man and it was plain he wasn't, and I could have told him how to run his ranch, but he'd been in the country for two years and he'd been in Cheyenne, and therefore he might be in a good position to say I was stupid or smart to invest money in town lots.

He didn't give me any horselaugh. He turned back to the stove and flipped the steaks over, then he said seriously, "You just might do it. It's my guess that Cheyenne is going to be *the* town. I wish to hell I had a little money to buy some of them lots. Right now the U. P. is selling 'em for $150 apiece. Of course that's gravy for the company because the lots didn't cost them nothing except to survey 'em. They can't afford to price 'em too high or nobody will buy 'em, but I'll bet you right now that within two, three months, when the track gets to Cheyenne, them same lots will sell for five hundred dollars."

That wouldn't be a bad deal for me, I thought. Hold

the lots a few months and make better than three-to-one
profit. I asked, "You don't think Julesburg will be the big
town?"

He gave me the horselaugh then. "Hell no," he said.
"There ain't no reason why it should be, set off by itself
the way it is in the northeast corner of the state like it is."

He waggled a forefinger at me. "It's different with
Cheyenne. They ain't gonna leave a town as big as
Denver high and dry, especially when there's a whole
territory depending on it with a lot of stuff to ship, so
there's bound to be a junction with a spur they'll run
south to Denver. It's on a direct line between Fort
Laramie and Denver, too. No sir, you can't miss investing
in Cheyenne property."

"It sounds good," I said, thinking he had been studying
the situation longer than I had.

"And another thing," he went on. "Cheyenne's been
named as a division point. That means jobs and jobs
mean men and men mean families and families mean a
market."

He shoved the steaks around on the bottom of the
frying pan. "Julesburg? Let me tell you about that place. I
was there a while back, and I was glad to get out alive.
When they call it hell on wheels, they ain't mistook. I've
seen some mean, tough burgs in my time, but that one
takes the cake. There's more whores and pimps and
gamblers and just plain sneak thieves over there than I
ever seen before. You get into bed with a whore and she
hands you a drink, and that's all you remember till you
wake up in an alley with your pockets picked clean. Stay
away from Julesburg, Mr. Glenn. It ain't safe for man or
beast."

"Chances are Cheyenne will be the same when it's the
end of track," I said.

"Mebbe." He shrugged. "Mebbe not. There ain't nobody in Julesburg that's interested in getting law and
order. It all depends on the kind of leadership they get in
Cheyenne. Now you look like a purty tough hand. You
willing to take the lead in handling gangs of thieves and

murderers? Get a vigilante committee to working if the law can't handle it? There's nothing like a few hangings to clear out the riff-raff."

The idea had not occurred to me before, but I guessed right then I'd be up against that decision sooner or later. If I bought lots in Cheyenne, I'd have a stake in establishing law and order. If the law couldn't keep it, a vigilante committee was the only answer.

I had never belonged to one. It hadn't been necessary in Black Hawk, though there had been plenty of talk about forming one several times. Denver had had a very active one. I guess it had been necessary there, but I had never been in favor of forming one in Black Hawk. When a vigilante committee is controlled by the wrong men, you simply exchange one form of lawlessness for another.

"I guess I'd be willing," I said after thinking about it for a minute. "If I'm a property owner in Cheyenne, I'd have to help establish law and order. If we didn't have it, I couldn't sell my property."

He nodded. "That's right. Well, I guess we can eat." He set the table, brought out a pot of cold beans, lifted a pan of biscuits from the oven, poured the coffee, and then forked the steaks into our plates. He was a better than average cook and I was more than average hungry, so the supper tasted like the banquet he'd said it wasn't.

When we finished eating, we went outside into the cool of the evening and filled our pipes and smoked. It was a real easy relationship, with me telling about living in a mining camp and Ed telling about working on a ranch near Trinidad and drifting north and finally deciding to start his own outfit here near the territorial line.

After a while we both yawned and he said he guessed we'd better roll in. I could sleep in the barn because he had only one bunk in the house. There wasn't much hay in the mow, but I raked enough together to sleep on. Then I lay there thinking about my idea.

A good ranch could be made out of the EB. Come to think of it, I wouldn't mind being a rancher. I'd be about as free that way as any way. I guess what I feared the most was being pinned down to a job. I was wondering what Ed would say about having a partner when I dropped off to sleep.

CHAPTER IX

I woke up sometime before dawn. I had no idea what time it was, but it was black dark. For a little while I didn't know why I had awakened; then I heard voices. I sat up and listened, and decided the men were at the corral gate. One voice was Ed Burke's. I had no idea who the other man was.

They were arguing about something, or actually quarreling, from the tone of their voices, but I couldn't make out any of the words. Presently they arrived at some sort of agreement. At least, they stopped talking. A moment later I heard the sound of a horse galloping away from the barn, headed west; then the thudding of hoofs faded and died.

I lay back on the hay, wondering about it. It was a fair guess that someone had ridden in during the night, got Ed out of bed, and swapped horses with him. When it was daylight, I left the barn and had a look at the horses in the corral. One of the blacks was gone and a strange buckskin was there. He'd been ridden hard, and judging from the way he stood with his head down, I had a hunch he might not be any good again.

Smoke was lifting from the chimney of the shack. The door was open, so I stepped through it and saw that Ed was standing at the stove frying bacon. He saw me and nodded, saying, "Howdy. You sleep all right?"

"Yeah, fine," I answered, "except that during the night I heard a couple of men talking. One of them sounded like you."

"Yeah, it was me," he said in an offhand way. "It's happened before. The U. P. has some surveying crews in the Black Hills trying to locate the best route over them

mountains. It's a purty good grade west of here, you
know. The story is that General Dodge discovered the
pass by accident one time when the Indians jumped him
and his party, but of course the route the railroad will
take has to be exactly the right grade, and be staked out
now so that the graders won't have no trouble following it.
They'll be laying rails over that summit before snow flies."

"What's that got to do with your night visitor?" I asked.

"Hell, didn't I tell you?" He wiped a hand across his
face. "Sometimes I think I'm getting old before my time.
You know, my pa was that way before he died. Of course
he was over sixty, and I'm only twenty-seven, but I'm
getting about as forgetful as he was. I recollect one time
when the sheriff stopped to get him for helping and
abetting an outlaw when he was trying to cross the line
into Mexico—"

"What's this got to do with your night visitor?" I asked
again, knowing by this time that he was trying to avoid
giving me an answer.

"Nothing," he said. "I was just aiming to tell you about
my pa. Say, the coffee's done. Why don't you get your cup
yonder and pour yourself a cup."

I did, and decided to quit asking questions. Maybe he
had his reason for not wanting to answer me. It wasn't
any of my business, but it did look queer, and I couldn't
help wondering about it. I guess he thought about it a
minute and decided it would be better if he told me.

"That feller who was here last night was a messenger
for the railroad," he said. "You see, General Dodge or
some of the other mucky-mucks who are east of here at
the end of track, wherever that is, or maybe clean back
in Julesburg, want the surveyors to do something or not
do something they've been doing, so they send a man in a
hurry to tell 'em. I don't know what kind of message this
bird had, but he was in an almighty fidget to get there."

"From the looks of that buckskin in the corral," I said,
"he must have ridden hell out of him."

"Yeah, I reckon he did," Ed admitted, "and I ain't sure
that I came out real good on the trade, but he gave me
some boot, so I won't lose much if the buckskin lays down

and dies. We augered some about how much boot I was to get, but I figured the railroad could afford to pay me purty good the way they throw money away on other things."

He poured coffee, then pulled a pan of biscuits he'd been warming up out of the oven and forked the bacon into plates and got out his jar of honey, so we ate pretty well again. We didn't say much as we ate, but I kept thinking about his story of the railroad messenger. Somehow it didn't ring quite right, but then maybe he accepted the story the fellow had told him. It didn't make any difference to Ed why the man was in such a hurry to get to the Black Hills as long as he got the money he wanted.

After we finished eating, I said, "Time I was moseying along."

"No sense you being in a hurry," he said. "I'll clean up the dishes and ride with you. I ain't been in Cheyenne for several days. Maybe it's growed since I saw it. Anyhow, it'll be plenty lonesome after you leave and I don't think I can stand it. Sometimes I feel like going outside and barking at the moon like a coyote."

"Sure," I said. "I've got no reason to hurry. I guess they won't sell all of their lots before noon."

He snickered. "No sir, they won't, and that's a fact. From all the streets and lots they've measured off, you'd think the U.P. was figuring on Cheyenne being another Chicago."

I went outside and filled and lighted my pipe. I strolled over to the corral and stood studying the buckskin. He didn't look any better than when I'd first seen him. I thought it was probable he'd do just what Ed said—he'd just lie down and die.

I didn't see the two men ride up until they were almost at the door of the shack. They didn't see me at all, and after I'd had a look at them, I decided maybe it was just as well they didn't see me until I wanted them to, so I stayed there at the corral with about half of it between me and them.

They both carried stars, but that didn't prove anything to me. They were two tough-looking gents, and I'd seen plenty of men toting stars who were just one jump removed from being outlaws. Some weren't even that one jump removed, so I figured it would be a good thing to find out what they were up to before they saw me.

They got off their horses and stood looking around. Ed either hadn't seen them or had decided to ignore them. Now one of them called, "Hello! Anybody here?"

Ed came to the door and stepped outside. "Yeah, somebody's here."

That was all he said, but he was wearing his gun now, which he hadn't been doing before, so I made a guess that he'd seen these men and decided he'd better not take any chances.

They looked him over, silent and cold and somehow threatening without saying a word. Ed looked right back at them, his hand close to the butt of his gun. I didn't know then how much he was figuring on me taking chips in the game, but even if I stayed out of it I had a notion he'd smoke both of them down before they could pull a trigger.

One of them, the taller one, said, "I'm Chip Rawls, United States Marshal. This is Harry Jones, a deputy United States Marshal. Who are you?"

"Ed Burke, if it's any of your business," Ed said. "What's on your mind? I don't have all day. I'm getting ready to ride into Cheyenne."

"You've got plenty of time to talk to us," Rawls said. "Did you see a man riding past here during the night by name of Poke Kelly? He was forking a buckskin."

"Not that I know of," Ed said. "Now if you'll get on about your business, I'll—"

"Easy," Rawls said. "Just take it easy. I told you that you've got plenty of time to talk to us. Did anybody ride through here last night?"

Ed stood looking at them for maybe thirty seconds, then I guess he decided it wasn't any good to lie, maybe thinking about the buckskin he had in his corral. Finally he said, "Yeah, a man stopped here during the night and traded me his tired buckskin for a fresh horse; then he rode on west."

"Why didn't you hold him?" Rawls bellowed angrily. "That was Kelly. He robbed a stage south of here and killed the messenger. What do you think we're here for?"

"He didn't tell me his name was Kelly," Ed said sharply, "and he sure didn't tell me the law wanted him for holding up a stage and killing a messenger. You take me for a mind reader or something?"

"I think you're either a damned fool or you're in cahoots with the pack of outlaws who are all over this country," Rawls said testily, "and you sure don't look like no fool. I'm arresting you for conniving with a known outlaw and giving him aid and sustenance in his flight from justice."

"You ain't arresting me for nothing," Ed said. "You can make up your own law and charges all you want to, but you can't make 'em stick around here. Just leave me out of it. If you try arresting me, you'll be buying yourself a hole in the ground."

Then Ed did a fool thing, or that was the way it seemed to me. He made a slow turn and gave the two lawmen his back before he stepped into the shack. Rawls started to go for his gun, but I moved away from the corral and yelled, "Hold it."

Rawls had his gun out of leather and almost leveled. I believe he would have shot Ed in the back, but when he heard me he froze, his gun within inches of being lined on the middle of Ed's spine. The hammer was back, so it must have been all he could do to keep from pulling the trigger.

"Mister," I said, "if you had shot Burke in the back like you were fixing to do, I'd have killed you right where you stand. I don't believe you are a United States Marshal. I never knew one who would shoot a man in the back."

Rawls turned around and eyed me for a while, so furious he was trembling. Finally he asked, "Who the hell are you, another member of this wolf pack?"

"I'm not a member of anything," I said. "My name's Jim Glenn. I lived in Black Hawk until I sold out a few

days ago. I'm headed for Cheyenne. I stayed here overnight and Ed Burke was kind enough to give me supper
and breakfast. It's a good thing I was here on this
particular morning or you'd have murdered him. Packing
a badge doesn't give you an excuse to murder a man."

"I wasn't going to shoot him," he said, sort of half-
hearted with his lie. "I was fixing to put a slug past his
head so he'd turn around and tell me what he knew about
Poke Kelly."

He eased his gun back into leather. I was still mad.
Either these men were pretending to be U.S. lawmen for
some reason of their own, maybe hoping to run Kelly
down and relieve him of any loot he had taken off the
stage, or they were disgraces as lawmen. Either way, I had
a feeling I'd just as soon kill both of them as not. I carried
my feeling a little further. I even had the notion that the
world would be a better place to live in if they were dead.

I dropped my gun back into leather. I said, "Rawls,
you are a God-damned liar."

I figured that would make him go for his gun. If he
had, I'd have killed him sure. I guess I was so mad I was
a little bit out of my head. I was hoping Jones would
draw, too. They were both facing me, and even if they
weren't very fast with their guns, one of them would
probably have plugged me, except for one thing.

Facing me, they had their backs to the shack, so the
situation was reversed to what it had been. They didn't
know whether Ed was standing there in the doorway or
not. As a matter of fact, he was, his gun in his hand, and
he could have smoked both of them down while they were
drawing on me.

Rawls stood there steaming for quite a while. His pride
was hurt, and pride was a vital part of a man like that. In
the end he wanted to live more than he wanted to recover
his pride, so he didn't force anything.

After a time Rawls said, "Harry, go take a look in the
corral."

I moved into the open, away from the corral toward the
barn, so there wasn't any chance that the deputy could get

behind me. I aimed to watch him and Rawls at the same time. Right then the weather was pretty sticky. It wouldn't have taken much to start the ball.

Jones must have sensed that because he didn't make any effort to get around to the other side of the corral. He walked to the gate, very slowly, had his look, and came back. Ed was still standing in the doorway and Jones couldn't help seeing him.

"The buckskin's out there, all right," Jones said.

Rawls swore. He said, "Let's ride, Harry. We're wasting time with these two buckos." He swung into the saddle, then he leaned forward and said to Ed, "I think you knew who Kelly was and I think you didn't want to stop him. If I ever get any proof that you're working with the outlaws, I'll be back."

"I'll welcome you," Ed said coldly.

He didn't say any more, but I think Rawls got the point that Ed would welcome him with a dose of lead. Anyhow, Rawls and Jones rode west, hoping, I suppose, that they'd pick up Kelly's trail. I walked to the shack, saying, "Ed, you are a complete idiot for turning your back to men like that. I don't know yet whether they were lawmen or not, but that's not the point. Rawls is a killer."

Ed wasn't offended. He just grinned at me as he said, "I knew you were out there."

"You're still an idiot," I said. "You didn't know me well enough to be that sure I'd take a hand in the game. A lot of men would have stayed out of it."

He shook his head. "I'm a good judge of horseflesh and men. It didn't take me long to size you up, Jim. You're a hell of a tough man and I figure we're gonna be friends. You couldn't have stayed out of the ruckus any more than you could fly. Now saddle up. I'll be finished up here in a little while and we'll light out for Cheyenne."

I turned on my heel and went back to the corral and saddled my horse. What could you say to a man who talked to you that way? I still didn't know whether Ed really believed what Poke Kelly had said about being a

Union Pacific messenger, or whether he just didn't give a damn and was perfectly willing to swap horses with an outlaw who was running from the law. Either way, I had a hunch Ed was right about us being friends.

CHAPTER X

We rode into Cheyenne before noon and I will have to admit I was disappointed. I had seen some primitive Colorado mining camps, but I had never seen any place as primitive as this. You couldn't dignify it by calling it a town.

I saw a few log houses, others built of cross ties which had been set on end to form the walls and were covered by canvas for roofs, a few with posts set in the ground for corners with nothing but canvas for walls; but most of the settlement consisted of plain, ordinary tents. I had the impression that Cheyenne looked more like a county fair than a town.

I groaned, and Ed looked at me and grinned. "I told you not to expect much of a town," he said.

I nodded agreement. "I know. But I did expect to see more of a town than this."

He threw out a hand in a wide, inclusive gesture. "You can see it's gonna be a big city. Look at the stakes marking the streets and lots. The signs telling you the names of the streets are all in place so you can't get lost among the tall buildings. I've heard the railroad has surveyed four square miles, so they're sure expecting it to be a city."

I could see that, and if I'd had any doubts about investing my money in Cheyenne lots, I lost them at this point. I was going to take my father's advice and gamble big. Either I'd be rich or I'd be starting over. All of a sudden I felt a thrill bigger than I had ever felt before in my life. I was getting in on the ground floor and the only way I could go was up.

Ed reined to a stop and dismounted in front of a big tent with a sign: HEAD QUARTERS SALOON. "I'll go in here and wet my whistle," he said. "You want a drink?"

I shook my head. "No, I'm going to buy some town lots and get rich."

He laughed. "You'll do it, Jim. You'll do it as sure as hell's hot. Well, I'll see you once in a while. I figure I ain't gonna stay out there on the EB and rot, so I'll come to town and turn my wolf loose."

"Thanks for putting me up and feeding me," I said.

"I enjoyed it." He laughed again. "The part I enjoyed the most was when you threw your gun on that bastard of a United States Marshal. I hate 'em. If I ever run into him in town, I'm likely as not to jump him."

"No sense getting in bad with the law," I said.

"If he is the law," Ed said. "So long."

He nodded and went into the big tent. I rode on down the street, noting that I was on Eddy. I rode quite a ways on it, clear past the last tent, not turning around until I came to 24th. Then I followed it one block to the next street, which was Ferguson, and rode back on it to 16th, where I had started.

It wouldn't be a tent city for long. I must have seen twenty buildings in the process of being built, and I had never heard so many hammers in my life. I wouldn't have any trouble getting a carpenter's job if I wanted it, but I was going to do my own carpenter work and hire some men to boot if I could find them.

I turned east on 16th to Hill and rode along it for eight blocks until I reached 24th again. It struck me that the business section would be in those blocks close to 16th on Eddy and Ferguson, and maybe Hill, and the lots farther out would be in a residential area.

I returned to 16th Street on Ransom, which paralleled Hill. By this time I knew what I wanted if the lots were still available, and I had a pretty fair notion of the way the town would grow, so I hunted until I found the Union Pacific land office. I tied my sorrel in front of the tent and went in, carrying my saddlebags.

"I want to see a plat of the city," I said.

"Certainly." The clerk turned, picked up the plat from a table behind him, and laid it on the counter in front of me. "You are interested in buying some lots?"

"I'm not just interested," I said. "I am going to buy some."

"Good." He rubbed his hands together the way a greedy banker would when he's taking a big deposit. "Very good. You won't go wrong, my friend. Cheyenne is destined to be the biggest city in the area. The railroad company has designated it as a division point, you know."

"How big are the lots?"

"Sixty-six feet by a hundred and thirty-two," he answered. "Very generous lots."

"Where will the tracks run?"

"South of 16th," he said.

"The lots colored black are the ones that are sold?"

"Correct," he said. "We have done very well for the short time we have been selling town property."

Most of the lots in what I had guessed would be the business section were sold, but I found a few that looked good, mostly on Eddy, and then I began picking up lots farther out that would be in the residential section. I figured I had got here just in time and that in a few days most of the lots that had a quick future would be gone.

When I had made a small pencil mark on my thirtieth lot, I said, "I'll take these."

Well sir, by the time the clerk had added up the number of small pencil marks I'd made, he had the goggle-eyed look of a man who was in a state of shock. He looked me over, very carefully this time, and asked, "You sure you can pay for them?"

That irritated me, but I held onto my temper. I said, "I'll pay for them."

"Cash for all thirty?"

"Right."

"That will be forty-five hundred dollars," he said as if he didn't believe there was that much money in the world.

I opened my saddlebags and began taking out money. By the time I finished, I had exactly $1,217.50 left. I walked out with empty saddlebags, all of my cash in my money belt, but I owned thirty pieces of Cheyenne property. I wished my father was beside me to look the lots over. I think he would have been proud of me.

I stepped into a tent restaurant on Eddy Street and had my dinner, then I spent the rest of the day looking at my lots. I picked one out on the corner of Eddy and 22nd where I was going to build my house, then I hunted up a lumber yard and asked if plenty of lumber was coming in.

"You bet," the dealer said. "We've got every teamster we can hire hauling lumber from Denver. We've got other stuff—windows and doors and hinges and nails and so on—coming in from Julesburg. Besides that, several small sawmills are starting to operate in the foothills southwest of here. Now what can I do for you?"

I had figured out the size house I wanted—not big, but big enough for me and a guest if I had one. Maybe I could return Ed Burke's hospitality some time. I told the dealer what I had in mind and where I was going to build, and he promised to have the lumber out there in the morning. They were short of windows and hinges, and I might have to wait a few days for them.

"Do you know of any carpenters I can hire?"

He gave me a derisive laugh. "Carpenters," he said. "Mister, have you listened to those hammers? Some of the hammers ain't in the hands of carpenters. They're just hammer-and-saw men who are earning carpenter's wages because there ain't any real carpenters to be had. No sir, I don't know of nobody you can hire."

"I'll build my house myself," I said, "but I want to put up a business building later on and I'd like to get it started as soon as I can. If you hear of any good men who want to work, send them to me."

"I'll do that," he said with a kind of a sneer. "Yes sir, I'll sure do that."

I didn't like him worth a damn. I went back to my horse and I stopped, flat-footed, my breath going out of me. Just as I reached the sorrel, three men left a tent saloon across the street. The big man in the middle was Bully Bailey as sure as I was a foot high. The other two were probably the men who had been with him in Black

Hawk, though I couldn't see them well enough to be sure.

It came as no real surprise to see Bailey in Cheyenne. A new wild town was bound to attract riff-raff like Bailey. Still, I was stunned to actually see him. I stood there watching him until he disappeared into another saloon down the street, then I mounted and rode to the Great Western Corral and left my horse there.

I walked to my lot on Eddy and 22nd where I intended to build, carrying my saddle blanket. The night was going to be a warm one and the blanket was all I'd need. I was determined to sleep on land that I owned the first night I was in Cheyenne. But I couldn't get Bully Bailey out of my mind. I didn't know whether he had seen me or not, but if he hadn't, he soon would in a town as small as this.

The truth was I was scared. I wasn't scared of any man alive that I could fight while I faced him, but I knew I'd never have a chance to face Bailey again. He wouldn't risk it, so he'd wait until he had an opportunity to smoke me down some night when the moon was full and light was strong enough for him to see me. He'd shoot me in the back and I wouldn't even know he was there.

I just didn't know how any man could defend himself against an attack like that.

CHAPTER XI

I worked practically every waking hour on my house during the first month I was in Cheyenne. I had a strange feeling about it. I don't know why I had it or where it came from, but the thought kept nagging me that time was running out for me.

Not that I was afraid to die. I just didn't want to die until I had accomplished something. It seemed to me that it was a great tragedy for a young man to die without making his mark in the world. It might be only a scratch, but he should have done something. So far I hadn't even made a scratch. I told myself I was going to finish the house, at least, then I was going to start living in Cheyenne, to become a part of the town.

I didn't believe in ghosts, I had never had the slightest interest in spiritualism, I had always believed that life took a different form after death and that anyone who had died could not communicate with those of us who still lived in the flesh. My belief hadn't changed, but still I could not rid myself of the notion that my father was prodding me with the familiar words, "The sun's on the wall, Jimmy."

So I worked as hard as I could and had the house finished late in August. Several times Ed Burke stopped by and gave me a hand. He was a fair carpenter and painter, and I was thankful for his help. Too, he was pleasant company and I enjoyed visiting with him.

It struck me that Ed was neglecting his ranch. He hated hard work, and that included putting up hay. I offered to go out and help with his haying, but he wouldn't let me. I had enough to do, he said, and of course I did. He finally got it cut and stacked, but I'm sure he fooled around so long that he lost some he could have saved.

I learned one thing about Ed very soon—ranching was really not his interest. But I will have to admit that I couldn't find out what was, unless it was women. Whisky, too, I guess, and maybe poker, though he never seemed to lose or win much. I think he played just to pass the time. He appeared to be satisfied if he came out even.

Ed Burke was pleasant and good-natured and easy to have around. He was perfectly happy if he had a place to sleep out of the weather and three meals a day. I was a little impatient with him because he never seemed to have a serious thought in his head. The notion that he had something to accomplish in this life never occurred to him.

Ed was a spectator of life, not a participant. He was amused by almost everything he saw. He laughed about the whores he bedded down with. He'd say, "They're cows, Jim. Just about as sensitive as any old cow you ever saw, lying on their backs and chewing their cuds with a far away look in their eyes as if they're thinking about what they're gonna have for breakfast, and all the time I'm working like hell. They don't want nothing but your money. Lazy—that's all they are. It's easier to make a living on their backs with their legs spread than it is to keep house for a husband."

He made some snide remarks about the men who were trying to set up a temporary government in Cheyenne. They were men who had some talent for leadership and honestly desired law and order in Cheyenne and didn't want it to become another Julesburg. Most of them owned property, and they knew that their property would not increase in value unless we had law and order.

I took as much part in setting up a town government as I could. Not that I had any ambition to be a leader. It was just that I had most of my money invested in Cheyenne property, and I wanted that investment to grow. I was perfectly satisfied to let the older, wealthier men assume leadership, so I didn't say much, but I attended all the meetings and voted when the time came.

The end of steel was moving steadily toward Cheyenne from Julesburg and would reach Cheyenne sometime in the fall. When it did, the riff-raff that made Julesburg a hell on wheels would move in on us. The trick was to be ready for them when the time came.

The first step was a mass meeting of the citizens of Cheyenne on August 7. A committee was appointed to draw up a charter. This was presented the following day. Two days later we held an election in Beckwith's store, the polls being open from three P.M. to ten P.M. There were three hundred and fifty votes cast, and I'm guessing this was mighty close to every man in town who was eligible to vote. H. M. Hook, who owned the Pilgrim House Hotel and the Great Western Stables, was elected mayor.

We finally had a Provisional Government, just about a month after the first permanent settlers had arrived in Cheyenne. It was a little better than no government, but not much, because it didn't have any legal power.

We were a part of Dakota Territory. Maybe that was better than being part of Colorado, which none of us wanted, but the seat of government of Dakota Territory was at Yankton, which was one hell of a long ways from Cheyenne. It was quite a while before the people in Yankton got around to making our government official. I guess they figured we weren't really a part of them.

Anyhow, Ed would be working along beside me and then for no reason at all he'd start a tirade about the men who were on the town council and the mayor and the marshal.

"Just like a bunch of overgrown kids playing a game," he'd say. "Somebody's got to be big and these are the jaspers who want to be it. Passing laws about paying good money for a license to carry on a business. Hiring policemen. Building a jail. My God, Jim, don't they have enough to do just running their own business?"

He was completely unreasonable about the whole thing. At times I thought he was an anarchist at heart who didn't want any kind of government. Actually he just wanted to be free, without any restraint, I guess, though I couldn't see how any of the laws passed at the council hurt him. Finally I told him he'd lose his cattle, and horses too, if there weren't some rules that men had to live by.

He snorted and said he guessed that wouldn't be much loss—just a dozen skinny old cows and a few horses. "Oh, I know we've got to have some rules," he admitted, "but a Vigilance Committee can take care of it. What we've got is a bunch of men wanting to lord it over the rest of us and playing at having a government. It ain't no answer. Sooner or later we'll get an official government and then we'll have our problem licked. We don't have it licked now and there's no use fooling ourselves."

"The men we've elected strike me as being responsible," I said. "I don't know when we'll get that official government you're talking about, and neither do you. What I do know is we've got to have something right now. That Julesburg bunch will be here in another two, three months, and they'll take the town over if we don't have some government."

"Get a vigilance committee together," he snapped. "I tell you a few hangings will straighten things out in a hurry."

I didn't argue any more about it, but I didn't know why he was so set on a vigilance committee handling the outlaws. A few hangings would straighten things out, all right, but there wasn't any guarantee about who would be on the rope-end of the hangings. It might be me. The truth was I was just as scared of vigilantes as I was of the Julesburg riff-raff.

Outside of this one subject, Ed was a reasonable man and we got along fine. I couldn't figure out why he was so irrational about the Provisional Government. And it wasn't just with me. He had several arguments in the saloons, especially after he'd had a few drinks, and he'd usually wind up in a fight. I got so I didn't even ask him how he received the black eye he was sporting, or the bruised lip. I just assumed he'd been holding forth on the Provisional Government again and had been talking to the wrong man.

The more I thought about it, the less I understood it.

Ed was a man who couldn't or wouldn't discuss politics or foreign policy or religion or philosophy. As I said, he didn't seem to have a serious thought in his head except on this one subject. Finally I got so I quit talking about it, figuring that everybody had an irrational streak if you looked for it long enough. This question of the Provisional Government was Ed's.

Before August was over I had speculators looking me up and trying to buy some of my lots. I was offered five hundred dollars for them, and although that had looked like a good price when Ed had mentioned the figure to me the night I'd stayed with him, I didn't think it was so good now. I had a hunch property values were going higher and that I'd do better to sell at the top of the market, if I could guess when that was going to be. I didn't know, of course, but I was dead sure it hadn't topped out yet.

More people were moving to Cheyenne every day. They lived in some of the damnedest places a man could imagine, sometimes nothing more than dugouts or wagon boxes or the poorest kind of frame houses that were no better than shacks.

Somebody said, "The houses of Cheyenne are standing insults to every wind that blows." It was true enough for most houses, but mine was different. I could have sold it for a good profit even before it was finished, but I wouldn't listen to any offer—I was determined to live in it myself. I guess I figured that a man was judged by the house in which he lived, and for a time I was close to being the Number One Citizen of Cheyenne, if a man is judged by his house.

Fort D. A. Russell was established on the northwest outskirts of Cheyenne. It became one of the major forts throughout the long period of the Indian wars on the plains and was retained as a permanent post after the others were given up. Camp Carlin was also set up near Cheyenne, a supply depot for fourteen forts within a radius of four hundred miles. It was always a beehive of activity, with its thousands of horses and more than one hundred freight wagons and pack trains and the five hundred men or better who worked there.

All of this added to Cheyenne's business, helped boost property values, and made a bigger demand for good houses. I could have done well just building houses that fall and winter, but I was bound to put up a business structure. I owned several good business lots, and I could do the work myself. There was a constantly growing demand for such buildings, and now that I owned considerable town property, my credit seemed to be unlimited.

I knew I could rent my building as soon as it was finished. I didn't know exactly how much rent I could get, but I was certain that any reasonably good building would be excellent income property and I was determined to make it big while I could. I was, as my father had once suggested, making the big gamble and I saw no reason to cash in now with luck running my way.

Building materials were pouring into town, so there was a better supply than when I had started working on my house in July. Freight outfits were on the move all the time between Cheyenne and Julesburg to the east and Denver to the south.

One interesting thing happened that I didn't see because I was still working on my house and never left it until it was too dark to work. Then I usually went to the business part of town for my supper and a drink. I always fixed my own breakfast and dinner, but more often than not I went to a restaurant for supper. By the time I quit work every day I was too tired to fool with building a fire and cooking a meal.

I didn't hear about this incident until it was over, but apparently a bunch of Julesburg speculators, judging Cheyenne to have a better future than Julesburg, came to town and squatted on several town lots, refusing to accept the fact that the railroad company owned the lots and had the authority to sell them.

I suppose the Julesburg men had been breathing the lawless air of their hell-on-wheels town so long that they figured they'd find the same air in Cheyenne. Their argument that the site of Cheyenne was public domain and they had a right to squat on it was stupid, but they did their damnedest to make it stick. They refused to move off the lots, so the Union Pacific men sent to Fort D. A. Russell for help.

Before the squatters knew what had happened, troops arrived and drove the settlers south at gunpoint. There wasn't any argument or debate about the matter until the squatters were across Crow Creek. After that there was a palaver, but the settlers were not allowed to return until they recognized the right of the Union Pacific to sell the town lots.

This affair wasn't particularly important except that it pointed up the need for tough law enforcement. The soldiers were stationed at Fort D. A. Russell to help the Union Pacific, especially against the Indians, but it has always been a question in my mind which was worse, savages who fought to protect their homes or white outlaws who were supposed to be civilized. In any case, the soldiers couldn't always be depended on; the garrison was never a large one, and if the men were chasing Indians, there might not be enough soldiers left at the fort to put down a riot.

I kept my eyes peeled for Bully Bailey and his friends, but I didn't see or hear anything more of them. Maybe Bailey had seen me at the same time I saw him and he wasn't ready for a showdown with me yet. That didn't mean it wasn't coming sooner or later, but at least I had a peaceful month.

That is, my life was peaceful until I met Preacher Frank Rush. I suppose that in a town the size of Cheyenne I was bound to meet Frank sooner or later, but sometimes I think there are absolute laws of cause and effect that dictate a man's destiny, laws we don't understand any more than we understand gravity.

Anyhow, my meeting Frank Rush marked the beginning of a number of important events in my life, and my month of peace came to an end.

CHAPTER XII

I had seen Frank Rush on the street a number of times and I knew he worked for the Cheyenne and Western Freight Company, but that was all I did know about him. He was a big man, a good six-foot three-inches tall and broad across the shoulders, with the biggest hands I ever saw on any human being. I guessed he weighed two hundred and twenty-five pounds, maybe more.

These were obvious facts I had noticed about the man when I would pass him on the street as I was going downtown for supper. I assumed he lived near my house because he was always walking north toward it, passing me going in the opposite direction.

He was a man you couldn't help noticing and I had been curious about him. I hadn't the slightest notion that he was a preacher until one evening in September when I stepped into the Head Quarters Saloon for a drink.

I'd finished my house and had found a couple of carpenters who were willing to work for me. They had just arrived in Cheyenne and hadn't found anything better. I had started my business building and was working on it by myself when they stopped by and asked if I could use a couple of good men. I said I'd find out how good they were and for them to show up at seven o'clock the following morning.

They were pretty good carpenters at that—better than I had expected—so I hired them. After that we moved right along with the building. Before we even had the roof on, three men who were looking for store buildings jumped me about renting it.

The Head Quarters Saloon had moved out of the tent

and into a frame buildir . The owner even hired a brass band that banged away every evening in front of the saloon. It made more noise than music, but it did pull in a crowd.

On this particular evening I had had supper and decided I needed a drink before I went home. I guess I was lonesome. I hadn't seen Ed Burke for several days, and although I worked well with my two carpenters, they were both family men and we didn't spend any time together after we knocked off work. I was never a man to pick up superficial friends the way Ed Burke did, so I think it was the need to be with people more than the hunger for a drink that drove me into the Head Quarters that evening.

The place was jumping. Several soldiers from Fort D. A. Russell and Camp Carlin were there, a bunch of freighters who operated between Cheyenne and Fort Laramie were bellied up against the bar, some others were playing poker, and a dozen or more graders had come in from the railroad camps, so altogether it was a motley crew, as the fellow said.

Several girls who had rooms upstairs were circulating through the crowd trying to drum up business. One of them propositioned me the minute I came through the batwings, but I didn't want any part of her. She was too fat for me. I remembered reading in the newspaper a sardonic article on the entertainment offered the men in Cheyenne. The author mentioned the Teutonic girls that one of the dance-hall operators had imported from St. Louis. He said they danced and stunk by turns, and after looking at these girls I could believe it. I couldn't help thinking of Ed Burke calling them cows.

Anyhow, I'd been working too hard to get horny, so I told the girl no, got my drink at the bar, and found an empty table over next to the wall. I sat down, thinking I hadn't had a woman for a long time and wishing Rosy and Flossie Martin would show up here. I had expected them before this and had even considered writing to them.

There was a lot of racket in the Head Quarters, all the kinds of noise that's natural for a crowded saloon. Several

men at the bar were trying to sing, but their music was
worse than the brass band out in the street. Some of the
racket was just loud talk. Now and then a man would yell
in anger and a fight would start, but the bouncers soon got
it stopped. Several card games were going on, and once in
a while when the big noise died down you'd hear the click
of chips or the banging of a glass on a tabletop.

I sat there and nursed my drink and looked and
listened, and all the time I was thinking what a waste of
time and money it was. On the other hand, a good saloon
like the Head Quarters was a kind of club, and I'm sure it
served a worthwhile purpose for many of the men who
were there.

I didn't see Frank Rush when he came in. The first I
was aware of him being in the saloon was when he raised
his hands above his head and shouted, "I want to talk to
you men this evening."

He got everyone's attention, all right. This was the first
time I'd ever seen anything like this happen in a saloon.
He had a great, booming voice that could be heard above
the din. Men stopped talking and drinking and playing
cards and turned to look at a man who had a voice like
that and the temerity to go with it.

The silence wouldn't last long, of course, but he took
advantage of the few seconds that it did last. Again his
great voice boomed out. "I'm Frank Rush. Some of you
know where I work at the Cheyenne and Western Freight
Depot. I'm doing that temporarily to feed my wife and
myself until I can get a church started. What I want to
talk to you about tonight is the gospel of Jesus Christ and
the great love He has for all of you."

The men were still listening, most of them not knowing what to make of this. One of the poker players who
had been sitting at a table next to mine jumped up and
started plowing through the crowd toward Rush. I judged
he was a professional gambler by the way he was dressed.

"Jesus Christ," the gambler yelled. "Who the hell is
he?"

"If you listen you'll find out," Rush said. "Go back to
your table and sit down. I won't take long. You men have

been worshipping Satan twenty-four hours a day. You always have an attentive ear for his siren call to sin. Now I'm asking you to listen for ten minutes to the gospel of Jesus Christ."

"Nobody wants to listen to that stuff," the gambler yelled. "Get out of here, you gospel-spieling bastard. I've got a game going and, by God, I don't intend to let you stop it."

He was a big man, but not as big as Rush. He had his share of guts, though, or maybe he was running a bluff, thinking that any man who called himself a preacher wouldn't actually stand and fight. But Frank Rush didn't back up an inch. When the gambler was a step from him, he swung a fist at Rush's face. The preacher didn't duck or turn away. He simply blocked the blow with his big left arm and hit the gambler with his right.

I guess Rush must have caught the man right on the button. From where I sat, it looked as if that punch actually lifted the gambler clear off the floor and launched him into flight. Anyhow, he surely went up and back down. His head hit the bar. He bounced off and sprawled flat out on the floor.

There was a thudding sound when Rush hit him—I'd heard the same sound in dozens of butcher shops when a butcher is softening up a piece of tough meat—and then the hard crack of the gambler's skull hitting the bar. After he lay sprawled on the floor I heard a strange sighing sound come out of the crowd. I guess a lot of breath was being let out all at the same time.

Rush held up his hands again and said, "I apologize for the interruption, gentlemen, but there are times when a minister has to strike and strike hard to get the opportunity to tell the gospel story. Most of you have heard it, probably when you were children. Apparently you have forgotten it or you wouldn't be in a place like this, sinning and sending your immortal souls to hell as fast as you can."

I guess the gambler had a partner at the table. I saw him get to his feet. But he didn't look the part of a gambler. As a matter of fact, he was dressed like one of the freighters. There were four others at the table. This one had a fine, tall pile of chips in front of him, so I figured he was a capper, working hand in glove with the gambler who had tackled Rush. The two of them, playing together, could and probably had been taking the freighters to a cleaning.

As I say, this was guess work, but it was plain he was up to something, although I didn't know what it was for a few seconds. He took two steps away from the table as Rush started to talk. I was on my feet and edging toward him, still not certain what he was going to do. I wondered why nobody else was interfering or was even concerned about his intentions.

Maybe the other men at the table wanted to get on with the game and didn't care what happened to Rush, or maybe they just didn't want to have anything to do with another man's fight. It was Rush's trouble. That was plain enough, and it was equally plain he hadn't noticed the fellow.

Then the man drew his knife, and of course there wasn't any doubt then about what he was going to do. I got to him just as he brought his arm back to throw the knife. He was quite a distance from Rush but I'd seen men who could be as dangerous with a knife at that distance as a gunman would be with a Colt .45. Put a piece of steel like that into a man's belly and he was dead. I figured Frank Rush didn't deserve it.

I caught the man's arm just before he was ready to let go, and I twisted it hard. He yelped and cursed me and tried to struggle, but I didn't give him much chance. I jerked him back and forth a few times and pulled him around as he dropped the knife, then I slugged him in the soft part of the belly.

He bent forward, his mouth springing open as he struggled for breath. I hit him a second time on the chin. He staggered back, sprawled over a chair, upset a table, and landed on the floor with a great clatter, his arms flung out. I had knocked him cold.

Rush stopped talking long enough to see what the commotion was about. For a few seconds there was silence again, and then that long, drawn-out sigh. A freighter over by the bar laughed shakily and yelled, "Look at 'em, lyin' there like a couple o' sleepin' babes."

Most of the men laughed and another one, a soldier this time, called, "Go ahead, preacher. It won't hurt to listen to a sermon. I guess most of us ain't heard one for a long time."

They listened better than I thought they would. I listened, too, and I was disappointed but not surprised by what he said. Although I didn't time him, it seemed to me he spent one minute on the love of Jesus Christ and nine minutes on the misery and horror and suffering of a soul burning in hell. I was reminded of my mother's funeral sermon and all the other sermons I had heard a long time ago.

Rush finished with, "Next Sunday morning I am holding religious service in front of my tent on the corner of Ferguson and Twenty-third Streets. You are all invited. Thank you for your attention."

He came to my table then. I was surprised because I wasn't sure he had seen what had happened. He had, all right, because when he reached my table he held out his hand, saying, "I'm obliged. I'm Frank Rush, as I'm sure you know."

"Jim Glenn," I said as I rose and shook hands with him. "I admire the way you handled yourself."

"I can say the same about you." He looked at me for a moment and then shook his head. "How can one man thank another for saving his life?"

"You don't," I said. "Forget it. I just thought you deserved to be heard."

That seemed to trouble him. He said, still looking straight at me, "You mean the gospel needs to be heard."

"I don't think you preached the gospel," I said. "In fact, I admire you and your courage for coming in here, but I don't give a damn about your theology."

That troubled him, too. He moistened his lips, and then he said, "You sound like a man who has given a good deal of thought to the subject."

"I have," I said.

"I see." He moistened his lips again. "This is not the time or the place to discuss it, but someday we will. You are erecting a building on Sixteenth Street, aren't you?"

"Yes," I said.

"I'm going to quit my job with the freight company," he said. "I'm an excellent carpenter. Can you use me?"

That floored me. I guess I stared blankly at him, because I couldn't make much sense out of it. I asked, "Why do you want to work for me?"

"Perhaps you will pay more than the freight company," he said. "Perhaps I like carpentry work better than loading and unloading freight wagons."

"There are a dozen men in Cheyenne who would give a good carpenter work," I said. "I don't understand why you've been working for a freight company until now and then decide you want to work for me."

He looked straight at me. He said without flinching or looking away or doing anything that would detract from the appearance of honesty that I'm sure he wanted to give, "Is it something you have to understand? Isn't it enough that I want to work for you? If you find that I'm not an excellent carpenter, fire me tomorrow night. My day's work won't cost you a cent if you don't like what I do."

"Fair enough," I said.

"I'll be a little late because I'll have to go to the freight depot and tell them I'm quitting," he said, "but I'll be with you before noon."

He was, and it didn't take me all day to realize he was as good as he said he was. I'll have to admit he was a better carpenter than I was. I didn't realize for quite a while that this was his way of thanking me for saving his life.

CHAPTER XIII

We made excellent progress with the building the following week. I could thank Frank Rush for that. He was a good man to have on my payroll any way I looked at him. He wasn't the preacher type. That is, he never tried to convert any of us and he didn't have that pious, holier-than-thou attitude of authority I had come to associate with preachers I had known.

One afternoon a carriage drove by that was filled with whores. They ignored us as well as all the other men who were on the street, so obviously they weren't trying to work up any new business. Apparently they were just out for some fresh air.

About an hour later the carriage returned. You never saw more sedate and dignified women in your life than this bunch. One thing was sure: they weren't going to get themselves arrested and kicked out of town for creating a disturbance.

The two carpenters who had been working for me before I hired Frank stared at the women both times they passed and made some lewd remarks. Frank stared, too, but there was nothing licentious in his expression. You can tell a good deal about a man's attitude toward women, good or bad, in how he looks at them and what he says when he looks. I guess I wasn't surprised when I saw an expression of sympathy on his face.

Frank didn't say anything when they drove by the first time, but when they returned, he said in a low voice, "Poor things," and turned back to the board he had been sawing.

After that I had a lot more respect for Frank than I'd

had before, but in a different way. I didn't agree with him that they were poor things. I'd had enough experience with whores to believe that most of them were like Rosy and Flossie Martin in at least one way: they preferred their profession to working for a living. Frank was probably as ignorant as hell about women like that, but he didn't condemn them. The way I saw it, he deserved a lot of credit for that.

After we quit working that evening, he said, "Jim, I want you to meet my wife Nancy. She asked me to have you come out for supper tomorrow evening."

I didn't want to go. I knew they lived in a tent and that it would be hard for a woman to cook a meal for company under such primitive conditions. Too, I just wasn't interested in meeting a married woman. Since she was a preacher's wife, I figured she'd be a dull, mousey woman who would be about as interesting as an Indian squaw whose conversational ability was limited to "ugh" and "how."

I couldn't turn him down, though, so I said I'd come. The next night I went home and washed up, changed to a clean shirt and walked to the Rush tent. I'd been past there a number of times and knew where it was, but I hadn't seen Mrs. Rush until that evening. I was amazed when I met her, astonished, even shocked. She was about as far removed from being the dull, mousey woman I had expected as a woman could be.

She gave me a good smile when Frank introduced us. By that I mean an honest, friendly smile. It wasn't the perfunctory smile that some women can put on and off as the situation demands just as they put on and take off a pair of shoes. It wasn't a phony, too-sweet smile, either. I'd seen plenty of times when a woman knew this was the reaction that was expected of her, so she performed to satisfy the expectation. With Nancy Rush it struck me that she smiled because she meant it and the smile came right from her heart.

"Frank has talked about you so much, Mr. Glenn," she said. "I know he's thanked you for saving his life, but I want to add my thanks, too."

She offered her hand and I took it, and found myself as tongue-tied as a bashful boy meeting a pretty girl. I was disgusted with myself, but I managed to mutter something about being glad that I'd been able to do it.

"Supper will be ready in a few minutes," she said, and turned back to the Dutch ovens and the coffee pot she had on the fire.

To cover my embarrassment I got my pipe out and filled it. When I glanced at Frank I thought he seemed amused. He said, "You see why I'm proud of her."

"Yeah, I sure do," I said.

I told myself that if I could find a woman like that I'd marry her tomorrow. I also thought that Frank Rush was a damned fool for making her live in a tent. Fall would be here soon and the nights would be cold, and then winter would be along.

Although I hadn't spent a winter in Cheyenne, I knew it could get almighty cold. With the kind of wind we often had, it would simply be unbearable in a tent. So far Frank had shown no intention of trying to find a house in which to spend the winter. At least he'd never mentioned it to me.

I lighted my pipe and puffed on it, my eyes on Nancy Rush. It's hard to describe her in words because I had a feeling about her that didn't come from anything that stemmed from my five senses. Oh, there were physical features I could mention. She was a pretty woman with strong physical features, dark brown eyes, and black, black hair. She was quite tall and had an excellent figure, with high, proud breasts and a slim waist and what must have been perfectly proportioned legs—judging from the bit of ankle that showed every so often. She looked a good deal younger than Frank, maybe by as much as ten years. I guessed she was about twenty-five.

Presently she handed me a plate and tin cup. There was humor in her dark eyes as she said, "I'm going to ask you to help yourself, Mr. Glenn, as soon as Frank asks the blessing. You'll find stew in one of the Dutch ovens and biscuits in the other. Coffee, of course, in the coffee pot. Don't be bashful. We're short on variety, but long on quantity."

I took the plate and cup, unable to keep my eyes off her. I saw the redness of her lips against her white teeth, but again, it wasn't her physical appearance that hit me so hard. I kept trying to pinpoint it, and then I had a hint of what it was. I sensed a maturity about her that went beyond her years; I noted the self-possessed curve of her lips, which I had never seen in another woman, but then I had never met another woman like Nancy Rush.

I guess Frank was as hungry as I was. Anyhow, his grace was a short one. Then he lifted the lids from the Dutch ovens and I helped myself. The stew had plenty of meat and several vegetables. I took a biscuit and poured my coffee and picked up my silverware from the pile she had placed on a napkin beside the fire.

The stew was excellent, the biscuits white and flaky, the coffee strong and black the way I liked it. As I ate, I kept glancing at Nancy, still trying to put into thought-words the feeling I'd had about her the moment I'd seen her. Gradually I worked out more than the hints I'd had of her maturity and self-possession.

She was a slim and shining girl who loved life. I thought she should have found it exciting—then I was stopped again because I suddenly had a very strong feeling she didn't. I don't know why this feeling came to me. It may have been my imagination, but I felt she was disappointed, perhaps frustrated.

We ate almost in silence, with only an occasional exchange of conversation. When I glanced at Frank, I had a notion he was quite satisfied with himself and with Nancy and with his life in general. I turned this over in my mind, but I failed to find any good answer as to why he would be satisfied and Nancy wouldn't. Again I realized that this could be my imagination, but I didn't think so. I had learned a long time ago to trust these hunches or feelings that came to me about people.

Nancy was an exciting woman, and it didn't make sense, if I was right, that she was unable to find excitement in her life with Frank. He was a hell of a good man. He should have been a good husband. I saw lines of discontent around her eyes and I became more certain I was right about them as the minutes passed.

When we finished eating, Frank rose from where he had hunkered beside the fire and dropped his plate and cup and silverware into the wreck pan. He said, "I've got a call to make, Jim. You'll have to excuse me, but I hope you'll stay awhile and talk to Nancy. She's alone all day and she doesn't have any friends here, so she gets pretty lonesome."

"Sure, I'll stay," I said. "I've got nothing to go home to."

After he left, I knocked my pipe out against my heel and filled it again. Nancy rose and poured water into a pan that was set on the fire, then glanced at me and smiled. She said, "I suppose you're wondering why Frank left to make a call when he invited you here for supper. Well, it's a man who has come to Christian service every Sunday since we've been in Cheyenne. His name is Ole Svensen. He's very sick. He was so sick last Sunday I didn't think he'd be able to stay here for all the service."

She shrugged her shoulders, her face turning grave. "If it wasn't Ole, it would be someone else. Frank is calling on somebody every evening. He has to call in the evening because he doesn't have time during the day." She laughed and added, "I guess you know that."

"I was wondering about something else," I said. "Why does Frank go off and leave a pretty wife with a man he doesn't know very well?"

"He knows you, or thinks he does," she said, "and he would never think of me doing anything wrong. You see, he always expects people that he loves or likes to do the right thing."

I had learned in the few days I had worked with him that he was a naive man in many ways, and this seemed additional proof of his naiveté. I didn't say that to Nancy, but it was plain that she thought the same of him. She washed the dishes and I sat puffing my pipe and wondering what was safe to talk about.

"You have a fine house," she said. "I've walked past

your place several times. I get so tired of nothing to do and just sitting here in a tent under a hot sun all day."

"I'm enjoying my house," I said, and then I asked the question that had been in my mind ever since I'd hired Frank. I just hadn't had the courage to ask it before. "How do Frank's religious services go? Does he have a crowd?"

She glanced at me, grimacing. "Would you say half a dozen people make a crowd? No, he will not get a crowd until he has a church building. He's saving every cent he can to put one up."

"Where?"

"On this lot," she answered. "It's the only property he owns."

"I thought he'd build a house on this lot," I said. "One to live in."

"Oh no." She smiled briefly. "A house to live in is not important. A church building where he can preach the Word is. He says he can't go on trying to preach in saloons where he interrupts men's sinning. They hate him when he does. He can't get people to come and stand in all kinds of weather, either."

"What will you live in?" I asked.

"The tent. He'll move it to the back of the lot when he starts his church building."

I couldn't believe it. I said, "You can't live in a tent all winter. It gets cold here. Awful cold."

"I know," she said, "but Frank doesn't. He won't know until the cold weather gets here."

I took my pipe out of my mouth and let it cool in my hand. Knowing that Frank Rush was impractical was one thing, but hearing it from his wife this way was something else. The strange part of it was that he was such a good craftsman, being practical in the material way of handling a saw and hammer. But on other matters in which he had to look ahead, he seemed just plain stupid.

"The end of steel will be here before long," I said, "and Cheyenne will be another hell on wheels. Aside from the cold weather, it wouldn't be safe for a woman to live in a tent. I don't know whether they'll get the rails past

Cheyenne and over Sherman Hill by this winter or not, but if they don't, this town will be jumping. You simply won't have a house to live in."

"I've thought of that," she said, "but Frank hasn't."

"Then tell him," I said. I guess I said it rather loud. I was out of patience with both her and Frank. Even a squirrel had enough sense to get ready for winter. "My God, tell him. If he can't look ahead by himself, you've got to do it for him."

She picked up her pan of dishwater and walked to the rear of the tent and threw it out. She came back, put the pan down, and wiped her hands on her apron. She said, "Mr. Glenn—"

"Jim," I interrupted.

She nodded. "Jim, there is one thing about my husband you might as well know right now. He never believes anything I tell him. I don't think he'd believe anything you would tell him. He has to see things for himself, and by that time it's usually too late. For instance, I told him it was dangerous to go into a saloon and preach, but he didn't believe it until that man tried to kill him with a knife—the one you stopped."

I put my pipe into my pocket and rose. She stood motionless, looking at me. I walked around the fire to her, wanting to take her hands, wanting to put my arms around her and tell her that her life could be filled with joy and pleasure and laughter, that it was what she deserved and she was being wasted on Frank Rush.

I didn't do any of those things. I stopped three feet from her and said, "Nancy, you shouldn't be living like this even in good weather. Why couldn't you and Frank move in with me? I have two bedrooms. You could keep house for me in exchange for a decent place to live. I wouldn't charge you any rent."

Most of the time since I had first arrived she had looked at me squarely if she looked at me at all, but now for the first time she lowered her eyes and shook her head. She said, in a tone filled with misery, "You know I couldn't do that and you know why."

"I'd better go home," I said abruptly. "Thank you for the good supper."

"You're welcome," she said. "I hope you'll come again."

I walked away quickly, not trusting myself to stay longer or to say anything else to her. I did not understand what had happened, but I knew very well that for the first time in my life I had met a woman I wanted. I also felt she wanted me. That was as far as it would go—just the wanting, never the fulfillment.

I saw an empty tin can in front of me. I kicked it halfway down the block, so far that I lost sight of it in the twilight. This was one hell of a note, I told myself. Well, one thing was sure. Frank Rush would never know how I felt about his wife.

CHAPTER XIV

Every day for several weeks I intended to say something to Frank about building a house for him and Nancy. I knew better than to suggest that they move into my house. I did indeed know what Nancy had meant when she'd said she could not do that and I knew why.

There wasn't any hope, either, that I could persuade Frank to build a house instead of a church, so I didn't try. The only plan that might work was for me to build a house on one of my lots and rent it to them. I would have made it rent free, but I suspected he had too much pride for that kind of arrangement.

They say hell is paved with good intentions. I guess it is. Anyhow, I just never got around to saying anything to Frank about a house. I had plenty of chances to talk to him and I wanted to, but I never did. Then, when my building was almost finished, something happened that took my mind off Frank and Nancy Rush.

I was standing in the doorway of the building looking around and wondering what I should do with it when Ed Burke stopped by. He had worked for me several afternoons and knew Frank and my other two carpenters, but it had been a week or so since I'd seen him. I thought he probably had not come to town during that week.

"Howdy, Ed," I said. "Haven't seen you for a while. I guess you've been busy."

He said, "Naw, I've been out of town. I mean, out of the country. I never work enough to be busy. I ain't like some jaspers I know who are working themselves into an early grave."

I was exasperated with him. I'd never had much use for

lazy men, and the better I got acquainted with Ed, the more I realized he was just plain lazy. This was true as far as his ranch work was concerned, certainly, although when he worked for me, he put out all the effort I could ask of a man.

"Oh hell," I said. "I don't work hard enough to end up in an early grave. On the other hand, there is an old saying about no work and all play makes Jack a dull boy."

He gave a short laugh. "Then I sure am a dull boy." He motioned to the interior of the building. "What are you fixing to do with this place."

"I haven't made up my mind," I said. "I've had plenty of opportunities to rent it, but I keep putting it off. It's big enough for a general store, only I've been thinking it would be better to run a partition down the middle and make two big rooms. I'd get more rent that way. That's why we put two doors on the street and two on the alley. I could rent half of it for a restaurant and the other half for a saddle shop or something of the sort."

He nodded in an absent-minded way and shifted his weight from one foot to the other. I don't think he heard what I said. He was nervous and I wondered why. Most of the time he acted as if he didn't give a damn about anything except getting his next meal or his next drink, but something was working on him now and I was curious about it.

He took a cigar out of his pocket and stepped back out of the doorway and stood with his back to the wall. He tried to light the cigar, but a sudden gust of wind sent a cloud of dust down the street and put his match out. He swore and moved past me into the building. This time he got his cigar going and flipped his match into the street.

"You know a tough bird named Bully Bailey?" he asked, trying to sound as if the question wasn't important, and failing.

That startled me, because I almost had succeeded in putting Bailey out of my mind. For a while after I'd seen him and his friends in Cheyenne I'd been plenty scared, Bully Bailey being the kind of man he was, but after all

this time I'd decided that the three men must have left the
country. Now, judging from Ed's expression and his tone
of voice, I guessed they were back in town.

"Yeah, I'm sorry to say I know him," I said. "Likewise
a couple of buckos who travel with him."

"They're still with him," he said. "They don't amount
to much, but Bailey's a bad actor. Take my word for it. I
know."

"So do I," I said. "He's a coward, but some of the most
dangerous men I ever ran into are cowards."

"Right," he agreed. "Well, it seems that all three came
to town about the time you did and then left for
Julesburg, but it got too hot for 'em there so they came
back to Cheyenne. Bailey's been drinking, and when he
gets enough coffin varnish in him, he gets a loose mouth.
Now he's been making some tall threats about you, saying
he's gonna stop your clock for good."

"I'm not surprised," I said. "I'm going to have to kill
the bastard. I saw him and his friends here, but when I
started looking for them, they had disappeared. I'd better
start looking again."

"I'll help you," he said.

"Oh no you don't," I said. "This is my fight and I'll
handle it."

He chewed on his cigar awhile, then he said grudgingly,
"All right, go ahead and get yourself killed of bravery.
That's what you'll do."

"No I won't," I said. "I never saw the day I couldn't
handle Bully Bailey and his friends."

"If you get a chance to see 'em," he snapped. "By God,
Jim, you are the mule-headedest man I ever seen. I don't
know why I waste my time worrying about you."

"Neither do I," I said. "I'll go get my supper. Afterwards I'll start looking for Bailey." Then I thought of
something and asked, "How come he's called Bully here
in Cheyenne? He always hated the name, but it got
fastened onto him in Black Hawk and he couldn't get rid
of it."

"It wasn't his idea. Some men besides you had met up
with him before he got here and knew what he'd been

called, so they pinned the name on him again. Fits him, too. I've met a lot of men I thought were tough birds, and liked them, but this damned Bailey ain't really tough. He's an animal." Ed shook his head. "No, I can't say that. It insults the animals. He's just plain mean."

"He is that," I said, remembering what he'd done to Rosy Martin. "Well, I'll go find some place to eat."

"Say, there's a new restaurant in town," he said. "It's called the Cheyenne Eatery. It's in a tent a block west of here, on Ferguson between 16th and 17th. Have you tried it?"

"No, I haven't," I said.

"It belongs to a young woman who just got to town. I claim she's the best cook in Cheyenne. Trouble is she's trying to run the place by herself, so the service is slow when she's crowded, but a meal is worth waiting for. Her name's Cherry Owens. A right purty filly, too."

"I'll try it," I said.

"You do that," he said. "If you don't get a good meal, I'll pay for it."

"Fair enough," I said.

He started off down the street, walking north. I wondered what he was up to. I stood there several minutes watching him until he disappeared. The saloons weren't in that direction. None of the brothels were, either, so I was curious about where he was going.

Finally I shrugged my shoulders and decided to hell with it. Anything he did was his business and none of mine. I liked him and enjoyed his company, but he didn't have the same goals I did and I often wondered what we saw in each other. Sometimes I wasn't sure what my goals were, but I had some, and more often than not I didn't think Ed had any.

I walked to the corner and turned toward Ferguson Street. I found the Cheyenne Eatery without any trouble. There were just two cowboys sitting at the counter, so the service wasn't as slow as it would have been if the place had been crowded.

Ed was right about the girl on two counts. She was a pretty filly, about twenty, I guessed, small, just about big enough to be called Watch Fob or Trinket or some such name, and she could move. She went on the dead run after she took my order and again when she brought my plate of food. I thought she'd wear herself out in a week at this rate, if she had to go on being both waitress and cook.

She was blond, and her eyes, a bright blue, had a way of taking a person in with one sweeping glance. Her hair was gold-yellow with touches of red in it. She had brushed it back from her forehead and tied it in a bun at the back of her head. It was a little too prim, I thought, and decided she would have been more attractive if she had used a little curl.

As for the food, Ed was dead right on that, too. I had never tasted a better steak in my life, the biscuits were light, the custard pie excellent, and the coffee wonderful. When I had finished eating, I sat there with my second cup of coffee, looking at her. The two cowboys had finished and left, so for the moment I was alone with her.

I guess she sensed I was staring at her. She had moved to the front of the tent and was standing there looking out into the street. Suddenly she turned and came back to where I was sitting. I was a little uneasy, thinking she might chew me out for staring rudely at her.

"Do I pass inspection?" she asked, smiling.

At least she wasn't irritated because I'd been staring at her, but I guess my face got red anyway. It felt hot enough to be red. I managed a wink and a weak grin.

"You certainly do," I said, "but I was sitting here worrying about you. You can't handle both sides of this business. You'll die of exhaustion."

She curtsied. "Thank you for your concern, Mr. . . ."

"Glenn," I told her. "Jim Glenn. We don't have many women like you in Cheyenne, so we treasure the few we do have."

She had been sarcastic, but now I realized she had turned serious. She studied me for a moment, chewing on her lower lip thoughtfully. Finally she said, "Maybe I misjudged you. I half believe you meant what you just said."

"Of course I meant it," I said testily. "And another thing. I don't know where you came from, but you can't run a restaurant in a tent in Cheyenne after cold weather gets here."

"I know that," she admitted. "I come from Denver, so I don't have any illusions about Cheyenne being in the tropics during the winter." She shook her head. "You see, I'm not in any position to be choosey. I couldn't find a building when I got here, not one that I could afford to rent."

She motioned toward the rear. "I have a small tent back there which I use for my living quarters. I can make out fine for another month or so. Buildings are going up all the time. I'll find something by then."

"I have a building we're just finishing," I said. "I can fix it up for you in a day or two. We'd just have to run a partition down the middle."

Her eyes narrowed and her mouth firmed out and I could feel the anger begin to build and then the outrage that took possession of her. "Mr. Glenn," she said, tight-lipped, "I know how men operate. You might as well get it through your head right now that I can't be bought by the best building in Cheyenne. I'll pay my way as I go, or I won't go. I'm not looking for any easy way."

I sat there looking at her and wondering what I'd said that had made her so mad. I guess it took me about thirty seconds to understand what she was saying. When I did, I got mad. I slid off the stool and tossed a four-bit piece onto the counter, then I walked out of the tent, leaving half a cup of coffee. I was tempted to go back and tell her to go to hell, that I wasn't trying to buy her as she seemed to think. If I wanted to buy a woman, I knew where to go.

I stopped and turned around, and then it struck me that she had been close to crying when she'd said all that about not being bought. She was young and pretty, and of course I had no way of knowing how many men had tried to take advantage of her. It was plain enough that to her all men were alike. Maybe that had been her experience with men.

After thinking about it a moment, I turned around and walked away. I didn't see any sense in begging her. If she thought this about me, she'd just have to think it. I doubt that any defense on my part would change her.

I walked along Ferguson to the nearest saloon, realizing that I should have sympathy for her. I knew a good deal about men, and I'll have to admit that many of them are exactly the kind she took me for.

It was dark when I began looking for Bully Bailey and his friends. I tried every saloon in town, but they didn't seem to be in Cheyenne. I didn't look in any of the brothels, thinking there wasn't any use. They'd be in bed with some of the whores if that was where they were. All I could do was to wait and try again tomorrow night. They were the kind of men who would show up in one of the saloons sooner or later if they were in town.

One thing did bother me. It seemed to me that I kept running into Ed Burke all evening. Or if it wasn't Ed, it was Frank Rush. I wasn't surprised at seeing Ed, because when he was in town he wandered around aimlessly from one saloon to another, but I knew Frank didn't drink and that he had given up trying to preach in the saloons, so I did wonder about that. I didn't ask either one what they were up to. It was their business. Certainly it wasn't any of mine.

By ten o'clock I knew I had to give up. I started north on Ferguson Street, tempted to stop at the Cheyenne Eatery and get a cup of coffee. If Cherry Owens gave me a chance, I'd tell her there was no price tag on my building as she had assumed.

I didn't get there. Not right then anyhow. Two men jumped me and a third one came at me from somewhere behind me. I guess it was that way, though I hadn't known I was being followed.

I didn't have any chance. I caught one of them with a good punch to the jaw that knocked him down. I kicked another one in the belly and drove the wind out of him, but the third one slammed a fist into my throat. I caught a glimpse of his face just as he hit me and saw he was Bully Bailey.

I was on my knees trying to breathe, but it seemed my throat had closed up and I was in the horrible, helpless condition of being unable to suck any air into my lungs. I felt as if my throat had collapsed or that my windpipe had been cut.

From a great distance I heard Bailey's voice: "I'm gonna kill the bastard."

One of them kicked me in the ribs. Pain knifed all through my belly, but I was breathing again. I started to get back on my feet when the roof caved in. I guess one of them slugged me with a gun barrel. Or maybe picked up a club. I didn't see him hit me, so I'll never know what he used. All I know is that the whole world turned black and I wasn't aware of anything until I came to in Cherry Owens' tent.

CHAPTER XV

I was unconscious for a long time, an hour or more from what Ed and Frank told me later. When I came to I was aware first of a whacking headache that I thought was going to split my skull any second, and at almost the same time I was aware that my chest hurt like hell every time I took a breath.

Later, when I was able to focus my eyes, I made out Frank's face. He kept shaking his head and saying something about wishing that Ed would hurry and get back with the doctor. Cherry Owens was kneeling beside me. She had a bucket of water next to the bed, which was just a mattress and a couple of blankets spread on the ground. She would wet a cloth in the water, then squeeze it as dry as she could, and finally lay it across my forehead. After a minute or two she would lift the cloth and repeat the process.

"The bleeding's stopped," she said. "I thought it would. The cut isn't deep, but I'm worried about that knot on his head. I'm positive he has a concussion."

"And some broken ribs to boot," Frank said worriedly. "Where is that doctor?"

"Don't expect the doctor to do any good," Cherry said. "All anybody can do is keep him quiet."

I looked at Cherry and then at Frank. I managed to say, "I'm all right."

I heard Frank's great sigh of relief. "Well, doggone it, Jim," he said. "That's not exactly your normal voice, but I'm sure glad to hear it."

Cherry smiled and sat back, her hands on her knees.

"It is indeed good to hear your voice," she said. "We wondered if you were ever going to come around."

I guessed I was in the tent that was her living quarters. I said, "I'm in your bed and it's time you were using it. Get me home, Frank."

"You can't be moved," Cherry said sternly. "I've had a little nursing experience, and one of the first things I learned was that anyone with a concussion has to be kept absolutely still, so don't roll around or move any more than you have to. You are staying here."

"Where will you be?" I asked.

"Right here beside you," she said. "I've got other blankets. I don't mind not sleeping on the mattress. The ground is just about as soft."

"Aren't you afraid to sleep in the same tent with me?" I asked.

She laughed softly. "I've had some experience with men," she said. "That's how I had my stint of nursing, if you could call it that. No, I'm not afraid to sleep here. Your spirit is probably willing, but your flesh will be weak for quite a while."

Frank was grinning from ear to ear, but I didn't see anything funny about what was being said. The girl was a fool; she didn't know men as well as she thought she did. But when I started to raise up on one elbow to tell her a thing or two that she didn't know about men, I could have sworn my head was splitting open, and I fell back on the pillow.

"You see?" Cherry said triumphantly. "You're going to be right there on that mattress for a while."

Ed came into the tent with a short pot-bellied man who carried a black bag and smelled of whisky. I told myself that every frontier doctor must be a drunkard. Maybe that was the only kind who came west, and their drinking was what had made them leave their home practice. I figured this one would want to operate right away, but he didn't.

He set his black bag on the ground, dropped to his knees and felt of my head. He said, "Hmmmm, he's got a concussion." Then he felt of my ribs, pressing too hard on my left side, and in spite of myself I let out a yip of pain and clenched my teeth. He said, "Hmmmm, he's got some broken ribs, too."

He rose, picked up his black bag, and turned to Ed. "Keep him here for at least twenty-four hours. Feed him lightly. Try to keep him from being active for a week or more. It'll be a month before he gets over this. That will be five dollars."

"You old fraud," Cherry cried. "You didn't tell us a thing we didn't know."

The doctor nodded amiably. "Certainly I'm an old fraud, my dear, but I have no idea how you found out. It wasn't my idea coming, you know. Your friend here used the muzzle of his gun as a gentle persuader to induce me to leave a very interesting poker game. Besides, I never suspected you would know so much about medicine. Now the five dollars please."

Ed handed him a five-dollar gold piece. He said, "Thank you," and left the tent.

"That kind of doctor makes me so mad," Cherry said.

"We don't have much choice of doctors," Ed said. "I guess I wasted my five dollars, but maybe it will help to keep Mr. Jim Glenn flat on his back where he belongs."

"For twenty-four hours," I said. "No more. Tomorrow evening you're taking me home."

"Well now," Ed said, "if I had a purty nurse like this one, I wouldn't want to leave."

"I've got to," I said, "because if I stay here I might get better, and if I did, the flesh might get as willing as the spirit."

"All right," Cherry said. "You'd better go tomorrow evening. Bring a team and wagon, Mr. Burke. He won't be walking for a few more days."

"The offer of my building had no strings attached to it," I said. "I'd still like to rent it to you."

"Very well, I'll accept your offer," she said. "I'm sorry I said what I did, but the words were out before I realized I should have explored your offer before saying anything. The only excuse I have is that I've lived my life among men since I was fourteen. I know exactly what most men are like. My mistake was not finding out that you are different from most men."

"Oh, he's different from other men," Ed said maliciously. "He's so different you can trust him any time and under any circumstances."

"Shut up, Ed," I said. "That's not true and it's why you're getting me out of here tomorrow evening. Frank, start putting a partition down the middle of our building and fix her half of it the way she wants it."

"With living quarters in the back?" she asked.

"Of course."

"Thank you, Mr. Glenn," she said. "Thank you very much."

I saw she was close to tears. Life had been hard on her, I thought. I wasn't sure she'd had all the experiences with men she claimed she had, but any young woman as attractive as she was who had made her own way in boom towns like Cheyenne and had kept herself decent was to be admired. I did admire Cherry Owens.

I didn't want to embarrass her any more than I had, so I looked at Ed and asked, "What happened? I thought Bully Bailey was going to kill me. He said he was."

"He was trying to when we got there," Ed said.

"Just how did you happen to get there?" I asked.

"I was worried about you," he said. "You're so damned stubborn. The way Bailey had been running off at the mouth I figured he was gonna try tonight, which same he did. He was purty drunk, and when a man like Bailey gets drunk, he gets mean, so I went after Frank as soon as I left you." He nodded at Frank. "You tell him what happened."

"Ed was pretty excited when he got to my tent," Frank said. "He told me you'd be dead before midnight if we didn't keep an eye on you. You might be dead anyway, Bailey being the kind of man he is, and you being stubborn and confident the way you are, so I came downtown with him and we tried to follow you as much as we could without being too evident about it. When you started home, we trailed along, but we were too far back to keep them from jumping you. We got there as soon as we could and gave them a little trouble. They got away, though."

"We gave 'em more'n a little trouble," Ed said, grinning. "You should of seen Frank. He was a one-man gang. He didn't need me. He went after 'em like a bull buffalo, banging heads together and throwing 'em around like rag dolls. At first we thought they had killed you. We packed you over here to Miss Owens' place and she looked you over and said everything the damned doc said."

My head still hurt as much as ever and I wasn't taking any deep breaths. I closed my eyes. I was just too tired to keep them open and I hurt too much to keep on talking. All I could think of was that Ed Burke and Frank Rush had saved my life. Maybe I was too stubborn and self-confident, but I had never depended on other men for help and I didn't figure on starting now.

As soon as I was able, I decided, I'd hunt Bailey and his friends down and kill them, but they'd probably be hard to find, and I'd probably be in the same position I had been in tonight, knowing they were around and that they were a daily menace to my life but still not able to find them.

"Thank you," I said. "Thank all of you. You saved my life. I won't forget it."

"Glad to have had the fun," Frank said. "I'll get back to my tent. We'll start work on that partition in the morning."

Frank left, but Ed stayed, staring down at me and scowling as if he couldn't make up his mind about something. Finally he said, "I think I ought to stay here with you, Jim. That bunch might be back."

"Not Bailey," I said. "Not if he took the beating you said he did. They're all out of town and ten miles away by now."

"I don't want you staying here," Cherry said sharply to Ed. "I can look after Mr. Glenn. Tomorrow evening you come with a team and wagon and take him home. Until then he's my responsibility."

Ed threw up his hands. "All right," he said. "I'll be here tomorrow evening."

After Ed left, Cherry opened one of her boxes and took out a pillow and some blankets and made her bed on the other side of the tent. She started to blow the lamp out, then drew back and looked at me. She asked, "Can I do anything for you?"

"Not tonight," I said.

"Time is a great healer," she said. "If you need anything during the night, wake me up."

She blew out the lamp, and a few minutes later I heard the steady rhythm of her breathing. She was right, of course. Only time would heal my ribs and head. Here I was, for the first time in my life, sleeping a few feet from a very attractive young woman, and I couldn't even get off the mattress.

The night was a very long one and I began to think the sun had forgotten to come up. I had never been sicker in my life. Maybe I was feverish, but sometime during the night I decided I was going to marry Cherry Owens. When it was daylight, she stirred and turned on her side, her eyes coming open.

When I saw she was awake, I asked, "Would you bring me a drink of water?"

"Of course," she said.

She got up and filled a dipper with water and brought it to me. She slipped a hand under my head, lifted it and held the dipper to my mouth. I drank greedily, for my throat was dry, my lips cracked. When she eased my head back to the pillow I said, "I'm going to marry you, Cherry."

"What?"

"You heard what I said, but I'll repeat it. I'm going to marry you."

"I thought that was what you said." She was on her knees beside me. Now she leaned forward and looked at me closely in the thin light. "You're feverish."

"Of course I am, but I'll get over it, and when I do, I'll marry you."

"Thank you for your decision, Mr. Glenn," she said, "but don't you think a girl ought to be asked?"

"Oh, I'll ask you," I said. "I just thought that now ought to be a good time to tell you."

"Do you always approach marriage like this?" she asked.

"I never have before," I answered, "but you're the first girl I ever saw that I wanted to marry."

"I'm complimented," she said, "but I'm not convinced it would be the proper thing to do. Maybe you think you compromised me by sleeping in my tent with me and you owe it to me to marry me."

"No," I said. "I never worry about things like that. It's just that I think you'd be a good wife for me and I'm sure I'd be the right husband for you. After we were married awhile you'd love me and I'd love you."

She laughed. "Oh, you are a romantic one, Mr. Glenn," she said. "I've always wanted a romantic proposal, and this is certainly one I'll remember."

I closed my eyes, thinking I'd boogered everything up, but feverish or not, I'd never meant anything more in my life than what I'd just said. When I opened my eyes a few minutes later, she was gone.

CHAPTER XVI

The twenty-four hours I spent on Cherry Owens' bed taught me one thing which I guess I had known, but only in an intellectual way, and that's entirely different from knowing something down in the bottom of my belly where the great compelling emotions are born. Time, I discovered, is entirely relative.

I had enjoyed the weeks I'd been in Cheyenne, enjoyed them more than I had ever enjoyed any other equal period in my life, so the days had passed quickly, each one of them equal to about one minute of the night and day I spent in Cherry's tent.

My head didn't stop pounding for one instant, and my chest hurt with every breath I took. If I forgot and took anything but the lightest of breaths, the agony was killing. All I could think of was, "God, get this over for me one way or another."

Cherry was in and out of the tent all day. She closed her restaurant, pinning a note on the flap of the big tent saying she would be closed until she reopened in bigger quarters, and gave her new address on Eddy Street. I told her she didn't need to do it on my account. She said she wasn't, that she just needed the rest. I decided it was a lie, but I didn't feel like arguing.

She didn't bother me by making me talk to her, and I appreciated that. It made me think more of her than ever. A silent woman, I thought, was a rare person. She fixed some chicken broth for me and brought a bowl to me in the morning and again at noon, but I had trouble swallowing even something as innocuous as chicken broth.

That evening I told Cherry not to bring me any of

the broth, that I couldn't eat anything. Not long after full dark I heard a wagon and knew they had come to take me home. I didn't want to go, simply because I hurt like hell if I moved, so of course it would be hell compounded when they moved me to the wagon and from the wagon into my house, to say nothing of the bumping of the wagon on the way. I had made up my mind, though, that I would not keep Cherry out of her bed for another night, so I'd grit my teeth and bear it.

Ed and Frank came in and asked me how I felt. I lied and said fine. Of course they both knew I was lying. They got me on my feet and held me upright. The tent spun around as if it had gone crazy. I thought I was going to faint, but I never had fainted in my life and I wasn't going to start now. It was touch and go for a while, though.

I groaned. I didn't know until we had almost reached the wagon that I was the one doing the groaning, although I had heard it from the moment they had lifted me to my feet. Cherry walked beside us, and after I was on my back in the wagon she promised to look in on me the following morning.

Somehow I survived the jolting trip home and being hoisted to my feet again and half carried into the house. They helped me lie down, and for a while after that I thought I was going to die and hoped I would. I didn't, but I'm sure that, even though I have suffered considerable physical pain a good deal during my life, I never hurt as much as I did that evening while I was being taken home.

I kept on hurting after I was in my own bed, too. I thought about some of the platitudes I'd heard, that time is a great healer and all that kind of thing. Well, it seemed to me that time was damned slow doing its job. The past twenty-four hours had been a century.

Frank took the team and wagon back to the livery stable and Ed stayed with me that night. I asked him if he wanted to sleep in my extra bed, but he just grinned and said no, he'd brought his soogans along.

"I'll be outside your window," he said. "It's a warm night. I'll sleep in my Tucson bed."

I knew enough cowboy jargon to recognize a Tucson bed as "using his back for a mattress and his belly for a cover." He was right about the night being warm; he probably wouldn't need his blankets. Frank had promised to stop by tomorrow evening and tell me how they had got along with the partition. He said Nancy would drop in, too.

I didn't really care much whether anybody came to see me or not. All I wanted was for time to get at the job of healing me. I guess it got started that night. I slept some, and the dark hours did not drag at quite the same slow rate they had the night before.

When it was daylight Ed came into the house and built a fire and made coffee. He cooked breakfast, but I didn't want anything except coffee. It tasted good, the first thing that had since I'd taken my beating. After breakfast Ed left, saying he'd see me later.

As he went through the door, I told him to let Bully Bailey alone, that he was my meat. He grunted and kept on going, but I knew he was going to hunt for Bailey. I was sure he wouldn't find him, that the three men had hightailed out of town. I was equally sure that I would have one hell of a hard time finding them when I started looking.

Cherry came in before noon, bringing another bowl of chicken broth. This time it tasted good, too, so I guess time was getting in a few licks. Nancy showed up late in the afternoon and poached an egg for me. It was awful. I had never seen a poached egg before. I told her to fry the next one she fixed for me.

She didn't stay long. Later, after Frank had eaten supper, he came in and said they'd got a good start on the partition, that Cherry had drawn him a diagram to show him how she wanted the place arranged. They'd have it finished in less than a week, he thought.

He looked at me a moment, then asked hesitatingly, "What are you going to do after it's finished?"

"Build another house," I said. "I'll be up and working with you in a week."

"Yeah, sure," he said, and grinned.

I wasn't working with him at the end of the week, but I was walking and taking care of myself, and I was able to sit up and talk and not get as tired as I had been. Nancy and Cherry saw me every day, but they didn't run into each other until the last day of the week. Cherry had told me the restaurant would be finished that afternoon. She would lay in her supply of food after that, and she would open the following morning. She cooked my dinner and said I was looking fine, all I needed was a shave. I guess I did look like a grizzly bear, but I just hadn't felt like bothering with anything as unimportant as shaving.

Cherry was ready to leave, but she stood across the table from me. I knew she wanted to say something, but I didn't prod her. I waited, and after a while she blurted, "Jim, you don't know how grateful I am for all you're doing for me. You're the first man I ever met who would do something without any thought of reward."

"Whoa now," I said. "You've got me wrong. I'm going to get my reward."

Her mouth firmed up the way it had that first time I'd seen her. Now that seemed a long time ago and it also seemed that I had known Cherry for a long time, and it surprised me that she took what I said the wrong way again.

She didn't blow up in my face this time, though. She said coldly, "And just what form is the reward to take?"

I still didn't feel well and that may be the reason I reacted the way I did, short-tempered and impatient. Besides, it was plain she was still taking what I said the wrong way, and there really wasn't any excuse for her being suspicious of me now.

"You know, Cherry," I said. "I told you I'm going to marry you."

She relaxed and laughed so hard she had to lean against the wall. Finally she wiped her eyes and said, "I'd forgotten that you were going to marry me. I'll have to wait until you shave before I decide whether I'm marrying you; then I can tell whether you're man or beast."

I sighed and said, "I suppose that right now I look more like a beast than a man."

"That's right," she said, and laughed again. "Well, I've got to go and buy my groceries. I probably won't see you tomorrow."

"I'll be down and test your cooking in a day or two," I said.

"You do that," she said, and turned and almost ran into Nancy Rush, who was coming through the front door.

It was the damnedest thing, almost comical, but ticklish, too, and for a moment I didn't know quite what to say or do. Then I remembered they had never met, so I introduced them. They nodded at each other and said something pleasant in an unpleasant way. Looking at them, I was reminded of two cats who had their claws out, ready to slash each other to bits.

Finally, after what seemed another century, reminding me once more that all time is relative, Cherry turned to me and said, "Don't forget where my restaurant is," and left the house.

Nancy didn't move for another full minute. She stood in the doorway watching Cherry until she was down the street a block or so, then she turned and came on into the house. She didn't say "Good morning," or "Howdy" or anything. She went to the stove and poured herself a cup of coffee and sat down at the table.

"So that's the notorious Cherry Owens," she said in a strange, brittle tone. "She's the woman you slept with, isn't she?"

This made me mad, but I didn't want to make Nancy mad. She was very special to me.

I got my pipe and tobacco out, the way I always did when I wanted to gain a little time. I packed the bowl of my pipe, lit it and pulled on it, and then I said, "You didn't get that quite right. She slept on one side of the tent and I slept on the other."

She looked right at me and sniffed. Then she leaned

forward as she said, "The woman's a fool to miss a chance like that. Don't expect me to stay on my side of the tent if we're ever in a similar situation."

So she was going to make it hard for me, I thought. I said, "Well, it wasn't that Cherry was a fool or missed a chance. She knew there wasn't any use to get any closer. She said the spirit might be willing, but the flesh was weak, and she was right. I didn't even think I was going to live through the night."

"I see." She walked nervously around the room for a time. Then she said, "Don't do it. She won't make you a good wife. Now then, can I get anything for you or do anything?"

"No," I said. "I'm getting along pretty well. I can almost take a good breath, and there are times when my head doesn't ache."

"Good." She returned to the table and looked down at me for a moment. Then she leaned toward me and kissed me.

I've kissed a good many women, but I'd never had the feeling I did right then. Like all great emotional experiences, it was not a feeling I could describe in words. I didn't know anything about electricity, but I supposed that getting a jolt of electricity would have hit me just about the same as Nancy's kiss did.

After she drew her mouth back from mine, she held her face close to mine for several seconds, her eyes wide and troubled. Then she straightened and said, "Good-by." She walked out of the house without another word.

I knew that if we both continued to live in Cheyenne there would be trouble. I had the utmost respect for the institution of marriage, and I knew that if I were married and another man touched my wife, I'd kill the bastard as easily as I'd kill a mad dog.

In my opinion, any man who would take another man's wife was the lowest kind of a human being and I had no use for him at all, but I also knew it depended on which side of the fence I was on. In this case I was on the wrong side of the fence.

These thoughts ran through my mind as I sat there, my

pipe going cold in my hand. Then suddenly a prickle ran
down my spine. I could see the pattern that destiny was
weaving for us. For the first time in my life I felt that I
did not have free will. I was a puppet, and some unseen
power was pulling the strings. I was scared then, scared all
the way down to the very bottom of my belly.

CHAPTER XVII

Frank came in that evening after he'd had supper. He wanted to know how I felt and if I'd eaten yet, and after he was satisfied that I was all right and able to take care of myself, he said, "A man came by today wanting to rent the other half of the building for a jewelry store. At least he called it that, but from what he said I guess he'll have other gadgets than jewelry to sell. He wanted some counters built and another room partitioned off in the back."

"Let him have it," I said, "if he'll sign a lease and pay six months rent in advance. I don't care to do all the work he wants done and then have him move out in a couple of weeks."

Frank nodded. "I'll tell him."

"How long will it take you to do the work?"

Frank shrugged. "I don't know. Most of the week, anyway."

"All right," I said. "Now, as soon as you get it done, you'll start on another house on that lot I own on the corner of Hill and 22nd Street. I want the house to be about the same size as this one—two bedrooms, a kitchen, and a living room. When you get it finished, you and Nancy are to move into it. You'll pay me whatever rent you can afford. Nancy tells me you're saving all the money you can to build a church. That's fine. Go right ahead and build, but I'm going to have a house for you two to live in."

He sat down and stared at me. He wiped his face, pretending that he was sweating. It was a fine warm evening, but not that warm, so I thought he was probably

wiping his eyes. Finally he said, "I don't savvy this, Jim.
You could have your choice of a dozen renters before the
house is finished."

"Sure I could," I said, "and you and Nancy are my
choice."

He shook his head. "No, there's more to it than that.
Somebody else could afford to pay you more rent than we
can. Now suppose you tell me why you're doing this for
us."

I didn't want to tell him that he was an absolute fool
for making Nancy live in a tent, although I'll admit I was
tempted to. I puffed on my pipe for a time and thought
about my answer for several seconds, then I took my pipe
out of my mouth.

"I owe you a hell of a lot, Frank," I said. "More than
I'll ever repay. For saving my life when Bailey and his
pals jumped me, and taking over the responsibility of the
building while I'm laid up. That's enough reason."

"You don't owe me anything," he said. "I'm glad to
have the work."

"There's another reason," I said. "I guess it's the main
reason I'm doing it. Nancy can't spend the winter in a
tent, as cold as it gets here. It's not safe, either. We'll have
hundreds of plug-uglies when the end of track gets here.
A woman like Nancy will get raped sure if she's living in
a tent, with you being gone as much as you are."

He stiffened and stared at the floor, his face going pale.
As ridiculous as it sounds, I don't think he had thought of
either the cold weather or Nancy's safety. He asked
without looking up, "Has Nancy complained to you?"

"Not a word," I said, "and I'll bet she hasn't complained to you, either. She's not the complaining kind, but
I know more about the winters here than you do. I think
I know more about the toughs who'll flock into Cheyenne
from Julesburg, too."

He sighed, still staring at the floor. He looked as guilty
as hell. I didn't know what was bothering him until he
said, "I suppose you think I ought to build a house to live
in instead of a church."

"No, I don't think that," I said. "It's up to you. It's not

my business to tell you yours. Right now building houses is my business. I want you and Nancy for renters. It's that simple."

"No, it's not that simple," he said. "I'm not like Ed Burke, who seldom has a serious thought in his head. I keep thinking about my eternal soul and what I owe to the Lord and what He wants me to do. I think about these hard cases I see in Cheyenne who are going to hell at a gallop. I've got to build that church, Jim. I've learned I can't do any good preaching in the saloons, and I can't get a congregation if they have to stand in the hot sun or out in the cold weather in front of my tent while I'm preaching. On the other hand, I realize I owe something to Nancy, too."

"Damn it, Frank," I said, "I'm not trying to tell you what to do. I just know what I want to do."

"I know, I know." He rose, walked to the door and stood staring into the twilight. After a long silence, he said moodily, "It's not easy to make decisions like this, Jim. I guess that's what I'm trying to say. You see, when we were first married, we had a little church in eastern Kansas. Nancy didn't like living there. The ladies in the church didn't like her, either. Maybe they were jealous, her being as pretty as she is and all. There wasn't one of the other women who came close to being as pretty as Nancy is. It didn't take me long to figure out we had to move. I'd always wanted to be a missionary and it seemed to me this was a good field, so I came here and I fetched Nancy with me." He shook his head. "It's not a good life for her, though, not a good life at all."

I didn't say anything. I couldn't. I agreed with him that it wasn't a good life for Nancy, but I knew he wouldn't like to hear me say it. I puffed on my pipe and he stared at the street in the fading light. Several minutes passed; then he turned to me and said, "All right, we'll take you up on your offer. I'll tell Nancy. I know she'll feel better when she hears. Good night."

"Good night," I said.

After he left, I sat there thinking about Frank and the ways a man should serve the Lord. I guess it's something we all have to decide in our own way and our own time, but I was damned sure that letting your wife freeze to death in a tent or run the risk of being raped by some tough was not the way to do it. The more I thought about what a fine woman Nancy was, and what a short-sighted man Frank was, the more patience I lost with him.

She came by the next day to thank me for the house and to see if I needed anything. She only stayed a minute. After she left, I was convinced more than ever that she wasn't happy with Frank. She never said a word against him or even anything that was critical, but I sensed that something was being left out of her life. After that day I didn't see her for a long time.

As soon as I felt like walking I went downtown to my building and met Jorgens, the jeweler who had opened his store a few days before. Then I went into Cherry's restaurant. She'd found an old man to wash dishes and had hired a woman to help out, although Cherry still did most of the cooking and liked to wait on her customers too, if she had time. It was early in the afternoon and her dinner crowd had left. The place smelled of new lumber and paint along with the stew and whatever else she had cooked.

When she saw me come in, she called, "Welcome, landlord. I wondered how soon you were coming down to check on your investment."

"I'm not here to check up on my investment," I said. "I just got hungry."

"Good," she said. "Come on back to my room. I haven't had dinner yet. We've been busy, and the crowd just cleared out a few minutes ago."

The other woman was cleaning up the counter. She was a big rawboned Swede, older than Cherry and not particularly attractive, but that wasn't important. She looked capable and strong, and that was important. Cherry introduced me to the woman, and then to the old man who was washing dishes. He had one short leg and must have been close to seventy. There wasn't much work for a man like that in a boom town, and I suppose he was glad to find a job that gave him a living.

Cherry had me fill my plate with stew and take a couple of biscuits and a cup of coffee, then led the way to her room. It was neat and clean, not big enough maybe, but it seemed adequate for her bed and bureau and several boxes she had not unpacked. She pulled a chair up to one of the boxes and motioned for me to sit down.

"A poor table," she said, "but it will have to do. Making things do is something I've got used to."

She sat on the bed and used the other side of the box for her table. The stew was good and I ate with relish. The truth was I had been getting mighty tired of my own cooking. Cherry watched me eat, smiling as if pleased, and sent me back to the kitchen for a second helping.

"It's a pleasure to see you eat like that," she said when I returned. "You were downright picky the last time I fixed something for you to eat."

"I'm glad I'm able to eat," I said. "I don't know how close I came to cashing in my chips, but I felt like I was going to. Now I think I can pick up a hammer in another week or so."

We talked about her business and she wanted to know what I was going to do next and how soon the end of track would be in Cheyenne. When I got up to go, she wouldn't let me pay. "Next time," she said. "This time I wanted to have you visit with me and just . . . well, just be company."

I started to leave; then I turned back and looked at her. She was a very attractive young woman, her gaze fixed on me, her moist red lips parted a little. I said, "Cherry, will you marry me?"

She gave a start and rose from the bed, her lips coming together, the smile going out of them. She opened her mouth to say something and shut it, then she said, "Jim, are you really serious this time?"

"I was never more serious in my life," I said.

She shook her head sadly. "You don't love me, Jim. I think you're just lonesome."

"You're right about me being lonesome," I said. "I don't love you the way the love stories tell about, but I learned to know you pretty well when I was flat on my back. The important thing is that I can take care of you and I admire you. Love will come, the right kind of love that makes a home. A lot of families start with less."

She nodded, the small smile returning to the corners of her mouth again. "You're a very honest man, Jim, and I admire you for it, but it's not enough. Not yet anyhow. Ask me again someday."

"All right, I will," I said.

When I got home, a man was sitting on the porch waiting for me. He was dressed up like a dude, with an elk-tooth charm dangling from a chain that was stretched across his vest. He was wearing a black derby hat and one of the biggest diamonds I ever saw in a ring on his right hand. He had a fine short beard, a carefully trimmed mustache, and he smelled of bay rum. He shook hands with me and said his name was Lucky Sam Bellew.

"I'm a land speculator," he said. "It's like playing poker. You've got to outguess everybody else in the game. Right now here in Cheyenne I'm trying to outguess the government and the railroad. I'm betting on the Union Pacific making Cheyenne one of the major cities on their main line. I want to buy your lots."

"They're not for sale," I said. "Not yet anyway. I'm playing a little poker with them myself."

"That's your right, of course," he said. "You were smarter than most. You got in on the ground floor and bought them cheap from the railroad. Now I may be a fool, and there is no sure way of knowing when land values will level off. I'm a little scared that I'd lose on these lots, with the end of track just a few miles east of town. They may shove the end of steel right on over Sherman Hill and winter in Laramie. Cheyenne might wind up a little burg of fifty people."

He irritated me. I'd told him plain enough that the lots were not for sale. I said tartly, "Mr. Bellew, I just got done telling you—"

"I heard you, but you haven't heard me," he said. "I'll give you a thousand dollars a lot. That's one hell of a big profit for you, if you stop and figure it."

The offer boggled my mind some. It was twice as much

as I had been offered before, and I'd thought five hundred was a good offer. I was tempted. I sat there looking at him for about thirty seconds, thinking that I had twenty-five lots I could and would sell. I'd still have two more I intended to keep on Eddy Street because they were good business sites and I wanted to build on them and have additional rental property. I'd have twenty-five thousand dollars, which was more than I had ever expected to have in my entire life.

Then I decided that if Lucky Sam Bellew intended to gamble, I could too. I shook my head and said, "No. They're not for sale."

Bellew nodded and shook hands and left. I stayed on my front porch for a time listening to the saws and hammers that were working all around me. I wasn't sure whether I'd been a fool or not, but I didn't worry about it. I still had the lots, and I could still sell them for a profit even if nobody else paid me a thousand apiece.

I started thinking about Cherry. She'd marry me in time—I was sure of it. I was also sure she'd make a good wife, which was important, but I couldn't help thinking how different it would have been if Nancy were free and I had asked her to marry me. I would have said flat out in the plainest words I could manage that I loved her. I couldn't say that to Cherry. I wanted to marry her, though. I wanted to very much, but I guess my motive was questionable, to say the least. I thought that if I married Cherry, I wouldn't get into trouble with Nancy.

CHAPTER XVIII

Steel reached Cheyenne on November 13. We knocked off work and walked down to the railroad grade to watch the rails being laid through town. Frank stopped at the tent and persuaded Nancy to go with us. I dropped by the restaurant and talked Cherry into going, too. I told her she wouldn't lose any business, that every man and his dog would be down there along the grade.

All the way to the grade Cherry walked beside me and Nancy walked beside Frank, and I don't believe either woman said a word to the other after the first cool greeting. When we arrived, we found that I was right. Every man and his dog were there, particularly the dogs.

Laying the rails was as interesting a show as I had been told. The surveyors, bridge builders and graders were all working miles west of Cheyenne. There had been a good deal of Indian trouble, even though soldiers out of Fort D. A. Russell were constantly patrolling the route the railroad would take.

Most of the men employed by the Union Pacific were Civil War veterans who worked with their guns close at hand, but we were constantly hearing of brushes with the Indians, particularly among the surveyors, who had to work far out ahead of everyone else. They were the most likely men to get killed, and many of them were.

The Casement brothers, General Jack and Dan, were responsible for laying the track, and much of the grading, too. Jack Casement had been a prominent general during the Civil War and had put together a well organized, disciplined group of men. Most of them were Irish, a tough, brawling, hard-working bunch of men who might have been very hard for someone else to manage, but the Casements handled them well.

As I stood in the crowd and watched the rails being put down, I was amazed at the proficiency and speed with which the job was done. A light car pulled by one horse came up to the end of steel, the car loaded with rails. Two men grabbed the end of a rail and moved forward. Other men took hold of the rail by twos, and when it was clear of the car, the men went forward on the run.

At exactly the right second someone yelled a command to drop the rail. They did, being careful to put it into place right side up. Another gang of men was doing exactly the same thing on the other side of the track. I held my watch on them several times, and noted that it took about thirty seconds per rail.

As soon as the car was empty, it was tipped to one side while the next loaded one moved up; then the empty car was tipped into position again and was driven back for another load, the horse galloping as if the devil was right on his tail. The gaugers, spikers and bolters kept close on the heels of the men dropping the rails.

Just a few minutes watching these men gave me an admiration for them I had never felt for a group of laborers before. I had not seen anything like it, and I never saw anything like it afterwards. It was cooperation at its best.

Then the thought came to me that I was going to make a fortune out of my lots and I owed it to these men who were putting the rails down and spiking them into place, along with the graders and bridge builders and surveyors. Of course, I owed something to the Union Pacific company and General Dodge and the Casement brothers, but the men on top were making good money. The Irishmen who did the sweating and ran the danger of getting an Indian bullet or arrow in their briskets weren't getting rich.

There was a hell of a lot of banging as the end of steel moved past us. I did some quick calculating as I watched. Three strokes to the spike. I counted ten spikes to the rail. Somewhere I had heard it took 400 rails for a mile of track. About that time I quit calculating, but one thing was sure: those sledges were going to swing a lot of times before the line was finished between Omaha and Sacramento.

We walked back to Cherry's restaurant in a kind of daze. The whole operation was incredible. Sherman Hill lay west of Cheyenne, then the desert, which offered a different kind of resistance, with the Wasatch Mountains on beyond the desert. Of course the Central Pacific, with its Chinese labor, had even a worse kind of terrain to cover, with the Sierras making an almost impenetrable wall.

Cherry invited all of us to dinner. At first Nancy said she had some things to do and couldn't stay. Then Frank said something in a low tone. I couldn't hear the words, but from the sound of his voice I knew it was something harsh, perhaps bitter. She said something back, her face turning red, but she went in and sat down at the counter, Frank on one side of her, a carpenter on the other.

Cherry's hired woman had dinner almost ready. We ate hurriedly because we'd heard that the first train to Cheyenne would arrive that afternoon, and of course the whole town would be down there on the tracks to welcome it.

It was a historic occasion, the day we had been waiting for, and I'll admit I had an uneasy feeling in the bottom of my belly every time I thought about turning Lucky Sam Bellew down when he'd offered me a thousand dollars for each of my lots. I just wasn't sure whether I had made a mistake or not.

I'd heard and read some wild tales about Julesburg. Early in the summer, or maybe it had been in late spring, there had been only about fifty people in Julesburg. By the end of July it had exploded to about four thousand, with streets of mud or dust depending on when it had rained last.

The prices the merchants had been able to charge for their goods were outrageous. Apparently it was the grab for money that had made Julesburg the town it had become, but the absence of law and order was what worried me. I think all of the businessmen of Cheyenne felt the same way.

We simply did not want Cheyenne to become another Julesburg, which had had more than its share of whorehouses, dance halls, gambling places and saloons. The women, so I had been told, walked around town with derringers carried on their hips. They would rob a man by putting something in his drink, but he would not be allowed to take proper measures against them after he came to.

One reporter wrote that Julesburg had people who would kill a man for five dollars. I believe it. Dead men had been found in town or close to it every day, their pockets emptied of whatever they were carrying, and yet the bulk of the people in Julesburg apparently were indifferent to what was happening.

All of this ran through my mind as I ate. I didn't say much to Cherry, who sat beside me at the counter, but the thought kept nagging me that Nancy wasn't safe in her tent and Cherry might not be safe in her restaurant if we allowed Cheyenne to go the way Julesburg had.

In the end, it was the good women like Nancy and Cherry who built the towns and brought civilization to the frontier, not the whores, who too often worked hand-in-glove with the sneak thieves and murderers who had made Julesburg a literal hell. Now that Cheyenne was the end of track, Julesburg would cease to exist as a town, and it would happen overnight.

I knew what Ed Burke would say if I told him what I was thinking. As we hurried back to the track I decided he was right—a vigilance committee was the answer. I knew he was right when the train pulled in, with the cars banging and the bell ringing and the whistle shrieking.

One of the men on the train yelled, "Gentlemen, I give you Julesburg." That was exactly right. While everyone else was whooping and hollering as the passengers left the train, I just stood there as if I was paralyzed.

Frank nudged me in the ribs and asked, "What's the matter with you, Jim?"

I shook my head and came out of it right away. I managed a weak holler, but it was easy to see that the train was carrying the frame shacks and poles and tents that had made up much of Julesburg, along with the barroom equipment and gambling devices that had given it the reputation of being the most notorious city of sin in the West.

Along with the railroad men, mule skinners and hunters who were on the train, there were the whores and the pimps, the professional gamblers and con men. Within a matter of hours Cheyenne would be a city of sin that would match the Julesburg of yesterday. It struck me that this historic occasion was not what I had expected it to be.

Cheyenne had planned a huge celebration, with a platform for speakers and big signs that read, "The Magic City of the Plains greets the trans-continental railway" and "Old Casement, we welcome you" and "Honor to whom honor is due." I wanted no part of it, and I couldn't help wondering if progress always meant that you had to swallow the bitter with the sweet.

I'd had more than enough. I said, "Cherry, let's get out of here."

She nodded. As we walked back along Ferguson Street she glanced at me and asked, "What's the matter, Jim?"

"It's a funny thing," I said, "how it is when you actually see something that you knew was coming. Cheyenne will be the hell on wheels that Julesburg has been and it scares me. Have you got a gun?"

"We've got three," she said. "I knew this was coming and I've been scared, too, so I bought three pistols the other day. I gave one to Olga and one to old Pete and I kept one. We'll use them if we have to."

"Good," I said. "If you need any help from me, get word to me as fast as you can."

She laid a hand on my arm and squeezed it. "Thank you, Jim," she said.

I left her at the restaurant and went on home, more worried and upset than I wanted to admit. We had policemen, and we had a civilian auxiliary police force, in which I had very little confidence. I knew damned well that our official law enforcers simply couldn't handle the number of toughs who had come in on that train. To make it worse, more would come. I had no doubt of that.

Frank stopped in later and said it had been a festive day. Then he gave me a close look and wanted to know why I was so glum. I told him, adding, "If you're looking for souls to save, a lot of them came in on the train today. I guess the people who have been in Cheyenne from the day the first settlers arrived haven't been angels, but we've been pretty close compared to the riff-raff that was on the train."

He frowned and scratched his chin. Then he asked, "How do you know the train was carrying people like that?"

"I saw enough of them to know," I said. "That kind is never hard to identify. We also saw the stuff they were bringing with them from Julesburg. Besides, we've known all along that Julesburg would pick up and move here as soon as Cheyenne became the end of track. I don't know of any way to keep the undesirables out. All we can do is control them once they get here."

He hadn't even thought about it, I guess. From what Nancy had said, and from what I had observed about him, he was that kind of man. Now he nodded and said, as if only half-convinced, "I guess you're right."

"Has Nancy got a gun?" When he shook his head I said, more sharply than I intended, "Damn it, Frank, get her one. You'd better stay with her every evening until we get your house finished."

He nodded again. "I guess I had."

I knew he wouldn't. If one of these hardcases ever so much as touched Nancy, I'd kill him, no matter what Frank said or did. I was plain disgusted by the naive way he looked at the situation, but killing a man after it was too late wouldn't help Nancy. I wished they'd move in with me, but I knew better than to ask them after what Nancy had said the last time I'd suggested it to her.

I had a visitor that night after it was dark, a man named Jess Munro. I'd seen him in town and knew him by name, but I had never actually met him or talked to him. One thing was sure: he was the kind of man you'd notice in a crowd.

He was about thirty, I judged, a dark-faced man with a black mustache and beard, and black hair. His eyes were dark brown, his jaw square, the kind of jaw you'd expect to see on a forceful man. He was stocky in build, with large hands and muscular shoulders. He'd be a hard man to whip, I told myself.

Munro carried himself with a straight-backed military stiffness and precision that I associated with an army man. I suspected he had been an officer on one side or the other during the war, probably with the Union because his speech gave no indication that he was a Southerner. I had never seen him without a gun on his hip. He had one now, and I wondered about it because he claimed to be a dealer in real estate and had an office on Ferguson Street.

He shook hands with me, his grip very strong. He pinned his gaze on my face as if making a judgment about me, then said, "Ed Burke tells me you're a tough hand. I saw you operate the night Frank Rush tried to preach in the Head Quarters Saloon. You saved his life. I think you'll do."

"Do for what?"

"You saw what the train brought in this afternoon," he said, ignoring my question. "Not that it is any surprise. The police can't do the job, even with the help of some of us who have been appointed law officers on a standby basis. You would have been contacted if you hadn't been laid up." He shrugged and added, "I guess we would be of help in case of a riot, but that's about all."

"I was laid up for a while, but I'm all right now," I said. "I've been working a full day for a week or so. I had thought about volunteering for police duty, but hadn't got around to it. I've been as concerned as anyone about what's going to happen."

"Good," he said. "Then you'll be willing to serve on the Vigilance Committee we're organizing. Some men, just four as a matter of fact, will act as chiefs. That's what we want you for. You'll have fifteen men under you to carry out any job that the Central Committee decides on. Will you do it?"

Here it was at last, laid right on the line. I had to make a decision one way or the other—now! I hesitated, looking straight at Jess Munro. I remembered all my old doubts and fears of the Vigilantes that had plagued me when I'd lived in Black Hawk, but this was a different situation. Something had to be done fast if Cheyenne was to be saved.

Still I hesitated, saying, "I've always been leery of vigilante rules. They operate outside the law. It can become mob rule very easily."

"That's right," he said grimly, "but we intend to take steps to safeguard against that happening here. I have appointed myself Chairman of the Committee for the simple reason that I've had some experience with vigilance committees and somebody has to get the ball rolling. Of course, I will be subject to removal by a majority of the Committee."

He paused, scratching his chin, then added, "Glenn, damn it, we just don't have much time. This bunch of toughs will be in control of the town before we know it if we don't do something. We've got to get on the job and do it quick."

It seemed to me that I had no choice, doubts or no doubts. I said, on impulse I guess, "I'll do it."

"Fine," he said. "We're meeting in the hall over Miller's store tomorrow night at eight o'clock. Don't mention this to anyone. Just be there."

"I will," I said.

We shook hands again and he left. I still wasn't sure I had done right. I wasn't even sure that Jess Munro wouldn't use the Vigilance Committee for his own purposes. So the old doubts were still there, but again it seemed I had no choice.

I couldn't just sit on my hind end and let the plug-uglies rule Cheyenne. I could do more to control the Committee by belonging than I could as an outsider, particularly if I was what Munro called a "chief." Tomorrow night I would know for sure.

Then my thoughts returned to Jess Munro. He was the type who enjoyed giving orders. Was he doing this just so he'd be in position to give orders, as he had as an officer in the army? I didn't actually know he had been an officer, but I thought it was a pretty safe guess.

Was he really a real estate dealer? Or was he on somebody's payroll? I had to admit that I might never know the answers to these questions.

CHAPTER XIX

We hadn't been working more than half an hour the next morning when a man came by and told us there had been two killings the night before. A railroad man had got into a brawl with one of the new gamblers named Tate Horn in the Head Quarters Saloon and Horn had shot him to death.

The other killing was plain murder any way you looked at it. A second railroad man apparently had been visiting one of the whorehouses—at least, the murderer wanted everybody to believe that was the case. The man had been stabbed in the chest and his pockets emptied. The body had been left back of one of the whorehouses.

My two carpenters did a lot of talking about it during the day, but Frank didn't say much. I hoped he was thinking about Nancy. I didn't say much either, but the doubts I'd had about the Vigilance Committee disappeared in a hurry.

I figured the first thing we'd do was to run Tate out of town. I didn't know whether he'd started the fight or not, but we didn't want him in Cheyenne and I was sure everyone who had lived in Cheyenne any length of time would agree with me. It was impossible to guess how many others he'd kill if we let him stay.

I climbed the stairs to the big room over Miller's store five minutes before eight that night and found that most of the men were there ahead of me. Three men sat at a table at one end of the room: Jess Munro, a banker named Fritz Thiessen, and the speculator, Lucky Sam Bellew. I didn't have any way of knowing who had been working with Munro to organize the Vigilance Committee, but I'll admit I was surprised to see a respectable banker and a land speculator joining Jess Munro.

For a time I stood just inside the door looking around. I knew a good many of the men. Some had been here before I'd come to Cheyenne; others had arrived about the same time I had. All of them had been here for quite a while, and all of them that I knew were men I would call solid citizens.

I saw Ed Burke standing on the right side of the room beside a window. I walked over to him and punched him in the ribs and said, "Howdy, Ed."

He turned, saw who it was, and slapped me on the back, a big grin stretching across his face. "Well, by God, I didn't know if Jess would talk you into joining up or not."

"I hesitated," I admitted, "and last night I had plenty of doubts, but this morning I figured it was the only thing to do."

The grin faded. "Hell of a note, ain't it? Two men killed the first night after the Julesburg bunch hits town."

Munro was on his feet and pounding on the table. When the rumble of talk died, he said in a loud, commanding voice that carried the length of the room, "Gentlemen, the meeting will come to order. As you all know, I'm Jess Munro. I'll serve as Chairman of this meeting." He motioned to Thiessen and introduced him, then Bellew, and added, "We are the self-appointed Central Committee of the Cheyenne Vigilantes, organized for the purpose of keeping law and order in Cheyenne. We appointed ourselves for the simple reason that someone had to get this group started."

He stopped, his dark eyes sweeping the room as if trying to decide how we felt, then he went on. "You all know what happened last night. I guess there won't be any argument about the necessity for speed, but I do want to assure you of one thing. Whenever our actions do not satisfy you, any five members of the Vigilance Committee can call for an election and we can be removed by a majority vote of the organization."

He picked up a sheet of paper. "First I'll read to you

the by-laws of the Cheyenne Vigilance Committee. I wrote them, but I claim no credit for them. They are based upon the by-laws of similar committees."

The document was a short one, stating the purpose of the Vigilance Committee, giving the method of removing the Central Committee as he had just stated, and saying that at no time would violence be used to keep the peace unless extreme conditions demanded it.

I was still thinking about that and telling myself that somebody, probably Munro, would have to decide what those extreme conditions were, when he laid the sheet of paper on the table and picked up another one.

"I will now read the oath we are asking all of you to take," Munro said. "We want you to know what it is before you take it. If any of you feel you cannot honestly take this oath, you will leave now. But remember one thing: you are not to inform anyone of the identity of the men you saw in this room. If you do, you will be dealt with in a manner that will make you regret you had ever opened your mouth."

I realized this was necessary, but again I wondered who would decide the manner in which the informer would be dealt with, and once more I had a notion it would be Jess Munro. We could be in for a bloodbath if he were a brutal man, and he could well be that kind. It was the old doubts that simply would not die.

Munro waited a good thirty seconds. When no one left the room, he read the oath. It stated that none of us would inform the regularly appointed law officers of our actions or of the actions of any other member of the Committee if he was doing Committee business, that we would not under any circumstances let our personal feelings or reasons enter into making our decisions as members of the Committee, and that at all times we would be reasonable and just in acting to preserve law and order in the city of Cheyenne.

After he had read the oath, Munro waited for another thirty seconds before going on. Still no one had left the room. Munro said, "Very well, I assume you are all satisfied with the by-laws and oath. Are you ready to take the oath?"

We said yes, a great rolling rumble of sound that came from all corners of the big room. Munro said, "We don't have enough Bibles for you to lay your hands on, but you will take this oath as a sacred obligation, fully as sacred as if you had placed your hand on the Bible. We will start by saying, 'I, John Smith,' or what your name is, 'do hereby swear,' and then you will repeat after me the oath word by word, and finish by saying 'so help me God.' If any man who takes this oath breaks his word, then God help him, because none of us on the Committee will."

If anyone had dropped a pin, I guess it would have sounded like a ten-penny nail. The room was that still, except for the heavy breathing of the sixty-odd men who were assembled here. We went through the oath just as Munro had outlined it for us.

I would have said it was impossible to get that many men to take anything with the deadly seriousness that we were taking this oath business, but I would have been wrong. The killings of the previous night had had the same effect on every man here that they'd had on me, I guess. Anyhow, there was no horseplay, no shuffling of feet, no laughing, no whispering.

When we finished with "so help me God," Munro nodded, smiling that brief half-smile of his, and said, "Good. The criminal element will never take control of our city."

Munro picked up a third sheet of paper. "Gentlemen, I will give you your teams. The Central Committee along with the four chiefs will constitute what we will call the flying wedge of the Cheyenne Vigilance Committee. We will undertake the drastic work that must be done and done quickly. There will be occasions when we will have to strike hard and fast after a vicious crime has been committed, before the crime has been forgotten by the people of Cheyenne.

"However, we need every man here to give us the appearance of strength that we must have if we are to function effectively. So tomorrow night all of you will gather at the town jail before eight o'clock. Bring your rifles and gunnysacks with holes cut in them for your eyes. We will parade along Cheyenne's principal streets. I have seen this done on a number of occasions, and I assure you it makes an impressive warning to the criminals. Many of them will leave town immediately."

He glanced at the sheet of paper in his hands, then went on. "The men who will serve as chiefs are Jim Glenn, Ed Burke, Charley Williams, and Bronco Stead. I will read Glenn's team first. When I finish reading the names of the four teams, I will designate the corners in which each of you will meet."

He read the names, then asked the chiefs to come to the table for the lists of names. We did, and again, and for no logical reason, I wondered how Munro had selected the chiefs. Williams owned the Star Saloon, and Stead operated the Western Livery Stable.

I understood how he had picked Ed Burke. Certainly Ed had been pushing the idea of the Vigilance Committee for weeks. I could understand why he picked me, with Ed recommending me, but I was puzzled over his choice of a saloon keeper and a livery stable operator. I shouldn't have been, I guess, because a saloon keeper and a livery store operator could be solid citizens the same as anyone else, but just the same I wondered about it, perhaps because I didn't know either man.

Munro designated the corners for each team to assemble, then gave us fifteen minutes to get acquainted with our men. I shook hands with the members of my team. I knew several of them and I made an effort to pin the right name to the right face of the ones I didn't know. I would not make a good politician because I always had trouble remembering men's names if I didn't have much to do with them.

Munro called us to order presently, asking, "Are there any questions?"

Apparently there were none, so Munro said, "I want the four chiefs to come to the table as soon as we adjourn. Remember, you are to assemble at the town jail with

gunny sacks and rifles tomorrow evening at eight o'clock.
No absence short of violent sickness will be accepted."

He paused, his dark eyes seeming to bore into every
man there. Then he said slowly, and with considerable
emotion, "Gentlemen, the one quality which every Vigilance Committee must have is loyalty to its officers and
the willingness to obey their commands. Meeting ad-
journed."

The men left the hall without talking, a grave and
unusual silence for so many men. I don't know why the
questions about Munro kept popping into my mind, but
there was no doubt about the real meaning of his words,
although he never actually stated it. What he intended to
say, and I was sure of it, was that the man who did not
obey his commands would be punished. Was he the one to
decide what the punishment would be? To my way of
thinking, murder inside a Vigilance Committee for diso-
bedience was just as bad as murder by one of the criminal
element we were trying to control.

The four of us who had been appointed chiefs moved
forward to stand across the table from Munro. As we
faced the men who were on the Central Committee, it
struck me that both Thiessen and Bellew were a little
nervous, but Jess Munro was not. I wondered if Thiessen
and Bellew were thinking along the same line I had been.

There was no doubt about one thing. This was Jess
Munro's party and he was enjoying every minute of it. I
knew then beyond the slightest doubt that before the
Vigilance Committee was disbanded I would be knocking
heads with Munro. We both might be sorry that he had
picked me as one of the chiefs.

CHAPTER XX

Munro waited until everyone had left except the members of the Central Committee and the four chiefs. Then he reached under the table and lifted out a wooden box. When he raised the lid, I saw that the box was filled with revolvers.

"We've got an ugly job to do tonight and I thought you might not be armed," Munro said, "so I brought these. Any vigilance committee's effectiveness depends upon how quickly and violently it reacts to a crime. Two murders were committed last night. We do not know the identity of one killer, but we do know the identity of the other. We are going after Tate Horn."

As soon as he had handed out the revolvers, he reached into the box again and took out a coiled rope with a hangman's knot on one end. There was no doubt about his intentions. He expected us to help him hang Tate Horn.

I looked at the three men standing beside me and then at the two men seated beside Munro. I sensed that they were as uneasy about this as I was, but I didn't see the slightest indication that any of them were prepared to challenge Munro. Either we'd play dead and roll over or I'd buck him, and I had no intention of rolling over and playing dead. I knew very well that if we went along with Munro and hanged a man, we'd be tarred with the same brush, and from then on Munro would have his way on everything.

"What are you going to do with that rope?" I asked.

He stared at me as if I were an idiot to ask such a

question. Then he said, "We're going to hang Horn with it."

I said, "No."

His expression changed. I guess he knew he wasn't looking at an idiot, but I don't think he was sure just what he was looking at or how far I'd go in opposing him. He glanced at the other men, then brought his gaze back to me, a hint of caution in his dark eyes.

"What do you mean by 'no'?" he asked.

"There are seven of us who will take part in the hanging," I said. "Who beside you decided that Tate Horn is going to hang?"

That seemed to shock him. I don't think the thought had entered his mind that anyone would oppose Horn's hanging, and he had promised himself the pleasure of seeing the man swing. Now he was sore, just plain mad, and I was certain that my previous suspicion of Jess Munro being a cruel man was correct.

I had always known that there were a good many people who enjoyed a hanging, that there were still places in the United States where people brought their lunch and made a public spectacle out of an execution, but it was a kind of recreation I had no stomach for, and I couldn't understand how any human being could be that way. From that moment on I had no real respect for Jess Munro.

Munro's face turned red right up to the roots of his hair. Several seconds passed before he managed an answer, but he finally got it said. "Nobody."

I was sure that had been the case, but before I could push the matter he demanded, "Why should there be?"

"Because you're one man," I answered, "and one man out of seven has no right to involve all of us in a hanging that might get us into trouble up to our necks. The law would call it murder. If this flying wedge as you called it is going to function as it should, all seven of us will make the decisions, not just you or any one of us."

Bellew said, "That's right, Jess." Thiessen nodded agreement. I couldn't see the faces of the men who stood beside me, but I had the feeling they were supporting me.

Munro couldn't speak for a moment. He sat back in his chair and glared at me. I believe he would have killed me on the spot if he'd thought he could. I'm convinced he had not expected resistance from any of us, and he found it hard to believe he was actually getting it.

"Well, by God," Munro said finally, "I didn't think you or anybody would object to hanging a man like Tate Horn. This is the way we scare the living hell out of every tough in Cheyenne. When they wake up in the morning and find Horn's body swinging from a cottonwood limb down by the creek, they'll be running over each other getting out of town." He stopped, glaring at me, then said, "Well?"

"I understand that," I said, "but the point is I don't know anything about Tate Horn or his fight with the man he killed or why he killed him. The murdered man may have been responsible for what happened. Just because he worked for the railroad doesn't put him in a class above Horn."

"No, but he was a working man and Horn is a gambler," Munro said, as if being a gambler was enough on the face of it to convict Horn of murder.

"I'm in favor of running Horn out of town," I said, "and that would be a warning to the rest of them who came to town yesterday, but if he killed the other man in self-defense, I'll have no part in hanging him."

"That's what he did," Bellew said. "I should have spoken up sooner. I was in the Head Quarters when he did it. His girl came from Julesburg with him. They call her Red Rose. She's a redheaded young woman who stands behind his chair when he's playing poker. He claims she brings him luck.

"Anyhow, the Irishman, a fellow named Mike Mulligan, came up and started talking to Rose. He'd been drinking and he was plenty ugly. He carried a gun, all right. I saw it under his waistband before the trouble started.

"Rose asked him to leave her alone, but he started to pat her on the shoulder. Then Horn told him to leave her alone. He just laughed and began feeling of Rose's breasts. She hit him a good wallop on the nose and started it bleeding. He backed up and went for his gun. I don't know whether he intended to shoot Rose or Horn, but Horn killed him before his gun was half leveled."

"Why hell, Jess," Ed Burke said, "we can't hang a man under those circumstances. I'm like Jim, though. I'm for running him out of town."

The rest of them agreed with that. Munro sat there fuming, the corners of his mouth working as he fought his anger, but by then there wasn't much he could do except give in. He nodded and got to his feet.

"All right," Munro said. "We'll go get him and tell him that if he's in town tomorrow night, we will hang him. If he is there, we'll have to do it. You savvy that?"

I didn't much like it, but it seemed a reasonable compromise, and I figured Horn would pull out without any more trouble. He'd be a fool if he stayed, and a man who makes his living playing poker couldn't be a fool. We all nodded our agreement. Munro reached into his box again and pulled out seven gunnysacks.

"We'll put these on, though sooner or later our identity will be known," Munro said. "We're going to have to expect that, and we'll probably have some attempts made on our lives. Sam, you lead the way because you know Horn by sight." Then Munro fixed his gaze on me. "Glenn, you'll back his play. The rest of us will string out behind you. If anybody pulls a gun or a knife or jumps either of you, we'll shoot him. We'll draw our guns when we go into the saloon."

We pulled the gunnysacks over our heads. Mine didn't smell good and it was rougher than a cob, but I could put up with it for a while. Munro blew out the lamps and we left the hall, with Munro still carrying the rope. I don't know why he kept it unless he wanted everybody in the saloon to see it. Or maybe he thought something would happen that would persuade us to hang Horn after all. Anyhow, he had it and kept it in plain sight.

We went into the Head Quarters, Bellew leading the way. I was two steps behind him, the other five behind us. We had our guns in our hands. It was almost comical to see the shocked expression on the men's faces as we came in. Within a matter of seconds the noise in the big room had stopped, and the silence was so complete that when someone coughed the sound was like thunder booming into a still summer day.

Bellew went straight to Horn's table. The man was a common type among gamblers, lean and thin-faced. with a neat black mustache and slate-gray eyes that told you nothing about what he was thinking or feeling. Red Rose was standing at his back, and she was, as Bellew had said, a young redheaded woman.

"Come with me, Horn," Bellew said.

For a moment the gambler didn't move. He stared at Bellew, then at me, and finally at our guns. He laid his cards on the table and rose, his gaze turning to the five men between us and the door. One of the men at the table said, "You're busting up our game, Mr. Gunnysack. We know what you're trying to tell us. Now get out."

Bellew hit him across the top of the head with his gun barrel, a short down-striking blow that knocked the fellow cold. He fell sideways out of his chair and lay motionless on the floor.

"All right," Horn said. "I'll go with you. Let's not have any more trouble."

"That suits me," Bellew said.

Horn walked to the door, his head high, his shoulders back. If he saw the rope in Munro's hand he gave no indication of it. Red Rose started to follow him, then stopped when I said, "Stay here."

We marched Horn into the street, no one else raising a hand to help him. The other five eased out behind us, Munro calling to the men in the saloon, "Sit pat if you want to stay healthy."

He stood in the street facing the door. When no one followed, he said, "We'll take him to the creek."

We walked him to Crow Creek, going down the middle of the street and across the railroad tracks so that anyone on the boardwalks could see what was happening. We stopped when we reached the first big cottonwood.

"I've got a right to a trial," Horn said. "I killed the fool in self-defense. Anyone who saw it will tell you that."

"We know," Bellew said, "so we're offering you a deal. If you will get out of town pronto, we won't hang you."

"If you're in town tomorrow night at this time, you'll swing," Munro said.

The light was so thin that I couldn't see his face, but I could almost feel the relief that rushed through him. "I'll be out of town before sunup," he said, and wheeled and ran.

We stood motionless until we couldn't hear his footsteps. Then Munro laughed shortly. "He will be, too," he said. "Remember. Tomorrow night. Bring your guns and gunnysacks."

We broke up then, with Lucky Sam Bellew falling into step beside me. We didn't say anything for a block; then we took the gunnysacks off our heads. I rubbed my face and said, "Feels good to get the damned thing off. Makes my skin itch."

"It does for a fact," Bellew said. "Thought any more about selling your lots?"

"No," I said. "I'll hold them for a while yet. I'm not going to sell all of them anyhow. I'm a builder, not a speculator."

"Give me first crack at them when you do decide to sell," he said. "I might raise my previous offer."

So he didn't think the market for town property had topped off yet. I felt good about that. I'd been uneasy about not selling, but now I was satisfied I had done right.

"I'll do it," I said.

We walked in silence for another block. Then he said in a low tone, "You had guts to stand up to Munro. He's a hard man to stand up to—I know from experience. I likewise know I should have spoken up about how Tate Horn happened to shoot the Irishman, but I was afraid to buck Munro. I would have, though. I mean, before we actually done the hanging."

He paused, then added doubtfully, "I think I would have. Anyhow, from now on Munro won't be quite so anxious to decide everything by himself. You've heard the saying about how total power corrupts totally or something like that. Well, I g ess Munro had total power until you challenged him. If you hadn't done it just when we're getting started, no one could have stopped him."

I was glad to hear him say that because I wasn't sure how the others felt about what I had done, even though they had supported me. I asked, "What does the man do? He claims he deals in real estate. Does he?"

"No," Bellew said. "I'd know if he did. It's just a cover-up. Nobody knows for sure who's paying him, but there's a rumor he's a troubleshooter for the railroad. It might be true—I don't know. Well, I turn off here. I'll see you tomorrow night."

I walked on home thinking about it. The rumor made sense and I was inclined to believe it. The railroad men didn't want Cheyenne to become another Julesburg, and this might be their way of stopping the toughs before they took control. In any case, I had made an enemy out of Jess Munro.

CHAPTER XXI

Tate Horn kept his word. He was out of town before sunup. At least I assumed he was, because no one in Cheyenne saw him the next day or any other day that I heard about. I would have heard about him, because news like that spreads in a hurry. By mid-morning the next day everybody in Cheyenne knew what had happened in the Head Quarters Saloon, and that made Tate Horn the best-known name in town.

I guess most folks expected to find his body swinging from a limb of one of the big cottonwoods. When it wasn't found, they assumed he had been murdered and his body hidden somewhere out on the prairie. Of course, none of us who had taken Horn out of the Head Quarters had anything to say.

He may have shown himself to some of his cronies after we let him go, but they kept mum about seeing him if they had. Apparently he took Red Rose with him because she disappeared that night, too, although there were some people in town who speculated that the Vigilantes had murdered her.

Any way we looked at it, his disappearance was almost as big a warning to the criminal element as his hanging would have been. It was interesting to listen to some of the talk around town. The police, of course, denounced the Vigilantes, saying they could handle any crime that was committed and that Horn's killing of Mike Mulligan had been investigated and was found to be an act of self-defense, and therefore it had not been a crime.

There were others who feared Vigilante rule as much as they feared rule by the criminal element, and they said so

frankly. On the whole, though, I think the people of
Cheyenne approved of us and what we had done and slept
a little sounder because of it.

I thought that Frank Rush and the two carpenters
looked at me a little speculatively, as if wondering
whether I had been involved in the Vigilante doings, but
they didn't ask and of course I didn't volunteer anything.
The carpenters talked frankly about favoring the Vigilante activity, saying that maybe their wives would be safe
now and they could go home from a saloon at night
without worrying about being knocked in the head and
robbed.

Frank only said, "Whenever you take the power to
enforce the law out of the hands of the duly appointed
officers, you run a risk of exchanging one set of rules for
another one that's worse. Who can say for sure which set
is best?"

I agreed with him one hundred percent. It was the
exact reason I'd had so many doubts about joining the
Vigilance Committee and why I had challenged Jess
Munro. I said nothing to Frank or the carpenters, however. They could make up their own minds about the
matter, and I was afraid that anything I said would make
them think one way or the other about my involvement.

It was, of course, the kind of problem in which I was
damned if I did and damned if I didn't. My very silence
might give me away. In any case, I was not in the habit of
being confidential with the carpenters, and Frank never
questioned me about it, so I didn't have to commit myself.

The next day we paraded exactly as Munro had
planned. At eight o'clock we assembled at the town jail on
Thomes Avenue. Every man was on hand. Munro organized us the way he wanted us, then we moved in a solid
mass to Eddy street, marching in columns of four, each
team making a solid block of sixteen men in four lines.
Munro, Bellew, and Thiessen were out in front. My team
came next. I was on the right end of the first line, the
same position that was occupied by the chiefs of the other
three teams.

Nearly all of us had been in one or the other of the two

armies during the Civil War, so marching was not new to us. From what I heard the next day, we put on a formidable show, our faces covered by gunnysacks and our rifles very much in evidence. After that we were known as "the gunnysack brigade," a facetious name perhaps, but one that put fear into the hearts of the undesirables.

We marched practically the full length of Eddy Street, took a cross-street to Ferguson and went along it, back on Hill, and then we returned to the jail. We scattered after that, taking off our gunnysacks in the darkness and circling to our homes. It was inevitable that some of us would be identified, but as Munro had said, that was to be expected, and I don't think any harm came from it.

I had a jolt as I approached my house. The lamps had been lighted in the front room and the blinds had not been drawn, so someone or several someones had moved in on me. I was sure Cherry wouldn't do it, and I doubted that either Frank or Nancy Rush would. There had been a rash of claim-jumpers in the last few weeks—lot-jumpers would be a better term, I guess—and I assumed I had a house-jumper on my hands just as I'd had when I returned to Black Hawk after my hitch with the First Colorado Volunteers.

I ran then, right into the front room with my rifle on the ready, so furious that it's a wonder I didn't start shooting the instant I saw anyone. But fortunately I didn't entirely lose control of myself. The moment I cleared the door, a woman sang out, "There's our man." And a second one cried, "It's Jim, all right."

I stopped and looked and swallowed, and I wasn't sure I was seeing what I thought I was seeing. Rosy and Flossie Martin had moved in on me. I wouldn't have been surprised if it had happened the first month I'd been in Cheyenne—in fact, I had expected them. But they hadn't showed up and I'd just about forgotten them.

The next minute they were all over me, hugging me and kissing me and acting as if I was their long lost sweetheart. I finally got my rifle laid down so I could cooperate, then I shoved them back and asked what they were doing in Cheyenne.

"Doing?" Rosy stared at me as if I had to be stupid to ask a question like that. "We're going into business as soon as you can build a house for us."

"Of course we're going into business," Flossie said. "We sold out in Black Hawk."

"We damned near starved the last month or so," Rosy said, "and we kept hearing about all the activity up here in Cheyenne, so here we are."

"We're going to get rich as soon as you build our house," Flossie said. "We had our driver bring us right here. Everybody knows you, so we didn't have any trouble finding the house."

"We'll live with you until our house is built," Rosy said.

"We'll use just one of your bedrooms," Flossie said, "except for the times you need us."

"We'll cook for you and keep house for you," Rosy said.

"Of course we will," Flossie said. "You'll have all the comforts and happiness of a husband and none of the responsibilities."

I sat down in my rocking chair and held my head. "My God," I said, "don't you think you'd better ask me about some of the things you're talking about?"

"Oh, we knew you wouldn't object."

"Of course not," Flossie said indignantly. "You're not the kind of man who would refuse an offer like this."

"Well, I can and I do," I shouted. "Now get out of here, both of you. Go to the hotel and get yourself a room. Tomorrow we'll talk business about the house you want built."

"Why, shame on you, James Glenn," Rosy said, pointing an accusing finger at me. "You wouldn't turn two innocent girls out into the night, would you?"

"To be attacked by wicked men while we walk the street?" Flossie demanded. "No, you wouldn't do that, Jim."

I looked at one and then the other, and damned if I

could tell from the hurt expression on their faces whether they were pulling my leg or not. Of course they were, but they were still serious about it. This was the way they always had been. There were times when I thought they were idiots and other times when I knew they were the smartest whores I had ever run into. Either way, they were a weird pair.

"Did you say innocent?" I asked. "And did I hear you call yourself girls?"

"Now don't get nasty, Jim," Rosy said.

Flossie shook her head at me reprovingly. "It isn't becoming of you, Jim. It really isn't like you."

I got up and faced them. I said, "Now look here, both of you. You are not going to make a whorehouse out of my place. Do you understand that?"

They nodded, suddenly subdued. "Yes," they said together. "We understand perfectly."

"And another thing. I have a good friend who is a preacher. I'm fond of both him and his wife. I wouldn't for the world have them know I was harboring two women like you."

"Oh, we wouldn't tell him you were harboring us," Rose said.

"And we wouldn't tell him what kind of women we are," Flossie added.

"And there's a third thing," I said, ignoring their remarks. "I've met a girl I intend to marry. If she ever found out I'd had any truck with you two, she'd throw me overboard so fast it'd make my head swim."

Rosy drew a cross over her heart. "We won't tell her."

"We promise," Flossie said. "We'll even lie for you."

"Now about the house," Rosy said. "We understand lots are expensive and hard to find."

"And that good carpenters are hard to find, too," Flossie said. "But we were told that you have some good men working for you and that you're one of the best builders in Cheyenne."

"I'd say that was all true," I agreed, thinking I was finally going to get rid of them. The red-light district was beginning to shape up on Eighteenth Street and I owned a lot in that block. "I'll sell you a lot for one thousand dollars and I'll build the kind of house you want on the lot. We'll work out the plans tomorrow when I can get to the hotel, probably early in the afternoon. I'm almost finished with the house I'm on, so I can start . . ."

I stopped. I thought I'd won and I'd be shoving them out of the house in another minute, but damned if they hadn't pulled the blinds and locked the front door as I was talking, and now they started to undress.

"What the hell are you doing?" I yelled.

"What does it look like?" Rosy asked. Before I could answer, she said, "We're going to bed—that's what. We've had a long day on the stage getting here from Denver and we're tired."

"We looked at your bed and it's big enough for all three of us," Flossie said. "Now get your clothes off and come to bed so you won't keep us awake any longer than you have to."

Every time I knocked heads with these two women I felt as if I were punching a feather bed. Of course I couldn't put two naked women out into the street. It was easier just to go to bed.

CHAPTER XXII

I got Rosy and Flossie out of the house at daybreak the next day. I knocked off work in the middle of the afternoon, found them in the lobby of the hotel, and took them to the office of Judge Eli Saunders, a lawyer I knew and trusted. They thought this wasn't necessary, but they didn't argue about it. Saunders drew up a contract, the women paid me one thousand dollars for the lot, and I promised to get started on their house by the middle of the following week.

That night after supper Lucky Sam Bellew called on me. The evening was a cold one, so we sat close to the heating stove and smoked, talking small talk that didn't amount to anything. We agreed that the town had been quiet after the Tate Horn business and that it was colder than hell and probably snowing hard on Sherman Hill and that chances were the railroad would be stopped in its tracks within a few days.

I thought he had come to talk Vigilante business, but he seemed to have trouble getting to it. I saw him knock his pipe out into the coal scuttle and slip it into his pocket. I heard him clear his throat and I watched him get up and walk to the other side of the room and finally turn and go to the stove. For a time he stood there with his hands jammed into his pants pocket, scowling as if there was something he had to say and couldn't find the words. By that time I had a pretty good idea he wasn't here on Vigilante business.

"Glenn," he said finally, "I asked you about selling your lots and you said you were going to keep them for a while. Now I'm not a man to push you, and you sure as hell have the right to do whatever you feel you should, but I'm going to make you an offer that sounds ridiculous. Maybe it is. Maybe I'd be better off if you turn me down flat.

"I can't even guess how high town lots are going. We do know that the Union Pacific is going to make a town out of Cheyenne, it being a division point and all, with a branch line running south to Denver. So the lots will always have some value. They won't go back to cow pasture like the lots in Julesburg."

He cleared his throat again. It seemed to me he was taking a roundabout way to get to what he meant to say, and I wondered about it. I decided he was so uncertain about Cheyenne's future that he had to talk himself into making an offer. I just sat there and pulled on my pipe and waited for him to dig his own grave, which he proceeded to do.

"You don't spend your time down on Ferguson and Eddy Streets playing poker with town lots," Bellew went on, "and that makes you smarter'n I am. My trouble is I don't have any lots to play poker with. That's why I'm making you this offer. As you said, you're a builder, not a speculator. On the other hand, I'm a speculator, not a builder, and I've got to have some lots if I'm going to sit in on the game."

He got his pipe out, filled it and lighted it. He still hadn't made any offer and I was convinced that he felt he had to try to buy my lots but the logical part of his brain was trying to put the brakes on telling him the lots weren't worth it and he might end up holding an empty sack. I still kept my mouth shut and waited.

After he got his pipe going, he said, "I'm not as good a gambler as I thought I was when I came to Cheyenne. The stakes are too high. I've got a pretty good sense of values and I know that the damned speculators—and I don't mean me—have bid the lots up until they're clear out of sight. I should warn you that they may go still higher and maybe you'd be smart to inquire around before you take my offer." He took the pipe out of his mouth and stared at it, his forehead furrowed by thought. "Has anybody come to you lately to buy?"

I nodded. "Several of them, but they struck me as fast-talking boys I didn't trust and I gave them no encouragement whatever. They just never got around to making me a firm offer. I guess I didn't let them."

"You haven't given me any encouragement either," he said, putting the pipe back into his mouth, "but I'm going to make you a firm offer anyhow. I'll give you a check tonight for part of it and I'll meet you at Judge Saunders' office at nine o'clock in the morning. We'll complete the deal there and I'll write you another check for the balance."

By that time my patience had worn out completely. I got up and waggled a finger under his nose. "My God, Bellew," I said in what must have been a threatening tone, "either do your job or get off the pot. What is your offer? You act as if you don't really want to make it."

"I don't," he snapped. "I'm scared to make it. Like I said, the stakes have gone too high, but I've got to have some property or I can't do any business. You own the best bunch of lots in town that haven't been built on. If I can buy them, I'll be back in business."

He took a long breath and gritted his teeth like a boy about to dive into a water hole for the first swim in the spring. "I'll give you twenty five hundred for all the residential lots you'll sell, and three thousand for the business lots."

My knees gave way and I sat down again. I couldn't believe he'd said what I'd heard. He must have gone completely crazy. I had expected an offer of maybe twelve hundred, or fifteen hundred at the most.

"I'll take it," I said quickly before he could change his mind. "I'll let twenty residential lots go and five business lots."

He nodded, still nervous, and walked to the table, sat down, and asked for pen and ink. I brought them to him and he wrote out a check for ten thousand dollars drawn on an Omaha bank. Then he said, "Tomorrow morning at nine in Judge Saunders' office."

"I'll be there," I said.

He walked to the front door, stopped and looked back at me. He said, "Two days ago a couple of women named Martin looked me up and asked about the price of lots and how much it would cost to build a house. Then they quizzed me about you. Did they ever find you?"

"Yeah, they found me," I answered, "but there's something wrong in what you just said. They didn't get to town until yesterday."

He shook his head. "I remember exactly when it was. It was day before yesterday. They'd been in town a day or so then."

"What did you tell them a lot was worth?"

"I said it was worth whatever you could get somebody to pay, but I thought any good lot would fetch around twenty-five hundred." He turned the knob, then asked, "What kind of work do they do?"

"They're whores."

"I'll be damned." He scratched his head. "They don't look like it. I was pretty well impressed with them. I thought maybe they were business women of some kind."

"Oh, they are," I said. "They're business women right down to their big toes."

He laughed shortly. "You never know. Usually I can spot one as far away as I can see her, but they fooled me. Well, I'll see you in the morning."

He went out, shutting the door. I looked at the check and then I thought of all the money I was going to get in the morning and I just didn't believe it. I wished my father could see this check. He'd given me some pretty good advice that had turned out better than either of us had guessed.

I was a rich man, and I hadn't turned my hand to earn it. I'd just invested my money and hung on for less than five months. Now I was looking at a check for ten thousand dollars, and in the morning I'd have another one for fifty-five thousand. I looked at the check again and told myself that when my father was alive, we had thought that ten thousand dollars was a fortune.

Then all of a sudden I thought of what Bellew had said

about Rosy and Flossie being in town for two days at least before they had seen me. They had plain out lied to me. More than that, they knew the lot they were buying was worth two-and-one-half times what they were paying. The good feeling went out of me and I was furious.

I went downtown on the run, stomped into the hotel, and banged up the stairs. I pounded on their door. When it opened, I was looking at Rosy, who had pulled a red robe over her gaily flowered nightgown.

"Why, it's Jim, Flossie," Rosy called. "He's come to see us."

"All you had to do was to send for us," Flossie said. "We can't do it here in the hotel—"

"I didn't come here to do anything but wring your God-damned necks." I pushed past Rosy and shut the door. "You sons-of-bitches lied to me."

They stared, their mouths sagging open. Then Rosy began to cry and Flossie dabbed at her eyes. Rosy whispered, "Honey, why are you calling us names?"

Flossie came up to me and put an arm around my waist. "Darling, I'm ashamed of you, calling us sons-of-bitches. Now you know that isn't true. We've always been good to you."

"Of course we have," Rosy said between sniffles. "You remember how it was in Black Hawk when we got you started building houses."

"You learned a lot on our house," Flossie said, "and we never complained once because you were slow and had to do some of your work over."

Rosy lay down on the bed and cried louder than ever, but somehow she managed to say, "We've always loved you, Jim. You're not like any other customers we ever had. You're special."

"You certainly are," Flossie said. "You're very special."

She kissed me, and then Rosy sat up and pointed a finger at me. "Why are you treating us this way? We don't deserve it at all."

"No we don't," Flossie said. "It makes me feel so bad that I think I'll . . . kill myself."

It was a hell of a good show, but calling me "honey"

and "darling" and telling me they'd always loved me didn't really change anything. I said, "You told me you'd just got in on the stage, but the truth is you'd been in town at least two days."

"Of course we lied to you, silly," Rosy said. "Don't you know why?"

"He wouldn't know why," Flossie said scornfully, "so I'll tell him plain out. We wanted to sleep with you and we knew you wouldn't let us stay unless we could make you think we'd just got to town and were tired."

I knew damned well they were twisting me around their little fingers into a good tight knot, and after I was gone and the door shut they'd probably laugh their heads off at how they had fooled me, so I said, "And another thing. You knew the speculators had run prices for town property up to twenty-five hundred dollars, but you only paid me one thousand for my lot."

"But honey," Rosy protested, "you made the offer."

Flossie nodded. "Now wouldn't it have looked funny if we had said, 'No, Jim, we won't give you your price of one thousand.'"

They had me. They were right as rain. It had been *my* offer. It wasn't their fault that they knew more about property values than I did. I swallowed, pulled the door open and began to back into the hall. "I'll tell you what," Rosy said. "We'll make up that fifteen-hundred-dollar difference in trade."

"Sure we will," Flossie said heartily. "You won't lose a penny and you'll enjoy yourself every minute."

"I accept your offer," I said, "but I'll be an old man before I pick up fifteen hundred in trade."

"No you won't," Rosy said.

"You'll be the best old man in the territory," Flossie said, "and it will always be waiting for you to come and get it."

"Are we forgiven?" Rosy asked.

"We've got to know or we won't sleep a wink tonight," Flossie said solemnly.

"Sure, you're forgiven," I said, and backed on out of the room and pulled the door shut.

I went down the stairs and across the lobby to the street, not sure why or how it had turned out the way it had. I should have known better than to go storming up the stairs to their room the way I had. I just wasn't any match for them.

When I went into the street it was snowing hard, the wind driving the flakes against me and stinging my face. I hurried home, my collar pulled up against my throat. I had a sour taste in my mouth, knowing I hadn't accomplished much. All I'd really succeeded in doing was to punch the feather bed again.

CHAPTER XXIII

I didn't sleep much that night. I had a funny feeling that I'd just had a pleasant dream and I'd wake up in the morning to find that Lucky Sam Bellew hadn't been to see me at all and I didn't have any check for ten thousand dollars. But when I woke up, the dawn light only beginning to touch my bedroom windows, there was the check on my bureau just where I had left it the previous evening. I was a rich man and I was going to be richer.

I got to Saunders' office five minutes early, but Bellew was already there. We finished our business before noon, so I had time to eat dinner and catch the east-bound 12:30 train, this time with a second check in my pocket for fifty-five thousand dollars.

Even after I was on the train with both checks in my wallet I couldn't get rid of the horrible feeling in the bottom of my stomach that it couldn't really have happened. Maybe the checks would bounce. Maybe Bellew didn't have that much money in his account.

He did. My worries fizzled out; I had no trouble cashing the checks. Then I got cautious, thinking that one of the banks in Omaha might go broke and it might be the bank that had all of my money, so I divided it, depositing it in three different banks, keeping out five thousand dollars, which I carried in a money belt buckled around my waist. All the way back to Cheyenne I fretted about being robbed.

As soon as I reached Cheyenne I went to Fritz Thiessen's bank, wading through six inches of snow that had accumulated on the ground since I'd left, and deposited most of the five thousand. I owed a big bill for

286

building materials, and this would give me enough to get squared away and still have some cash left in the bank.

Thiessen was in his private office when I deposited the money. He happened to see me and called me back into his office. He shut the door and waved me into a chair, then he sat down behind his desk and leaned forward.

"Do you know where Munro, Burke, Williams and Stead went to?" he asked.

"I just got back to town from Omaha," I said. "I didn't know they had gone anywhere."

"They have," he said solemnly. "I don't like it. They saddled up and left about sunup, riding west. Bellew told me about it. If you've been out of town, they couldn't have told you if they'd wanted to—but damn it, they should have told me. If it's Vigilante business, we should be informed. All of us."

I nodded agreement. "Bellew doesn't know?"

"Not a thing. He's a man who always gets up early, and he'd just finished breakfast and had left the restaurant when he saw them riding out of town. He hollered at them, but they kept going, pretending they didn't hear him."

This made me about as uneasy as it had made Thiessen. Still, if something had come up since I'd left town, they couldn't have consulted me, and I could see why they hadn't told Thiessen and Bellew. Both men were soft, and I doubted that they could stand a hard ride if that was what the four men had in mind. I didn't feel like telling Thiessen that, but I agreed that he and Bellew should have been consulted.

"Maybe they aren't going on Vigilante business," I said.

"Maybe," he grunted, "but the odds are that's exactly what they're up to. You may not have heard about the holdup. The Denver stage was robbed south of the Colorado line yesterday. The guard was killed and the driver wounded. The robbers got away with the strongbox and cleaned out the passengers. I heard there was three of them."

Thiessen leaned back and shook his head. "The trouble is it isn't within the jurisdiction of the Cheyenne officers.

By the time the Colorado lawmen got on their trail, the outlaws were out of the country. A hard wind blew all of last night, so any tracks that were in the snow were covered up before morning."

I hadn't heard, but it struck me right off that the four men had left Cheyenne to run down the outlaws. I didn't try to argue with Thiessen. I just spread my hands and shook my head. "I don't know what to say, Fritz. Chances are Ed Burke picked up some information and told Munro. You know Munro wouldn't let a chance like that slip by."

"We'll have it out with them when they get back," Thiessen said angrily. "I thought you set Munro straight the other night, but maybe he's so bullheaded he can't learn."

"He's a bullhead, all right," I said.

It was late in the afternoon when I left the bank. I built a fire when I got home and cooked supper, but the house was cold and I couldn't get it warmed up for quite a while. I thought about what Thiessen had said. In fact, I didn't think about anything else for a while.

I could guess what Munro would say when we jumped him. For one thing, he'd claim that the holdup had been on the other side of the line and wasn't the proper business of the Cheyenne Committee. He could also argue that he had a majority of the seven with him, so if we'd had a meeting and taken a vote, he had the four votes he needed for whatever action they had taken; the other three of us might as well save our wind. He could also have said, as I'd thought when I was talking to Thiessen, that I was out of town and he knew Thiessen and Bellew couldn't make the ride.

These were all facts we couldn't deny, but there was another aspect of this business that bothered me. I knew Ed Burke well, and by this time I felt I had Jess Munro sized up. I didn't know Stead and Williams very well, but it was my guess that they were four of a kind, tough men who would hang stage-robbers without hurting their conscience. Munro would have his hanging, and now he could do all the talking that he wanted to about making an example of these outlaws as a warning to the others.

In spite of all I could say to myself about the validity of Munro's arguments, the old doubts were right back in my mind again. Not that I was against hanging men who would hold up a stage and kill the guard and wound the driver. It was just that I would have to be absolutely sure of their guilt before I'd have any part of a hanging, but I was convinced that Jess Munro would hang men he *thought* had committed the crime just to get the warning over to the hardcases he wanted to get rid of.

Frank Rush dropped in after I'd finished my supper. He said the house was finished and he and Nancy would move in tomorrow morning. Barely in time, too, with the cold snap here and the snow on the ground. He was grateful to me, of course, for making the house available, and he was sure Nancy was too.

He didn't look at me while he said this. I wondered if he knew how I felt about Nancy, and that it was only my concern for her comfort and safety that had forced me to make the Quixotic gesture that I had. I knew very well I could have rented the house ten times and had cash coming in, and I knew equally well that I'd get little cash for the rent from Frank.

I'm not intimating that Frank meant to be dishonest about it. Rather, he felt impelled to put his money into his church building. He probably told himself that later on, after the church building was finished, he would see that I got all the rent that was coming to me.

I would not, of course, make an issue out of it and I told him so. I said that he had done fine work for me and he was not to worry about the rent. Then I said, "I've got a contract to build a house on that lot I own on Eighteenth Street. We'll get started on it in the morning. I guess it's not too cold to work."

"No, it's not too cold." He cleared his throat, swallowed, and finally blurted, "I'm sorry, Jim, but I've got to start on my church. I'm going to have to quit working for you."

I guess I should have seen this coming, but I hadn't,

and it struck me that he was being disloyal, that he should stay with me as long as I had work that was pressing. I didn't say anything, though. I took time to fill my pipe and light it, something I had learned long ago to do when my temper began crowding me.

Before I struck the match, the thought occurred to me that Frank knew what the house on Eighteenth Street was going to be used for and he didn't want any part in building it. For some reason the notion comforted me and took away the feeling that he was disloyal.

"Good luck with it," I said. "I hope you'll come back and work for me after the church is finished."

"I hope I can," he said.

He rose and we shook hands. He never did work for me after that. As a matter of fact, I didn't see much of him after that, because I didn't go to church and he didn't come to see me. When he had scraped some rent money together, he sent it over with Nancy.

Nancy was ashamed and apologized for being so far behind in the rent. It hurt me to see a proud woman like Nancy brought down to the position where she had to apologize for Frank. I told her not to say anything about it, that I had been determined to get her out of the tent and into a house, and that it was all right with me if I never got a nickel of rent.

She stood at the door and looked at me, and I looked at her. I wanted to tell her that the only reason I had built the house was that I loved her and couldn't stand the thought of her freezing to death in that damned tent and being in danger of getting raped every night by the hardcases who roamed the Cheyenne streets, in spite of all that the police and Vigilantes had done.

I didn't say any of it because I knew she understood that, even though I had never actually said it. I was convinced she loved me for it, even though she had never said that either. She turned and walked away. I went to the door and watched her as long as she was in sight.

I'm not sure of the exact thoughts that were in my mind as I looked at her, but I don't think I ever, at that or any other time during those months, entertained the hope that someday I would have her. I despised men who butted into another man's marriage—an attitude that never really changed.

Frank's leaving me didn't hurt as much as I was afraid it would. I was lucky enough to find another carpenter the next day, but now I stayed on the job almost all the time, whereas before, I had known that Frank would do a good job of overseeing the work if I wanted to go somewhere. Now I had to do it, so I was tied down far more than I had been.

Less than a week after I returned from Omaha, Munro and the other three men rode back into town. The weather had warmed up and most of the snow had gone off the ground, so we had mud, which was what had held them up, according to Ed.

He came into Cherry's restaurant as I was eating supper and told me they'd just got in. He ordered a steak and I sat beside him at the counter and drank coffee until he finished. Then he walked home with me. I built up the fire and offered him a drink and a cigar, and when we were comfortable I said, "I want to hear about this trip you and Munro and the other men made. Thiessen and Bellew are sore because they weren't informed."

"Is that so?" He seemed surprised. "Hell, Jim, it just wasn't any of their put-in. If it had been Cheyenne Vigilante business, we'd have told them, but this was out of town. I got wind of what had happened through one of the outlaws who knocked the stage over. He came by for a horse and told me the other three had hightailed for Dale City and had holed up there. I rode into town as soon as I could and told Munro. He asked Williams and Stead to go with us because we needed at least four men."

"You knew they'd go, and you knew they wouldn't kick about hanging three outlaws," I said.

He was surprised again. He pulled on his cigar for a moment, then said, "That's right ... You know, it never occurred to Munro that Bellew and Thiessen would feel that way. I'll tell him and he can talk to 'em. He's a tough bastard, that Munro, but he'll keep Cheyenne clean. You can count on that."

"I believe it," I said, and I sensed then that my trouble with Jess Munro wasn't over by a long shot. I'd known all the time, but for some reason I was reminded of it right then very forcibly.

"You know," Ed said, "I'm guessing that the railroad is gonna have to stop work for a while on Sherman Hill. We seen a lot of snow up there on top."

Dale City was a little burg about forty miles west of Cheyenne, so I understood why they'd been gone so long, what with the snow and then the mud. I just waited, figuring that he'd get around to telling the whole story if I gave him plenty of time.

He never did get around to telling the whole story, though. I guess I didn't give him enough time. What he said next set me off. "We surprised 'em. They probably figured they were so far from Cheyenne that nobody from here would bother 'em, and being in Wyoming, they didn't count on nobody chasing 'em from Colorado. We got 'em under our guns and we took 'em down to a railroad trestle and strung 'em up."

He stopped and looked at me, grinning. "You know who it was? Well sir, you wouldn't guess. I was surprised because I didn't think they had it in 'em. It was your old friend Bully Bailey and his two sidekicks."

I was stunned. I blinked, and the blood began to roar in my head. Before I knew what I was saying, I yelled, "You son-of-a-bitch! Bailey was my meat. You knew that. Why did you hang him?"

He'd looked as if he thought I'd be pleased with what they'd done, but what I said wiped the grin off his face. He stood up and jammed his hands deep into his pockets.

"Jim," he said, "if anybody else had called me a son-of-a-bitch I'd have cleaned his plow for him good, so don't repeat it. But I will say one thing to you. You are a God-damned fool. Bailey would never have faced you in a gunfight. Sooner or later they'd have come into Cheyenne and dry-gulched you. They'd have killed you the other time by kicking you to death if me and Frank Rush hadn't saved your life. You're too much of a gentleman or a fool—I ain't sure which—to have shot Bailey in the back, and that's the only way you could have killed him. Now you're safe and you call me a son-of-a-bitch for doing you a favor."

He got up and stomped out. He was dead right and I knew it, but I couldn't find enough guts to tell him until Sunday, when I rode out to his ranch and told him. He laughed and said, "Get off that horse and come inside. I've got a bottle that needs killing."

That's the kind of man Ed Burke was.

CHAPTER XXIV

Those of us who had been prophesying that the railroad would mire down in the snow on Sherman Hill were proved right. Chief Engineer Dodge had named Fort Sanders on the western side of the Black Hills as his objective, but he didn't quite make it.

Any way you looked at it, Dodge and the Casements and the others had to be given "A" for effort. They must have done the greatest job of railroad building the world had ever seen. At Cheyenne they had built 517 miles from Omaha, and 87 miles had been laid in the last three months. Besides that, there was always extra work to be done, such as putting in the sidings and switches.

The distance from Cheyenne to the start of the climb was fifteen miles, with the summit of the Black Hills another fifteen miles farther west. Dodge's goal, Fort Sanders, was only twenty more miles downhill from the summit.

They reached eight thousand feet on the pass and there the snow stopped them, still ten miles from the summit and thirty miles short of Fort Sanders. But the Union Pacific had laid 240 miles of track in 1867, and if any of us in Cheyenne had been asked, we would have said it was a hell of a good job.

Even though the laying of track had stopped, a lot of work was done through the winter months for the big final push to Ogden and beyond. All kinds of materials were piled high along the track and the Casements' warehouse in Cheyenne was packed with stores ready to be used the following spring.

Tons of iron rolled in; ties were piled up like young

mountains, and more were being cut in the Black Hills
and Medicine Bows. All of this was fine for business, and
for a few months Cheyenne prospered. But we had our
headaches, too: before we knew it we were a city of
ten thousand people.

Rosy and Flossie were crying for their house to be
finished. They were losing money every day, they said,
and I knew they were. I hired two more men and we
rushed it through. From the night they opened both
women were kept busy with crowds of Irish graders and
track-layers who had been called in from the end of steel,
and the new men who were pouring in on every train
from Omaha.

Again I was reminded how the things that happen to us
are never unmixed blessings, and that the pill of success
may be sugar-coated, but the pill can be mouth-prickling
sour when the sugar is gone. It was fine to have so much
business in Cheyenne, so much money to spend, but there
was the other side of the coin: lots and building costs too
high, crowds on the streets twenty-four hours a day, rents
too high, people living in tents and shacks that were a
health hazard and a disgrace to Cheyenne, and an increase in the criminal element along with the booming
population.

As soon as I finished the Martin women's house, I
started a new business building, this one on Eddy Street. I
could have rented it a dozen times over if I'd had it
finished, but first the house for Frank and Nancy Rush
had delayed me, then the Martin house, and the upshot of
it was that I simply didn't get my building done in time to
cash in on the big boom.

Still, I didn't complain. I had sold my lots to Lucky
Sam Bellew at close to the top of the market. The boom
price of lots had leveled off, although I think some of the
corner business lots did bring as much as thirty-five
hundred after I sold to Bellew.

I don't know how Bellew came out. Within a month
from the time he bought my lots he sold out and left
town. Probably he ended up about even, the slump not
coming until early in the spring. I suspect he put every

nickel he had into my lots, knowing, as we all did, that when the boom was over prices would drop as fast as they had sky-rocketed. The question was not *if*, but *when*.

I think Bellew found the game too much for his nerves, so he probably got out when he could by selling for about the same figure he had paid me. He didn't go broke, though there were plenty who did. Later in the year I was able to buy back some of the lots I'd sold to Bellew for five hundred dollars apiece.

Speculators had given me a fortune, and for that I was thankful, but I had no reason to lose sympathy on the ones who lost their shirts off their backs. It was the same in any gamble—they knew the possible consequences when they sat in on the game. Some won and some lost, but when the slide came, the ones who did lose lost big.

As I said, we had an increase of the criminal population with the boom in the overall population. We had more whores, more pimps, more con men, and more sneak thieves. There was no way to keep this element out of town, but I don't know what would have happened to Cheyenne if we had not organized the Vigilantes.

I still had some doubts, I still kept my eyes and ears open waiting for Munro to go off half-cocked, but to my knowledge he never did. Somehow we kept the lid on. I'm not saying we didn't have some murders and robberies. We did, of course, and we had men mugged and rolled and beaten, but Cheyenne did not become another Julesburg. Most of the stories written about Cheyenne's lawlessness were exaggerated by reporters who, when the facts failed to give them a good story, simply made one up.

I was busy and so was Cherry, and for that reason we didn't see each other as much as I would have liked. Maybe Cherry wanted to see more of me than she did—at least, I wanted to think that. Many times when I dropped into her restaurant for supper she only had time for a quick smile when she saw me. Later in the winter she did sometimes invite me back into her living quarters to eat supper with her, or more often simply to have a cup of coffee with a piece of cake or pie she had set aside for me.

From the day the first train from Julesburg had arrived with all the toughs who were moving to Cheyenne, I had worried about Cherry. Now, with the bridge-building and track-laying crews called in for the winter, conditions were far worse.

As far as I know, there was only one time when she had any serious trouble. By sheer good fortune I was on hand to save her from what might have been a tragedy. I had worked late that evening. Then, to make me still later, Munro had called a meeting of the Central Committee along with the four chiefs, so I hadn't had time to get any supper.

Munro called these meetings at least once a week and sometimes oftener because he had spies among the hardcases. Ed Burke seemed to know what the plug-uglies were planning, too. Munro always put before us the names of men he thought should be run out of town. He gave us chapter and verse along with the names. If we all agreed that they had to leave town, and we practically always did, they were warned. They usually pulled out before their time was up and that was the end of it.

The way we operated was to locate our man, usually in a saloon when he was drinking at the bar. Then one of us would go into the saloon and tap him on the shoulder and say, "You're wanted outside." Or, "There's a man out here who wants to talk to you."

When we got him into the street, we'd escort him around the saloon building to the alley, where a bunch of us would be waiting, and tell him to be out of town before sunup. All of us except the Vigilante who had gone into the saloon would be wearing our gunnysack masks.

If our man was still in Cheyenne after we delivered our warning, we'd go after him a second time. We would show him a rope, then give him a hell of a beating. After that he'd pull up stakes as soon as he was able to travel. It didn't fail once, so the bad ones were on the move out of town almost every day, and the others heard about it and stayed inside the law. They knew they'd be next if they didn't.

I didn't take part in any of the hangings, though there

were some. And I never knew for sure that Munro or any of the Vigilantes were involved in these hangings. I always believed that the toughs were the ones who were responsible, doing it to get rid of their rivals. Of course, they expected the blame to fall on the Vigilantes, which it did.

Anyhow, I was hungry that evening. I wouldn't have been surprised if Cherry had locked up and gone to bed, but she hadn't; she was still looking for me to drop in. The evening crowd was gone and she had sent her help home, so she was alone, except for a big red-bearded bastard who'd had enough to drink to make him mean.

He should have gone to a whorehouse, as horny as he was, but he'd lingered over his coffee, watching Cherry as she cleaned up. Finally she told him to leave. That was what triggered him. When I came in he had her backed into a corner and was trying to kiss her. She was fighting him off, but he was too strong for her. In the fracas before I took a hand, he had torn her blouse clear down across her right breast.

I seldom lost my temper—I mean, lost it to the place where I had no control over myself. But this time I lost it completely. I guess I was a madman when I tackled the fellow. He didn't know I'd come in, he was that busy with Cherry. If I hadn't showed up, I'm convinced he would have raped her right there on the restaurant floor, and perhaps killed her.

I caught him by a shoulder and yanked him around. He was so surprised that he released his grip on Cherry. She ducked away from him and backed into the kitchen, trying to hold her blouse together. I hit the man in the mouth, knocking his front teeth out, cutting his lip, and flattening his nose so that blood spurted in a fine red stream.

He went back and down, his head hitting a corner of a table. I jumped on him, my knees driving the wind out of him. I got a handful of hair and banged his head against the floor. I wasn't doing any thinking. Afterward I couldn't remember what I had done, but Cherry told me I was hammering a tattoo on the floor with the back of his skull. Once in a while, for good measure, I'd slug him on the jaw with my free hand.

I don't know how Cherry got through to me, but she finally did. When I realized what I was doing, I stood up and stared down at the man. His face looked like a piece of raw beef. I got him by the feet and dragged him into the street. The night was a cold one, and I knew that if he laid there awhile he'd freeze to death. I didn't give a damn if he did.

For a moment I stood in the doorway and watched him. I guess the cold air revived him—or maybe it was the snow. Anyhow, he got up on his hands and knees and started to crawl away. He spilled out flat on his belly, then struggled up to his hands and knees again and crawled a few more feet before he fell again.

I turned and closed the door. Cherry was standing motionless, one hand clutching the front of her torn blouse, her eyes on me as if she had never seen me before in her life.

I went to her, asking, "Are you all right? Did he hurt you?"

"I'm all right," she whispered. "You got here just in time."

I put my arms around her and kissed her long and hard. I'd kissed her before, but never like this. When we finally drew apart, I said, "Cherry, marry me. Marry me right away. I don't want you to take any more chances staying here by yourself."

She looked at me, her moist lips quivering. "I'll marry you," she said, "but not right away. I've got to think about it some more."

"Why?" I demanded. "You've had all winter and part of last fall to think about it."

"I'm afraid, Jim," she said. "Afraid of what you might do sometime. You'd have killed that man if I'd let you alone."

It was my turn to stare at her. "Sure I would," I said. "He deserved killing."

"I didn't know you had a temper like that," she protested. "It scares me."

It didn't make any sense to me. I'd saved her from a raping. Very likely I saved her life. I turned on my heel and strode to the door. I was afraid to stay there—I'd have lost my temper again if I had. She was scared of me because I'd lost my temper. I guess she thought I could come in and see her being abused and beat hell out of that bastard and be my cool, calm self while I was doing it.

Before I slammed the door behind me, I yelled, "Lock up."

"Wait, Jim," she cried out. "Don't go."

But I didn't wait. I shut the door with a hard slam and walked home through the snow. I built a fire and cooked my own supper, then I sat at the table and smoked my pipe. I felt as if I had eaten a plateful of rocks. After a time I calmed down and my stomach felt better.

When I could think straight again, I began to wonder if I really wanted to marry Cherry. I wasn't sure right then. I wasn't sure at all.

CHAPTER XXV

I didn't sleep much that night. Cherry crowded into my thoughts and refused to leave. I knew I had to make a very important decision. Either I was going to marry Cherry or I wasn't, but if I was, I had no patience with her stupid remark that she had to think it over some more. She'd had all the time in the world to think about it, and if she still had her doubts, then marrying me wasn't the thing for her to do.

Nothing had changed for me. I knew, as I had all along, that I didn't love her. I had never told her that I did. It was a simple proposition for me of having reached the age in which I felt a need to settle down and raise a family. I needed a wife, I needed a housekeeper, and I needed a woman to entertain. Good business required entertaining, and I was very much aware that when Cheyenne settled down to a town's normal routine, I would have to answer many demands that weren't evident now.

From my point of view, I had a great deal to offer a woman. I could give Cherry a comfortable home and a life with far more luxuries than she was used to, more than the average woman had. I had big plans for the future. I would do more building as time went on and Cheyenne grew on a permanent basis.

The Indian problem on the plains was far from settled and wouldn't be for a long time, so I was convinced that Fort D. A. Russell and Camp Carlin would be here for years. The army was going to need beef and wood and hay, and I intended to get my share of the contracting business. I didn't know anything about it, but I could learn just as I had learned to build. Other men had grown rich dealing with the army, and I saw no reason why I shouldn't, too.

I had spent a lot of time in the last few months dreaming about the future. Now I had the money to do anything I wanted to. I could hire crews of men to cut wood and hay and haul them to the fort. I could buy a herd of cattle in Colorado and hire cowboys to drive it to the fort. Once a man has money to deal with he can turn a dream into reality, and that was exactly what I aimed to do.

Before this I'd never allowed myself to dream big because I didn't have the money I needed to work with, but now the sky was the limit for my dreams, and I needed a woman to fill out the dreams, to share my good fortune. I'd lived long enough by now to realize that the really fine things of life do not come to men who live alone.

I considered myself a practical man, and love is always a part of being practical. I had offered Cherry a proposition, a fair exchange. I was sure she understood. But if she kept her part of the bargain, she had to trust me. The fact that I had lost my head and almost killed a man should not make her afraid of me. I resented it. No wife could be an adequate wife if she was afraid of her husband. I had seen wives who were afraid of their husbands, and she had hurt my pride when she had said in effect that that was the way it would be with us. Men like that were bullies, and I hated them.

By the time it was dawn I'd made up my mind to have it out with her. We'd make our rules; we'd know what to expect out of each other. If these rules didn't suit her, then by God she wasn't the woman for me to marry.

Apparently I was in a daze that day as I worked. One of my men asked me if I was sick, and another remarked that I must have been up all night tomcatting around. When it was supper time I went to Cherry's restaurant and sat down on a stool at the counter. Apparently the waitress had told Cherry, because she came out of the kitchen within a minute or so from the time I sat down. She walked behind the counter until she came to me.

Leaning forward, she whispered, "Jim, come back to my room. I want to talk to you."

The Irishmen who sat on both sides of me snickered and winked at each other, but I slid off the stool, ignoring them, and followed Cherry to her room. She closed the door after me, then turned and put her arms around me and kissed me.

It was the first time she had ever made the first move, and it knocked my plans right out of my head. I wanted her. This was the first time for that, too. I guess I had never thought she wanted me physically, but now I felt she did.

Then when she drew back and whispered, "I've been looking for you all day, Jim. I'm so glad you came tonight."

I looked at her, puzzled, and not quite knowing what she expected. From the expression on her face I wasn't even sure she knew what she had done to me. Then, quite suddenly, the feeling came to me that she hadn't wanted me that way at all, that she was seeking forgiveness and letting me know she didn't want to lose me.

Whether I was right or wrong about what was in Cherry's mind, I decided I couldn't say any of the things I had intended—things I would have said if I'd been talking to Nancy Rush and she had been free to marry me.

Nancy would have known exactly what was in my mind, and the same hunger would have been in her that was in me. But Cherry was different. In some strange way she seemed to live apart from the ordinary human world of passion and love and all the other strong human feelings that make life worth living for most of us.

"I'll get our plates," she said, and disappeared into the kitchen.

She returned with two plates of stew, went back after bread and butter and coffee, then brought two slabs of dried apple pie and set them on the bureau. We didn't talk much as we ate, but as soon as we were finished she took the dirty dishes back into the kitchen, then returned and pulled her chair close to mine. She reached for one of my hands and held it as she talked, squeezing it now and then to emphasize what she was saying.

"I want to apologize for last night, Jim," she said, "but first I must thank you for saving me perhaps from a fate worse than death. I mean that literally, not as a joke as people so often make it. I would rather be dead than to have been violated by that man. The part I want to apologize for was saying I was afraid of what you might do. I'm not afraid of that at all. I can only say I was so worked up—I mean just plain scared—that I didn't know how it sounded."

She took a long breath that was really a sigh. She was close to crying when she went on: "Jim, you are a fine man; I'm proud to be asked to marry you. Just give me a little more time. I've hated men all my life. My father was a monster and my mother hated him. She taught me to do the same and I guess I saw my father every time I looked at a man. I'm getting over it. You've helped me get over it, but I still need more time."

I saw tears running down her cheeks. She brushed at them impatiently with her free hand. She said, as if angry at herself, "I'm sorry, Jim. I hate bawling women and it isn't often it happens to me. It's just that I want you to understand and I'm not sure you can. I'm not like any other woman in the world. I don't want to be different, but I am."

She was silent then for a full minute or more, staring at the wall in front of us. Then she burst out, "Of course I don't want to be like some women. I mean, like the ones on Eighteenth Street who sell themselves to men. They're animals. A man buys a woman and she sells herself like a . . . a piece of merchandise. I have no sympathy for those women."

"They're still people," I said. "It's just that they've chosen that way to make their living."

"Are you defending them?" she demanded.

"No," I said. "All I'm saying is that they're people."

"They're animals," she snapped. "They chose that way of making a living because they are too lazy to work. I've had trouble hiring help, but there have always been plenty of those creatures in town who have not wanted to work." She took another long breath. "I never intended to get on that subject. I know you're not the kind of man who has anything to do with them, and of course you've known all the time I'm not that kind of woman."

I didn't tell her about my relationship with Rosy and Flossie Martin, and I hoped she would never find out. She was too innocent to understand, I thought, and of course once we were married I wouldn't need them and I'd never see them again.

"Well then," I said, "are we still getting married?"

"Oh yes," she said quickly. "Of course we are."

"When?"

"I don't know," she answered slowly. "I told you I still need a little time. Part of it, I think, is to prove to myself that I can make my own living, not just when there's a boom on, but during ordinary times when we have to scratch for a living."

I couldn't and wouldn't press her, but I wasn't really satisfied by her explanation of why she wanted to wait. I thought she just couldn't bear to pin the date down, that what she had said about hating men was probably true, and that this had been responsible for some of her attitudes and actions.

Now I remembered how suspicious of me she had been at first. She had been kind and compassionate when I had been beaten up by Bully Bailey and his friends, but I had been helpless then. When I looked back over these last months, I was struck by the time it had taken me to wear down her suspicions.

"I'll buy you a ring tomorrow," I said. "I'll stop in about the middle of the afternoon when you aren't busy."

The following day I took her next door to the jewelry store and bought her the biggest diamond in the place. She liked it and admired it, but somehow I was disappointed in her reaction to it. I'm not sure why, except that I had an idea she was saying all the right words but wasn't really feeling what she was saying.

That evening when I ate supper she was nowhere to be

seen. I didn't ask about her. I thought that if she wanted to see me she'd make herself known. I walked home through the twilight, wondering why she had stayed out of sight.

The sky had cleared and the stars were beginning to come out. The air was biting, with a hard wind driving down from the Black Hills across the prairie and drifting the snow in places up to my knees or higher.

I was chilled when I went into the house. The instant I opened the door, the warm air rushed at me. I stepped inside quickly and shut the door. Then I saw Nancy sitting in a rocker beside the window. It was the first time I'd seen her for nearly two months. She had brought the rent money in February and now it was almost April.

"I didn't want to sit here in the cold," she said, "so I built a fire. I made some coffee."

I pulled off my sheepskin and hung it up, then slapped my hat onto a nail beside the front door. I said, "I'm glad you did. Do you want some coffee?"

"No, I had a cup just now," she said, "but I'll pour you some if you—"

"I just left the restaurant," I said. "I'll have a cup after while."

"The rent is on the table," she said bitterly. "I don't know whether it's in advance for April, or whether Frank is paying some of the back rent. He didn't say."

"It's all right," I said. "I've told you that."

"No, it's not all right," she said. "I've always paid my own way, but now I'm forced to live on your charity. On Zach Dunlap's, too. We have a big bill at his store . . . I don't know, Jim. I don't think I can stand it much longer."

"How's Frank?" I asked.

"Fine," she answered, the bitterness still in her voice. "You know he's working for Fred Stallcup?"

"I'd heard that he was," I said.

Stallcup was the biggest builder in Cheyenne and probably paid better wages than I did. He was a man who would appreciate a good worker like Frank Rush. I was a little put out with Frank for not coming back to work for me, but I guess I didn't have any right to be.

Probably Frank hadn't been sure I'd do any more building. As a matter of fact, I wasn't either. It was only a matter of days until the railroad would send its crews out again and Cheyenne's boom would peter out. Frank probably thought he had a better chance to have a permanent job with Stallcup than with me.

"His conscience hurts him," Nancy said, "so he's afraid to face you, owing rent like he does. That's why he has me bring it to you. But the church is almost finished, so maybe he'll do better in the future. I'd like to get a job, only Frank won't let me. But if he doesn't pay you off, I will get a job, no matter what he says. I'll see that you're paid."

"Nancy, don't . . ."

I stopped. I could go on telling her a dozen times not to worry about the rent, that I didn't need the money, but it wouldn't have done any good. It seemed to me that nothing could do any good for her as long as she lived with Frank. He would never change.

I had purposely stayed away from Nancy because I did not trust myself. Now that I was engaged to Cherry, I had still more reason to stay away from Nancy. Still, I found myself walking toward her, slowly, not by choice, or by any decision on my part—I was moved by some compelling force that had not been willed by me.

From where I stopped, close to her, I could see only the side of her face. She was a beautiful woman—Frank Rush did not deserve her. He did not even realize how great a treasure he had. She was not cut out to be a preacher's wife. She had known that for a long time, but I don't think Frank did. He probably hadn't thought about it any more than he had thought about Nancy's safety when the Julesburg crowd had rolled into Cheyenne last November.

Then for the first time I was aware that in one way Frank was like Cherry. Neither had any understanding of the world in which they lived—Cherry, who hated men, and Frank, who thought of very little except the saving of men's souls.

"Divorce him, Nancy," I said. "Don't go on bruising yourself this way. There's no future for you living with Frank."

Slowly she tipped her head back to look at me. I saw misery in her face, complete and absolute misery such as I had never seen on the face of any other human being. She said, "I know that, Jim, but I can't divorce him."

"Why?" I demanded. "Why, when you know—"

"Several reasons," she interrupted. "One's enough. He's a kind and gentle man who would never injure me in any way. He lives the best he can with the understanding he has. He would never know why I divorced him. It would kill him."

She rose and walked to the door, then turned to look at me. "Jim, the Bible says it's as great a sin to think adultery as it is to do it. That makes me a great sinner."

What she said startled me. Before I could say anything, she had added. "Good-by. I just wanted to see you for a few minutes."

"I'll walk home with you," I said.

"No, it isn't dark yet," she said. "I'll be all right." She turned the knob and pulled the door open, her gaze still on me. Then she asked, "Are you going to marry Cherry Owens?"

"I think so," I answered. "I bought her a ring today."

"Don't do it, Jim," she said. "She's the wrong woman for you."

"Why?"

She stepped outside and shut the door, not answering. I stood at the window and watched her until I couldn't see her any more. I didn't have any idea why she had said that about Cherry.

CHAPTER XXVI

During the winter General Dodge had been called back to New York to confer with the top men of the Union Pacific. Get to moving in the spring as fast as you can, the top men had said, comfortable in their heated offices and homes. Hang the expense! Push the end of steel on west with all possible speed.

Time! That was all that counted. Beat the Central Pacific to Ogden. Get as close to the California border as you can. Maybe we can shut the Central Pacific out of the rich trade of the Salt Lake valley. To hell with anybody else. We'll take every nickel we can.

This was the law of the jungle. On beyond the Black Hills was the Laramie Plains, then the Red Basin and the Bitter Creek country, and finally the snow-covered Wasatch Range. After that, of course, there was the Utah and Nevada desert—if the Union Pacific could lay track fast enough to beat the Central Pacific and get there first. The reward was to the swift, not to the honest, the compassionate, or the idealistic.

To the fat and comfortable planners and plotters in New York, it made little difference how many surveyors and bridge builders and graders and track layers froze to death or were killed by Indians or died from exposure or drinking bad water in the Bitter Creek desert. The old mountain-man legend said that a jack rabbit had to carry a canteen and a haversack to make it across that desert. True or not, it made no difference to the big men in New York. Get the rails laid any way you can. Time! Nothing else counted.

So General Dodge gave the surveyors their marching

orders. They left Cheyenne late in February and crossed the Wasatch Range in sleds, the snow so deep that it covered the tops of the telegraph poles. Spring came slowly that year, so slowly that much of the equipment and many of the animals were lost. The miracle was that any of the men survived.

When April 1 came, the army of graders, bridge builders and track layers that had wintered in Cheyenne moved out, even though the ground on Sherman Hill was still frozen as hard as cement, too hard for the picks and shovels of the graders to work.

It took a month for the railroad to reach Laramie, near Fort Sanders. For a time Laramie was the end of steel, and many of the problems that we had faced in Cheyenne all winter simply moved west to face the people of Laramie. Later Benton, on the edge of the Red Basin, was hell on wheels, then Rawlins, and after that Green River and Bryan, which was thirteen miles away.

Within a matter of days we saw Cheyenne change from the roaring boom town to a quiet city scattered along the Union Pacific tracks, the tents and many of the shacks gone, fifteen hundred people instead of ten thousand. Most of the fifteen hundred who remained were solid citizens who had made a decision, many of them months ago, to cast their fortunes with Cheyenne—win, lose, or draw. I was one of them.

Early in April Jess Munro called the leaders of the Vigilance Committee together in his office. There were six of us, the same men with the exception of Lucky Sam Bellew, who had persuaded Tate Horn to get out of town last November.

I had not seen much of Jess Munro for several weeks. The first impression I had of him as I stepped into his office was that he had not changed from the time we had taken Tate Horn out of the saloon and told him to leave Cheyenne. He was as tough and tight-lipped as ever. He leaned back in his chair and looked us over. It seemed to me he was almost smiling—as close to smiling as I ever saw him.

"Gentlemen, our job is nearly finished," Munro said.

"From now on, with one exception the police can handle the problems that come to Cheyenne. I think we have done very well, and the town owes more to us than anyone knows."

Then he leaned forward, the ghost of a smile gone from his lips. "However, you will continue to serve as Vigilante officers until such time as I disband you. That will not be for some time, not until I know the danger of lawlessness is gone . . . The fact that the mass of laborers has left Cheyenne does not mean that peace and harmony will prevail. We have had some organized crime, and we will continue to have it for a while. That is the exception I mentioned which the police will not be able to handle."

Munro sat back in his chair. "Believe me, gentlemen," he went on in a subdued voice, "I am better informed on this matter than any of you, because I have contacts among the undesirables who will sell information to me for a price. The reason I asked you to come here tonight was to tell you to be prepared for a call to duty at any time, even though you may think the need for our organization is passed . . . We will not, of course, make a show of force as we did last November. You men are the key to our success. I expect you to respond when I need you. The call may not come for several weeks, but it will come. Now are there any questions?"

"I've got a problem," Bronco Stead said, "although I'm not sure anybody can help except to give me some advice."

"Let's hear it," Munro said.

"I've bought about a dozen Kentucky horses," Stead said. "In a few weeks I'll be leaving Cheyenne to bring them here by train. They're worth a fortune. Fact is, I'm spending a fortune for them. They're mostly brood mares, though I'll have three studs in the herd. I expect to make a good deal of money selling them to some of the Englishmen who've started cattle ranches around here. They have more money than sense, and they appreciate good horseflesh. My problem is how to keep them from being stolen. Some of the organized crime you're talking about is horse stealing, and if I'm any judge, horse thieves never turn down an opportunity like this."

Munro nodded as he reached for a cigar, bit off the end and lit it. He didn't say anything for a time, but he looked at us as if thinking some of us were the horse thieves Stead was talking about. He pinned his gaze on me, then on Ed Burke, and went on along the half-circle of men who faced him.

"What do you men think?" he asked finally. "Have you got any advice to give Bronc?"

We didn't. At least, we didn't have anything to say. Munro took the cigar out of his mouth. "I told you we have had some organized crime in this country in spite of all we could do. The truth is we haven't done a damn thing so far to smash the organization. All we've done is to cut off a few limbs, but the roots are as sound as ever."

Munro waggled a finger at Stead. "I'll tell you one thing, Bronco. These horses you're bringing in will tempt the same outlaws who have been robbing the stages."

"I know, I know," Stead said sharply, as if insulted because Munro was telling him something he already knew. "If they can get my horses across the line into Colorado, they can drive them into Denver, and I'd have one hell of a time finding them, let alone proving ownership."

"All I can tell you is to keep a heavy guard on them as long as they're in Cheyenne."

"How heavy is heavy?" Stead asked.

"Whatever you want to pay," Munro said. "Good men will cost you money, and you're the only one who can decide whether you can afford to hire enough men to guard them adequately."

"I can't afford not to," Stead said in a tired voice. "I wish now I'd waited for a while, but I've made my deal and I've got to go through with it."

We broke up a moment later. I walked out of the building with Ed Burke, more troubled by the meeting than I liked to admit. When we reached the boardwalk, I said, "Ed, I had a bad feeling about Munro. Looked to me like he suspected some of us of being in cahoots with the outlaws."

Ed laughed shortly. "Sure he did. Still does, probably. He looked at you first, then at me, which got me to wondering if you're his Number One suspect and I'm Number Two."

"He's got no grounds to suspect us," I said, getting more angry by the second as I thought about it. "For all we know he's into it up to his neck. This might be his way of turning suspicion to one of us."

We reached the door of the Head Quarters Saloon and stopped. Ed pulled thoughtfully at an ear, then said, "That hadn't occurred to me, but you could be right. I'd sure like to turn the tables on that bastard." Then he shrugged, as if dismissing the thought. "Come on in. I'll buy you a drink."

"Thanks," I said, "but I'll get along and see if Cherry's still up. Maybe she'll have some coffee on the stove and a piece of pie put away for me."

"You're a lucky man, Jim," he said in what struck me as a tone of envy. "I see she's wearing your ring. She'll make you a good wife." He hesitated, then added, "I guess you didn't know it, but I've been purty sweet on that girl myself." He shook his head. "Hell, you had the inside track all the time. I should of known that."

"I'm just lucky," I said, and went on along the street.

He'd given me quite a start. I had known, of course, that Ed took his meals in Cherry's restaurant when he was in town, but I hadn't known that he'd ever given her a romantic thought. He'd never even hinted at it to me.

Cherry's restaurant was still open. She was glad to see me, as she nearly always was when I dropped in. She locked the front door and told me to come on back to her room. She brought coffee and pie, and I enjoyed myself until I remembered what Ed had said, so I asked her about it.

She looked at me, troubled. "I'm surprised he mentioned it to you," she said. "He's proposed a dozen times. Just a day or so ago he wanted me to leave the country with him. He said he had plenty of money for me to live in style."

"He's lying," I said angrily. "He's never made a nickel on that ten-cow spread of his. He plays some poker, but he's not a very good player and I never knew him to win any big pots."

"I thought he was lying," she said, "and I thought it was funny he tried to persuade me to leave with him, knowing I'm engaged to you and being a friend of yours and all."

"It's funny, all right," I agreed.

But it wasn't laughing funny. I thought about it as I walked home. I couldn't make it out. I'd never understood Ed anyhow, though there wasn't any mystery about that. I never understood people who didn't work and were as happy and easygoing as Ed. The point was it didn't seem like him to try to steal my girl, especially after she had started wearing my ring. It might have made sense if Cherry had been the flirty kind, but there wasn't a flirty bone in her body.

I lay awake a long time that night, but I couldn't make it add up right. Before I dropped off to sleep I told myself I'd ask him plain out the next time I saw him, but I didn't have a chance. I never saw him in town again.

CHAPTER XXVII

Through the following weeks we had to adjust to a changed Cheyenne—no crowd on the streets, plenty of room in the hotels for transients, very little crime, and not much business. All of us, I think, were glad to see the tents and the worst of the shacks go. We noticed more soldiers in town, too. Actually there weren't any more, but before they had been a small minority. Now we were aware of them simply because fewer people were on the streets or in the saloons.

The red-light district was cut down to a few houses on Eighteenth Street. Of course, one of them belonged to the Martin women. I still dropped in about once a week, sometimes just to talk. They were always glad to accommodate me, whether it was business or talk. They cried poormouth to me about how their business had gone downhill.

I told them to move to Laramie, but they refused to do that. They were comfortable here, they liked the house I had built for them, and they claimed their trade was from the best businessmen in Cheyenne and the best officers from Fort D. A. Russell and Camp Carlin.

Maybe they were lying to me, but I let them enjoy their lies, even to telling me how much they thought of me. They said they wouldn't leave here unless I married Cherry, and if I wasn't going to marry her, how about marrying one of them?

I didn't take them seriously, but I liked them, and I usually wound up at their place Saturday night and often slept there until late Sunday morning. Cherry never wanted me to stay with her after ten or eleven o'clock.

I didn't know what Ed Burke was doing, but I didn't see him. I thought maybe he didn't come to town any more, or maybe he did come and I just never ran into him. Anyhow, he didn't look me up the way he used to. Possibly he was hurt because he hadn't got anywhere with Cherry. I didn't think he was that sensitive, but then I hadn't thought he was in love with Cherry, either.

A couple of times I dropped in on Nancy and Frank Rush, but I didn't feel comfortable with them. Nancy was quiet and withdrawn, and Frank never looked at me while we were talking. He always looked past me for some reason, so I decided I wasn't really welcome there.

Perhaps it was exactly as Nancy had said—Frank's conscience hurt him. He wasn't working, because Stallcup had quit building and there weren't many good jobs in Cheyenne. Frank had finished his church and had good crowds most of the time, so I supposed he was busy with his congregation.

Cherry attended Frank's Sunday morning service and told me about it. She accepted his brand of religion without question. This was something we seldom talked about, and I was very much aware that it would be an issue between us if we had any children. I would never under any circumstances allow my children to go to a church that was as strong on hellfire and brimstone as Frank's was.

I refused to worry about it, though. The truth was I had just about given up on marrying Cherry. I didn't press her any more to set the date. It was up to her. Maybe she wanted to be begged, but I had made up my mind I wouldn't do it.

I spent a good deal of my time at Fort D. A. Russell. I knew most of the officers and I had started to dicker with them for a wood contract—or hay, though I preferred a deal in wood. We hadn't quite come to terms. The truth was I had to feel my way, this being something new for me. I wasn't real sure how much I'd have to pay men to cut wood and then haul it to the fort. The situation was a good deal different from hiring carpenters to build houses.

When my second business building was finished, I

rented it to a man who started a saddle and harness shop. He said now that the railroad boom was over, Cheyenne would become a center of cattle raising, and I thought he was right, though maybe a little premature. I built a room in one corner of the building and used it for an office. I furnished it with a desk and several chairs, so it was comfortable enough, but I didn't spend much time there.

Like most of the other businessmen in Cheyenne, I was on the streets or in the saloons more than I was in my office. Of course, we kept tabs on the progress of the railroad. The end of steel had gone past Laramie and was now moving across the Laramie Plains.

Then near the end of May, Bronco Stead returned from Kentucky with his horses. They were in the corral behind his livery stable, and as soon as the word spread every man in town except Frank Rush hurried to the corral to get a look at the horses we'd heard so much about.

They were fine animals and I would have loved to have owned one, but I was never a fool over horses as some men are and I had no intention of spending a fortune for one of them. I suppose they were worth their weight in gold, though Stead got cagey when anyone asked what he wanted for them. My guess was he hadn't decided what to ask, perhaps because he didn't know how much he could get out of the Englishmen.

That night they were stolen. I never heard all the details, although I'm sure that if Stead had put an adequate guard on his corral, as Jess Munro had told him to do, it wouldn't have happened. I assume he was trying to save money. Or it might have been a trap for the thieves. That seemed a crazy idea, using a fortune in horses to trap a gang of thieves. I was inclined to accept it as a possibility, though, knowing how anxious Jess Munro was to get the deadwood on the men who were involved in what he called "organized crime."

Anyhow, Stead and two men were guarding the horses when they were surprised by the outlaws. Stead claimed there were a dozen men in the outfit, but when the sheriff looked the ground over he said he doubted that the gang had over four men. In any case, they got the drop on

Stead and the two guards, slugged them with their gun
barrels, and drove the horses off, leaving the three men
lying on the ground beside the corral.

I tried to go down there that morning as soon as I
heard about it, but the sheriff had several deputies and
city police guarding the place, so no one could get within
fifty feet of the corral gate.

Jess Munro saw me and came to me. He said in a low
tone, "Be ready to ride tonight. We're going after those
horses."

"Not me," I said. "We've got a sheriff and a police
force. They're paid to enforce the law."

"Glenn, sometimes I wonder how smart you are,"
Munro said contemptuously. "You know what'll happen.
The sheriff will snort around here till noon talking and
getting ready. Finally he'll ride out with a posse and get as
far as the Colorado line; then he'll be back, all tuckered
out and saying he didn't have any authority to go over the
line."

"Which same is true," I admitted, "but he can wire the
Colorado lawmen and—"

"We won't be held up by any line," Munro interrupted.
"I need your help, Glenn. You took an oath. What do you
think I've been staying around Cheyenne for? I aim to get
those bastards and you're going to help me."

"So you'll get your hanging after all," I said sourly.

That remark didn't set well with him. His eyes narrowed and his lips squeezed together and his face got red.
He said, "I don't have to ride all night to manage a
hanging—I can go to Laramie and have a dozen. I'm
going to bust up this gang of outlaws. I knew they
couldn't pass these horses up."

"All right," I said. "I'll be ready if it works out with
the sheriff the way you say it will."

It did. I should have known it would. This kind of
thing was old business to Jess Munro, and he was an
expert at it just as he was in judging men.

I had finished supper and gone home when Munro
showed up with Stead and Williams and a half-breed

named Red Buck. I'd seen Buck around town and had talked to him a time or two, but I didn't know him well.

After the exodus around the first of April, Buck had stayed out of town. At least, I hadn't seen him. He claimed to be half Cheyenne and half French, and maybe he was. He was a tall, very thin man, with a dark face and black hair and the high cheekbones of a Cheyenne.

He was an excellent horseman and a good tracker, but I was surprised when Munro said, "Saddle up, Glenn. Red Buck knows exactly where the horses are. If we can get there before dawn, we'll have 'em. We'll get our men, too."

I didn't feel any great obligation to help recover Stead's horses, and I felt even less obligation to keep my oath, because I figured the time that bound me to it was past, but I was interested in breaking up the gang of thieves. If I continued to live in Cheyenne, which I intended to do, I wanted it to be a law-abiding town and I wanted a safe road between Cheyenne and Denver.

I had built a small shed on the back of my lot. I kept my sorrel there instead of at the livery stable where I had left him when I first came to Cheyenne. I saddled him and rode into the street within a matter of minutes.

"Where's Ed Burke?" I asked. "He always wants in on a deal like this. We could use another good man."

"We could at that," Munro agreed. "We'll stop at his place. It's not out of our way."

It was dark by the time we crossed Crow Creek. The weather had turned cold in the afternoon and now a chill wind was driving down from the Black Hills. We were all wearing coats. It was hard to talk above the wind, so we didn't try. The sky was clear and the stars gave us some light even though there was no moon.

We reached Ed's place sometime before midnight. I stepped down as Munro said, "See if he's home, Glenn. The last time I was out here he was gone."

I opened the door and yelled, but no one answered. I struck a match, found a lamp, and held the flame to the wick. I looked around, appalled by the dust that had drifted in around the door and windows. I went into the bedroom and realized immediately that he hadn't been here to st___ for a long time. He had cleaned out the things he'd need if he was traveling. He hadn't left much in the house, not even any grub in the kitchen.

I blew the lamp out and went back to the waiting men. "He's not here," I said. "Looks like he hasn't been home for a while."

"That's the way it looked to me the last time I was here," Munro said. "Mount up and we'll get to moving."

We rode southwest. I'd never been in this country and I had no idea when we crossed into Colorado. The wind continued to knife us. Still no one tried to talk, maybe because of the wind, or maybe because we all knew we were taking on a dangerous job. If it went as expected, men would be hanged, and I didn't think anyone except Munro would enjoy it.

We didn't stop to rest our horses until almost dawn, when the word came back from Red Buck, who was leading the procession, that we were almost there and we'd leave our horses here. We stepped down and tied our mounts.

In the darkness I couldn't make out exactly what the country was like, but there were willows here and I heard water running a short distance from where I stood. We followed Red Buck for a quarter of a mile. I had a feeling we were in a narrow ravine, with very steep sides. It would make a good place to hole up, the walls likely hiding the corral and what buildings there were from anyone who might be riding by.

Presently Red Buck stopped us. He said in a low tone, "The outlaws are asleep in that shack. The horses are in a corral behind the shack. At least, that was the plan. They're heading out for Denver as soon as it's daylight if nobody stops 'em."

I had no idea how he knew this, but I didn't ask. Munro said, "We'll stop them. We'll move up to the shack, easy and quiet. Bronco, you and Glenn take the far side. The rest of us will stay on this side of the door. We'll wait till one of them shows himself. Bronco and Glenn will handle him. The rest of us will go in after whoever is inside. Red tells me there should be only three men."

I could see the first hint of dawn in the eastern sky. In a few minutes there would be some early light, enough for the outlaws to spot us if they woke up and looked out through the windows. But maybe there weren't any windows and maybe Red Buck knew that. He did seem to know a great deal about these men, so much that I began to wonder if he had helped steal the horses.

We made it to the front of the shack. Stead and I moved past the door and slipped around the far corner. I'd been right about the windows. There were none, at least on the front and east side of the building. We waited for ten, perhaps fifteen minutes—it's hard to say because time drags in a situation like that. Presently a man inside the shack coughed. Then I heard him cross to the door, a board in the floor squeaking under his weight.

He stepped outside to relieve himself. We waited until he was done and had turned back toward the door, one hand buttoning his pants. I wasn't showing much of myself, just enough to watch him. I punched Stead with an elbow, then rushed the man, getting a hand over his mouth as I pulled him back around the corner of the shack.

In spite of all I could do, the man made a strangled kind of grunt. One of the men inside called, "What's the matter with you, Hamp. It ain't time—"

The three men outside the door lunged through it. The man I'd nabbed wasn't as big or strong as I was. I had him on the ground face down, one hand on the back of his head, his face in the dust. He flounced around, trying to get me off his back. Finally I drew my gun and rammed the muzzle into his neck. When he felt the gun, he quieted down in a hurry.

"I've got him," I said to Stead. "Go inside. They may need you."

They didn't. There were only two men inside the shack. They were out of their bunks and had their revolvers in their hands, but they didn't have time to use them. Munro and Red Buck, the first through the door, got them before they could fire a shot. Munro slugged his man with his gun barrel. Buck didn't touch his. He said, "You're covered," and the man froze.

A moment later Stead was back with me. "No trouble," he said. "Like taking candy from a baby."

I got off my prisoner and stood up just as Munro came out of the shack. He and Williams were carrying a man. The sun wasn't up, and the light was still very thin, but there was enough of it for me to see that their captive was Ed Burke.

CHAPTER XXVIII

I was stunned. For a few seconds I just stood there, staring at Munro, then at Ed. As soon as I found my voice, I yelled at Munro, "What's the matter with you? That's Ed Burke. You know him as well as I do."

They laid Ed down in the grass. Munro said to Red Buck, "Get the ropes." Then he turned to me. "I guess I know him better than you do, Glenn. He's the brains of the wolf pack we've been trying to run down. Now we've got the deadwood on him and we're going to hang him."

"Oh no you're not," I said. "Are you out of your head? He's got a ranch. We stopped there tonight. He's been in and out of Cheyenne ever since I've been there. You appointed him a Vigilance Committee officer. You act like you've forgotten all of this."

Munro shook his head. "No, I haven't forgotten it, and I'll admit that appointing him a Vigilante officer was the biggest mistake I've made for a while. I wasn't onto him then. He used his position to know what we were planning and to give me some bad advice. Like hanging the three men at Dale City. He was one of the outlaws who robbed that stage, but by blaming the other men and getting them hung he got suspicion turned away from him and his friends."

"I don't believe it," I said. "Anyhow, he's my friend. You're not going to hang him."

"You try to stop it and you'll get yourself beefed," Munro said. "Go take a look at what's in the corral. You'll find the horses there." When I hesitated, he snapped, "Go on. We won't string them up till you get back."

I ran past the shack to the corral. There was enough

light for me to see that Stead's horses were there all right. I ran back, not knowing what I was going to do, but dead sure I was going to stop the hanging. Even if Ed was as guilty as hell—and it looked to me as if he was—I aimed to see that he had a trial.

When I got back to where Munro and the others were waiting, Ed was conscious. Then he saw me and said, "Well, so you caught up with me too, Jim. I shouldn't have come back from New Mexico, but I kept thinking of those damned horses that Munro and Stead had been waving in my face. I had to show 'em we could take 'em. We did, too."

"And you got yourself caught," Munro said roughly. "Now you'll hang."

"It wasn't you that caught us," Ed said. "It was that God-damned double-crossing bastard over yonder." He motioned toward Red Buck. "How come you're dealing with a man like him, Munro? He'll sell you out just like he did us if he gets a chance."

"He won't have a chance," Munro said. "I'm paying him off and he's getting out of the country pronto. If he doesn't, I'll see he winds up in the jug."

"You're getting purty low," Ed jeered.

"Not any lower than I ever did," Munro said smugly. "I've always had spies among the toughs. You know that. It's not hard to find men who'll sell out for a price."

I glanced at Red Buck. The sun was almost up now and the light was good enough to see the expression on his face. He wasn't ashamed one bit. I guess a man like that is never ashamed of what he does. He was scared, though. Maybe he thought Munro wouldn't keep his bargain and would end up hanging him too.

Stead and Williams were standing a few steps behind me, holding their guns on the other two horse thieves, who looked like any of a hundred hardcases I'd seen come and go in Cheyenne all winter. I'd get no help from either Stead or Williams. I didn't know how I could buck four men of the caliber of these four, particularly Jess Munro, who was just about as hard as they came. I had to do it someway. I kept telling myself that Ed Burke was not going to hang.

Ed and Munro were still jawing back and forth, Ed needling Munro about being so low he could crawl under a snake's belly with his hat on for dealing with a double-crosser like Red Buck, and Munro, as smug as a cat lapping up cream, saying he didn't mind being that low as long as he got his man.

"We couldn't have found either the horses or you," Munro said, "if it hadn't been for Red Buck, so he turned out mighty useful."

"He helped us take the horses," Ed said. "He's as guilty as any of us. He was in that stage robbery that we strung Bully Bailey up for. He's been in most of the robberies and killings that I know anything about, and you admit you're using him."

"Sure I'm using him," Munro said. "He comes pretty high, too, but he's worth it. With you out of the game, your pards will hightail out of the country."

"Most of 'em are over in Laramie now," Ed said. "You'll have it all to do over again."

"Not exactly," Munro said. "I don't often run into a man like you, sitting out here on a little spread innocent as all hell and pretending to be an honest rancher and doing your best to get the Vigilantes organized. You were cute, Burke, cuter'n a scheming female trying to get her man. You even fooled Jim Glenn there."

All the time they were gabbing, Munro taking the opportunity to brag a little and Ed just using up time in the hope that something would turn up, I was thinking about Ed and how he had managed to fool me. I had thought of him as a friend, but now I wondered if he hadn't just used me for his own advantage.

He was the first man I'd met in this country. He'd put me up for the night almost a year ago and he'd ridden into Cheyenne with me the next day. He'd helped me when I'd started to build. He'd saved my life when he and Frank Rush jumped Bailey and his friends, and even though I'd been sore about the hanging of Bully Bailey, everything he'd said had been true. If they hadn't strung

Bailey up, he would have dry-gulched me sooner or later and I'd be dead.

On the other hand, Ed had lied to me and pretended to be something he wasn't. I'd always had a certain amount of respect for an outlaw who didn't deny what he was, but I had damned little respect for a man who claimed to be an honest rancher and was robbing stages and killing people all the time. He'd even tried to steal Cherry while she was wearing my ring.

Well, I didn't respect Ed, who was a first-class hypocrite, but I liked him. He had saved my life—nothing could change that.

"Let's get on with the hanging, Jess," Stead said.

"All right," Munro said. "We've wasted enough time. There's several limbs on those big cottonwoods that are stout enough to hold a man. Toss the ropes over them and then fetch up the horses."

"There'll be no hanging," I said. "We're taking these men to Cheyenne for trial."

"Well, by God," Munro said as if he didn't believe he'd heard right. "You never learn, do you, Glenn. Well sir, you're bucking me for the last time. I'm running this show and don't you forget it."

"You always give a condemned man one last request, don't you, Munro?" Ed asked.

Munro looked at him, the almost grin coming to his lips again. "Sure, Burke," he said, "but we're not taking time to build a fire and cook you a meal. You're going to have to swing on an empty stomach."

"That ain't my last request," Ed said. "I want to talk to my friend Jim. I've got some advice to give him about not throwing his life away for a no-good piece of scum like me."

"All right," Munro agreed. "That's more sense than I expected to hear from a man like you, but remember that Red Buck is going to have his gun on you all the time. If Glenn tries to hand you his iron, you're both dead."

"I believe Buck would do it," Ed said. "I've seen the bastard kill a child just to watch him die. Compared to him the rest of us are angels."

Munro had turned to the cottonwoods and was ignoring Ed as he gave Stead directions about the ropes. Ed was on his feet, reeling a little. His head must have been splitting, but he came on to where I stood halfway between the shack and the cottonwoods.

When he reached me, he said in a low voice, "That was right. I meant what I said while ago. You're a good man, Jim. You'll take care of Cherry. Better'n I could. Don't give 'em any excuse to kill you. Munro hates you from your boot-heels right on up to the top of your head. You keep bucking him and he'll have the best time of his life killing you."

"Why didn't you put guards out?" I asked. "You wouldn't have been surprised if you had."

"Because I never thought that damned, sneaking Red Buck would sell us out," Ed said. "We was figuring on moving out early this morning and I didn't dream Munro would have any dealings with a bastard like Buck. If he hadn't guided you here, Munro wouldn't have found this place for a week. By that time I'd have been in New Mexico." He paused, then added, "Stupid, wasn't it? You should always figure the worst from a man like Buck."

He was about three feet from me, blood trickling down his forehead. Buck stood ten or twelve feet from us, close enough to hear most of what Ed was saying, but he gave no sign he was insulted or sore over what Ed had said about him. He had the same impassive expression on his dark face I've seen a lot of Indians have. They can hate you enough to kill you, just as if you were a bug to step on, but you'd never know it from the way they look at you.

Suddenly Ed's knees gave way and he fell against me. I grabbed him, and as I eased him to the ground, he whispered, "Dig in front of the manger in the first stall in the shed at my ranch. Give the money to Cherry. It's all I've got to leave her."

He acted as if he'd fainted, going loose all over and closing his eyes. I pulled my gun and I lined it on Munro. "You heard what I said a while ago," I told him. "We're taking these men in for trial. If one of the others shoots me, I'll get you before I hit the ground. That's a promise."

Munro chewed on his lower lip, then said, "Glenn, you're either a hero or a fool. You're not holding a good enough hand to play your bet out."

"I'm neither a hero nor a fool," I said. "You know I believe in the law handling cases like this. I've had my doubts about the Vigilantes all the time, particularly because of bastards like you who enjoy hanging men. Now have a couple of your boys saddle the horses that belong to Ed and his friends and we'll start back for Cheyenne, just like you said."

"I kind of admire you even if you are a fool," Munro said. "I've been in this business for a long time. I've belonged to several Vigilance Committees and I've done my share of hanging, but I never met a man before who was a stickler for law the way you are, and who was willing to back up his beliefs with his life. You've got a big future in Cheyenne if you live."

That was the point, I thought. Munro had no intention of letting me live. Red Buck would have shot me in the back if Ed hadn't got to his feet and rushed him. At least Stead told me that later, though at the moment I couldn't take my eyes off Munro to look around to see what had happened.

I heard the shot and started to move to one side so I could keep my gun on Munro while I figured out what was going on behind me. If I'd known, I'd have smoked Munro down. As it turned out, I didn't have a chance to find out what was happening.

I got around just enough to see Buck standing there looking surprised, smoke from his gun barrel drifting away into the early morning stillness. Ed was bending forward, one hand gripping his chest; then he toppled over on his face. The next instant the roof fell on me and I dropped into a bottomless well, turning head over heels as I fell. It lasted only a moment; then there was nothing but complete and absolute darkness.

CHAPTER XXIX

I don't know how long I lay there, but when I came to I was immediately conscious of two things: a headache that threatened to split my skull right down the middle, and the bright sunlight in my eyes. I sat up and rubbed my face, turning so that my back was to the sun. Then I opened my eyes, and I saw them.

Munro had done his job, all right. Ed and his two friends were dangling from cottonwood limbs, swaying just a little in the breeze that came down the ravine, the limbs groaning as the ropes scraped against the wood. I'd seen men after they'd been lynched and it always made me sick. The sight of these three would have made me sick even if Ed hadn't been one of them.

I suppose it was the complete loss of human dignity that came to a human body when death was from hanging that gave me that feeling. I never felt the same when I saw a man who had been shot to death; shooting never gave a body the grotesque, macabre look that hanging did: the twisted head, the gaping mouth, the purple face. Maybe, too, I have always felt that hanging was a horrible way to die.

Whatever the cause, I was sick. I got up and staggered toward the shack, the ground turning in front of me. It seemed to have waves, like the surface of a lake when it is driven by a hard wind. I almost fell before I reached the shack. When I did reach it, I put a hand against the wall to steady myself, and then I began to retch.

It went on for what seemed a long time. I continued to do it long after there was nothing left in my stomach to come up. When it finally stopped, I went to the stream, lurching back and forth like a seasick man. I got down on my hands and knees and washed my face and took a drink of water, but it was quite a while before I felt like getting back on my feet.

I knew what I had to do, whether I felt like it or not. Jess Munro had left the bodies here for the magpies to peck at, but I couldn't. I cut them down and removed the ropes from their necks. I wasn't sure about Ed—he didn't look like the other two. He had a bullet hole in his chest, and I wondered if he was dead before they had put the rope on his neck. It would be like Munro, I thought, to hang a dead man because that was supposed to be the fate of a horse thief.

I hunted around the shack and the shed behind it and finally found a pick and shovel. I spent most of the day digging the graves. They weren't as deep as they should have been, but I was too tired to dig any deeper. I found a tailgate in the weeds back of the shed. I carved Ed's name on it, birthdate unknown, and below that: *May 30, 1868*.

Not that anyone would ride by here and look at the graves, or read what I had cut on that tailgate, but I felt better doing it. I guess I thought it was the least I could do for Ed Burke. I hadn't saved his life. I hadn't even been able to get a trial for him, but I had done all I could and I could not blame myself for what happened to him.

I rolled the bodies into the graves and shoveled the dirt on them. I set the tailgate into the earth at the head of Ed's grave, and then I stood there for a while, thinking I ought to sing a hymn or pray for them or maybe recite some scripture.

I didn't, because I couldn't. It wouldn't make any difference to them anyhow, but I got to thinking about Frank Rush's brand of religion and how he thought he was saving men's souls. I wondered if he had ever tried to save Ed's. I asked myself if Ed was bad or good, and how could I tell if any man was bad or good, including myself. I could think of a lot of good things to say about Ed.

On the other hand, if he had held up that stage and killed the guard and wounded the driver, then he was bad by almost any standard. But then maybe he hadn't been the one. Somebody else, a man like Red Buck, might have done the shooting. Somehow I just couldn't see Ed Burke ever shooting a man he didn't have to.

Munro had left my horse in the corral, which surprised me. I saddled up, so tired and weak I didn't think I'd ever make it into the saddle, but I did. I hadn't had anything to eat all day, but I couldn't have eaten if a banquet had been spread before me. My stomach was still too queasy.

The sun was almost down by this time, but I figured I'd find Ed's ranch by dark. I wondered if Red Buck could have heard what Ed had whispered to me as he fell against me. If he had, Ed's money would be gone. Or, even if he hadn't heard, he might have suspected what Ed was telling me. Maybe he was hiding out somewhere around Ed's place, waiting to get the drop on me and make me tell him where the money was.

I didn't feel like riding hard, so I didn't get to Ed's place as soon as I thought I would. The sun was down and the dark was moving in fast when I reined up beside his shed. I swung down, looking around and listening while I hung onto the horn. I think I would have fallen on my face if I hadn't.

I didn't see or hear anything out of line. As soon as my dizziness left me, I opened the door and led my horse inside. Then I closed the door and listened some more. It was all right, I thought. Probably, Red Buck was twenty miles away by now.

Ed had always kept a lantern hanging just inside the door. I found it and lighted it. Then I led my horse into the second stall, tied him and offsaddled, and decided to wait until morning to hunt for the money.

I lay down in the straw of the first stall, thinking I was probably lying on the loot that Ed had hidden there. I'd take it to Cherry when I found it, just as he had told me to do. There was no way of finding out who it belonged to, and I certainly had no intention of keeping it.

I couldn't go to sleep for a long time after I blew the lantern out. I woke up several times before dawn; I just couldn't get rid of the feeling that Red Buck was around there somewhere. If he had heard what Ed had told me, he wouldn't tell Munro. He'd take Munro's money and say he was leaving the country; then he'd come out here and wait for me to show up.

I kept my gun in the holster, knowing that if I pulled it out and laid it beside me I wouldn't be able to put my hand on it if I needed it right away, and then I'd be in a hell of a fix. I don't know how many times I woke up and listened and dropped off into a light sleep again. I had some wild dreams, and maybe it was the dreams that kept waking me up. I thought I was gunning Red Buck down, and then I was trying to find Jess Munro and shoot him.

When I woke the last time I saw that the first light of dawn was showing through the knotholes and the cracks between the boards on the east side. The next instant my heart began to pound. I heard the hinges of the door squeak. Someone was opening it very slowly and carefully.

I have never made any claims about being a seventh son, or the seventh son of a seventh son, but I think I had known all the time that Red Buck would try this. I eased my gun out of the holster. Then I caught a man's movement as he slid through the door. I had no intention of lying there and being shot to pieces, or having that bastard get the drop on me and shoot off my fingers and toes until I told him where Ed's money was. He was enough Indian to do exactly that.

As soon as I could pinpoint the man's position, I started shooting. I didn't wait to see if it was Red Buck. I put the first slug just about where I figured his chest was and I lowered each shot a few inches so my fourth one would drill him in the belly.

I held the last shell in my gun so I'd have one more load if I needed it. I moved quickly to one side and then I listened. The man was down, all right, but I couldn't tell whether I'd killed him or not. When I didn't hear any groans or hard breathing, I figured I'd got him, so I edged toward him, keeping close to the wall of the shed. Holding my gun in one hand, I fished a match out of my pocket. I struck it and moved it so the light fell on the man's face.

My breath went out of me the same as if someone had hit me a hard blow in my belly. It wasn't Red Buck at all. I had shot and killed Jess Munro.

I blew out the match and sat back on my heels and tried to figure out how this could have happened. Munro had been too far away to hear what Ed had said to me. Buck was the only man who could have heard, so how had Munro found out?

One thing seemed certain: Red Buck wasn't a man to give anything away. The more I thought about it, the more sure I was that Buck had sold his information to Munro and left the country, figuring that getting a few dollars from Munro was better than taking a chance on staying around.

Anyhow, I had to think that Munro had come here to get the money for himself. For some stupid reason, maybe selfish, I was gratified to think that he was as big a thief as anybody when the chips were down. I could only guess, of course, but I figured that Munro must have thought that I'd remain at the other place and bury the bodies, and then I'd be too tired to ride, so I'd stay there until morning.

He was a smart man and he had me pegged right. I hadn't felt like riding so far, and I wouldn't have done it if I hadn't been afraid that Red Buck would beat me to the money if I spent the night at the hideout.

One thing I did know: I was in trouble if anyone found out I had killed Munro. He wasn't a man who made many friends, but he was respected in Cheyenne. If he had been working for the railroad, I'd have somebody on my tail in a hurry.

I led his horse inside the shed, tied him in the last stall, and shut the door. I watered my horse, looking around and listening as my horse drank and wondering if Munro had come alone. No one seemed to be around. I'd have known it by now, because whoever had been with him would have heard the shooting and made a try for me. Anyhow, if Munro had bought the information, he wouldn't be likely to share it with anyone.

As soon as I could, I got my horse back into the stall,

tied him, forked hay into his manger and gave him a bait of oats. I closed the door and lighted the lantern. Using a shovel Ed had left in the corner beside the pitchfork, I started digging.

It didn't take me more than ten minutes to find a metal box. I lifted it out of the hole, flipped the lid back, and looked at more money than I had ever seen in one place in my life before. No sense in counting it, but I judged the box contained at least $10,000. I wondered what Cherry would do with so much money.

I hunted around the shed for something to put the money in, and ended up by emptying the half-sack of oats. I moved the money from the box to the sack and tied it. Then I stood looking at Munro's body for a while and a happy thought struck me. I'd bury him where I'd found the box. It would make him happy, I thought, to share the same hole with the empty box.

I don't know what had got into me. Maybe all the things that had happened in the last twenty-four hours had made me a little crazy. Or maybe it was because my head still ached and my stomach was still queasy. I hadn't eaten anything for about thirty-six hours, but I don't think a meal would have stayed down if I had eaten one.

Sometimes I am convinced that people's emotions bring about their sickness. I hurt worse, and had been hurting even before I'd been slugged, than any time I could remember, at least since I'd had the beating that Bully Bailey and his friends had given me. To find out what Ed Burke really was, and then try to save his life or at least get a fair trial for him, to fail and end up by cutting him down and burying him—all this did more to make me sick than the whack I'd received on my head.

Somehow I found the strength to enlarge the hole until it was big enough to hold Munro's body. I dropped him into it, then lifted his head and shoved the empty box under it so it served as a pillow. After I filled the grave and raked litter over it, I didn't think anyone would suspect that a man was buried there.

I tied the sack of money behind my saddle, led my horse outside, and went back after Munro's horse. Halfway between Ed's place and Cheyenne I turned Munro's horse loose. Someone would find him and bring him in, or just keep him.

In any case, I didn't know what else to do with him. I couldn't see that finding Munro's horse would lead anyone to his body. Even if it did, it wouldn't throw any suspicion on me unless Cherry did some unnecessary talking, and there was no reason for her to do that.

When I reached Cheyenne, the first thing I did was go to Cherry's restaurant. It was close to noon and the smell of cooking food was just about more than I could stand, but I went on back into the kitchen, trying to ignore my stomach's announcement that it had been empty for a long time.

Cherry was standing beside her big range frying meat. She smiled when she saw me and spoke a greeting. I said, "I've got a present for you."

She frowned as she looked at the gunnysack. "I haven't got time to look at it now, Jim, but if you'll—"

"You'd better take time," I interrupted. "Ed sent it to you."

"Ed Burke?" She turned to a woman who was working for her and handed her a fork, motioning for her to watch the meat. As she led the way to her room she asked, "Why didn't Ed bring it?"

"He's dead," I said.

She whirled to look at me, to see if I was telling the truth. "What happened?"

"He had an accident."

"What kind of an accident?"

"He dropped off his horse."

"How could he drop off a horse?"

I didn't want to tell her what had happened, so I lied a little. I said, "I mean he fell off his horse."

She closed the door as I dumped the money on the bed. I said, "Ed asked me to bring this to you."

She froze, her lips parting, her eyes wide as she stared at the money. She walked slowly to the bed, then fell on her knees and began fingering the greenbacks and the gold and silver pieces as if she didn't believe they were real.

All she could say was "My God, Jim, look at all this money. Just look at it!"

I turned around and strode out of her room. I went home and put my horse up, then walked into the house and made coffee. I was plenty hungry, but I didn't think I could keep anything down yet, so I didn't try to cook.

After I drank two cups of coffee I fell asleep in my chair. I slept a few minutes, then woke enough to stagger into my bedroom, take off my boots and gun belt and fall across the bed. I slept the clock around, and when I woke up it was dark.

I cooked a meal, my stomach having settled down to where I could eat, though I was careful not to eat very much. I thought about Jess Munro, and how I had killed him. It surprised me to discover I did not feel at all guilty. My feelings were quite the opposite, in fact. I was struck by the thought that by accident a strange sort of justice had been brought about, with Munro meeting his death by trying to steal Ed Burke's stolen money.

If I had known it was Munro, not Red Buck, who was slipping into the shed, I probably would not have fired. But I didn't know, so Jess Munro had died.

CHAPTER XXX

Sometimes I've had the idea that my life has been marked by different periods, periods that were determined by events more than by time.

For instance my childhood while my mother was alive, my growing-up years with my father, the wood-cutting and building era in Black Hawk, interrupted by the brief interlude with the First Colorado Volunteers, then my move to Cheyenne and my engagement to Cherry. This chapter, at least my engagement to Cherry, came to a final end on the second Sunday morning in June, 1868. Not that it was any surprise. But I had not wanted to make the absolute and complete break. Cherry did.

After leaving the money with Cherry, I decided not to go back. I felt that the next move was up to her. I'll admit I had been irritated by the way she'd acted when I gave her the money. Apparently she had been hypnotized by it. She hadn't even said, "Thank you." "Why did Ed want me to have it?" The ugly thought occurred to me that she had agreed to marry me because she knew I had some money, and now she was indifferent because she had enough money of her own to do what she wanted.

I was aware that she might have been temporarily knocked off her moorings when she saw the money, but she could have come to my house later to talk about it. But I didn't see anything of her. The chances were that I'd have been home if she had come, because I stayed pretty close for several days. I simply didn't feel like doing anything.

I had gone to Bronco Stead's livery stable and talked to him. That was when he told me that Ed had seen what

Red Buck was aiming to do and had got to his feet and jumped between us, so that he took the bullet which was meant for me.

Stead also said that he was the one who had knocked me cold with his gun barrel. He said it was better for all concerned than killing me, which is what Buck or Munro would have done if I'd stayed on my feet and kept prodding them about a trial.

He was more than likely right, because Munro had had all he could stand of me and sooner or later would have given Buck the signal to try again. Stead went on to say that killing me would have created some problems, as well known and liked as I was in Cheyenne. He also claimed he was the one who had persuaded Munro to bring my horse up and leave him in the corral. How much of this was a lie was more than I could tell.

I asked Stead why Munro had insisted on me going along. He said they wanted to be sure I knew why they were hanging Ed. Unless I had actually seen Stead's horses in the corral with my own eyes, they knew I would never believe Ed had helped steal them. They were dead right about that, but they hadn't guessed I'd raise so much hell about Ed and the other two getting a trial. The reason they missed their guess on this, I think, was that Munro would never admit he couldn't handle another man, no matter who he was.

Finally, Stead told me that Munro had left Cheyenne for Laramie to help the Vigilantes there. When he failed to show up, I guess they wondered what had happened to him, but as far as I know his body was never found, so his disappearance remained a mystery.

Aside from going to Stead's livery stable and the grocery store and the post office, I stayed at home. It was not so much that my stomach still hurt, or that I was tired. I recovered from my physical ailments, but I didn't get over my mental and emotional problems so easily. I simply could not get the picture of Ed Burke swinging from a limb out of my head.

Knowing as much as I did about Ed, I realized he was a paradox, both good and bad, and I wasn't at all sure he took Buck's bullet to save my life. The more reasonable explanation was that he wanted to avoid a hanging. Being shot to death was certainly better than hanging. Still, what he had done saved my life, along with Bronco Stead knocking me cold.

In any case, Cherry did not come to see me. I had decided not to see her, so our relationship was one hell of a failure as far as romance went. As I thought about it more, it occurred to me that Cherry would have left town with Ed if she had known he had as much money as he had. I may be doing her an injustice, but I had expected her to come to see me, and when she didn't I was hurt, and then angry.

When I thought about her dropping to her knees and fingering the money, and the greedy expression that came to her face, I sensed that she had given up any serious thought of marrying me and that it was only a question of time until something happened to make a formal break.

Oddly enough, I felt relief. I didn't want a wife and family enough to beg her to marry me, even if she was the only woman in Cheyenne I knew who was eligible and I would consider marrying. The formal end came the Sunday morning I've mentioned, a little before eleven o'clock.

I'd gone to the Martin house the night before and had stayed there, as I did quite often. Rosy and Flossie had welcomed me, as they always did, telling me I was their favorite customer and asking why I'd stayed away so long. They'd cooked breakfast for me. After we'd eaten I remained at the table, smoking and talking to them while they did the dishes. The truth was I hated to go home to an empty house and I didn't have anything else to do.

I found myself thinking of Nancy Rush and how pleasant it would be to go home to her, and then I considered how it might have been with Cherry if we had really loved each other, or even if she had welcomed marrying me and wanted to be my wife, as I had first thought she did. I had to face the truth that I had expected too much of her. The way she had kept putting

me off and saying she needed more time was ample proof
that she had not wanted to marry me at any time.

Finally I got so churned up just thinking about Cherry
that I couldn't sit there and listen to Rosy's and Flossie's
chit-chat about nothing of importance. I got up and
walked out of the house and down the path to the street.
For some reason, my father's old saying about the sun
being on the wall came back to me.

It was the first time I had thought of that statement in
months. I felt guilty. I had all this money and so far I
hadn't done much with it. I remembered the parable
about the three servants whose master had given them
varying amounts of talents. I knew I had to find something to do.

I didn't see Cherry until I reached the boardwalk that
ran parallel to the street. I almost collided with her. She
stood motionless, staring at me, her face so white I
thought she was deathly sick and was going to faint.

I said, "Good morning, Cherry."

She pointed to the Martin house with a trembling
finger. "Jim, you ... you didn't come out of there, did
you?"

She knew damned well I did. She couldn't have helped
seeing me walk down the path. I was just plain sore
because she was so quick to condemn me for something
she didn't approve of when she had postponed marrying
me as long as she had.

"You bet I came out of there," I said, my tone sharp.
"Those women are my friends."

She jerked my ring off her finger and shoved it into my
hand. "I never want to lay eyes on you again," she said
and, whirling, ran back the way she had come.

I suppose she had been headed for Frank's church and,
being a little late, had come this way because it would
save her a block or so. By walking fast, she had probably
assured herself it wouldn't contaminate her.

I stood there staring after her, feeling quite satisfied
now that it was over. Actually, it had been over for quite
a while—maybe it had never really started. I knew one
thing for sure: this was better than getting married and

then having our marriage turn out a failure, as I was sure it would have done.

Cherry's holier-than-thou attitude toward whores had got to me before. I had a notion that for all of their sinning, Rosy and Flossie were better human beings than Cherry was.

Turning, I walked back into the house. I called, "Break out the champagne. My engagement is over. Finished. Done."

"Glory be," Rosy cried as she ran out of the kitchen. "That does call for champagne."

"It calls for a real celebration," Flossie said. "What do you want to do, Jim?"

"Oh, I don't know," I said. "Drink the champagne and then go home."

"I've got a better idea than that," Rosy said. "Let's go back to bed."

"Of course," Flossie said. "That's lots better than going back home. There's nobody waiting for you there."

That was exactly what we did.

The following Monday morning I saddled up and rode out to Fort D. A. Russell. I signed a contract that afternoon to cut and deliver two hundred cords of wood by November. The next morning I hired a crew. By noon we were on our way to the Black Hills.

CHAPTER XXXI

Even now I do not know any more than Pilate did exactly what truth is. I've read that the knowledge of truth comes from inside a man. If so, then this is the truth. If Cherry were telling the story, the events of the past year would be different. I mean, they would appear to be different to a third party. The same thing would be said if Nancy or Frank Rush were telling what had happened. I am convinced that no one can tell his life history and be completely objective.

I would not ask anyone to believe I was innocent of all wrongdoing. I have read and talked and listened about free will, yet I am not certain how much free will we have. On the other hand, I do not believe that all the events of our lives are planned before we are born, that we move through life as so many puppets while some great, unknown power pulls the strings. Perhaps we act from instinct, driven by some inner compelling power of which we are not fully aware.

Still, I am sure we make our own destiny. Only the foolish ask, "Why did this happen to me?" Only the foolish deny their responsibility for the fate that comes to them—good, bad or indifferent. So, inadvertently, I chose my destiny. It may seem strange, but if I were given the opportunity of living the months of September and October over, I would not do anything different than I did, even with the wisdom of hindsight.

Through the summer I worked as hard, probably harder, cutting and hauling wood to the fort, than any of my men. This being my first contract, I wanted to meet my deadline with time to spare. I was sure that a satisfactory performance would bring additional contracts. I always left my sorrel at the fort, so after I had pulled into the fort on Saturday afternoons with my load, I would unharness my team, saddle my sorrel, and ride into Cheyenne.

This was the routine I had followed every Saturday from the time I had started hauling wood early in the summer. In Cheyenne I would get my mail, take care of whatever items of business were pressing, and then heat water and bathe before I went to bed. I was always sweaty and dirty, and I always felt thoroughly gummed up by pitch, which seemed to cover my clothes like a suit of sticky armor.

We'd had some rain during the summer, but nothing like the gulley-washer that hit Cheyenne not long after dark the evening of the first Saturday in September. Lightning started flashing just about the time I put my sorrel away. I heated the water, as I did every Saturday, poured it into the washtub, which I had brought into the kitchen from the back porch, and added a couple of buckets of cold water. I undressed and tossed my pitch-stiffened clothes across the room, then stepped into the water and lathered my body, enjoying the muscle-relaxing heat of the water. That was when the storm hit.

I had known the storm was coming for an hour or more, judging by the black clouds that had rolled up over the Black Hills and then moved eastward, and the slashing lightning and booming thunder that I'd been hearing for the past hour. I was thankful that I was in for the night and had not been caught in the open with my team and load of wood, or in the saddle between Fort D. A. Russell and Cheyenne.

Not that I thought I was sugar or salt and would dissolve in the rain. It was just that it would have been damned uncomfortable—that's all. I'd been out in storms like this one both in Colorado and Wyoming, and I avoided one every time I could.

It's not only getting wet. It's the wind and the sudden sharp drop in temperature, along with the searching fingers of lightning, which act as if they are actually trying to touch a man and fry him to death. I've had lightning hit trees very close to me, suddenly, without warning, giving the impression of an exploding shell. It is, to say the least, mighty damn scarey.

When I stepped out of the tub and started toweling myself dry, I saw a flash through a kitchen window that must have hit very close. Immediately after, I heard the jarring blast of thunder that rocked the house. A moment later the back door opened and Nancy Rush stepped into the kitchen. She shut the door and leaned against it; then she closed her eyes and seemed to freeze there.

Never in my life have I seen a more thoroughly soaked person than Nancy, or one who had a more woebegone expression on her face. Water ran down her cheeks, strands of wet hair were plastered against her forehead, her dress clung to her body, and she was shivering violently. More than that, she was scared. I wasn't sure whether she was shivering from fear or the cold.

For a moment I stood motionless, staring at her, as completely surprised as I ever had been in my life. She looked at me, but I had the feeling she didn't really see me or know that I was absolutely naked.

She tried to say something and couldn't, and then closed her mouth. She was breathing hard. I suppose she had been running, but I don't think her failure to speak was due to being out of breath. I guessed that a combination of the cold downpour along with that close flash of lightning had completely unnerved her.

I came out of it in a moment. I threw the towel down and ran to her. "Get over to the fire," I said. "You've got to take your clothes off. Come on, I'll help you."

Water ran down her·legs and off her shoes onto the floor. She wiped her face with her wet hands, and this time when she tried to speak, she said in a tone that was barely audible, "I got caught."

"You sure did," I said.

I took her hands and led her to the stove. I ran into the bedroom and returned with a clean towel. She was trying to unbutton her dress, but she was still shivering so much that her fingers were all thumbs and refused to obey her mental commands. There was no doubt about her being caught in the storm, but why she had started out in the first place was the part I wondered about.

"Let me do it," I said, and handed the towel to her.

She dried her hands and face and wiped her hair with the towel while I unbuttoned her dress. My fingers weren't much better than hers, and she must have been carrying ten gallons of water that had been soaked in by her dress and petticoats and long drawers. Somehow I got all her clothes off her chilled body, then rubbed her with the towel until her skin was pink.

She was still shivering when I pulled a couple of chairs up to the stove. I wrung as much water as I could from her clothes, then hung them over the chairs to dry. I took one of her hands and led her into the bedroom. She went willingly and without protest.

I threw back the blankets and helped her into bed. As soon as she lay down, I got into bed beside her and pulled the blankets over us. I put my arms around her and drew her to me and held her against my warm body. It must have been at least ten minutes before she quit shivering.

"I take long walks every evening," she said. "Sometimes in the middle of the day, too. When I left home this evening, the clouds didn't look so bad. It was warm then. Real pleasant. As soon as I realized the storm was coming, I started to run, but the rain caught me and then the lightning struck. Just a block or two north of here, I think. I was so scared I couldn't keep running, so I came in here."

She giggled and I knew she was feeling all right again. "Excuse me for bursting in on you when you were taking a bath. I didn't intend to embarrass you."

"You didn't," I told her. "As a matter of fact, I've spent a good deal of time daydreaming about a situation like this, but I never expected it to be anything more than a daydream. Now you're here in my arms, I'm not so sure about that. Maybe I really did expect it to happen."

"Oh Jim, I know, I know," she said. "I tried to keep it from happening, but I knew it would. Someway, somehow."

Then she kissed me and the door swung open for us. It was an experience I cannot describe any more than I can describe a brilliantly colored sunset to a man who has been born blind. I have known of only a few human experiences that are beyond words. This was one, the spirit soaring to the mountain top, the total feeling far greater than any human being could experience from his five senses.

It has been said that when all conditions are right, the physical level of feeling transcends the usual mundane experience of life and becomes spiritual, that in reality the physical and spiritual are very close and all of life is one.

Some of the great lovers of the ages have discovered this. If they were poets, they have recorded it, saying in effect that only stupid people divide life into separate categories and contend that they always remain separate. If a person is filled with nothing but lust, or has a compelling appetite for food and drink, or is driven by an insensate hunger for power, this might be true. It was not true of either of us. We didn't lie there and exchange sentimental words of love, but the love was there. We both knew it without the words.

Nancy slept for a few minutes. I held her in my arms all the time she was in bed with me, thinking how I had hated men who took other men's wives. It had been a foolish judgment, because I had not understood how it could happen without guilt, without blame. Now, with her warm flesh close to mine, I knew what Frank would think if he ever found out. Still, I felt no guilt. If he had truly and properly loved her, she would not have been in bed with me.

She woke with a start and threw the blankets back with a violent gesture. She sat up, looking around and breathing hard. I said, "You're all right, Nancy. You're safe and you are loved."

She took a long breath and said in a tone of wonder, "Why, it is true, Jim. I thought for a few seconds I had been dreaming again."

"It really happened," I said.

"I've got to go," she said. "I want to get home before Frank does."

"It's raining," I said, "and your clothes are probably still damp."

"It's not raining so hard now," she said, "and I won't be in my wet clothes very long."

She got out of bed and ran into the kitchen. She started to dress. I followed her and stood in the doorway watching her, not wanting her to go but knowing it would be wrong to try to keep her. I wondered if she would ever come back, and again I knew it would be wrong to urge her, that it was a decision she had to make.

She smiled as she slipped on her dress. She said, "Thank you, Jim. I'll sleep tonight. I haven't slept well for a long time. It is something Frank has never understood. I have tried to explain it to him, but he won't listen. I don't try any more."

My fists were clenched so tightly the nails pressed into the flesh of my palms. It was hard for me to breathe. I felt as a man must feel who has had a very brief glimpse of Paradise and then sees the curtain pulled together in front of him, cutting off the view.

I asked, "Where is Frank?"

"Calling on the sick," she said bitterly, "or just visiting members of his flock. He has time for them even though he may not have time for his wife. He has become a successful minister and there are many who love him."

"Divorce him, Nancy. Marry me."

Right or wrong, the words came out of me in a kind of desperate cry. I could not let her go, so I tried to keep her. She shook her head at me, smiling again, the bitterness gone from her. "I can't, Jim. It's something else he could never understand. It would destroy him. I just can't do it."

She walked to the door, put her hand on the knob, then turned to me. "You are my love," she said. "I'll be back."

"Saturday night?"

She nodded. "Next Saturday night."

She left, closing the door behind her. I looked at the

wet spots on the floor where she had stood when she had first come in. The puddles the rain had made had not dried up, but they would soon be gone. They could not last, and I knew, too, with deep regret, that this new relationship with Nancy could not last either.

CHAPTER XXXII

Nancy kept her promise and came to my house every Saturday night through September and October, but she seldom stayed very long. She would usually sleep a little while and then lie in my arms for a few more minutes. After that she would get up and dress and hurry home, saying she did not want Frank to come back to the house and find her gone.

We never talked about ourselves and the future. I had a strange feeling of unreality during those weeks. I wanted it to last through eternity, but my rational mind kept reminding me that it was the most futile of hopes, that each Saturday night might be the last one.

After she left, I would continue to feel her presence. I would sit by the stove and smoke and think of her, of all that had happened while she had been with me, of every word she had spoken, and then how transient this relationship was.

She would never be my wife no matter how much I wanted it to be that way. I knew this with the same certainty that I knew the sun would come up in the morning. I accepted each Saturday for what it was—a few minutes, an hour or two—and I accepted the inevitability of the fact that soon I would have only memories.

It was not until the middle of October that Nancy stayed most of the night with me. We got out of bed near midnight and I built up the fire and made a pot of coffee. We drank and I smoked, and I looked at Nancy with the heart-sinking feeling that this might be the last time she would be here. I don't know why the feeling was so strong that night, unless it was the fact that our relationship had lasted longer than I had thought it would and I could not believe it would continue much longer.

We sat in silence for a long time, and then I burst out, for no reason except that I wanted her to know, "Nancy, do you know how much I love you?"

"Yes." She put her coffee cup down on the table and reached out and took my hand. "Do you know how much I love you and how long it has been?"

"I know how long," I answered. "From that first evening when Frank had me to supper and you cooked a good dinner over the fire in front of your tent."

She nodded. "Except that through all of that evening and all the other times I have seen you I resolved not to let my love overcome my honor. I married Frank for better or for worse. I had every intention of keeping my marriage vows. I would have succeeded if I hadn't been caught in the storm that night."

I got up and walked to the stove, not as sure of that as she was. For some reason I had a crazy notion that what had happened was inevitable, that if the storm hadn't brought us together, something else would. I lifted a lid and knocked my pipe out and replaced the lid. Then I said, "Nancy, I have always condemned men who slept with other men's wives. To me they had no honor, but it was a judgment I should never have made."

"Don't have any guilty feelings," she said quickly. "I owe you an explanation."

"You don't owe me anything," I said, "and I don't have any sense of guilt. Even if I had a choice and could live these last six weeks over, I wouldn't change anything we have done. It's just that when I consider how I used to feel I get pretty damned humble. I guess it bears out what the Bible says about not judging."

"Yes, I guess it does," she said. "Anyhow, I want to tell you one thing about Frank. I loved him very much when we were married even though I wasn't interested in being a preacher's wife. I was willing to try and I did the best I could. No matter how hard I tried, I was constantly criticized for doing too much or not doing enough or wearing the wrong dress or flirting with one of the men of the church when I hadn't done anything more than to say good morning."

She poured another cup of coffee and sipped it for a moment. "I think I could have stood that if everything had been right between me and Frank. I have never understood why he feels the way he does about a man's and woman's physical love. He never comes to me until he has to just for enough relief to go to sleep . . . It's always over in about ten seconds—then he goes to sleep. That's why I told you the first night I was here that I could sleep. It was the first time since I married Frank, and it's why I take the long walks I do—but walking doesn't do any good. Frank believes it is wrong unless we do it to have children. It's immoral. It's . . . it's surrendering to the flesh and the devil. Well, I've given up any hope of having children."

She sat staring at her coffee, tears running down her cheeks. She asked in a low tone, "Why does he feel that way, Jim? Why?"

"I don't know," I said, "except that it is an old teaching which is part of the Christian dogma. It was Adam's and Eve's original sin in the Garden of Eden, they say, a carnal sin that comes from man's lower nature. I say it is a false doctrine. I don't believe they sinned and I don't believe we have sinned."

"Neither do I," she said, "but I do know we can't keep on. It's got to the place where I'm afraid to look at Frank for fear he'll guess about us. If I continue to come here, he'll find out sooner or later."

"I've asked you to divorce him," I said. "I'll tell him if you want me to."

"No, Jim," she said. "I can't do it."

We were silent again for a while. Then I remembered a question I had been wanting to ask her and just never thought of it when I had a chance. "Why did you tell me not to marry Cherry?"

"She's too tight-lipped. She won't make any man a good wife." Then Nancy laughed. "Well, it was more than that. I was jealous. I didn't want you to marry anyone else."

"But if I can't marry you . . ." I began.

"I'm just a dog in the manger," she said, "and I hate myself for being that way."

Later, as she was getting ready to go home, she told me that Frank was sitting up with Grandma Carruthers. The old lady had been one of the most steadfast members of Frank's flock. For a month or more she had been bedfast; then about a week ago she had taken a turn for the worse. She couldn't die and she couldn't get well, and she had to have someone to take care of her all the time. Her daughter, with whom she lived, was completely worn out, so Frank was taking the nights and Nancy spent part of each day with her.

"We can't go on much longer," Nancy said. "We just can't last. Frank has had very little sleep for a week." She stood by the door, her hand on the knob as she looked at me. "I love you, Jim. I love you very much and I can't live without you, but if I ruined Frank's life, I would feel guilty."

"You've got yourself to think of, too," I said.

She nodded. "I know, and I've got you to think of. I can't forget that. I should never have let it start."

"No," I said, remembering my thoughts about the memories. "What we've had has been good. It can't be taken from us no matter what happens now."

"I've thought about that," she said, "but in my saner moments I know I've got to make a decision." She stopped, biting her lower lip, then added, "Jim, I don't know how I could go through a week if I didn't have Saturday night to look forward to, but I can't keep coming, either."

She opened the door and left the house. I stood there for a time before I went back to bed, thinking about it. I told myself again that she was the one to make the decision. If she decided not to come here again, I would sell my property and leave Cheyenne.

I could not stay here and know she was in the same town I was in and leave her alone. I would end up going to Frank and bullying him into divorcing her. She wouldn't like it, and if it ruined Frank, she might refuse to marry me. For the only time in my life I wished I had the gift of second sight. I just could not look ahead and see any solution to our problem.

I finished the wood contract on Thursday and spent Friday winding up the odds and ends such as paying off my men and promising them work the next contract I had. Besides that, I had letters to write and several business deals to explore, so I had plenty to do, but on Saturday I couldn't settle down. I fidgeted around all day, wondering if Nancy would come and what decision she had made.

Perhaps I was unduly fearful about it, but I had no real hope—that was all. I would not even try to force her to see it my way. If she came to me, it had to be of her own free will, accepting all the risks there were in making that decision.

She came not long after dark, bright-eyed and eager. As she took my hand and led me into the bedroom, she said, "Frank was home when I got back last Saturday, but he didn't suspect anything. I told him I couldn't go to sleep and had gone out walking. I've done it before, so he wasn't surprised."

The evening was so warm we lay on top of the blankets. She did not go to sleep, but stayed in my arms and pressed her body very hard against mine as she hugged me.

"I've decided, Jim," she said. "All of my married life I've thought of Frank and tried to do exactly what he wanted me to—at least until the night of the storm. I even took the rent money to you because he was too big a coward to face you. He was willing to live in your house, though. I kept thinking it would be better after the church was finished and he'd pay what he owed you, but he hasn't.

"Well, I've thought about it all week, about you saying I had you to think of. Myself, too. I'm going to Denver. I'll divorce Frank. I kept telling you I couldn't do it, but I know I can. I'll write to you and let you know how I'm getting along and where I'm staying if you want to see me."

"Of course I want to see you," I said. "You'll need some money."

"Oh, I'll work," she said. "I couldn't just sit still and do nothing."

"You'll still need money to get started," I said. "If you need more, or if you don't find a job, let me know. Money is one thing I have plenty of."

She sat up on the edge of the bed. "All right," she said. "Give me lots of money and I'll spend it. After we're married I'll spend all of your money."

"Now wait a minute. You don't need to go whole hog." I reached over and patted her stomach. "Have I told you lately what a beautiful body you have?"

"No, not lately," she answered. "You never tell me often enough."

"I'll do better in the future," I promised.

"I'd better get home," she said. "I don't want Frank to find me gone again. He had several calls to make, so he told me he'd be away two or three hours."

I got up and crossed the room to my bureau. I had quite a bit of money left after paying off my men. I opened the top drawer and picked up a roll of bills. I asked, "Will $500 be enough?"

She didn't answer. I heard her heavy breathing. I turned to ask her again, thinking she hadn't heard. I froze, dropping the money back into the drawer. Frank stood in the kitchen doorway, staring at me, his face dark with fury. Hate, too, I guess. I had never seen an expression on his face like the one I saw then.

He was not the Frank Rush I had known for more than a year. He was a madman. A gun in his right hand dangled at his side. I knew he would use it.

"You bastard," he said. "I'm going to kill you."

Nancy was putting on her clothes as fast as she could. I don't think Frank saw her. Maybe he didn't even know she was in the room. I couldn't think of anything I could do except distract him. Then maybe Nancy would be able to slip out of the house. She could go for help. At least she could save her own life.

"You're a sick man, Frank," I said. "Let me have the gun. Then you come and lie down."

I started walking toward him, one hand extended. He backed into the kitchen. "Don't come any closer," he said. "I'm sick all right. You made me sick. You're a great man in Cheyenne, and all the time you've been committing adultery with my wife. You've bought her. You've got money and property and you contract wood for the army. I trusted you and you steal my wife."

He was in the kitchen now. I saw Nancy slip around the bed to a window and ease up the lower sash. Frank couldn't see her from where he stood, about halfway between the back door and the door into the bedroom. She'd get away.

I took another step toward him, my hand still extended. Then I knew from the expression on his face, the sudden tightening of his lips against his teeth, that nothing could save me. He was ready to pull the trigger.

Still, I had to try. At least I could buy a little more time so Nancy could get farther away from the house. I said, "Give me the gun, Frank. You don't want them to hang you."

He fired. I seem to remember a burst of flame, the roar of the gun, and I reeled back, trying to stay upright and knowing I couldn't. I thought he had killed me, that he had blown off the top of my head.

I had a weird feeling I was in two worlds. I was falling as I tried to hold to this world and at the same time I was reaching into another with the other hand. Then there was nothing but blackness.

CHAPTER XXXIII

Paul Lerner laid the manuscript down. He leaned back in his chair and closed his eyes, thinking it was a strange place for Jim Glenn to end his story. There was much that Glenn had left unsaid. Perhaps that was the reason he had asked Lerner to see Cherry Owens Lind, Nancy Rush and Frank Rush. He would start with Cherry in the morning, he told himself as he rose and went downstairs for supper.

He ate an early breakfast the following morning, then walked to Stead's Livery Stable and rented a rig. He wondered if this Stead was the Bronco Stead that Jim Glenn had mentioned. He didn't ask because Glenn had not said for him to talk to Stead. The less attention he attracted the better.

"Do you know Cherry Lind?" Lerner asked the hostler. "I believe she lives up Crow Creek about five miles from town."

"Mrs. Lind?" the hostler said. "Sure, I know her. She always leaves her horse here when she comes to town. She lives on the CO ranch. It's marked. You won't have any trouble finding it."

Lerner thanked him and drove away. He took the Crow Creek road out of town, wondering what Cherry Lind would be like. From Jim Glenn's journal he had a clear picture of the three people he was to see, and he could not keep from wondering how true the picture was. He was sure he would not like Cherry and he was equally sure he would like Nancy Rush. Frank was a question mark. It would depend on what the years in prison had done to the man.

It was still early in the morning when he saw an arch

across a lane that turned off the road to the right, the big black letters CO showing up clearly at the top of the arch. The buildings were about a quarter of a mile from the road. Lerner studied them carefully as he approached them.

The ranch had the look of a working spread, with its pole corrals and sprawling log barn and slab sheds. Still, it was not like most of the ranches he had seen in Wyoming and Colorado, which had been built strictly for utility and were lived on only by men. A woman's touch was evident in the washing on the line, the grass and flowers inside the fence that surrounded the house, and the white lace curtains at the windows.

He pulled up in front of the house, wrapped the lines around the brake handle and stepped down. As he turned toward the gate, a man yelled, "Hold it."

Lerner stopped, one hand on the gate. The man who strode toward him was more boy than man, probably seventeen or eighteen. He had the long-legged look of a boy who had shot up fast the last year or so, his muscles not having caught up yet with his bones.

"What do you want?" the boy asked.

"I'm Paul Lerner from Denver," Lerner said. "I drove out here to see Mrs. Lind."

"You still haven't said what you want," the boy said impatiently.

"I'm a reporter," Lerner said. "I want to interview her."

"Oh hell," the boy said scornfully. "Now why would you want to interview her? She's just another ranch woman. You can find a hundred of 'em hereabouts."

Lerner hesitated, wondering if the boy was her son. If so, how much would he know about Jim Glenn and his mother's relationship with Glenn. If he did know, his reaction might not be favorable.

"She was one of the early settlers in Cheyenne," Lerner said carefully. "I understand she ran a restaurant when it was hell on wheels. I want to talk to her about her experiences."

The boy scratched an ear, glanced at the house, then

back at Lerner. "I dunno," he said dubiously. "She's not much on talking about those times. Besides, she's busy, this being wash day and all."

Lerner opened the gate. "I can ask her," he said.

"I'll call her," the boy said.

He strode past Lerner, stepped up on the porch and pulled the screen open. He yelled, "Ma." For a moment there was no answer. The boy went into the house and Lerner followed, taking off his hat and remaining near the door.

The room was furnished with a black leather couch, one leather chair, several rockers, and a claw-footed oak stand in the center of the room. A number of magazines and catalogs were piled neatly on top of the stand.

A rag carpet covered the floor. There was no fireplace. Instead, Lerner noted the big heater, which would be adequate in the coldest winter weather. The wallpaper had a pattern of small red roses against a silver background. A pronghorn rack hung near the door. Everything, Lerner saw, was spotlessly clean.

The boy started toward the kitchen, then stopped beside the stand as his mother came into the room. She looked at Lerner, then at the boy, and said, "Well?" Her tone was not a friendly one, and Lerner sensed that he would learn very little from her.

At least he was seeing Cherry Owens Lind. He recalled Glenn's description of her: bright blue eyes, gold-yellow hair with touches of red, and a small enough body for her to be called Watch Fob and Trinket. The description fitted her now as well as it had more than twenty years ago, even to her hair, which was brushed back from her forehead and pinned in a bun at the back of her head.

The only difference would be in the lines in her face. They seemed particularly deep around her eyes. Then he saw that her lips were thin and pressed tightly together. He was reminded of what Nancy Rush had said about Cherry not making a good wife for Glenn.

"This fellow is from Denver," the boy was saying. "He's a reporter. His name's Paul Lerner. He wants to interview you about the early days in Cheyenne when it was hell on wheels."

"I don't remember a thing about those days," she said sharply. "Good day, sir."

She whirled toward the kitchen door, her skirt whipping away from her trim ankles. "Wait," Lerner said. "Jim Glenn asked me to talk to you."

She whirled back to face him, her lips parting, plainly surprised to hear him say that. "Why on earth would Jim ask you to talk to me?" she demanded.

"He's written a journal about the first fifteen months he lived in Cheyenne," Lerner said. "About his early years, too. I suppose an autobiography would be a better word. Anyhow, he asked me to talk to you of the events he tells about. I think he wanted this interview to be checked for authenticity against what he wrote."

She opened her mouth, then closed it without saying a word. Her eyes moved to the boy, who had backed to the front door and now stood motionless, listening. She said sharply, "Bud, did you finish the chores?"

"No, I saw this fellow drive up—"

"All right," his mother said. "You saw him and you brought him in. Now go finish the chores."

He hesitated, not wanting to leave, but after a few seconds he reluctantly turned and walked away.

She waited until the boy left, then asked, "Why did Jim write all of this? Is he trying to justify himself for his affair with the Rush woman?"

"No," Lerner said. "I would not attempt to say what his motives were, except that he feels other people can learn from his mistakes."

"They should," she said tartly. "He made enough."

"I would guess there is another reason," Lerner went on, "one that is common to many men. All of us have a desire to be immortal. Leaving a book that survives after a man's death is one way to achieve immortality."

"I see," she said with cold contempt. "Yes, Jim Glenn would want to be immortal. I suppose he didn't have anything to say that was complimentary about me."

Sun on the Wall

"On the contrary," Lerner told her. "He had many complimentary things to say about you."

"You're lying," she said. "Have you seen the Rush woman?"

"No, but I will."

"Have you seen Frank Rush, who put Jim in his wheelchair?"

"No, but I plan to see him too."

"You do that," she said. "They'll have plenty to tell you. I have nothing to say."

"But Mrs. Lind—"

"Good day, sir," she said.

Turning, she disappeared through the door. She was still quick-moving, just as Glenn had said she was when she had her restaurant. She had kept her figure too, he saw, her waist so tiny that a man could almost encircle it with his hands.

This time Lerner did not attempt to call her back. There was nothing to do but leave the house, get into the rig, and drive back to Cheyenne. He told himself that Jim Glenn had foreseen how Cherry Owens Lind would perform. She had not mellowed with age. As a matter of fact, he guessed she was more determined, more dominating, more certain of her judgments than she had been as a young woman.

It struck Lerner as interesting that she had not wanted to recall the events that Glenn had related. He decided that the lines around her eyes were evidence of discontent. She had not, he thought, lived a happy life. She probably could not keep from wondering what her life would have been if she had married Jim Glenn.

Thinking about his short interview with her, it occurred to Lerner that she had not asked him to stay for dinner. She had not asked if he would like a cup of coffee. She had not even asked him to sit down. She had not inquired about Jim Glenn, either, although Lerner was sure she had not seen him for years.

Lerner would have to write an epilogue to Glenn's book. Glenn, of course, had known that. Lerner doubted that he had expected Cherry Lind to tell anything new or different, or add to what he had written. He simply wanted Lerner to see her, to get an impression of her.

Well, he had the impression all right, he told himself with wry amusement. His impression was that Cherry was an unhappy and unfriendly person, and Glenn had been lucky not to marry her. This, he realized, was exactly the impression he'd had of her after reading what Glenn had written.

CHAPTER XXXIV

Lerner returned the rig to the livery stable before noon, ate dinner at his hotel, and walked to Nancy Rush's place on the corner of 16th and Russell. Everything was exactly as he had expected it to be: the white frame house, the picket fence, also painted white, the green lawn and flowers growing close to the front of the house, and the window box with the red geraniums.

As he stepped up on the porch and gave the bell-pull a tug, he pondered something he thought he had discovered. He was convinced that few people change over the years. Given a certain combination of dispositions, ambitions and attitudes, a young person would be the same kind of person in middle life and old age, at least until senility set in.

He mentally admitted that a great traumatic experience, through some strange inner alchemy, might transform a man or woman and give him or her a new direction, but he considered it unlikely to happen. His theory had held up with Cherry Lind. Now he sensed a warmth, a loving care that Nancy Rush gave her home. That, too, was a feeling he had expected to have.

She opened the door and looked at him questioningly. He said, "I'm Paul Lerner. I'm a Denver reporter. Jim Glenn asked me to talk to you."

"Of course," she said. "I should have guessed. I knew you were coming." She held the screen open. "Come in."

He stepped inside and she let the screen close behind him. She shut the door, then motioned to a hat rack on the wall. "Hang your hat up and come on back. I'm busy this afternoon so we'll talk while I work."

He hung his hat on the rack and followed her along the hall to a room that held a cutting table, a dressmaker's dummy, a sewing machine, two chairs, remnants of several pieces of dress goods, and an unfinished red-velvet gown that had been draped across the cutting table.

"This is the working part of the house," she said. "I hope you don't mind visiting in this room."

"Of course not," he said.

"As a matter of fact, I seldom use the parlor," she said. "I spend most of my time in this room, partly because I like to work, but mostly because the parlor is too stiff and formal for me. Sit down." She motioned to a rocking chair. "Go ahead and smoke if you want to. Oh, can I get you a cup of coffee? I have a pot on the stove."

"No, I just got up from dinner," he said as he sat down. He drew a cigar from his pocket and bit off the end. "As you seem to know, Jim Glenn wrote to the editor of the *Rocky Mountain News*. As a result I was sent here. I talked to Mr. Glenn yesterday and he gave me the manuscript of an autobiography he has—"

"I know," she interrupted. "I've read it. Jim wanted you to talk to me about what happened during those first fifteen months he lived in Cheyenne when I knew him. I am not familiar with all the events he relates, but I know about many of them, and I can assure you that, to the best of my knowledge, everything he has written is true."

Lerner watched her as she talked, and he told himself that again his theory was right. Nancy Rush was in her middle forties, but she was still a very attractive woman, with only a trace of gray in her black hair. She had kept her figure, although not as perfectly as Cherry Lind had. She had the same high, proud breasts that Glenn had mentioned, the same nicely proportioned ankles, but the years and perhaps her hours of sitting as she worked on dresses had given her a spread across her buttocks that she probably had not had when Glenn first knew her.

The fault was a minor one. Lerner could understand why Glenn had called her a slim and shining girl. Now she was no longer a girl, but a mature woman, and there was still an air of excitement about her. He saw, too, the self-possessed curve of her lips, and he sensed the outgoing warmth that he was sure Glenn had felt. Cherry Lind had been embittered by life; Nancy Rush had not, and that, Lerner told himself, was a part of the difference between the two women.

Nancy had taken a chair near the cutting table. Now she picked up her needle and thread, replaced her thimble, drew the velvet gown off the cutting table, and began to sew. Lerner watched her for a moment, then said, "If you've read what Mr. Glenn wrote, you know he didn't finish his book. I'll have to, but before I can do it, you'll have to tell me what happened. I'm curious, too, why he didn't finish it."

"He got too sick," she answered. "He intended to finish it. He worked very hard on it the last two years, writing and rewriting and of course trying to recall the events he relates. Recalling some of his feelings, too, which I believe is even harder than recalling events. He was a very busy man up until about two years ago. He bought and sold Cheyenne property and he continued to do a great deal of business with the army.

"He was always fortunate in finding good men to work for him, and he had a great talent for instilling a sense of loyalty in them. He began to fail two years ago. That was when he decided to write this journal or whatever you call it. He should have started sooner. A few weeks ago he told me he couldn't finish it. Just didn't have the strength to hold on to his pencil and paper. Besides that, he said his mind was getting fuzzy.

"That was why he wrote to Alex Dolan, the *News* editor. He had to have help from a qualified person, he said, or the book would never be published. He wanted it published, Mr. Lerner. It's the one thing he wanted above all others. A great deal depends upon you."

"I appreciate that now," Lerner said. "I didn't when I talked to Dolan in Denver. I saw Mrs. Lind this morning and she asked me why he wrote his autobiography. I said he told me he hoped people would profit from his mistakes, and also that he may have chosen this way to reach for immortality. I told her it was common to all men in one way or another."

"You are very discerning, Mr. Lerner," Nancy said. "That's exactly right. He wanted a wife and children as a young man. Having children, of course, is the way most people seek immortality, but after he was shot he couldn't have children, so he wrote a book."

She sewed for a moment, then looked up and asked cautiously, "How was Cherry?"

"It seemed to me she was unhappy," he answered. "She wouldn't tell me anything."

"I didn't think she would," Nancy said. "Jim didn't think so either, but he wanted you to try. You see—and God forgive me because I'm making a judgment that perhaps I shouldn't make—I firmly believe she would never have accepted Jim's ring in the first place if he hadn't had money and she thought she could get her hands on it by marrying him. She had to have a husband she could control and she knew Jim was a strong man, one she could not control. I think that was why she put off marrying him."

She bit her lower lip and was silent for a time. Then she went on. "As you probably gathered from reading Jim's book, I didn't like Cherry. Part of it was because I was jealous of her, and it was also because I sensed there was this side of her that escaped Jim. She couldn't give or bend. She had to dominate. Life with her would have been hell for Jim. He would never bow to any woman.

"Anyhow, after Ed Burke left her that money she didn't need Jim. She would have found some excuse to have broken the engagement even if she hadn't seen him come out of the Martin house that morning. She ran the restaurant for several more months, then she sold it and bought the CO on Crow Creek. She married one of the cowboys, made him her foreman, and five years later he was dead. She never married again."

He had been rolling the cigar between his finger tips. Now he lighted it. When Nancy stopped talking, he said, "Well, let's go back to what happened the night Jim was shot."

She glanced at him, her expression grave, then went on with her sewing. She said, "You must understand, Mr. Lerner, that I am a bad woman, a woman of loose morals. I betrayed my husband by sleeping with another man. Most people in Cheyenne have forgotten it or never heard the story, but at the time I was the scarlet woman and it would have been very easy for me to have joined the sisterhood on Eighteenth Street. But I knew enough about their lives to be sure I couldn't live that way. I nearly starved, though, before Jim was well enough to be concerned about me and to send for me.

"He gave me money to live on and later he deeded this house to me. I have always enjoyed sewing and I'm quite good at it. In time, I was able to start a dressmaking business. I've made a living over the years and I'll continue to make one, I think. Jim will leave me something, but I won't get much aside from the trust fund he set up for me, which will be administered by one of the local banks."

She did not, Lerner thought, want to answer his question, but it had to be answered if he was to write the epilogue to Glenn's book, and she was the only one who could answer it. He said, "Now about that evening Glenn was shot."

She glanced up again, smiling. "I know. You can't talk to Jim again. You probably haven't heard, but he slipped into a coma this morning. He won't live much longer—a matter of hours, I think. I hope he goes soon. He had always been such a strong man. It's been hard to see him go downhill the way he has the last two years. Up until then he had retained his strength, even though he was held to his wheelchair.

"He saw lots of people and he kept on making money. As I told you, he was involved in a good many business deals and he enjoyed them. He gave much of his money away. You know his father's saying about the sun on the wall. Well, Jim had a feeling he wasn't going to live a long life and he had to be doing whatever he was going to do. Giving money away was something from which he gained great satisfaction, but he was always careful about it. He never gave money to anything or anybody until he had looked into the situation carefully."

Lerner pulled gently on his cigar, waiting patiently until she finished. Then he tried again. "Mrs. Rush, would you tell me—"

"Yes, I will because I'm the only one who can and you have to know," she said. "I'm like everyone, I guess. I put off doing what I don't want to do. This is a painful memory and I don't like to bring it back into my mind. Perhaps it's the real reason Jim didn't finish his book. It was painful to him, too. When you're doing something which you know isn't right and then you're caught at it, the experience is hell.

"Jim and I loved each other and kept on loving each other right up to the moment he lost consciousness. I've told him many times that I would marry him. I started telling him as soon as I had my divorce, which wasn't long after Frank went to prison, but he wouldn't have me. He kept telling me to find another man. I could never convince him that I didn't want any other man. All I wanted to do was to take care of him, but he didn't want me to do that, so I've been able to visit him and that was all."

This time when she stopped Lerner said nothing. He waited, and presently she said, "There is only one thing I would say in criticism of Jim's book. He doesn't give himself enough credit. For instance, he had great physical courage, like the time in the Head Quarters Saloon when the man was going to knife Frank. Jim saved Frank's life at the risk of his own, because the crowd was hostile and it's a miracle those men didn't turn on him and kill him."

She paused again and for a moment he thought she was going to cry, but she went on, her tone firm. "It was the same the night Frank caught us. I was sitting on the edge of the bed just starting to put my clothes on when I heard something in the kitchen. We usually locked the doors and I don't know why we didn't that night. I looked up and there was Frank with the gun in his hand.

"My heart just quit beating. I thought he was going to kill both of us right then. As soon as I could begin to think straight, I put my clothes on. Jim started talking to Frank, who backed into the kitchen, and I got out through the window. I ran for help. I heard two shots. I came back with a policeman and a doctor.

"Jim was lying on the floor with blood on his forehead. I thought he was dead. Frank just stood there as if he was frozen, still holding the gun in his hand. We lifted Jim to the bed and the doctor saw that one bullet had grazed his head and knocked him out. I don't know how the second bullet could have hit him the way it did, but it struck his spine and that's what has paralyzed him all this time. I don't know what Frank was aiming at, but maybe Jim was turning and falling when that bullet hit him.

"Well, a few people blamed Jim and said Frank had a right by the unwritten law to do what he did, but most folks didn't agree. Jim was better known and better liked than he realized, and the feeling was very strong against Frank. There was even some talk of lynching. When Frank was being tried, Jim insisted that he be carried into the courtroom on a stretcher. He wasn't able to be in his wheelchair yet. He asked that Frank be found not guilty, that he did what any man would have done under those circumstances, but that didn't change the jury's mind. They found Frank guilty and sent him to prison for a long term."

Again she was close to crying when she finished. Lerner waited for a time, and when he saw she was finished talking, he rose. "Thank you, Mrs. Rush. If I'm still in Cheyenne when the funeral's held, would you like for me to go with you?"

She glanced up and nodded. She said in a low tone, "Yes, that would be nice. I'll have to go alone if you don't come for me. You know, I won't even be able to help with the funeral arrangements. Ron Ballard and Ella Evans will do that. They have always been very honest in disliking me."

She went to the door with him. As they walked along the hall, she asked, "Have you talked to Frank?"

"I'll see him tomorrow."

"He's not in prison," she said, "but I think he's still in Laramie. They can tell you at the prison where he is."

Lerner paused in the doorway. "Is there anything in the book you don't want published? Or in what you've told me?"

She shook her head. "No, nothing can hurt me now. Besides, it's all in the record. There's no use for me to deny anything even if I wanted to."

"I'll see you again before I leave Cheyenne," he said.

He walked away, thinking that she had been a lonely woman and would be even more lonely now that Jim Glenn was dead or soon would be. Life had been unjust to her, and yet it had not made her bitter.

Again his theory had proved correct. He had found her to be the kind of woman Jim Glenn had made her out to be. With any kind of luck, her sin, if that was what it had been, would never have become public knowledge. The strange part of the whole business was that Jim Glenn's image in the community had not been tarnished, whereas Nancy had become, as she had said, the scarlet woman, and it would never really change as long as she lived here.

CHAPTER XXXV

Lerner took a morning train to Laramie. As the train rolled across the summit of Sherman Hill, he thought of what Glenn had written about that hard winter of 1867–8 when there had been so much snow here that construction had been stopped and the crews had wintered in Cheyenne. He thought, too, of the hunger for profit, and how the survey crews had been sent on west in the dead of winter and the construction crews had been ordered out when the ground was still frozen too hard to be worked by pick and shovel.

The profit motive, Lerner reflected, was still one of the most powerful of all human drives, and human nature had certainly not changed during the years that had followed the building of the Union Pacific. But whatever motives had driven the men who built the transcontinental railroad, the actual physical labor of laying the rails still seemed a tremendous accomplishment twenty years after it was done.

One question had been cleared up by Glenn. Previously Lerner had read everything he could lay his hands on about the Vigilance Committees, for a book he hoped to write. He had suspected that there had been some thread connecting the Cheyenne Vigilantes with the earlier organizations in the Montana gold fields and in Denver.

Now he realized that there could be no such connection unless the man Glenn knew as Jess Munro had been in Denver or the Montana mining country and had helped organize those committees as well as the one in Cheyenne. Lerner would never have an answer to that question, but it seemed possible that Munro was involved with all three, particularly since he had admitted having experience with other Vigilance Committees.

Lerner arrived in Laramie before noon. He ate dinner, then hired a cab to take him to the prison. When he arrived he was told that Frank Rush had served his term and had been released several years before, but that he still returned to the prison once a week to work with some of the convicts.

"He's a good man," the official said. "He's done a great deal for several of our prisoners. He's an excellent carpenter. If you're going to give him work, he'll do a good job for you."

"No, I just want to talk to him." Lerner hesitated, then said cautiously, "Jim Glenn asked me to talk to him."

"Glenn?" The official was shocked. "He's the man who was sleeping with Frank's wife, wasn't he? Hell, I don't see why Frank didn't kill the bastard."

"I believe he tried," Lerner said.

"Well, he should have tried harder," the man said. "I consider it a miscarriage of justice, sending Frank here. Any man with red blood in his veins would have done exactly what he did. I'll tell you one thing. If I ever found my wife in bed getting screwed by some bastard like that Glenn fellow, I'd kill him. I can't understand a jury convicting Frank like they done."

That wasn't the way Frank Rush had found Glenn and Nancy when he had entered Glenn's house with his gun, but Lerner saw no purpose in arguing the point. It was evident that the man had a high regard for Frank Rush, and therefore saw the incident from Frank's point of view.

"Could you give me Rush's address?"

"Sure, but when you mention Jim Glenn, Frank will kick your ass right through his front door." The man wrote the address down and handed it to Lerner. "He lives about a block from the depot. It's your funeral, mister."

Lerner thanked him and returned to the cab. The official's reaction was interesting to him and he wondered if his mental picture of Frank Rush would hold up as well as his picture of Cherry Lind and Nancy Rush had. After reading Jim Glenn's book, it seemed to Lerner that Rush had been a very impractical man who had put his career as a preacher above everything else.

The way Lerner looked at it, this was absurd. He had no sympathy for a man who did not have the practical sense to know that his wife should not have to live in a tent all winter. The way Glenn told it, that was the kind of man Rush had been. Still, he must also have been good-natured and kind, with the best of intentions. With Ed Burke, he had saved Glenn's life the night he had been attacked by Bully Bailey and his friends.

He seemed, then, a complex man who registered high on the scale of human values in some areas and very low in others. In trying to probe his own feelings about Frank Rush from what Glenn had written about him, it seemed to Lerner that he was basically a good man, certainly with more good traits than bad.

Perhaps he didn't have any really bad traits. He just had blind spots. The question, of course, was what had prison done to the blind spots. It occurred to Lerner that Rush must still have his good traits or he would not be going out to the prison to work with some of the prisoners.

When Lerner met him and shook hands with him, he was surprised first by Frank Rush's appearance. He could not have been over fifty-five, yet he appeared to be twenty years older. He was a large man, as Glenn had said, and he looked as if he had retained his strength, but he was stooped, his hair was completely white, and he talked very slowly, as if uncertain what the next word would be.

"I got your address from the prison," Lerner said. "I'd like to talk to you for a few minutes if you have the time to spare."

"Come in," Rush said. "I have plenty of time. I have eternity."

The house was a small one with a single bedroom, a kitchen, and a living room. No more. The outside needed paint, the yard had grown up in weeds, and dust on the furniture was so thick a person could print his initials on it. Rush was clean and his clothes were clean, but he had not shaved for several days, his white stubble adding to his appearance of age.

A moment later, after Lerner was seated in the only rocking chair in the living room, Rush said, "You may not know it, but at one time I was a minister. I started a church in Cheyenne. I had even put up a building and had an excellent congregation when a friend and my wife betrayed me. Perhaps you know that was the reason I went to prison."

"Yes, that's why I'm here to talk to you," Lerner said.

He sensed bitterness in the man and he knew then that in this case his theory had failed him. Frank Rush was a changed man from what he had been twenty years ago in Cheyenne. He'd had the traumatic experience that Lerner realized would or at least could change a person. Yet perhaps the theory hadn't failed after all—this was simply the exception that proved the rule.

Rush leaned forward, his big hands spread on his knees. "Just what do you want of me?"

Lerner remembered what the prison official had said and he sensed he could not tell Rush the full truth if he expected to get the man to talk. He said slowly, phrasing each sentence carefully, "I'm a reporter, as I told you when I introduced myself. The editor of the *Rocky Mountain News* is interested in historical incidents. You and your wife and Jim Glenn and Ed Burke and of course many others were among the first settlers in Cheyenne."

Rush nodded. "That's true. So you know about those people?"

"I've made myself familiar with the early history of Cheyenne," Lerner said. "What I want from you is an account of what happened the night you shot Jim Glenn. It may be a painful memory, but—"

"It is a painful memory," Rush interrupted, "but I'll be glad to tell you about it. I don't know what you can do with it. I hope you'll write it for the world to read and know what happened. I've always wanted an opportunity to talk to someone who would make the truth public. I realize now that I look at some things in a different light than I did at that time. You see, I had worked very hard to build up my congregation. As I saw my place in life, it was to help other people. I know now that the way I lived day by day was more important than anything I ever said from the pulpit on Sunday morning."

Lerner nodded agreement. "I'm sure that's right."

"My wife had never been happy as a preacher's wife," Rush went on. "I should have known that she would not go on even pretending to be my wife, but I loved her and trusted her. I trusted Jim Glenn, too, although I did not see much of him after I quit working for him. You knew I had worked for him as a carpenter?"

"Yes, I know about that," Lerner said.

Rush stared at Lerner as if wondering how the reporter happened to know so much about him. Then he shrugged his muscular shoulders and hurried on. "At this particular time an old lady called Grandma Carruthers was dying. Both my wife and I sat up with her because she had lingered so long her relatives were worn out. The night she died I came home earlier than I had expected to. It was certainly earlier than my wife expected. She was gone when I got home and she did not come in until very late. She said she couldn't sleep, so she had taken a walk.

"Now this was reasonable, because she often had trouble sleeping and she did walk a great deal, but never so late at night. I knew something was going on from her expression. She had often seemed discontented and un-happy, even nervous—but not that night. She was the happiest I'd seen her for months. She was humming a tune when she came into the house—I don't remember what it was. She smiled at me and called a greeting as she went on back to her bedroom. It was such a reversal from the way she had been for so long that I couldn't understand her. I didn't even tell her that Grandma Carruthers had died. Not until the next morning.

"At first I didn't suspect what had happened, but my suspicion grew through the following week because she seemed anxious and impatient and asked me more than once what I was going to do Saturday night. For the first time in our married life I decided to spy on her. I told her I had several calls to make and I'd be gone for two or three hours. I hid outside and followed her when she left the house a few minutes later.

"She took the alley and went into Jim Glenn's house through the back door. I waited until I saw around the edge of the blind that there was a light in his bedroom. I slipped up to the window and found a narrow opening beside the blind, enough to see what they were doing. I could not believe what I saw. At first I was sick, because I loved Nancy and I respected Jim Glenn, but a moment later I realized I had been betrayed, and I became a madman.

"I went back home and found the pistol I had bought for my wife a few months before, when Cheyenne was a very tough town and I was worried about her safety. I returned to Glenn's house and slipped in through the back door. I crossed the kitchen and stood in the doorway and looked at them.

"They had finished what they were doing and were talking. Both of them were naked. When they saw me, my wife started to dress and Glenn came at me telling me to give him my gun. I backed into the kitchen. I found it hard to shoot a man I considered my friend, but he kept coming and then the truth swept over me.

"He had seduced my wife; he had destroyed my home. He was a thoroughly evil man who had given himself to the devil. I shot him twice, the second time as he was falling. I thought I had killed him. I stood staring at him, not believing this was real. It was a terrifying nightmare. Even now, after all these years, when I remember what happened there is a kind of nightmarish fog over it.

"My wife had got out of the house through a window and she came back later with a doctor and a policeman. I hadn't tried to escape. I was arrested. Glenn lived, as you probably know, and I was sent to prison. I was just an ordinary person, a preacher with a small congregation composed mostly of women—but Jim Glenn, you see, was a very important man.

"Glenn had money and property. He had been one of the leaders of the Vigilance Committee, which was common knowledge by that time, and he was doing a contract business with the army at Fort D. A. Russell. I didn't have a chance. I was found guilty and sentenced before the trial ever started. Maybe Glenn paid the jury to find me guilty. He had enough money that he could have done it. I have no proof that he did, but I still cannot understand how a jury could have found me guilty unless something like that was done."

Rush was silent for a moment, his brooding gaze fixed on the floor. He had taken a long time to tell his story, speaking as slowly as he did. Lerner said nothing, but sat watching the expression on Frank Rush's face, the way his hands gripped his knees, the tension that held him, the intensity of his feelings as he dredged his mind for the events that had happened on what had been a terrible night for him.

Again the thought came to Lerner that an act of this kind depends for interpretation upon the point from which anyone looks at it. To Rush there was no justice in the sentence that had been given him; to Glenn the bullet that had put him in a wheelchair was not deserved. Nancy would see it the way Jim Glenn had. She had intended to marry Glenn after she divorced Rush. They would have been happy, Lerner thought, a happiness that an inadequate husband had stolen from them by making Glenn an invalid for life.

Now, thinking about what Rush had said, it occurred to Lerner that no mention had been made of the fact that Glenn had saved Rush's life in the Head Quarters Saloon, that it had been Glenn, not Rush, who had been concerned about Nancy's safety, no mention of the rent he had owed Glenn, of his inadequacy as a husband, although it was possible he didn't even know he had not been a satisfactory husband. Perhaps the jury had not made a just decision, but Lerner questioned whether it was possible for any man or group of men to make a just decision in a case like this.

"That's all I can remember," Rush said finally. "It's in the past now. Whatever mistakes I made cannot be undone. I have not seen either my wife or Glenn since the trial. I don't want to. I tried to make something of my life when I was in prison, and since I was released I have gone back to work with men they thought I could help."

He wiped a hand across his face and began to tremble. "I don't know, Mr. Lerner," he said in a shaky voice. "This is something I cannot make a judgment about. The Lord will have to do that and I know He will. All of my life I have tried to do what the Lord wanted me to do, but sometimes it's been hard to know what He wants. I cannot believe I did wrong when I shot Jim Glenn. It is true that the Lord says vengeance is His, but the only hands the Lord has are our hands. I believe I was serving as the hand of the Lord when I pulled the trigger."

Lerner rose and shook hands with him. "Thank you for talking to me," he said. "You don't object to anything you've said being published?"

"No," Rush said in a tired voice. "I hope it will be published. It's the reason I talked to you. It seems to me that the Lord's part in solving the troubles of the world is never published for people to read, but the devil's side always gets into the newspaper."

When Lerner left the house Rush was still in his chair, a defeated and worn out man, still trying after more than twenty years to justify what he had done as the Lord's work.

On the train returning to Cheyenne, Lerner ran Rush's story back through his mind. He could not escape one fact, which seemed certain to him: if Frank Rush had really worked at being Nancy's husband, she would never have started the affair with Jim Glenn.

When Lerner reached his hotel, he went into the dining room for supper. He sat down at the table with a folded copy of the *Daily Sun,* left by some previous diner, in front of him. He opened the newspaper and saw the headline: JIM "MR. CHEYENNE" GLENN IS DEAD.

CHAPTER XXXVI

Lerner stayed in Cheyenne for the funeral, partly because he wanted to pay his respects to a man he had come to admire, and partly because he wanted to see what Cheyenne would do for one of her most beloved citizens. Also, he wanted to see and talk to Nancy Rush again after interviewing Frank.

He read everything the newspapers said about Jim Glenn. Nothing was derogatory, much was complimentary, some of it too sugar-sweet. Lerner did not catch any glaring errors of fact. A great deal was made of his gifts, along with statements to the effect that many of his gifts were not publicized and therefore not known.

Lerner was amused by the fact that, after having read Glenn's autobiography, he could have told the Cheyenne reporters several exciting events in Glenn's life that they didn't know. His efforts to obtain a trial for Ed Burke, for instance, and his shooting Jess Munro. Nothing was said about Nancy Rush, and Lerner was pleased by that. He had been afraid the old scandal would be dragged out again and attention focused on Nancy, as it had been when the shooting occurred.

He hired a rig and picked Nancy up shortly before one. The funeral was still more than an hour away, but she was ready, so they left her house at once. It was fortunate that they arrived at the Methodist Church early, because even then they had trouble finding seats. Long before the first prayer was prayed, people were standing along the sides and in the back of the sanctuary. Afterwards Lerner heard that hundreds were massed in the street outside the church.

378

Lerner saw nothing unusual about the funeral. He suspected that Glenn would not have approved of it. The smell of hellfire and brimstone was in the air, and Lerner was reminded of what Glenn had written about his mother's funeral, which he had remembered so well even though he had been only six at the time.

The one thing that made Lerner marvel was the great mass of flowers. Surely there could not have been that many in Cheyenne, he thought. Some must have been sent by train to Cheyenne from Denver.

One other thing surprised him: Nancy did not shed a tear. She sat beside him, her face grave, her hands folded on her lap. He could not keep from thinking what a handsome woman she was, even at a time like this. He wished he could have seen her when she was young and Jim Glenn had first fallen in love with her. Lerner could understand why Glenn had done what he had, but he could not understand how Frank Rush could have neglected her and been so unaware of her needs.

Lerner and Nancy drove to the cemetery with the funeral procession, a very long one. Afterwards the newspapers commented on its being the longest in Cheyenne's history. The graveside service was short, and as people began moving away, Nancy's elbow prodded Lerner in the ribs. He glanced at her and she gave him a bare half-inch nod to two women who had been crying visibly and loudly. They were middle-aged, plump, and looked exactly alike in their black dresses and floppy-brimmed black hats.

Nancy put her mouth to Lerner's ear. "The Martin women," she whispered. "Rosy and Flossie. They moved to Denver and got married and became respectable."

Lerner had to struggle to hold back a smile. That would be exactly like them, he thought. The chances were they had married well and were making two men very happy.

Lerner still had two hours before train time, and when Nancy asked him to come into the house for a cup of coffee, he accepted. She did not go into the parlor, but again led him back to her sewing room.

One of the things he wanted to settle was the disposal of the earnings that Glenn's book would return in royalties. "We'll get it published somewhere," he told her. "As to how much it will make, your guess is as good as mine. There are sections I will use for the *Rocky Mountain News*. I suggest that I keep what the *News* pays me for my time, and whatever comes in from book publication will go to you."

She was startled. "Why should I have any part of it, Mr. Lerner?"

"This is something I had no chance to ask Jim Glenn," Lerner said. "It may not even have occurred to him that the book might make money, and that if it did some would come to him. A number of things impressed me when I read it, and one of them was the fact that he loved you very much. Whether what you and he did was right or wrong has nothing to do with the fact that he loved you. There i no question about that, so I'm equally sure he would want the royalty money to go to you."

She cried for the first time that day. When she could speak, she said, "You are a very kind man, Mr. Lerner. If you want to give me this money, I will take it and be thankful for it."

Lerner gave her his card. "You'll get it," he said. "If anything comes up or you want to contact me for some reason, write to me at that address. When you come to Denver, look me up. I would be proud to take a woman as beautiful as you to supper."

"I won't forget it," she said.

"I don't want to go into my talk with Frank Rush in detail except to say that he justified himself by claiming his hand was the hand of God when he pulled the trigger that night."

She stared at Lerner blankly for a moment until the full impact of what he had just said got through to her. Then she cried, "Why, he never used to talk that way. He's gone mad."

"I had that feeling," Lerner said. "He's brooded about it for so long and felt for so long that he didn't deserve the prison sentence he received that he isn't completely sane. But the point I wanted to ask you about is this. He claimed Jim Glenn was an important man in town with money and property, whereas he was a man of no importance, with only a small congregation composed mostly of women. He believes that Glenn bribed the jury to find him guilty."

Nancy bowed her head, struggling with her temper for a time. Then she said, "There is not a word of truth in it. Frank has really lost his mind to even think that. I told you that Jim was carried into the courtroom on a stretcher to plead for Frank, asking that he not be found guilty—but the jury didn't listen."

"I was sure there was no truth to it," Lerner said, "but I wanted you to know what he was thinking."

She looked directly at him. "Just what are you going to say in the epilogue that you will write, Mr. Lerner?"

"I will say as little as I can, just enough so the reader will know that Glenn lived after the shooting and that Rush went to prison," Lerner said. "Perhaps also a few paragraphs about his gifts and what the people of Cheyenne thought of him."

"Don't you forget that that is what you will write." She rose and, walking to a window, stared at the lawn and row of hollyhocks that ran along the edge of her yard. "Jim read the Bible a good deal, particularly during the last two years, when he sensed he didn't have long to live. There is a passage in James that bothered him. It bothers me, too. It goes something like this: 'What is your life? It is a vapour that appeareth for a little time, and then vanisheth away.' Jim used to say it was such a waste if a man's life vanished away. I don't believe it does, Mr. Lerner. Not a life like Jim's. I like to remember what his father said, that there is no death. We keep right on living."

"I believe it," Lerner agreed. "Well, I've got to go or I'll miss my train."

She turned to him and kissed him on the cheek. "Thank you," she said. "Thank you very much."

"What will you do now?"

"I don't know," she said. "I spent a great deal of time with Jim the last two years while he waited to die. Now there doesn't seem to be anything to do that's worth doing."

"You'll find something," he said.

Later, after he had stowed his bag in the rack above the seat, he sat down and leaned his head against the red plush seat in the coach. He heard the train whistle and the bell clang, then felt the jolt of the car as the train began to move.

His mind went back to his talk with Alex Dolan and Dolan asking what Jim Glenn had meant by saying the sun is on the wall. He knew now, of course, and he would tell Dolan, but it would not really mean anything to the editor until he read Glenn's book.

What an extraordinary assignment it had been, Lerner thought, and then the quotation from James came into his mind. He smiled as he remembered what Nancy Rush had said about it. She was right, he told himself. Some lives might be like vapour and vanish away, but Jim Glenn's life would not be one of them.

Social welfare: 252005, Kyiv, Bankivska St., 6.

Shevchenko State Prizes: 252008, Kyiv, Sadova St., 3; tel. 293-07-62.

National Olympic Committee of Ukraine: 252023, Kyiv, Esplanadna St., 4; tel. 220-02-00; 220-13-09; fax: 220-95-33; telex: 13-18-66 Tennis.

Writers Union of Ukraine: 252024, Kyiv-24, Bankova St., 2 tel. 293-45-86; 293-95-52

STATE COMPANIES

Radio and Television Company of Ukraine: 252001, Kyiv, Khreshchatyk St., 26; tel. 228-33-33; 226-31-44.

Foreign Tourism Joint-Stock Company: 252034, Kyiv, Yaroslaviv Val, 36; tel. 212-55-70; fax: 212-46-24.

SELECTED STATE INSTITUTIONS

"Book Palace": 253094, Kyiv, prospekt Gagarina, 27; tel.: 552-01-34.

General Procurator: 252601, Kyiv-11, MSP, Riznytska St., 13/15; tel. 226-20-27; 290-10-20.

Religious Affairs Council: 252021, Kyiv, Hrushevsky St., 14; tel. 293-23-94.

Supreme Court: 252601, Kyiv — 24, MSP, Orlyk St., 4; tel. 226-23-04; 293-33-13.

Republican Center for Exhibitions and Markets: 252085, Kyiv, prospekt Hlushkova, 1; tel. 261-74-24; fax: 261-76-77.

Political Parties of Ukraine

DEMOCRATIC PARTY OF UKRAINE (DPU)
Tel. 216-85-91; 293-75-56

GREEN PARTY OF UKRAINE (PZU)
Kyiv-70, Kontraktova Ploshcha, 4, Hostynny Dvir; tel. 417-02-83.

LIBERAL PARTY OF UKRAINE (LPU)
340037, Donetsk, Kirov St., 147-a.

PARTY OF THE DEMOCRATIC REBIRTH OF UKRAINE (PDVY)
Kyiv, Instytutska St., 27/6, suite 31.

PEASANT PARTY OF UKRAINE (SelPU)

PEOPLE'S PARTY OF UKRAINE (NPU)
Dnipropetrovsk, Naberezhna Lenina St., 1; tel. (0562) 58-80-32.

"RUKH" POPULAR MOVEMENT OF UKRAINE (NRU)
Kyiv, Shevchenko Blvd., 37/122; tel. 224-91-51; 216-83-33; 274-20-77.

Government

Supreme Rada: 252019, Kyiv, Hrushevsky St., 5.

Council of Ministers: 252008, Kyiv, Hrushevsky St., 12/2; tel. 293-52-27.

SELECTED MINISTRIES

Communications: 252001, Kyiv, Khreshchatyk St., 22; tel. 229-12-71.

Culture: 252030, Kyiv, Franko St., 19; tel. 224-49-11; 226-26-45; fax: 225-32

Defense: 252005, Kyiv, Bankivska St., 6; tel. 291-54-41.

Economy: 252008, Kyiv, Hrushevsky St., 12/2; tel. 293-61-41.

Education: 252001, Kyiv, Khreshchatyk St., 34; tel. 226-32-31; fax: 226-33-2

Environment: 252001, Kyiv, Khreshchatyk St., 5;
tel. 226-24-28; 228-40-04; fax: 228-06-44.

External Economic Relations: 252053, Kyiv, Lvivska Ploshcha, 8;
tel. 226-27-33; 212-54-23; 212-53-59.

Foreign Affairs (MZS): 252018, Kyiv, Mykhaylivska Ploshcha, 1;
tel. 212-86-60; fax: 226-31-69.

Health: 252021, Kyiv, Hrushevsky St., 7;
tel. 226-22-05; 293-61-94; fax: 293-69-75.

Investments and Construction: 252008, Kyiv, Sadova St., 3;
tel. 293-26-89; 292-04-70.

**Protection of the population from the after-effects
of the accident at the Chornobyl Nuclear Power Station:**
252196, Kyiv, ploshcha L. Ukrayinky, 1; tel. 226-30-67; 296-83-95; 296-86-77

Youth and Sports: 252023, Kyiv, Esplanadna St., 42; tel. 220-02-00; 220-14-6

AGENCIES

Ukrainian National Information Agency (Ukrinform): 252001, Kyiv,
Khmelnytsky St., 8/16; tel. 226-32-30; 229-81-52; fax: 229-24-39.

COMMITTEES

Tourism State Committee: Yaroslaviv Val, 36; tel. 224-81-49, 212-55-70.

State Customs: 252055, Kyiv, Politekhnichny Provulok, 4-a;
tel. 446-92-41, 274-81-94.

SOCIAL-DEMOCRATIC PARTY OF UKRAINE (SDPU)
Kyiv, Tolstoy St., 16/24; tel. 229-08-16.

SOCIALIST PARTY OF UKRAINE (SPU)
Kyiv — 9, Bankova St., 6, suite, 638.

UKRAINIAN CHRISTIAN-DEMOCRATIC PARTY (UKhDP)
Lviv, Papanivtsi St., 10-a; tel. 33-13-25.

UKRAINIAN PEASANT-DEMOCRATIC PARTY (USDP)
Kyiv — 024, Bankivska St., 2; tel. 224-17-92.

UKRAINIAN REPUBLICAN PARTY (URP)
Kyiv — 034, Prorizna St., 27, tel. 228-03-06; fax: 228-04-09

UNITED SOCIAL-DEMOCRATIC PARTY OF UKRAINE (OSDPU)
Kyiv, Tolstoy St., 16/24; tel. 225-11-46.

Diplomatic Representatives of Ukraine

Permanent Mission of Ukraine to the United Nations.
136 East 67th St., New York, N.Y. 10021, USA.
Code: (1-212); tel. 535-3418; Telex: 22-32-22-25-40; Fax: 288-5361.

**Permanent Mission of Ukraine to the United Nations
and other International Organizations in Geneva.**
Ambassador: Oleksander Slipchenko.
15, Avenue de la Paix 1211, Geneva, Switzerland.
Code: (41-22); tel. 734-38-01, 740-32-70; Fax: 734-40-44.

Permanent Mission of Ukraine to the UNESCO. Permanent Representative:
Yuriy Kochubey.
1, rue Miollis, 75015 Paris 7-e, France.
Code: (33-1); tel. 40-72-86-04; Fax: 45-04-17-65, 40-72-82-54.

Permanent Mission of Ukraine to the International Organizations in Vienna.
Permanent Representative: Yuriy Kostenko.
Erzherzog Karl Strasse 182, 1220 Vienna, Austria.
Code: (43-222); tel. 22-93-52, 22-33-52; Telex: 471-36129; Fax: 586-34-24.

Consular division
Elizabetstrasse 13, 1010 Vienna, Austria.
Tel. 586-97-17.

EMBASSIES OF UKRAINE

ARGENTINA. Ambassador: Oleksandr Nikonenko.
Calle Latinur 3057, 1425 Buenos Aires, Argentina.
Code: (54-1); tel. 802-7316; Fax: 802-38-64.

AUSTRIA. Ambassador: Yuriy Kostenko.
Erzherzog Karl Strasse 382, 1200 Wien, Austria.
Code: (43-222); tel. 22-93-52; Fax: 585-34-24.

BELARUS. Ambassador: Volodymyr Zheliba.
Minsk, vul. Kirova, 17, Belarus.
Code: (0172); tel. 27-70-04, 27-23-54; Fax: 27-28-61.

BELGIUM (Netherlands and Luxembourg). Ambassador: Volodymyr Vasylenko.
Blvd. Paul Emile Yanson 33, 1040 Bruxelles, Belgium.
Code: (32-2); tel. 534-93-91, 534-92-65, 534-91-63; Fax: 534-86-95.

BULGARIA. Ambassador: Oleksandr Vorobyov.
Symenovsko Shosse, 53, Sofia, Bulgaria.
Code: (359-2); tel. 441-671.

CANADA. Ambassador: Victor Batiuk.
331 Metcalfe St., Ottawa, Ont. K2P 1S3, Canada.
Code: (613); tel. 230-2961, 230-2410; Fax: 230-2400.

CHINA. Ambassador: Anatoly Plyushko.
San Li Tun, Dongliujie, 11, 100600 Beijing, China.
Code: (86-1); tel.532-63-59, 532-40-14.

CUBA. Representative: Oleksandr Hnyedykh.
Calle 46, No. 503, Miramar, La Habana, Cuba.
Code: (53); tel. 33-23-74; Fax: 33-23-41.

CZECH REPUBLIC. Ambassador: Roman Lubkivsky.
Praha-1, ul. Priskope, 6, Czech Republic.
Code: (42-2); tel. 32-22-66; Fax: 322-966; Telex: 661-222-54.

EGYPT. Ambassador: Viktor Nahaychuk.
El-Saraia Str., 9, Cairo, Egypt.
Code: (20-2); tel. & Fax: 349-1030, 700-942.
Consular Department: 718-932.

ESTONIA. Ambassador: Yuriy Olenenko.
Code: (014-2); tel. 51-64-95.

FINLAND (Denmark, Norway and Sweden). Ambassador: Kostyantyn Masyk.
Punavuorenkqtu, 21-F, 00150, Helsinki, Finland.
Code: (358-0); tel. 608-563, 607-050; Fax: 607-968; Telex: 571-255-77.

FRANCE. Ambassador: Yuriy Kochubey.
21, avenue de Saxe, Paris 75007, France.
Code: (33-1); tel. 43-06-07-37; Fax: 43-06-02-94.

GERMANY. Ambassador: Ivan Piskovy.
Waldstrasse, 42, 5300 Bonn 2, Germany.
Code: (49-228); tel. 31-19-95, 31-21-32;
Telex: 41-88-56-15; Fax: 31-83-51.
Berlin. Embasy Representative: Vadym Petrenko.
Unter den Linden 63-65, 10117 Berlin, Germany.
Code: (49-30); tel. 229-16-18; Fax: 229-17-45.

GREAT BRITAIN. Ambassador: Serhiy Komisarenko.
78 Kensington Park Rd., London W11 2PL, Great Britain.
Code: (0-71); tel. 727-63-12; Fax: 792-17-08.

GREECE. Ambassador: Borys Korniyenko.
17-A Paritsi Str., 15451 N. Psychiko, Athenes, Greece.
Code: (30-1); tel. 687-58-85; Fax: 67-16-652.

HUNGARY. Ambassador: Dmytro Tkach.
H 1062, Budapest, Ut. Nogradi, 8, Hungary.
Code: (36-1); tel. 155-96-09, 156-86-97, 155-24-16; Fax: 202-22-87.

INDIA. Ambassador: Heorhiy Khodorovsky.
176, Jorbagh, New Delhi 110 003, India.
Code: (91-11); tel. 461-60-86, 461-60-19; Fax: 461-60-85.

IRAN. Ambassador: Ivan Maydan.
Vanaka (Bahak) Str., 101, Tehran, Iran.
Code: (98-21); tel. 675-148; Fax: 800-71-30; Telex: 112-374.

ITALY. Ambassador: Anatoliy Orel.
Via Castelfidardo, 50, Roma 00185, Italy.
Code: (39-6); tel. 447-001-72, 447-001-74;
Fax: 447-001-81.

ISRAEL. Ambassador: Yuriy Shcherbak.
12 Stricker St., 62006 Tel-Aviv, Israel.
Code: (972-3); tel. 604-0141, 604-0313, 604-0311; Fax: 604-25-12.

LATVIA. Ambassador: Volodymyr Chorny.
LV 1050 Riga, Kalpaka b. 3, Latvija.
Code: (013-2); tel. 325-583, 332-046.

LITHUANIA. Representative: Rostyslav Bilodid.
2016 Vilnius, Turniskics, 22, Lithuania.
Code: (012-2); tel. 76-36-26.

MOLDOVA. Ambassador: Vitaly Boyko.
277012 Kishinev, 31 August St., 127, Hotel "Kodru", Room 727, Moldova.
Code: (04-22); tel. & Fax: 23-79-15.

POLAND. Ambassador: Hennadiy Udovenko.
00580 Warsaw, Aleja Szucha, 7, Poland.
Code: (48-22); tel. 29-32-01; Fax: 29-64-49.

ROMANIA. Ambassador: Leontiy Sandulyak.
Bucuresti, Sector 1, Str. Rabat-1, Romania.
Code: (40-0); tel. 312-45-47; Fax: 312-45-14.
Consular Department: tel. 312-67-02.

RUSSIA. Ambassador: Volodymyr Kryzhanivsky.
103009 Moscow K-9, Stanislavsky St., 18, Russia.
Code:(7-095); tel. 229-76-77, 229-55-81, 229-69-22; Fax: 229-35-42.
Consular Department: tel. 229-07-84; Fax: 229-16-03.

SWITZERLAND. Ambassador: Oleksandr Slipchenko.
Feldeggweg, 5, 3005 Bern, Switzerland.
Code: (41-31); tel. 44-23-16; Fax: 21-27-07.

TURKEY. Ambassador: Ihor Turyansky.
Cinnah Caddesi, Alabas Sok. 3/2, Cankaya/Ankara 06690, Turkey.
Code: (90-4); tel. 439-99-73; Fax: 440-68-15.

UNITED STATES OF AMERICA. Ambassador: Oleh Bilorus.
3350 M Street, NW, Washington, D.C. 20007, USA.
Code: (1-202); tel. 333-0606; Fax: 333-0817.

YUGOSLAVIA. Ambassador: Vadym Prymachenko.
Ulica Beligradska br. 32, 11000 Beograd, Yugoslavia.
Code: (38-11); tel. 65-75-33, 65-82-51; Fax: 75-29-21.

CONSULATES OF UKRAINE

AUSTRALIA. Melbourne. Honorary Consul: Zina Botte.
4 Bloom St., Moonee Ponds, 3039, Melbourne, Australia.
Code: (61-3); tel. 326-0135; Fax: 326-0139.

GERMANY. Munich. Consul: Anatoliy Ponomarenko.
Pienzenauerstrasee, 15, 8000 Munich 80, Germany.
Code: (49-89); tel. 982-87-71; Fax: 982-71-41.

UNITED STATES OF AMERICA. Chicago. Consul: Anatoliy Oliynyk.
2247 W. Chicago Ave., Chicago, IL. 60622, USA.
Code: (1-312); tel. 384-66-32; Fax: 371-5547, 384-6750.
New York. Consul: Viktor Kryzhanivsky.
240 East 49th St., New York, NY 10017, USA.
Code: (1-212); tel. 371-5690, 371-5000; Fax: 371-5547.

Foreign Embassies and Consulates in Kyiv, Ukraine

ALGERIA. Nemanska St., 4, suite 20; tel. 295-71-26; Fax: 295-32-97.

ARMENIA. Hotel "Moskwa"; tel. 229-08-06, 229-08-07.

AUSTRALIA. Malopidvalna St., 8; tel. 229-54-26.

ARGENTINA. Staronavodnytska St., 8, kv. 11; tel. 295-11-19, 295-68-72;
Fax: 294-98-20.

AUSTRIA. Lypska St., 5, kv. 408; tel. 291-88-48, 291-88-40; Fax: 291-89-60.

BELGIUM. Shovkovychna St., 26; tel. 293-21-10; Fax: 226-36-47.

BIELARUS. Kutuzov St., 8; tel. 294-82-12, 294-80-06.

BULGARIA. Hospitalna St., 1; tel. 224-53-60, 225-51-19,
225-22-02; Fax: 224-99-29.

CANADA. Yaroslaviv Val St., 31; tel. 212-22-35.

CHINA. Hrushevsky St., 32; tel. 216-02-15; Fax: 227-84-02.

CROATIA. Volodymyrska St., 45; tel. 224-41-18; Fax: 229-32-02.

CUBA. Bekhterivsky Provulok, 5; tel. 216-29-30, 211-02-37, 216-26-08.

CZECHIA. Yaroslaviv Val, 34; tel. 212-00-20, 212-19-12.

DENMARK. Volodymyrska St., 45; tel.: 229-33-40, 228-10-56, 228-11-40; Fax: 229-18-31.

EGYPT. Staronavodnytska St., 4-b, kv. 49; tel. 294-98-90.

ESTONIA. Kutuzov St., 8; tel. 296-28-86; Fax: 295-81-76.

FINLAND. Striletska St., 14; tel. 228-43-39, 228-70-49; Fax: 228-20-32.

FRANCE. Reytarska St., 39; tel. 228-87-28, 228-73-69; Fax: 229-08-70.

GERMANY. Chkalov St., 84; tel. 216-74-98, 216-78-54; Fax: 216-78-54.

GREAT BRITAIN. Desyatynna St., 9; tel. 228-05-04, 229-12-87; Fax: 228-39-72.

GREECE. Lypsky St., 4; tel. 291-88-77.

HUNGARY. Reytarska St., 33; tel. 212-40-04 /39/, 225-02-98, 212-41-34, 212-41-04.

INDIA. Hospitalna St., 4; tel. 227-83-25, 227-83-26, 227-88-56.

IRAN. Kruhlouniversytetska St., 12; tel. 229-44-63; Fax: 229-32-55.

ISRAEL. L. Ukrayinka Blvd., 34; tel. 295-62-16, 295-69-25; Fax: 294-97-48.

ITALY. Lypska St., 5; tel. 291-88-99, 291-89-52; Fax: 291-88-97.

JAPAN. Lypsky St., 5; tel. 293-45-37, 291-89-04; Fax: 293-26-16.

KIRGIZIA. Kutuzov St., 8; tel.: 295-53-80, 295-96-92.

KOREA (North). Saperne Pole, 28, kv. 24; tel. 268-49-49.

KOREA (South). Volodymyrska, 43; tel. 224-83-31, 224-23-19; Fax: 224-51-32.

LATVIA. Chkalov St., 41; tel. 224-95-27, 244-29-75.

LIBYA. Staronavodnytska St., 4, kv. 74; tel. 296-85-66.

LITHUANIA. Gorky St., 22; tel. 227-43-72.

MOLDOVA. Lypsky St., 5; tel. 291-87-44, 291-87-60.

MONGOLIA. M. Kotsyubynsky St., 3; tel. 216-88-91, 216-87-51.

NETHERLANDS. Turgenyev St. 24; tel. 216-19-05, 216-98-16; Fax: 216-81-05.

NORWAY. Striletska St.,15; tel. 224-00-66.

POLAND. Yaroslaviv Val, 12; tel. 224-63-08, 291-80-40.

PORTUGAL. Hotel "Dnipro"; tel. 229-77-17.

ROMANIA. M. Kotsyubynsky St., 8; tel. 224-52-61, 224-43-16.

RUSSIA. Kutuzov St., 8; tel. 294-63-89, 294-66-31.

SLOVAKIA. Yaroslaviv Val, 34; tel. 229-79-22, 212-03-10.

SOUTH AFRRICA. Khreshchatyk 1/2; tel. 229-66-29, 229-40-61, 229-57-27.

SPAIN. Dehtyarivska St., 38-44; tel. 213-04-81; Fax: 213-00-31.

SWEDEN. Lypsky St. 5; tel. 291-89-19, 291-89-69; Fax: 291-62-33.

SWITZERLAND. Hospitalna St., 4; tel. 220-44-61, 227-86-62; Fax: 227-86-88.

TUNISIA. Hotel "Rus'", kv. 419; tel. 227-81-16, 227-81-19.

TURKEY. Lypsly St., 5; tel. 291-88-45, 291-88-84, 291-88-72.

UNITED STATES OF AMERICA. Yu. Kotsyubynsky St., 10; tel. 244-73-49, 244-73-44, 244-73-54; Fax: 244-73-50.

VATICAN. Chervonoarmiyska St., 96; tel. 269-91-03; Fax: 268-24-17.

VIETNAM. Avtozavodska St., 78; tel. 430-67-84.

UNITED NATIONS REPRESENTATIVE IN UKRAINE:
Sichneve Povstannya St., 6; 293-93-26; Fax: 293-26-07.

UNESCO-CHORNOBYL PROGRAM COORDINATOR:
Instytutska St., 1, kv. 78; tel. 228-46-72.

WORLD BANK. Shovkovychna St., 26, kv. 2-3; tel. 226-35-21; Fax: 226-35-25.

EUROPEAN BANK. Shovkovychna St., 15/1; tel. 291-88-47, 291-88-48, 291-62-46.

INTERNATIONAL MONETARY FUND. M. Hrushevsky St., 12/2, kv. 812; tel. 293-40-68; Fax: 293-84-45.

Travel Agencies

USA:

AIR UKRAINE
1620 I St., N.W., Suite 810
Washington, D.C. 20006
Tel. (202) 833-4648; Fax: (202) 833-4676
*Non-stop service from Washington, D.C.
to Kyiv.*

AIR UKRAINE
551 5th Ave., Suite 1010
New York, N.Y. 10176
Tel. 1 (800)-UKRAINE (857-2463);
(212) 557-4044
Non-stop service from New York to Kyiv.

BALKAN AIRLINE
41 E. 42nd St., #508, New York, NY 10017
Tel. (212) 573-5530; Fax: (212) 573-5538

BRAVO INTERNATIONAL
1320 Hamilton St., Allentown, PA 18102
Tel. (800) 822-7286; Fax: (215) 437-6982

DIASPORA
220 S. 20th St., Philadelphia, PA 19103
Tel. (215) 567-1328; (800) 487-5324
Fax: (215) 567-1792

West Orange, NJ, Tel. (201) 731-1132

*Travel & Discover the Historic, Cultural
and Architectural treasures of UKRAINE.
We offer individual, group, professional,
and custom designed tours. Fly Air Ukraine.*

DUNWOODIE TRAVEL
771-A Yonkers Ave., Yonkers, NY 10704
Tel. (914) 969-4200

EUROPE-OKSANA
1045 N. Western Ave., Chicago, IL 60622
Tel. (312) 489-9225; Fax: (312) 489-4203

FREGATA TRAVEL
250 W. 57th St., Suite 1211,
New York, NY 10107
Tel. (212) 541-5707; Fax: (212) 262-3220

HAMALIA
43 St. Mark's Place, Suite 6-E,
New York, NY 10003
Tel. (212) 473-0839; Fax: (212) 473-2180

HANUSEY MUSIC & GIFTS
244 W. Girard Ave., Philadelphia, PA 19123
Tel. (215) 627-3093

KOBASNIUK TRAVEL
157 2nd Ave., New York, NY 10003-5765
Tel. (212) 254-8779; Fax: (212) 254-4005

LANDMARK, Ltd.
6102 Berleen Drive,
Alexandria, VA, 22312-1220
Toll-Free: (800) 832-1789; Tel. (703)
941-6180; Fax: (703) 941-7587
*Landmark, Ltd. provides personalized travel
services for independent travelers and
businessmen, delivers flowers for special
occasions, provides rapid transmission of
messages, assists with visas and legalization
of documents, and provides other support
and personal services.*

MIR Corporation
85 S. Washington St., Ste. 210,
Seattle, WA 98104
Tel. (800) 424-7289; Fax: (206) 624-7360
Wholesale tour operator specializing in
custom-designed group and individual
ancestral village programs to Ukraine,
Russia, Poland. Also offering unique,
special-interest itineraries and complete
travel services throughout Newly
Independent States and Central Europe.
Offices in Moscow, St. Petersburg, Kyiv.

LOT POLISH AIRLINES
Offices in the USA:
500 5th Ave., New York, NY 10110
Tel. (212) 869-1074
333 N. Michigan Ave., Chicago, IL 60601
Tel. (312) 236-3388
6100 Wilshire Blvd.,
Los Angeles, CA 90048
Tel. (213) 934-5151
Toll free: 1 (800) 223-0593

RAHWAY TRAVEL
35 E. Milton Ave., Rahway, NJ 07065
Tel. (800) 526-2786; (908) 381-8800

SCOPE TRAVEL
1605 Springfield Ave., Maplewood,
NJ 07040; Tel. (800) 242-7267
(201) 378-8998; Fax: (201) 378-7903

SHIPKA TRAVEL
5434 State Rd., Parma OH 44134
Tel. (800) 860-0089

TRANS EUROPA
8102 Roosevelt Blvd., Philadelphia,
PA 19152; Tel. (215) 331-9060
Fax: (215) 331-7747

UKRAINIAN CUSTOM ASSN.
JFK International Airport
167-43 Porter Rd., Jamaica, NY 11434
Tel. (718) 244-0036; Fax: (718) 244-5528

NORTHWESTERN TRAVEL
849 North Western Ave., Chicago, IL 60622
Tel. (312) 278-8844.

AUSTRALIA

BALTIC & EAST EUROPEAN TRAVEL
1st Floor, 2 Hindmarsh Sq., Adelaide, 5000
Tel. (61-8) 232-1228; Fax: (61-8) 232-0279

BOHEMIA TRAVEL
188 Commercial Rd., Praham, 3181
Tel. 510-8717

GATEWAY TRAVEL
48 The Boulevarde, Strathfield, N.S.W. 2135
Tel. (61-2) 745-3333; Fax: (61-2) 745-3237
We can book accommodation and
Homestays. We can also arrange invitations
to visit relatives. Discount airfares to/from
Kyiv/Lviv. Individual and group travel. Busi-
ness contacts. Inbound tours available. We
have partbers in Ukraine.

LIDCOMBE TRAVEL
31 Market St., Sydney, NSW
Tel. (2) 261-5051

MAGNA CARTA TRAVEL
309 Glenhuntly Rd., Eisternwick, Vic. 3185
Tel. (3) 523-6981; Fax: (3) 523-0695

SAFEWAY TRAVEL
322 Lt. Lonsdale St., Melbourne, Vic. 3000
Tel. (3) 670-8420; Fax: (3) 670-8812

ST. MARTINS TRAVEL
31 Market St., Sydney, 2000
Tel. (2) 261-5051

CANADA:

ALLEGRO TRAVEL
103-167 Lombard Ave.,
Winnipeg, Man. R3B OV8
Tel. (204) 944-9430

ASTRO TRAVEL SERVICE
2206 Bloor St. W., Toronto, Ont. M6H 1N2
Tel. (416) 766-1117

BLOOR TRAVEL AGENCY
1190 Bloor St. W., Toronto, Ont. M6H 1N2
Tel. (416) 535-2135

BON VOYAGE TRAVEL
10226 — 140 St., Edmonton, Alta. T5N 2L4
Tel. (403) 451-0263; Fax: (403) 451-2016

CARAVEL TOURS: TRAVEL LTD.
Box 277, Stony Plain, Alta. T0E 2GO
Tel. (403) 963-4575

DOMAR TRAVEL
2985 Bloor St. W., Toronto, Ont. M8X 1C1
Tel. (416) 236-7546

EUROPA TRAVEL
1008-103 Ave, Edmonton Alta. T5J OG7
Tel. (403) 424-6481

E-Z WAY TRAVEL
Stan Blazosek, Manager
20, 301 Hwy. 33 W., Plaza 33,
Kelowna, BC V1X 1X8
Tel. (604) 765-2922; Fax: (604) 765-2910
"For Business or Pleasure"

EAST WEST TRAVEL
12952 — 82nd St.,
Edmonton, Alta. T5E 2T2
Tel. (403) 476-1577

EURO-SUN
2011 Lawrence Ave. W., Suite 20,
Toronto, Ont. M9N 3V3
Tel. (416) 249-2011; Fax: (416) 249-0903

FIRCHUK'S
610 Queen St. W., Toronto, Ont. M6J 1E3
Tel. (416) 364-5036; Fax: (416) 364-3864

INTER-NATION TRAVEL
2017 Centre St. N., Calgary, Alta. T2E 2S9
Tel. (403) 276-8128

LONDONERRY TRAVEL
56 Londonerry Mall,
Edmonton, Alta. T5C 3C8
Tel. (403) 475-9281

PACIFIC AVENUE TRAVEL
388 Pacific Ave., Toronto, Ont. M6P 2R1
Tel. (416) 763-6700

PEKAO INTER. TRAVEL
1610 Bloor St. W., Toronto, Ont. M6P 1A7
Tel. (800) 387-0325

TIME TRAVELLERS
93 Lombard Ave. R. 100,
Winnipeg, Man. R3B 3B1
Tel. (800) 665-9935

TRAVEL UNLIMITED
869 Main St., Winnipeg, Man. R2W 3N9
Tel. (204) 942-5114

WESTERN OVERSEA TRAVEL
219 Selkirk Ave., Winnipeg, Man. R2W 2L5
Tel. (204) 586-8059

BOOKSTORES:

UKRAINIAN BOOK STORE
10215-97 St. P.O. Box 1640.
Edmonton, Alta. T5J 2N9
Tel. (403) 422-4255; Fax: (403) 425-1439.
The biggest and best selection of Ukrainian Books and English Books on Ukrainian subjects.

СКЛАД ЦЕРКОВНИХ РЕЧЕЙ CONSISTORY CHURCH GOODS SUPPLY
9 St. John's Avenue,
Winnipeg, Manitoba R2W 1G8
Tel. (204) 589-1191; Fax: (204) 582-5241
Specializing in Church Articles of the Eastern Orthodox Rite: Books, Icons, Crosses, Vestments, Clergy Shirts, etc.

GREAT BRITAIN:

PILMAR INTERNATIONAL
Abacus Buss. Cen.,
West Ealing, London, W13 OAS
Tel. (061) 810-9742; Fax: (061) 810-9743

ROCHDALE TRAVEL CENTRE
66 Drake St., Rochdale, Lancs. OL16 1PA
Tel. (0706) 311-44/46; Fax: (0706) 526-668

TRADE WINGS
Morley House, Suite 18/20, 5th Floor, 320 Regent St., London, W1R 5AG
Tel. (071) 631-1840, Fax: (071) 636-1705

TRIDENT GROUP TRAVEL
Royal Crimea House, 354 Uxridge Rd., London, W3
Tel. (081) 992-1068; Fax: (081) 992-1068

UKRAINIAN TRAVEL
27 Henshaw St., Oldham, Lancs.
Tel. (061) 633-2232

TEMPERATURES

Fahrenheit	Centigrade	Fahrenheit	Centigrade
212	100	60.8	16
104	40	57.2	14
100.4	38	53.6	12
98.6	37	50.0	10
96.2	36	46.4	8
93.2	34	42.8	6
89.6	32	39.2	4
86	30	35.6	2
82.4	28	32.0	0
78.8	26	28.4	-2
75.2	24	24.8	-4
71.6	22	21.2	-6
68	20	17.6	-8
64.4	18		

METRIC SYSTEM

Linear measurements:

1 yard	=	0.914 meter
1 foot	=	30.48 centimeters
1 inch	=	2.54 centimeters
0.62 mile	=	1 kilometer
1 mile	=	1.6 kilometer
1.09 yards	=	1 meter
3.28 feet	=	1 meter
0.39 inches	=	1 centimeter

Solid weights

1 lb.	=	0.4536 kilogram
1 oz.	=	28.35 grams

Liquid measurements:

1 gallon	=	3.785 liters
1 quart	=	0.946 liters
1 pint	=	0.473 liters

CONVERSION CHART FOR CLOTHING

Women's Dresses and Blouses

US	Ukraine
10	40
12	42
14	44
16	46
18	48

Men's Suits

US	Ukraine
37-38	48
39-40	50
41-42	52
43-44	54
45-46	56

Women's Suits

US	Ukraine
30	40
32	42
34	44
36	46
38	48

Men's Shirts

US	Ukraine
14-14 1/2	37
15-15 1/2	38
16-16 1/2	39
17-17 1/2	40

Women's Shoes

US	Ukraine
4	34
5	35
6	36
7	37
8	38

Men's Shoes

US	Ukraine
6 1/2- 7	38
7 1/2- 8	39
8 1/2- 9	40
9 1/2-10	42
10 1/2-11	44

TELEPHONE AREA CODES IN UKRAINE

CITIES AND VILLAGES	CODE	CITIES AND VILLAGES	CODE
Altchevsk	06442	Blyznyuky	05754
Alupka	0654	Bobrovytsa	04632
Alushta	06560	Bobrynets, Kirovohrad Region	05257
Amvrosiyivka	06259	Bohodukhiv	05758
Ananyiv	04863	Bohorodchany	03471
Andrushivka, Zhytomyr Region	04136	Bohuslav, Kyiv Region	04461
Antratsyt	06431	Bolekhiv	03477
Apostolove	05656	Bolhrad	04846
Arbuzynka	05132	Borodyanka, Kyiv Region	04477
Artemivsk, Donetsk Region	06274	Borova, Kharkiv Region	05759
Artsyz	04845	Borshchiv, Ternopil Region	03541
Askania-Nova	05538	Boryslav	03248
Bakhchysarai	06554	Boryspil, Kyiv Region	04495
Bakhmach	04635	Borzna	04653
Balakliya, Kharkiv Region	05749	Bratske, Mykolayiv Region	05131
Balta, Odesa Region	04866	Brody, Lviv Region	03266
Bar, Vinnytsya Region	043410	Brovary, Kyiv Region	04494
Baranivka, Zhytomyr Region	041444	Brusyliv, Zhytomyr Region	04162
Barvinkove	057572	Bryanka, Luhansk Region	06443
Baryshivka, Kyiv Region	04476	Bucha, Kyiv Region	04497
Bashtanka	05158	Buchach	03544
Baturyn, Chernihiv Region	04635	Burshtyn	03438
Berdyansk	06153	Buryn	05454
Berdychiv	04143	Busk	03264
Berehove	03141	Chaplynka, Kherson Region	05538
Berezanka	05153	Chechelnyk, Vinnytsya Region	04351
Berezhany	03548	Chemerivtsi	03859
Berezne, Rivne Region	03653	Cherkasy	0472
Bereznehuvate	05168	Chernihiv	04622
Bershad	04352	Chernihivka, Zaporizhzhya Region	06140
Beryslav	05546	Chernivtsi	03722
Bila Tserkva	04463	Chernyakhiv, Zhytomyr Region	04134
Bilhorod-Dnistrovsky	04849	Chervonoarmijsk, Rivne Region	03633
Bilohirya, Khmelnytsky Region	03841	Chervonoarmijsk, Zhytomyr Region	04131
Bilohorsk, Crimea	06559	Chervonohrad	03249
Bilokurakyne	06462	Chervonozavodske	05356
Bilopillya, Sumy Region	05443	Chop	03137
Bilovodsk	06466	Chornobai	04739
Bilozerka, Kherson Region	05547	Chornobyl, Kyiv Region	04493
Bilyaivka, Odesa Region	04852	Chornomorske, Crimea	06558

Chornukhy, Poltava Region	05340	Hlobyne	05365
Chortkiv	03552	Hluchiv	05444
Chudniv	04139	Hlyboka	03734
Chuhuyiv	05746	Hnivan	04355
Chutove	05347	Hola Prystan	05539
Chyhyryn	047302	Holovanivsk	05252
Debaltseve, Donetsk Region	06249	Holuba Zatoka	0654
Derazhnya	03856	Horlivka, Donetsk Region	06242
Derhachi, Kharkiv Region	05763	Hornostayivka, Kherson Rgion	05544
Dmytrivka, Chernihiv Region	04635	Horodenka	03430
Dniprodzerzhynsk	05692	Horodnya, Chernihiv Region	04645
Dnipropetrovsk	0562	Horodok, Khmelnytsky Region	03851
Dniprorudne	06175	Horodok, Lviv Region	03231
Dobropillya, Dontetsk Region	06277	Horodyshche, Cherkasy Region	04734
Dobrovelychkivka	05253	Horokhiv	03379
Dolyna, Ivano-Frankivsk Region	03477	Hoshcha	03650
Dolynska, Kirovohrad Region	05234	Hostomel	04497
Domanivka	05152	Hrebinka, Poltava Region	05359
Donetsk	0622	Hulyaipole, Zaporizhzhya Region	06145
Drabiv	04738	Hurzuf	0654
Drohobych	03244	Husyatyn Ternopil Region	03557
Druzhkivka	06267	Ichnya	04633
Dubno, Rivne Region	03656	Illichivsk	04868
Dubrovytsya, Rivne Region	03658	Illyintsi, Vinnitsa Region	04345
Dunayivtsi	03858	Irpin, Kyiv Region	04497
Dvorichna	05750	Irshava	03144
Dykanka	05351	Ivanivka, Kherson Region	05531
Dzerzhynsk, Donetsk Region	06247	Ivanivka, Odesa Region	04854
Dzerzhynsk, Zhytomyr Region	04146	Ivankiv, Kyiv Region	04491
Dzhankoi	06564	Ivano-Frankivsk	0342
Enerhodar	06139	Ivanycni, Volyln Region	03372
Fastiv, Kyiv Region	04465	Izmayil, Odesa Region	04841
Feodosiya	06562	Izyaslav	03852
Foros	0654	Izyum	05743
Frunzivka	04860	Kaharlyk, Kyiv Region	04473
Hadyach	05354	Kakhovka, Kherson Region	05536
Haisyn	043348	Kalanchak, Kerson Region	05530
Haivoron, Kirovohrad Region	05254	Kalush	03472
Halych, Ivano-Frankivsk Region	03431	Kalynivka, Vinnytsya Region	04333
Haspra	0654	Kalyta	04494
Henichesk	05534	Kamin-Kashyrsky	03357
Himyak, Donetsk Region	06237	Kamyanets-Podilsky	03849
Hirnyak, Lviv Region	03249	Kamyanka Buzka	03254
Hirnyatske, Donetsk Region	06256	Kamyanka, Cherkasy Region	04732

Kamyanka-Dnistrovska,	03736	Kostopil	03657
Zaporizhzhya Region	06138	Kostyantynivka, Donetsk Region	06272
Kaniv	04736	Kotelva	05350
Karlivka, Poltava Region	05346	Kotovsk, Odesa Region	04862
Katerynopil	04742	Kotsyubynske	04497
Kazanka, Mykolayiv Region	05164	Kovel	03352
Kehychivka	05755	Kozelets	04646
Kelmentsi	03732	Kozelshchyna	05342
Kerch	06561	Kozova	03547
Kharkiv	0572	Kozyatyn	04342
Khartsyzk	06257	Kramatorsk	06264
Kherson	0552	Krasni Okny, Odesa Region	04861
Khmelnytsky	03822	Krasnoarmiysk, Donetsk Region	06239
Khmilnyk, Vinnytsya Region	043388	Krasnodon	06435
Khorol	05362	Krasnohrad	06556
Khorostkiv	03557	Krasnohvardijske, Crimea	057442
Khotyn, Chernivtsi Region	037312	Krasnokutsk, Kharkiv Region	05756
Khrystynivka	04745	Krasnoperekopsk	06565
Khust	031422	Krasnopillya, Sumy Region	05459
Kiliya	04843	Krasny Luch, Luhansk Region	06432
Kirovohrad	0522	Krasny Lyman	06261
Kirovsk, Luhansk Region	06446	Krasyliv	03855
Kirovske, Crimea	06555	Kremenets	03546
Kirovske, Donetsk Region	06250	Kreminna, Luhansk Region	06454
Kitsman	03657	Krolevets	05453
Kivertsi	03365	Krynychky, Dnipropetrovsk Region	05617
Kobelyaky	05343	Kryve Ozero	05133
Kodyma	04867	Kryvy Rih	0564
Kolomyya	03433	Kryzhopil	04340
Kominternivske	04855	Kuibysheve, Zaporizhzhya Region	06147
Kompaniyivka	05240	Kulykivka, Chernihiv Region	04643
Komsomolsk, Poltava Region	05348	Kupyansk	05742
Komsomolske, Donetsk Region	06217	Kuznetsovsk, Rivne Region	03636
Komsomolske, Kharkiv Region	05747	Kyiv	044
Konotop, Sumy Region	05447	Ladyzhyn	04343
Kopychyntsi	03557	Lanivtsi, Ternopil Region	03549
Korets	03651	Lazurne	05537
Koreyiz	0654	Lebedyn, Sumy Region	05445
Korop	04656	Lenine, Crimea	06557
Korosten	04142	Letychiv	03857
Korostyshiv	04130	Lutun	04347
Korsun-Shevchenkivsky	04735	Livadiya, Crimea	0654
Koryukivka	04657	Lokachi	03374
Kosiv, Ivano-Frankivsk Region	03478	Lokhvytsya, Poltava Region	05356

Lozova, Kharkiv Region	05745	Murovani Kurylivtsi	04356
Lubny	053615	Mykhailivka, Zaporizhzhya Region	06132
Luhansk	0642	Mykolayiv	0512
Luhyny	04161	Mykolayiv, Lviv Region	03241
Lutsk	03322	Mykolayivka, Odesa Region	048572
Lutuhyne	06436	Myrhorod	05355
Lviv	0322	Myronivka, Kyiv Region	04474
Lypova Dolyna	05452	Nadvirna	03475
Lypovets, Vinnytsya Region	04358	Narodychi	04140
Lysyanka	04749	Nedryhailiv	05455
Lysychansk	06451	Nemyriv, Lviv Region	03259
Lyubar	04147	Nemyriv, Vinnytsya Region	04331
Lyubashivka	04864	Nesteriv, Lviv Region	03252
Lyubeshiv	03362	Netishyn	03848
Lyuboml	03377	Nizhyn	04631
Mahdalynivka,		Nikopol, Dnipropetrovsk Region	05662
Dnipropetrovsk Region	05611	Nosivka, Chernihiv Region	04642
Makariv, Kyiv Region	04478	Nova Kakhovka	05549
Makiyivka, Donetsk Region	06232	Nova Odesa	05167
Mala Vyska	05258	Nova Ushytsya	03847
Malyn, Zhytomyr Region	04133	Nova Vodolaha	05740
Manevychi	03376	Novhorod-Siversky	04658
Mankivka, Cherkasy Region	04748	Novhorodka, Kirovohrad Region	05241
Marhanets	05665	Novi Sanzhary	05344
Mariupil, Donetsk Region		Novoarkhanhelsk	05255
(for 5-digit numbers)	06292	Novoazovsk	06296
Mariupil, Donetsk Region		Novohrad-Volynsky	04141
(for 6-digit numbers)	0629	Novomoskovsk,	
Markivka, Luhansk Region	06464	Dnipropetrovsk Region	05612
Maryinka, Donetsk Region	06212	Novomykolayivka,	
Masandra	0654	Zaporizhzhya Region	06144
Mashivka	05364	Novomyrhorod	05256
Melitopol	06142	Novopskov, Ludansk Region	06463
Mena	04644	Novoselytsya, Chernivtsi Region	03733
Mezhova, Dnipropcetovsk Region	05670	Novotroyitske, Kherson Region	05548
Milove, Luhansk Region	06465	Novoukrayinka, Kirovohrad Region	05251
Mizhhirya, Zakarpattya Region	03146	Novovolynsk	03344
Mlyniv, Rivne Region	03659	Novovorontsovka	05533
Mohyliv-Podilsky	04337	Novy Aidar	06445
Monastyryshche, Cherkasy Region	04746	Novy Buh	05151
Monastyryske	03555	Novy Rozdol	03261
Morshyn	032456	Novy Svit, Crimen	06566
Mostyska	03234	Nyzhni Sirohozy	05540
Mukacheve	03131	Nyzhnyohirsky	06550

Obukhiv, Kyiv Region	4472	Polonne	03843
Ochakiv	05154	Poltava	0532
Odesa	0482	Popasna	06474
Okhtyrka, Sumy Region	05446	Popilnya	041372
Olevsk	04135	Pryazovske, Zaporizhzhya Region	06133
Olexandriya, Kirovohrad Region	05235	Pryluky, Chernihiv Region	04637
Olexandrivka, Donetsk Region	06269	Prymorsk, Zaporizhzhya Region	06137
Olexandrivka, Kirovohrad Region	05242	Pustomyty, Lviv Region	03230
Onufriyivka	05238	Putyla	03738
Orativ	04330	Putyvl	05442
Ordzhonikidze,		Pyatykhatky, Dnipropetrovsk Region	056510
Dnipropetrovsk Region	05667	Pyryatyn, Poltava Region	05358
Oreanda	0654	Radekhiv, Lviv Region	03255
Orikhiv, Zaporizhzhya Region	06141	Radomyshl, Zhytomyr Region	04132
Orzhytsya	05357	Rakhiv	03132
Oster, Chernihiv Region	04646	Ratne	03366
Ostroh	03654	Rava-Ruska	03252
Ovidiopil	04851	Reny	04840
Ovruch	041483	Reshetylivka	05363
Pavlohrad, Dnipropetrovsk Region	05672	Rivne	0362
Perechyn	03145	Rohatyn	03435
Peremyshlyany	03263	Rokytne, Kyiv Region	04462
Perevalsk	06441	Rokytne, Rivne Region	03635
Pereyaslav-Khmelnytsky,		Romny, Sumy Region	05448
Kyiv Region	04467	Rovenky, Luhansk Region	06433
Pershotravensk,		Rozdilna, Odesa Region	04853
Dnipropetrovsk Region	05673	Rozdol, Lviv Region	03241
Pershotravneve, Donetsk Region	06297	Rozdolne, Crimea	06553
Pervomaysk, Luhansk Region	06455	Rozhnyativ	03474
Pervomaysk, Mykolayiv Region	05161	Rozhyshche	03368
Pervomayske, Crimea	06552	Rubizhne, Luhansk Region	06453
Pervomaysky, Kharkiv Region	05748	Ruzhyn, Zhytomyr Region	04138
Petropavlivka,		Ripky, Chernihiv Region	04641
Dnipropetrovsk Region	05671	Rzhyshchiv	04473
Petrove, Kirovohrad Region	05237	Sakhnovshchyna, Kharkiv Region	05762
Pidhaitsi, Ternopil Region	03542	Saky, Crimea	06563
Pidvolochysk	03543	Sambir	03236
Pishchanka, Vinnytsya Region	04349	Sanatorne	0654
Planerske	06566	Sarata	04848
Pochayiv	03546	Sarny, Rivne Region	036552
Pohrebyshche	04346	Savran	04865
Pokrovske, Dnipropetrovsk Region	05678	Selidove	06237
Poliske, Kyiv Region	04492	Semenivka, Chernihiv Region	04659
Polohy, Zaporizhzhya Region	06165	Semenivka, Poltava Region	05341

Seredyna-Buda	05451	Stavyshche, Kyiv Region	04464
Sevastopol	0692	Storozhynets	03735
Shakhtarsk, Donetsk Region	06255	Stryy	03245
Sharhorod	04344	Sudak	06566
Shatsk	03355	Sumy	05422
Shchors, Chernihiv Region	04654	Svalyava	03133
Shepetivka, Chmelnytsky Region	03840	Svatove, Luhansk Region	06471
Shevchenkove, Kharkiv Region	05751	Sverdlovsk, Luhansk Region	06434
Shklo	03259	Svitlovodsk, Kirovohrad Region	05236
Shostka	05449	Syeverodonetsk	06452
Shpola	04741	Simferopol	0652
Shumske	03558	Synelnykove	05615
Shyroke, Dnipropetrovsk Region	05657	Talalayivka, Chernihiv Region	04634
Shyryayeve, Odesa Region	04858	Talne	04731
Shyshaky, Poltava Region	05352	Tarashcha	04466
Simeyiz	0654	Tarutyne, Odesa Region	04847
Skadovsk	05537	Tatarbunary	04844
Skole	03251	Telmanove	06279
Skvyra, Kyiv Region	04468	Teofipol	03844
Slavske	03251	Teplyk	04353
Slavuta	03842	Terebovlya	03551
Slavutych, Kyiv Region	04479	Ternopil	0352
Slovyanohirsk	06262	Tetiyiv, Kyiv Region	04460
Slovyanoserbsk	06473	Tlumach	03479
Slovyansk	06262	Tokmak, Zaporizhzhya Region	06178
Smila	04733	Tomakivka	05668
Snihyrivka	05162	Tomashpil	04348
Snizhne, Donetsk Region	06256	Torez	06254
Snyatyn	03476	Trostyanets, Sumy Region	05458
Sofiyivka, Dnipropetrovsk Region	05650	Trostyanets, Vinnytsya Region	04343
Sokal	03257	Troyitske, Luhansk Region	06456
Sokyryany, Chernivtsi Region	03739	Truskavets	03247
Solone, Dnipropetrovsk Region	05616	Tsarychanka	05610
Sosnytsya, Chernihiv Region	04655	Tsuman	03348
Sovyetsky, Crimea	06551	Tsyurupinsk	05542
Sribne	04639	Tulchyn	04335
Stakhanov, Luhansk Region	06444	Turiysk	03363
Stanychno-Luhanske	06472	Turka, Lviv Region	03269
Stara Synyava	03850	Tyachiv	03134
Stara Vyzhivka	03346	Tysmenytsya	03436
Starobesheve	06217	Tyvriv	04355
Starobilsk	06461	Ukrayinka, Kyiv Region	04472
Starokostyantyniv	03854	Ulyanovka, Kirovohrad Region	05259
Stary Sambir	03238	Uman	04744

Ustynivka, Kirovohrad Region	05239	Vynohradiv	03143
Uzhhorod	03122	Vynohradne, Crimea	0654
Uzyn	04463	Vyshhorod, Kyiv Region	04496
Valky, Kharkiv Region	05753	Vysokopillya, Kherson Region	05535
Varva	04636	Vyzhnytsya	03730
Vasylivka, Zaporizhzhya Region	06175	Yahotyn, Kyiv Region	04475
Vasylkiv, Kyiv Region	04471	Yakymivka, Zaporizhzhya Region	06131
Vasylkivka, Dnipropetrovsk Region	05679	Yalta, Crimea	0654
Velyka Bahachka	05345	Yalta, Donetsk Region	06297
Velyka Lepetykha	055431	Yampil, Khmelnytsky Region	03841
Velyka Mykhaylivka	04859	Yampil, Sumy Region	05456
Velyka Novosilka	06213	Yampil, Vinnytsya Region	04336
Velyka Olexandrivka,		Yaremcha	034342
Kherson Region	05532	Yarmolyntsi, Khmelnytsky Region	03853
Velyka Pysarivka	05457	Yasynovata	06236
Velyky Berezny	03135	Yavoriv, Lviv Region	03259
Velyky Burluk	05752	Yelanets	05159
Verkhni Rohachyk	05545	Yemilchyne	041494
Verkhnyodniprovsk	05618	Yenakiyeve	06252
Verkhovyna,		Yevpatoria	06569
Ivano-Frankivsk Region	03432	Yuzhnoukrayinsk, Mykolayiv Region	05136
Vesele, Zaporizhzhya Region	06136	Zachepylivka	05761
Veselinove	05163	Zalishchyky	03554
Vilnohirsk, Dnipropetrovsk Region	05653	Zaporizhzhya	0612
Vilnyansk	06143	Zarichne, Rivne Region	03632
Vilshanka, Kirovohrad Region	05250	Zastavna	03737
Vilshany, Kharkiv Region	05763	Zbarazh	03550
Vinkivtsi	03846	Zboriv, Ternopil Region	03540
Vinnytsya	04322	Zdolbuniv	036522
Volnovakha	06214	Zelenodolsk	05655
Volochysk	03845	Zhashkiv	04747
Volodarka, Kyiv Region	04469	Zhmerynka	04332
Volodarsk-Volynsky	04145	Zhovti Vody	05652
Volodarske, Donetsk Region	06216	Zhurivka, Kyiv Region	04470
Volodymyr-Volynsky	03342	Zhydachiv	03239
Volodymyrets	03634	Zhytomyr	0412
Volovets	03136	Zinkiv	05353
Vorzel, Kyiv Region	04497	Zmiyiv	05747
Vovchansk, Kharkiv Region	05741	Znamyanka, Kirovohrad Region	05233
Voznesensk	05134	Zolochiv, Kharkiv Region	05764
Vradiyivka	05135	Zolochiv, Lviv Region	03265
Vuhlehirsk, Donetsk Region	06252	Zolotonosha, Cherkasy Region	04737

INTERNATIONAL TELEPHONE COMMUNICATIONS

COUNTRY AND CITY CODES

Country	Area codes	City	Area codes	Time difference: with Kiev (hrs.)
Albania	355	Tirana	42	-1
Algeria	213/ 214	Algiers	2	-1
Argentina	54	Buenos Aires	1	-5
Australia	61	Sydney	2	+8
		Adelaide	8	+7.5
		Brisbane	7	+8
		Melbourne	3	+8
		Perth	9	+6
Austria	43	Vienna	1	-1
		Graz	316	-1
		Salzburg	662	-1
		Innsbruck	512	-1
Belgium	32	Brussels	2	-1
		Antwerp	3	-1
		Ghent	91	-1
		Liege	41	-1
Bolivia	591	La Paz	2	-6
Brazil	55	Brasilia	61	-5
		Rio De Janeiro	21	-5
		San Paulo	11	-5
Bulgaria	359	Sofia	2	0
		Varna	52	0
		Pernik	76	0
Canada	1	Ottawa	613	-7
		Vancouver	604	-10
		Montreal	514	-7
		Toronto	416	-7
		Edmonton	403	-9

Country	Area codes	City	Area codes	Time difference: with Kiev (hrs.)
Chile	56	Santiago	2	-6
China	56	Beijing	1	+6
		Shanghai	21	+6
Czech Republic	42	Prague	2	-1
		Brno	5	-1
		Karlovy Vary	17	-1
		Olomouc	68	-1
		Pilzen	19	-1
Denmark	45			-1
Egypt	20	Cairo	2	0
Finland	358	Helsinki	0	0
France	33	Paris	1	-1
		Bordeaux	56	-1
		Lyons	78	-1
		Marseilles	91	-1
Germany	49	Berlin	30	-1
		Bonn	228	-1
		Bremen	421	-1
		Dusseldorf	211	-1
		Dresden	351	-1
		Leipzig	341	-1
		Potsdam	331	-1
		Hamburg	40	-1
		Hannover	511	-1
		Magdeburg	391	-1
		Munich	89	-1
		Nuremberg	911	-1
		Frankfurt/Main	69	-1

Country	Area codes	City	Area codes	Time difference: with Kiev (hrs.)
Great Britain	44	London	1	-2
		Birmingham	21	-2
		Bristol	272	-2
		Glazgow	41	-2
		Liverpool	51	-2
		Leeds	532	-2
		Manchester	61	-2
		Edinburgh	31	-2
Greece	30	Athens	1	0
Hong Kong	852			+6
Hungary	36	Budapest	1	-1
Iceland	354	Reykyavik	1	-2
India	91	Delhi	11	+3.5
		Bombay	22	+3.5
		Calcutta	33	+3.5
Indonesia	62	Jakarta	21	+5 & +6
Iran	98	Teheran	21	+1.5
Ireland	353	Dublin	1	-2
Israel	972	Tel Aviv	3	0
		Ben Gurion airport	3	0
Italy	39	Rome	6	-1
		Bologna	51	-1
Italy	39	Venice	41	-1
		Genoa	10	-1
		Milan	2	-1
		Naples	81	-1
		Turin	11	-1
		Florence	55	-1
Japan	81	Tokyo	3	+7
		Kawasaki	44	+7
		Kyoto	75	+7
		Kobe	78	+7

Country	Area codes	City	Area codes	Time difference: with Kiev (hrs.)
Jordan	962	Amman	6	0
Korea, PDR (North)	850	Pyongyang	2	+7
Korea, Republic (South)	82	Seoul	2	+7
Liechtenstein	41 75			-1
Luxembourg	352			-1
Mexico	52	Mexico City	5	-8
Mongolia	976			+6
Morocco	212	Rabat	7	-2
Netherlands	31	Amsterdam	20	-1
		The Hague	70	-1
		Rotterdam	10	-1
New Zealand	64	Wellington	4	+10
Norway	47	Oslo	2	-1
Pakistan	92	Islamabad	51	+3
Peru	51	Lima	14	-7
Philippines	63	Manila	2	+6
Poland	48	Warsaw		-1
		7-digit-nos.	2	
		6-digit-nos.	22	
		Bialystok	85	-1
		Gdansk	58	-1
		Katowice	32	-1
		Krakow	12	-1
		Lodz	42	-1
		Poznan	61	-1
		Sopot	58	-1
		Szczecin	91	-1
Portugal	351	Lisbon	1	-2
Romania	40	Bucharest	0	0
Saudi Arabia	966	Riyadh	1	+1

Country	Area codes	City	Area codes	Time difference: with Kiev (hrs.)
Slovak Republic	42	Bratislava	17	-1
South Africa	27	Pretoria	12	0
Spain	34	Madrid	1	-1
		Barcelona	3	-1
Sweden	46	Stockholm	8	-1
		Goteborg	31	-1
		Malmo	40	-1
Switzerland	41	Berne	31	-1
		Basel	61	-1
		Geneva	22	-1
		Zurich	1	-1
Syria	963	Damascus	11	0
Taiwan	886	Taipei	2	+6
Tunisia	216	Tunis	1	-1
Turkey	90	Ankara	4	0
United Arab Emirates	971	Abu Dhabi	2	+2
Uruguay	598	Montevideo	2	-5
USA	1	Washington	202	-7
		Detroit	313	-7
		Los Angeles	213	-10
		New Orleans	504	-8
		New York	718	-7
			212	
		San Francisco	415	-10
		Philadelphia	215	-7
Venezuela	58	Caracas	2	-6
Yugoslavia:	38			
Serbia	381	Belgrade	1	-1
	382	Novi Sad	1	-1
	383	Kragujevac	4	-1

Country	Area codes	City	Area codes	Time difference: with Kiev (hrs.)
Slovenia	386	Ljubljana	1	-1
Bosnia, Hercegovina	387	Sarajevo	1	-1
Montenegro	388	Podgorica	1	-1
Macedonia	389	Skopje	1	-1

INDEX OF CITIES AND VILLAGES

UKRAINE: A Tourist Guide

Compiled
by Osyp Zinkewych
and Volodymyr Hula

Translated and Edited
by Marta D. Olynyk

Papir ofcetnii

Підписано до друку 16. 06. 1994. Формат 60 x 90 1/16. Папір офсетний.
Друк офсетний. Умовних друк. арк. 28. Зам. № 4-171. Тир. 10 000.

Umovnih Druk

Druk Ofsetnii

Видавництво "Смолоскип"
253053, Київ, вул. Артема, 1-5, к. 802.
Тел. і факс: (044) 212-08-77

Київська книжкова фабрика, 252054, Київ-54, вул. Воровського, 24.

Vorovs kogo

Printed and Bound in Ukraine

Kievska knizkova Fabrika